William Pynchon, Fitch Edward Oliver

The Diary of William Pynchon of Salem

A picture of Salem Life, Social and Political, a Century ago

William Pynchon, Fitch Edward Oliver

The Diary of William Pynchon of Salem
A picture of Salem Life, Social and Political, a Century ago

ISBN/EAN: 9783337019389

Printed in Europe, USA, Canada, Australia, Japan

Cover: Foto ©Raphael Reischuk / pixelio.de

More available books at **www.hansebooks.com**

THE DIARY

OF

WILLIAM PYNCHON

OF SALEM

*A PICTURE OF SALEM LIFE, SOCIAL AND
POLITICAL, A CENTURY AGO*

EDITED BY

FITCH EDWARD OLIVER
MEMBER OF THE MASSACHUSETTS HISTORICAL SOCIETY

BOSTON AND NEW YORK
HOUGHTON, MIFFLIN AND COMPANY
The Riverside Press, Cambridge
1890

ERRATA.

On page 19, note, for Daye, read " Dodge."
On page 26, note, for Gardiner, read " Gardner."

PREFATORY NOTE.

THE compliance of the editor with a request often urged, that the Diary of Mr. Pynchon be put in a more permanent form, has led to the publication of the present volume. Written in Salem during the war of the Revolution, and the years immediately succeeding, this journal may serve to bring to view the persons and scenes of that memorable period. Those especially who have associations with the Salem of the past may learn from this record something of its earlier social as well as political history, and the manners and customs of the time.

The Diary covers the whole period, with the exception of the year 1779 and four months of the year 1780, from near the opening of the war to the final establishment of our nationality. Beginning with the year 1776, the last entry was in March, 1789, a little more than a month before the inauguration of Washington. Although not, perhaps, of great historical value, it contains many items of local and general interest, not to be found elsewhere. The political, and sometimes unpopular, sentiments occasionally expressed by the author, it should be remembered, were uttered at a time when there were wide and

PREFATORY NOTE.

THE compliance of the editor with a request often urged, that the Diary of Mr. Pynchon be put in a more permanent form, has led to the publication of the present volume. Written in Salem during the war of the Revolution, and the years immediately succeeding, this journal may serve to bring to view the persons and scenes of that memorable period. Those especially who have associations with the Salem of the past may learn from this record something of its earlier social as well as political history, and the manners and customs of the time.

The Diary covers the whole period, with the exception of the year 1779 and four months of the year 1780, from near the opening of the war to the final establishment of our nationality. Beginning with the year 1776, the last entry was in March, 1789, a little more than a month before the inauguration of Washington. Although not, perhaps, of great historical value, it contains many items of local and general interest, not to be found elsewhere. The political, and sometimes unpopular, sentiments occasionally expressed by the author, it should be remembered, were uttered at a time when there were wide and

honest differences, among all classes, on the great ques-
tions of that day, and were, moreover, not intended for
the public eye.

The editor begs to express his thanks to the Rev.
Andrew Oliver, of New York, to the Rev. T. R. Pynchon,
of Hartford, and to Mr. Harrison Ellery, of Boston, for
valuable aid in the revision of proofs and the verifica-
tion of names and dates.

WILLIAM PYNCHON.

WILLIAM PYNCHON, of Salem, the author of the following diary, was born in Springfield, Massachusetts, December 12, 1723. He was the son of William Pynchon, who married Catherine, a daughter of Rev. Daniel Brewer, and grandson of John Pynchon, whose wife was the daughter of Rev. William Hubbard, the historian of New England. His great grandfather was John, who married Amy, daughter of Governor Wyllys, of Connecticut, and whose father was William Pynchon, one of the patentees of the Colony of Massachusetts Bay, and the founder of the town of Springfield. Through his mother, Catherine Brewer, Mr. Pynchon was descended from the Chauncys, and among his ancestors were many names closely connected with the earlier annals of New England.

Since the settlement of Springfield, the town had been the home of the family, and here Mr. Pynchon's boyhood was passed, and his preparation for college completed. He entered Harvard College, where many of his family had been graduated, in 1739, and received his degree in 1743, in the class with Foster Hutchinson, James Otis, and the Rev. Dr. Samuel Cooper, with whom he seems to have been on terms of intimacy through life. Two years after his graduation he went to reside in Salem with Mitchell Sewall, at that time clerk of the Superior Court. At the death of Mr. Sewall he became an applicant for the place now vacant, but

failing to obtain this appointment, he applied himself
more assiduously to the study of the law, and commenced
its practice in Salem, where he soon became prominent
as a counsellor and advocate. The Essex bar at this
time, as well as during the Revolutionary war, was noted
for its learning and legal ability, and, of the names that
gave it lustre, not the least conspicuous was that of Mr.
Pynchon. He was distinguished, says Washburn, for
his skill as a special pleader, and as a counsellor united
great subtlety with the utmost fairness and liberality.
As an instructor in jurisprudence he was remarkably
successful, and, as schools of law were then unknown, he
had many pupils who owed their success largely to his
teachings, among whom may be mentioned the Hon.
Jeremiah Smith, of New Hampshire, afterwards distinguished on the Bench and in the State. In 1774, on the
death of Judge Ropes, he became a candidate for the
vacant seat on the Bench of the Superior Court of the
Province, which was, however, filled by Judge William
Browne, one of the Justices of the Court of Common
Pleas, whose larger judicial experience may have determined the Council in his favour.

In his political views Mr. Pynchon was conservative,
and during the critical period of the Revolution was not
always in harmony with the popular voice ; but, if opposed at first to the war as a measure of doubtful expe-
diency, he was in these views by no means alone. "The
eminent lawyers of this time," says the late Ellis Ames,
in a paper read before the Historical Society,[1] "mostly
adhered to the British administration, and were all citi-
zens of great uprightness, integrity, and ability." To
this respectable class Mr. Pynchon belonged, and no
one could have borne the treatment he received with

<hr>

See Society's *Proceedings*, vol. xiv., p. 396.

greater patience and forbearance. He suffered much during the war from the general stagnation of business, and although he rarely, if ever, mingled in political controversy, he was not a little disturbed by the hostility of former friends, and the malevolence of party feeling. If he is sometimes emphatic in his language, it is rather from his intolerance of every species of political trickery than from an honest difference of opinion on the part of his opponent. He was as true to what he believed to be the true interests of his native country as any man that then lived ; and when the new government was finally established, he accepted it with all the heartiness of a loyal citizen. He was a member of St. Peter's Church, and one of its firmest supporters, and the names of two of its rectors, McGilchrist and Fisher, often appear in the pages of his diary. Although decided in his religious views, he was liberally inclined to those who differed from him. Among his frequent guests were men of every shade of religious and political opinion, and with many of the Congregational clergy he was on the most friendly terms. Few men he held in higher esteem than Dr. Andrew Eliot, " that excellent preacher and truly good man," as he calls him. Mr. Pynchon was of a generous and kindly nature, given to hospitality, and during his many years in Salem won the esteem of the community by his urbanity and public spirit.

It is not a little remarkable that a name honoured from the earliest days of the Colony, and now borne by one, its chief representative, who had passed the larger part of his life in Salem, eminent in his profession, and of singular purity of life, should have been selected to be sullied in the pages of a modern romance. A more repulsive character has rarely been portrayed by writers of fiction than that of Judge Pynchon in " The House of the

Seven Gables ; " and when it is remembered that William Pynchon was the only one of the family who had ever resided in Salem, and that from his learning, and fitness for the judicial office, he was sometimes accorded the title of Judge, it was but natural that the author of that attractive story should have been asked for an explanation of what seemed so unwarrantable a liberty.

In the following reply to a letter addressed to him by a descendant of Mr. Pynchon, and one who bore his name, Mr. Hawthorne frankly admits the ground of offence to be a reasonable one, and expresses regret that he should have been led, through unfamiliarity with the later history of Salem, to the selection of an honoured name to fasten upon an "imaginary villain " : —

LENOX, *May* 3d, 1851.

SIR, — It pains me to learn that I have given you what I am content to acknowledge a reasonable ground of offence, by borrowing the name of the Pynchon family for my fictitious purposes in " The House of the Seven Gables." It never occurred to me, however, that the name was not as much the property of a romance writer, as that of Smith, for instance ; while its unhackneyed singularity, and a certain indescribable fitness to the tone of my work, gave it a value which no other of the many sirnames, which suggested themselves to me, seemed to possess. Writing the book at a distance from Salem, I had no opportunity for consulting ancient records or the recollections of aged persons ; and I beg you to believe that I was wholly unaware, until the receipt of your letter, that the Pynchons, at so recent a period as you mention, if at any former one, had been residents of that place. Had this fact been within my knowledge, and especially had I known that any member of the family had borne the title of Judge, I should certainly have considered it discourteous and unwarrantable to make free with the name. I would further say that I intended no allusion to any Pynchon now or at any

previous period extant ; that I never heard anything to the
discredit, in the slightest degree, of this old and respectable
race, and that I give the fullest credence to your testimony
in favour of your grandfather, Judge Pynchon, and greatly
regret that I should have seemed to sully his honourable name,
by plastering it upon an imaginary villain.

You suggest that reparation is due for these injuries of my
pen, but point out no mode in which it may be practicable.   It
is my own opinion that no real harm has been done, inasmuch
as I enter a protest in the preface of "The House of the Seven
Gables" against the narrative and the personages being considered as other than imaginary.   But, since it appears otherwise to you, no better course occurs to me than to put this
letter at your disposal, to be used in such manner as a proper
regard for your family honour may be thought to demand.

Respectfully, Sir,

Your obedient Servant,

NATH'L HAWTHORNE.

Mr. Pynchon was married in 1751 to the daughter of
Mitchell Sewall, of Salem, by whom he had two sons
and three daughters. The eldest daughter, *Elizabeth*,
born January 26, 1752, married Timothy Orne, Esq. ;
the second daughter, *Catherine*, born February 25,
1754, married William Wetmore, Esq., whose daughter,
by a second wife, Miss Waldo, married the late Mr.
Justice Story ; *Sarah*, the youngest daughter, born February 6th, 1757, married the Rev. Thomas Fitch Oliver,
and died in March, 1832 ; *William*, the eldest son, born
July 24, 1759, married Martha Elkins, March 4, 1780,
and died without issue ; *John*, the youngest son, born
November 27, 1766, died unmarried.

THE DIARY

OF

WILLIAM PYNCHON.

———◆———

1776. *January* 1. *Monday.* Are they not pitiful statesmen who, by one act (the emission of paper currency), increase the publick expense and lessen the means of defraying it ? At least of supporting it ?

3. Elijah [1] and John Williams came, and set out again for Deerfield on Sunday the 7th.

8. *Monday.* Capt. Glover and Bartlett came for Libel. Bro. Stephen Sewall lodged here at night.

9. News came from Charlestown that Bunker's Hill was taken last night by the Provincials ; on inquiry it proved to be the burning of some houses at the bottom of the hill, and the taking four or five prisoners. Mr. Farnham [2] came here, and returned on Wednesday. At night a violent wind.

11. *Thursday.* Cloudy and cold. Mr. Higginson here from Newburyport. Mr. Farnham from Cambridge.

[1] Elijah Williams, of Deerfield, married Margaret, a sister of William Pynchon.

[2] Daniel Farnham, of Newburyport, was one of a group of eminent lawyers more or less distinguished at the bar and in public life. He was a graduate of Harvard College in the class of 1739, and died in 1776. Among others mentioned in this diary are Nathaniel P. Sargent, afterward Chief Justice of the Superior Court, John Chipman of Marblehead, the Cushings, Theophilus Parsons, and John Lowell, afterward Chief Justice of the first U. S. Circuit Court.

12. Mr. Higginson here. News from England into Falmouth that Lord Littleton and the Duke of Grafton had deserted the ministry, and joined the opposite party ; and that, since the King's speech, many others had also joined, so that the King had doubled his guards, and friends to America daily increased. *Quære de toto.*

13. I spoke to Stephen and Sam. Webb about Mr. Orne's ropewalk, desiring the consideration of the matter a few days.

15. Took Puffendorf, Grotius, and Burlimagnè out of the library.

17. *Wednesday.* Two prizes said to be brought into Newbury, and two into York, by the Newbury boats, etc. Quebec said to be stormed and taken, with the loss of a great part — one third — of the Provincial army. Disturbance at N. York for supplying [the] King's ships with provisions.

22. News came that General Montgomery and his aid-de-camp [1] [were] killed, and Col. Arnold wounded at Quebec, and the army repulsed ; and, on the 24th, we hear that the army miss about 1200 men, killed, taken, and deserted.

25. That two vessels, a [ship] and a   , were taken by our privateers near the Lighthouse, and carried into Plymouth.

26. Sent Mrs. Grant's letter by Major Frazer to Col. Moylan,[2] for J. Grant at Boston. Dr. Warren and Dr. Waldo [3] here from Cambridge, and say Boston is very soon to be bombarded. Snowed, and helped the sled-

---

[1] McPherson.

[2] Stephen Moylan was appointed by Washington one of his aids-de-camp, and afterward was made commissary-general.

[3] Jonathan Waldo, a son of Jonathan and Mary Waldo, was born in Boston, June 21, 1754. He was druggist, mayor, and selectman.

ding, so that on Saturday, the 27th, wood fell to 20 shillings a cord.

27. The militia was mustered for enlisting of men for the Provincial army, but not one enlisted. Very cold day.

28. *Sunday.* Clear and cold, very severe, and went into our own pew on that account.

30. *Tuesday morning.* Mrs. P. came to my house, and told me that Mr. T. proposed to pay her some paper money on a bond for silver, and asked what she should do ; for if she took it, she was afraid she could not let it, and should be a great loser and displease her husband ; and if she refused it, she might meet with trouble. I told her it was dangerous to give any advice in the matter ; however, advised her to do whatever she thought would be agreeable to her husband's mind ; that I apprehended he would blame her taking paper money which would not procure any remittances which he might have need of to London. Mr. T. told me that he must push the matter, if Mrs. Pointer should refuse the money. This I think affrighted Mrs. Pointer. Returned Grotius and 1 vol. Burlimagnè. I took two vols. of the Adventurer and four vols. of the World and two vols. of Ulloa to Mrs. Curwen's.

February 1. *Thursday.* Fair and very warm. A great number of heavy guns fired at Boston, at Admiral Graves' departure.

2. *Fryday.* At night heavy guns heard.

6. *Tuesday.* J. Williams came.

8. *Thursday.* J. Williams for Deerfield.

12. *Monday.* Clear and cold. Mr. Vans[1] assured me last evening in the street that he *disliked the proclama-*

---

[1] William Vans, a merchant of Salem, who seems to have been for a time in doubt as to which side it would be wisest to espouse.

tion read at meeting, it being too much for independence on G. B.

20. *Tuesday.* Clear and moderate. Mrs. Anderson went to Newbury.

22. *Thursday.* We hear of orders of Continental Congress to the Gen'l not to attack B.

29. Mr. Burke[1] and Capt. Lawrea sailed from Beverly harbour with the Privateers ; had a smart wind at N. W. News came that Dr. Gilson and others broke out of Plymouth jail and got into Boston ; and by advices from Dr. Eliot and Mr. Payson that the Regulars at B. are preparing to quit the town ; and from others that the Provincials are busy in preparing to bombard the town, and to erect works for that end on the hill at Dorchester, near the Neck.

March 2. Saturday. Mr. Hitchburn, Dr. Holten,[2] and Dr. Short, here. Boston to be attacked within 60 days, as Mr. H. declares. At night, bombs were thrown from Lechmere's Point.

3. *Sunday.* An engagement between Dawson, a cruiser, and 4 American Privateers. Query the event? The action seen from Salem steeples and tops of houses. Dawson outsailed the Privateers ; near 100 guns [were] fired, but no damage yet heard of ; they were very distant from him.

---

[1] Captain Burke commanded the schooner Warren. *History of Marblehead*, p. 174.

[2] Dr. Samuel Holten, sometimes mentioned in this Diary, was a prominent physician of Danvers. At the commencement of the Revolutionary struggle, he abandoned the practice of medicine and became an ardent supporter of the Revolutionary cause. He held many important offices, having been one of the delegates to the Congress for framing the confederation, and several times representative to the General Court. In 1796, being in feeble health, having served his country in public stations for forty-seven years, he accepted a commission as Judge of Probate, which office he held until 1815. He died the following year.

4. *Monday.*   It is said that three mortars were broke yesterday in Provincial firing, and one at Boston by the Regulars ; very little hurt done by the breaking bombs ; and firing of cannon was heard most of the forenoon, also some in the afternoon.

5. *Tuesday.*   A few bombs only thrown to-day.   In the evening, it rained a little ; in the night was a violent gale of wind with rain ; the man of war in harbour here driven.

6. *Wednesday.*   Clear and windy.   No firing heard in the forenoon.

7. B. went to Cambridge, Charlestown, Roxbury, and Dorchester, and returned on Saturday.

8. News came that the regular army was about to leave Boston.

9. *Saturday.*   In the evening, at about 8 o'clock, heavy guns were heard, and frequently, and for great part of the night, and on Sunday morning at 5 and 6 o'clock ; supposed to be from Boston, to prevent the Provincials from advancing to Dorchester Hill.

10. *Sunday.*   No firing at Boston, and in Regulars' intrenchments.

11. *Monday.*   Returned Puffendorf, and took it out again ; also returned the World, 4 vols., and Ulloa, 2 vols., and Adventurer, 2 vols., and took out Puffendorf, and his Introduction, 3 vols., Dodsley, two vols., and Adventurer,[1] 1 vol.

14. *Thursday.*   Capt. Foster returned from Cambridge.

15. *Fryday.*   A fine fair day ; wind N. W.   News that the regular army at Boston, with the inhabitants and effects, etc., are going off — whither is uncertain ;

---

[1] The *Adventurer* was a series of papers published in London, the first having appeared in 1752, and the last, two years later, in 1754.

and that part of the Provincial army hath marched Southward, expecting to oppose the Regulars at New York or Virginia.

16. *Saturday.* A firing of cannon at Boston and Dorchester during a great part of the night was heard by several.

17. *Sunday morning.* The troops at Boston embarked and went down to Nantasket, and the American troops took possession of the town and the fortifications at Bunker's Hill, where were found some wooden men and wooden guns and cannon, mounted, pointed, etc., etc., in due order.

18. *Monday.* A fine fair day. The fleet seen at Nantasket and King's Road from Leggs hill; the wind at N. E., they could not sail. The Court of Justices, Jurors, etc., summoned to attend this day at Ipswich, did not proceed, there being no act published for holding the court; in judicial matters hasty proceedings are seldom, if ever, so successful as moderate.

19. *Tuesday.* In the evening, about   o'clock, a great light was seen in the horizon, supposed to be the burning of the Castle, as since is proved.

20. *Wednesday.* [At] eve, at about 9 o'clock, another great light was seen, supposed to be at the burning of the buildings at Point Shirley; this light appeared to me, as I sat looking from the scuttle door, to be exactly in the midst between the two posts of the ballusters, at the top of the house, and a little south of Philips' house.[1]

24. *Sunday.* Clear and cold; wind brisk at N. W. The Fleet sailed from King's Road and Nantasket very early, and was out of sight at sunrise. News that they had taken prizes from the Americans during the week, and that they continued at Nantasket.

---

[1] Probably the burning of the block-house and barracks at the Castle by the British. See the *Boston Gazette*, March 25, 1776.

27. *Wednesday.*   The remainder of the Fleet at Nantasket and King's Road sailed from thence; whither bound is yet unknown.   Mrs. Browne, it is said, set out for Newport by land with Mr. Wickham.

29. *Friday.*   A great smoke at the southward is seen from Boston and Salem hills : said by some to be the woods on fire; by others, some ships; by others, a town.

30. *Saturday.*   Passage into Boston is allowed without passes at the ferries and at the Neck.   Training at Salem.

April 5.   *Friday.*   News came that Manly had taken (near Halifax) a vessel bound there from Boston,[1] with W. Jackson and other inhabitants, and a great quantity of goods.   Mitchel Sewall came.

7. *Sunday.*   Mr. Bromfield in town with his daughter from Boston.

10. *Wednesday.*   News by Capt. Browne that Quebeck was taken by the Provincial army, who lost therein 700 men, and that an express had arrived with the news. Mr. Vans proposes that Col. B., being a very worthy and good sort of man, should return to his country, and on his knees beg pardon of his countrymen; and he doubts not but he might, in such case, be received again.

11. *Thursday.*   Wm. Jackson, merchant,[2] and others, with some regular soldiers, went thro' Salem on foot for Boston, under guard; 't is said they were much insulted by the people (it must be presumed to be the rabble) at Newburyport, in their way hither; that Jackson was

---

[1] John Manly was one of the bravest and most successful of our commanders at this time.   He made several important captures, and was afterwards put in command of a 32-gun frigate.   It is asserted that "the first American flag was hoisted by him, and the first British flag was struck to him."   See Roads' *History of Marblehead*, p. 120.

[2] See *Hutchinson's Diary*, ii. p. 61.

stopped and obliged to leave his carriage, and walk on foot from Newbury to Salem, and thence to Boston ; that in Newbury street he was stopped again and obliged, after his hat was knocked off, to fall.on his knees and beg pardon of the mob and of the Country, and to say whatever was required of him.

14. *Sunday.*   Capt. Bowie, Foster, Hunter, Mess. Douglass, Hastie, and Savage, sailed for London.

15. *Monday.* Court of Admiralty at Ipswich. The new act produced was signed but by eleven of the Council.

22. [*Monday.*] Went in stage for Plymouth ; on Tuesday morning reached Wales' in [Hanover], and Plymouth on Wednesday, at sunset ; returned to Salem on Saturday P. M. the 27th.

30. *Tuesday.* Morn, and last night a plentiful rain. A salute of guns heard from Nantasket, as said.

May 6. *Monday.* Returned Puffendorf, 3 vols., Dodsley, 2 vols., Adventurer, 1 vol., to the Library ; and took out the 6th vol. of the Statutes, and returned it the 29th, election day.

13. *Monday.* Set out for Plymouth, and returned on Thursday, the 16th.

16. Received letter from Bro. Pynchon[1] of 14th of March.

17. *Continental Fast.*   News came of the Provincials' retreat from the works before Quebeck.

29. *Election day.* Tom. Bufton without notice left us in the morning and did not return till Thursday morning. Nat. Vickery came to live in the family, of which Tom had notice on Thursday morning. News of a skirmish at New York.

June 10.   *Monday.* Set out for Plymouth, Court of

---

[1] Joseph Pynchon, of Guilford, Conn.

Admiralty, and returned Saturday the 15th. Thursday night, the 13th, the militia went to Pt. Alderton and the islands by Nantasket, and placed some cannon ; and on Friday morning, they fired on the men of war and transports in the roads, on which they hoisted sail and departed.

16. *Sunday eve.* A heavy firing of cannon and small arms was heard at Lynn and Salem, and said to be at and from the Islands, Nantasket, etc., and from 3 or 4 Privateers, at an armed transport going for the Fleet, supposed to be at Boston.

20. *Thursday.* Mrs. Pynchon and myself being at Ipswich, B. with several of his companions went on board Capt. Fisher's vessel for a frolick, and did not return till   ; and, in the evening of the same Thursday, Mr. W. went on board, but could not persuade B. to return.

23. *Sunday.* A fleet of 10 or 11 sail of ships, some of them armed, were seen from Marblehead and Salem, steering towards Boston ; Capt. Fisher in a privateer kept ahead of them ; 3 others astern ; at about 3 P. M., the Fleet tacked and stood southward. On Monday they returned and kept in the bay, sailing backward and forward, and then stood eastward.

29. *Saturday.* By Col. Farley disagreeable news from Canada, New York and Albany. Very hot and dry all this week.[1]

30. *Sunday.* Easterly wind and foggy from the sea, and a prospect of rain ; thunder at a distance heard.

---

[1] *Quære,* whether the title of *Mr.,* *Esq.,* *Honour,* or *Lordship* be most proper in addressing J. Marston, [he being] Judge of Admiralty, of Common Pleas, of Court of Quarter Sessions, Justice of the Peace, County Register, Conveyancer and Scrivener, Colonel of the Regiment, Town Clerk, Parish Clerk, Representative, Selectman, Chairman of three Committees, High Sheriff, Brigadier, County Treasurer, Stated Preacher, Committeeman for Supplies, etc.

News of a conspiracy at New York for blowing up the magazines of the Provincials there, etc.

July 14. *Sunday.* Moderate rain. Mr. Wetmore and Mrs. Pynchon set out for Boston to consult Drs. Lloyd and Putnam.

15. *Monday.* The weather fine and fair. Upon return of Mr. Wetmore and Mrs. Pynchon from Boston, we dined and set out, and arrived there in good season, and myself and John were inoculated at Dr. Lloyd's house at ten o'clock in the evening ; he gave me six powders, to be mixed with molasses, and taken, one each night and morning ; and three for John, Monday, Wednesday, and Friday nights.

Was delivered into my hand the C. Congress' declaration of the Independence of the Colonies on G. Britain. Query, the consequences of this measure. God's chosen people, though governed by himself, desired a King of their own ; he gave them a King in his anger. We Americans, *God's favorite people*, desiring no King, have set ours aside ; but, wiser than the Israelites, who, having nothing, did every man what was right in his own eyes, we have preferred many to one, and subjected ourselves to   . We have had our ages of gold and of silver, but, not contented, we rejected both, and have lost them, and with them our copper and most of our brass and iron. What then ? Have we not PAPER in plenty ? Are we not wiser than the Israelites ? Charles the 12th of Sweden, a despot, wanted gold and silver, and his wants arose from his passion for war ; he took from his subjects all the silver they had, and in its stead returned them copper pieces, ordering them to pass as silver dollars. It was Baron Gortz' invention which cost him his life after the death of Charles. These pieces, as we are told, now pass for their real worth, which is less than a *Farthing*.   But our paper is an invention of our own.   Are we not wiser than Baron Gortz or his master ?

16. *Tuesday*.   Went to see Mr. Vassal's fine garden, also Mr. Lowell's ; eat our fill of fine fruit.   Visited the Salem patients in K[ing] and Q[ueen] streets, and find that they take powders but once in two days ; that I am favoured as to medicine, but expect to pay for it in pocks.   Dined at our lodgings.

17. *Wednesday*.   Dr. Putnam took the bandage, etc., off my arm this morning ; was satisfied that the incision, etc., were effectual ; went to Dr. Lloyd's, and he was of the same mind.   Visited our friends, patients, etc., in K. street and Q. street, also Dr. Pemberton and Dr. Mather; dined at Mr. Thomas Russell's with Dr. Putnam, Mr. Sparhawk, and Mr. Coleman ; P. M. eat fruit at Mr. Sheriff Greenleaf's fine garden — I mean S. Greenleaf, Esq. ; wrote to Mrs. Pynchon by Capt. Peale for some currants, etc.   Dr. Putnam and bro. Sargent at my lodgings in the evening ; drank tea at Dr. Putnam's.[1]

18. *Thursday*.   Took a glass of senna this morning instead of the powder ; John took half a glass of it, also, and within two hours each of us took another glass. Wrote to Mrs. Pynchon by Mr. Johnston and by Mr. Sparhawk for currant syrup instead of the fruit ; met Dr. Goodhue riding out.   He is breaking out, and is re-lieved by it ; his symptoms have been very high these three days ;   they appeared the ninth day from the in-oculation.[2]

---

[1] Dr. Aaron Putnam here mentioned was a physician of Charlestown. He was the great-grandson of Benjamin, the grandson of John and Pris-cilla Putnam, and the great-grandfather of Judge Samuel Putnam.

[2] The following is an extract from a letter of this date, written by Mr. Pynchon while in Boston : —

"We sleep finely, and our time passeth most agreeably indeed. We meet with much kindness from the gentlemen and all the inhabitants excepting

At noon the Congress Declaration of the Independence of the Colonies on Great Britain was read in the balcony of the Town house ; a regiment under arms, and artillery Co. in King Street, and the guns at the several batteries were fired, three cheers given, bells ringing, etc.; [in the] afternoon the King's arms were taken down and broken to pieces in King street, and carried off by the people.   P. M., cloudy and some rain.   Dr. Lloyd came to see me, and ordered me to continue taking the powders and senna, but John to omit the powders till Saturday night.   In the evening I received a letter from Mrs. Pynchon and a box of jellies, etc., by Mr. Knox.   Otis, I hear, curses me for a scoundrel.

19. *Fryday.*   Took another glass of senna ; John took one also ; at 12 took a powder.   Mr. Hunts at tea ; met Mr. Otis, and was introduced by him to Mrs. Otis in the street ; he left us, telling her that I was once a handsome fellow.

20. *Saturday.*   Took, each of us, a glass of senna before breakfast ; at 11 I took a powder ; wrote to Mrs. Pynchon by W. Sanders.   A. M., was at Mr. Bromfield's, and at Mr. Hutchison's and Watson's lodgings in Q. Street ; also at Mrs. Sparhawk's.   P. M., we went over to Bunker Hill ; met Mr. Barret and wife at the Ferry, who had been at my lodgings to see us, and were going to Salem on Monday.   On our return from Charles-

the tailors and barbers ; their squinting and fleering at our clothes, and especially our wiggs, begin to border on malevolence.   Had not the caul of my wigg been made of uncommon stuffe and workmanship, in my conscience I think my barber would have had it in pieces ; his dressing it greatly resembles the farmer's dressing his flax, the latter of the two being the gentlest in his motions. . . . We are told that Dr. P[arke]r will be called to answer for praying last Sunday for the King ; order is soon to be taken by the Congress, if not already done, as to publick prayers.   Yesterday we dined at Mr. Russell's ; visited Mr. Greenleaf's Gardens, and Dr. Pemberton and Dr. Mather."

town, found that Dr. Lloyd had been to see us. In the evening I went to advise with him as to medicine for tonight and tomorrow, but could not see him ; met there Mrs. Otis, and she urged me to come and see him. At 10 John took his powder, and I a glass of senna. Plentiful rain P. M.

21. *Sunday.* Cloudy and rain and sunshine by turns. John complains of swelling under his arm and in his gums, and toothache ; each of us took a glass of senna at 9. Dr. Lloyd called and left 6 more powders for me, and some salts for John ; the powders to be taken evening and morning as before, the salts twice, $\frac{1}{2}$ an oz. at a time. A Transport with beef and butter, from Ireland, was convoyed in to Nantasket by a fisherman ; on discovering the imposition, would have gone, but was prevented by the Fort at Point Alderton ; on her coming to the wharf, guns were fired and three cheers were given.

22. *Monday.* A very hot day. The militia being mustered for procuring   men — this town's proportion, for Canada and New York, drew us all into the Common, and the great heat brought on John's symptoms, to wit, headache and fever, which took away his appetite ; took a glass of senna ; dosed all the rest of the day ; at night took a small draught of nitre dissolved in water ; went to bed, having [had] but one dish of tea and a little piece of cake since breakfast. Was at Mr. Brimmer's in the afternoon ; tea at lodgings. John was very feverish and restless all night.

23. *Tuesday.* Cloudy and cool. Each took his glass of senna ; I took my powders as usual. Attended the Court of Inquisition. S. Greenleaf, Esq., Erwin, Esq., N. Cary, merchant, and —— Green, merchant, had each his trial. Mr. Erwin, of 83 years, and deaf, bound ; Mr.

Greenleaf bound to his good behaviour for   in £2000 himself, and £2000 his sureties ; Mr. Cary banished the town for four months, and to reside at [some] inland town, and bound to his good behaviour for   months. Tea, self and John, at Dr. Putnam's ; attended Mr. Winthrop for copies, etc., writs at his office. John's fever very high all night ; vomited in the evening.

24. *Wednesday.* Warm. Headache and loss of appetite early, yet assisted and gave directions to Mr. Elliot's commanders of the privateers ; walked only to Winnesimet Ferry this morning ; both languid and weak, — effects of medicine ; drank today only two dishes of tea and about four spoonfuls of milk porridge, being sick at the stomach. John continues to break out. Mrs. Pynchon came and brought some fruit, and dined with me.

25. *Thursday.* Warm. Sickness and headache continue ; John is easier than yesterday, and continues to break out ; eat today about a gill of milk and water, and a little piece of milk biscuit — the like at night ; headache and pain in my limbs abates in the cool of the evening, and I rested well. Dr. Lloyd had his trial this afternoon before the Court of Inquisition. Began to shave myself in the morning, but being obliged to desist through weakness was shaven by barber. Messrs. Sargent, Lowell, W. P. and ladies, Dr. Elliot and neighbour Giles, and Misses Onichs made us visits.

26. *Friday.* Warm. Headache and pain in my bones return, without any appetite ; eat only some broth at noon ; a dish of tea and one of coffee P. M. ; sleep well. Note — Lobden lives at the corner, near the place where Mrs. Bean lived in K. Street, and the Salem Stages, Warner, etc., put up there ; also at Newhalls.

27. *Saturday.* Weather moderate. Symptoms con-

tinue; eat some milk and water with some cake for breakfast. Dr. Lloyd much affected with the illness of his children, having the throat distemper. Hear from Salem that Derby's prize was retaken near Newbury bar; by J. Grafton and Mr. Lowell that some of the fleet in landing men at   were shattered and disabled.

28. *Sunday.* Fair. Symptoms continue; rose and walked about the house till sunrise; then walked to Charlestown Ferry; eat some whitpot for breakfast, also a cup of coffee and cake. Dr. P. says my fever is much abated. At noon Mr. Wetmore and Caty came to see us, and brought a most friendly letter from Mr. Goodale. Broth for dinner; John eat, in addition to his broth, a little lamb and cucumbers, notwithstanding my objections. Mr. Parsons procured me some fine cherries in the morning, and Mr. Lowell brought me some gooseberries and cherries. [In the] afternoon Father Kent [1] called and drank tea with me; hear that a transport [was] brought into Marblehead, bound from Halifax to New York, with B. Davis and others of this Town and Province on board, and a large quantity of goods.

29. *Monday.* Moderate, and rain by turns all day. Waked and rose at 3; walked to Charlestown Ferry; $1\frac{1}{2}$ dish of coffee for breakfast, pudding for dinner. John's fever increaseth; my fever abates; Dr. Lloyd here. Mr. Wetmore and Caty set out for Salem about 9 o'clock, just before the shower. John's fever and soreness increasing; Dr. Lloyd and Dr. Putnam came in the evening.

30. *Tuesday.* Fair. Pain in my head not entirely

---

[1] Rev. Benjamin Kent, H. C., 1727, was educated for the ministry, and was settled for a while at Marlboro, but afterwards abandoned that profession and studied law. At first a Whig, he subsequently espoused the other side, and died a refugee in Halifax in 1788. " He was an eccentric man," says Sabine, "and a wit."

gone ; for breakfast one dish of coffee, two dishes of milk and water, with milk biscuit and a bunn. John took electuary. Dr. Lloyd's trial finished —his condemnation.[1] I eat for dinner pudding and some buttered peas. Mr. Sargent went with me to see Judge W. Cushing whose pock was about turning. Mr. Russell and Colo. Frye to see me in the evening.

31. *Wednesday.* Fair. Billy came from Salem, brought some fruit, and dined with us; returned P. M. with young West. Dr. Lloyd here to see us.

August 1. *Thursday.* Fair and warm. Fast day. Rose with headache. Dr. Lloyd came, and allowed of eating meat, oysters, etc., moderately. Mr. Elliot from Ct. at Salem says old Mr. Barnard declines fast (if living), having had another paralytic turn. Went with Dr. Putnam to hear Dr. Elliot. Coddled apples and milk supper. Thundered and rained in the night ; at eve Mr. Blodget and co. visited us.

2. *Friday.* Cloudy and warm. Of Mr. Giles, two quarts whortleberries — milk supper ; go to bed, but cannot sleep ; rise again and walk the room some hours. Mr. Russell and lady and Dr. Elliot to visit us in the evening, also Blodget and co.

3. *Saturday.* Fair. Rise with the headache ; chocolate for breakfast ; walked up to K. Street, Mr. Lowell, and co. By way of Dr. Putnam we were asked to Dr. Lloyd's this afternoon, but were not well enough to wait on him. Supped on coddled apples and milk. Hear that Mr. Barnard of Salem died yesterday.

---

[1] Dr. James Lloyd seems to have been a moderate loyalist, and it is difficult to determine why the hard measures alluded to were taken against him. There is no mention of this trial in the biographical sketches of him.

Henry Lloyd prosecuted and banished in 1775 ; went to Halifax in 1776 ; and died in 1795, æt. 86.

4. *Sunday.* Fair and fine. Slept well last night;
[had] my usual headache ; rode in Dr. Pemberton's
chaise to the fortification and back with son John, which
almost cured my headache ; dined on w. berry pudding,
butter sauce, stringed beans and peas, and roast pigeon,
and eat heartily without inconvenience, and drank a
beaker of wine and water. Hear that Parson Barnard is
yet living. Tea at home ; Mrs. Pynchon and John at Miss
Gerrish's. Dr. Loring and the Miss Hunts spend the
evening with us. Supper w. and milk.

5. *Monday.* Fair and fine. Rose at 6 almost free
from headache ; chocolate for breakfast ; at 8 went over
the Neck with Mr. Coburn's horse and chaise ; a glass
of senna before breakfast ; mutton, squash and turnips for
dinner, with a little flip at landlady's desire, and it did
no harm ; tea at Dr. Lloyd's, where were Dr. Pemberton,
and N. Dowst, and Mrs. Temple and daughter ; visited
at Mr. Russell's afterwards, and at Mr. Hunt's in the
evening ; chocolate for supper ; took electuary first.
N. Ropes came with chaise for Dr. Putnam and Eben.

6. *Tuesday.* Fair and fine. Rose without headache ;
to Charlestown Ferry with Dr. Putnam, who with N.
Ropes went for Salem ; took a glass of senna ; chocolate
for breakfast ; received a present of sermons from Dr.
Pemberton ; at eleven took electuary. B. and S. came
and dined with us at two ; tarried the night. I went to
visit Parson Cooper, and he not at home ; went to Mr.
Kent's, and he absent ; thence to Mr. Coburn's ; went
to neighbour Giles'.

7. *Wednesday.* Fair and warm. Rose without the
headache ; took a glass of senna ; chocolate for breakfast. B. and S. tarried at breakfast and dinner, and they
with John set out for Salem after dinner, with S. Cabot
and Deb. Higginson about 4 o'clock from Winnisimet.

2

Mr. Vans with me in the evening, also Dr. Whittaker; I was at Dr. Clarke's in the afternoon, and eat fruit in his garden.

8. *Thursday.* Fair and warm. For breakfast, chocolate; dinner, mutton. P. M. at Mr. Sparhawk's, Dr. Pemberton's, and Mrs. Ropes' in K. Street; in the evening I came home in the rain.

9. *Fryday.* Cloudy. Rose at 7. Mr. Goodhue here; Mr. Wetmore dined here; attended P. M. the trial of a vessel bound from Jamaica for London.

10. *Saturday.* Fair. I rose at $\frac{1}{2}$ past 8 o'clock, too late to breakfast at Mr. Elliot's, who invited Mr. W. and myself; we all dined at Mrs. Chadwell's, and about 2 set out for the ferry; Mr. W. and Mrs. Pynchon for Charlestown, myself and B. for Winnisimet; and we all met at Newhall's and baited, and reached Salem about 7 o'clock, self and John having recovered of Small Pox.

12. *Monday.* The news of the dissolution of the English and Irish Parliaments in part confirmed, to wit, as to Ireland; as to England, [it is] said to be only a prorogation of Parliament. Several large showers today of rain. Received a letter from G. Deblois dated Halifax in July.

14. *Wednesday.* Rained and very warm. Dr. Smith and Mr. West in the evening here.

19. *Monday.* The Court of Admiralty; the " Queen of England " tried.[1] In the evening, Mr. L. and Mr. Wetmore set out for Portsmouth.

24. *Saturday.* Mr. Lowell and Mr. Wetmore return from Portsmouth. Milford frigate came into the harbour.

25. *Sunday.* At Church in the afternoon.

---

[1] This ship was advertised in the papers of the day to be sold at auction, October 3, 1776.

September 3. *Tuesday.* News from Boston that last week there were two engagements on Long Island ; in one, that 2000 regulars were killed ; in the other, that 5000 Provincials were killed by Hessians, who rushed on them sword in hand, throwing aside their muskets. *Credat Judæus Apella !* Mr. Vans prophesies that there will be no battle at New York this year ; his word for it.

6. *Fryday.* Mr. Vans present on Mr. Lee's and A. Cabot's [1] arrival from Boston, with news by way of Connecticut and Providence that the Provincials had gone off Long Island with artillery, etc., and that it was doubted whether they could secure New York against the regular army.

7. *Saturday.* The news confirmed by Mr. Hopkins and Lowell [2] from the General Court, Watertown ; and that Gen. Sullivan and P. Stirling [were] taken prisoners. It is said that Gen. Sullivan is at New York on his parole. Mr. Lowell returned in the rain from Boston. Mr. Wetmore and Caty returned last night ; they went on last Wednesday.

---

[1] Andrew Cabot was a son of Joseph and grandson of the first John Cabot. He was born December 10, 1750. He married Lydia Daye April 28, 1773, and died May, 1791.

The Cabots so often mentioned in this volume are descendants of John Cabot of Beverly, who came from St. Heliers, Jersey, in 1700, and was the son of François Cabot. He seems to have had nine children : 1. *John,* who married first Sarah Higginson, and secondly Hannah Clark. 2. *Hester,* who married John Higginson. 3. *Mary,* who married Mitchell Sewall, the father-in-law of William Pynchon. 4. *Anna,* who died unmarried. 5. *Margaret,* who married Benjamin Gerrish, who died in 1752, governor of Bermuda. 6. *Elizabeth,* who married Stephen Higginson. 7. *Francis,* who married first Mary Fitch, and secondly Mrs. Gardner, leaving by the latter no issue. 8. *Joseph,* who married Elizabeth Higginson. From Joseph are descended the Cabots, Lees, Jacksons, Winthrops, and Lowells of Boston.

[2] Daniel Hopkins of the Council, and John Lowell of Newburyport, one of the General Court.

8. *Sunday.* Mrs. Ste. Higginson[1] had her two daughters christened at Church ; the eldest about $2\frac{1}{2}$ years
old, named Barbara Cooper ; the other, six weeks old,
called Elizabeth ; sponsors, herself, with W. P. and ux.
Very warm, P. M.

17. *Tuesday.* The maritime Court sat at Salem until
Saturday afternoon.

22. *Sunday.* Fair wind, S. W. B. went on board
about 7 o'clock to go to sea when the tide should serve.
News from Boston by post from New York that the
city was in the possession of regular troops.

23. *Monday.* Fair and serene ; wind N. W. I sent,
enclosed to Captains Foster, Bowie, Hunter and Lawrea,
the decrees of condemnation of their several ships and
vessels by Capt. Pringle, bound from Boston for London.

October 1. *Tuesday.* Toast given by a Continental
agent to some prisoners at his table, " D——n to K.
George's head and pluck."

3. Capt. Sam. West was buried ; his age was [85]
years.[2] Mr. T. Fitch Oliver came to study law at my
office on this day.

22. News from Gen. Schuyler that Gen. Arnold's
fleet was beat and almost destroyed on the Lake ; that
Gen. Arnold blew up his ship, and escaped himself, and
some of the men, by swimming to shore ; that about 300
were taken prisoners, and dismissed with the blankets,
etc., to go home and not to take up arms again this   .

---

[1] Stephen Higginson was the son of Stephen Higginson and Elizabeth,
daughter of the first John Cabot. Their eldest daughter, Barbara Cooper,
who was born January 15, 1774, afterwards married Samuel G. Perkins,
whose daughter Barbara married the late Dr. Walter Channing of Boston.

[2] Captain Samuel West was the son of Samuel, the son of Henry West,
born in 1629. He was born in 1691, and married first Mary Gale, and
secondly Esther Brentnal. His son William married Mary Bickford, and
had Nathaniel, an eminent merchant of Salem, who left descendants, and
Edward, who died unmarried.

December 15. *Sunday.* News that Lord Howe and Gen'l Howe, are yet at New York, and that Earl Percy only with 6000 troops is on the Jersey side, without any design of proceeding to Philadelphia; and that part of a body of 15,000 foreign troops had arrived at Halifax, said to be about half of them; that Capt. Mussy and others had taken the   and carried her into   .

18. *Wednesday.* Cloudy, and south wind. Orders came for imprisonment of masters of vessels and others who had been taken as prisoners and were abroad on their parole, etc. ; some absconded and others were taken up. Mr. Dowst's family affrighted by soldiers with bayonets fixed, inquiring for prisoners. Colo. Frye's house searched also, as it is said.

21. Mr. Seton ordered by the Committee to be confined at D. King's and not to go without the yard. Lord and Gen'l Howe's proclamation to the Americans to come and surrender within [sixty] days.

23. Na[than] Bowen, Esq., Marblehead, deceased, aged 80.

24. Jos. Blaney, Esq., wife, deceased.[1] Weather severely cold. Prize said to be carried into Dartmouth ; 10,000 stand of arms, and 10,000 to 14,000 suits of clothes for soldiers.

25. *Christmas.* Very cold. My windows at Church broken, agreeable to threats of Cook and comp. for assisting the countryman to get the apples stolen from him.

26. *Thursday.* Snow and rain spoil the sledding. General Lee surprised and taken.

[1] Mrs. Abigail Blaney was the daughter of Samuel Browne, H. C. 1727, whose wife was Catherine, a daughter of John Winthrop, whose second husband was Epes Sargent. She married Joseph Blaney in 1757. Mr. Blaney was a prominent citizen of Salem at this time. He was born February 12, 1730, was graduated at Harvard College in 1751, and died in 1786.

27. Gen'l Howe defeated, and lost 7000 men, baggage, etc.

29. *Sunday*. Fair and moderate. News from Dr. Putnam at Providence, where he and Salem company had arrived well.

Threats and Wishes.

That Parson Gilchrist might drop down dead when he enters his pulpit ; that every tory was banished off the face of the earth ; that he, J. Dodge, could wring his hands in the heart's blood of every tory in the land — he could kill them as soon as he would eat ; that they did not deserve to live.

News of the fight at Jersey ; 12,000 British troops routed, and more taken prisoners than Gen'l Howe had taken since the arrival of Regulars.   News by vessel from France that more was done at F. Ct. last June than could be expected ; that great preparations were making in France and Spain, in Fleet and Army, in favour of America.   Newport submitted to British troops without opposition.   It rained but once in November and before the 12th of December.

1777. *January* 1.   News that the Farmer, Mr. Dickenson of Philadelphia, was gone over to Gen'l Howe with some other gentlemen ; that the Congress had sent off their papers, etc., and were preparing to depart from Philadelphia for Baltimore ; that on Christmas eve, Gen'l Washington with 3000 Americans crossed the Delaware, and, it being very stormy in the night, surprised and routed a party of 1500 or 1600 Hessians, a Colo. and other officers, cannon, baggage, etc. ; that about 900 of them were taken prisoners, some killed and some escaped.

9. That R. T. Paine, Esq., [is] returned from Congress, and contradicts the account of the Farmer's departure, and confirms the account of Gen'l Washington's action.

10. J. Adams and J. Lovell, Esqs., set out for the Congress.

12. Mr. Hastie[1] returned to Salem.

14. *Tuesday.* Lost my pocket book [in] Danvers. News that Newport is burnt by Regulars.

17. News from Capt. Cleaveland, by Mr. J. Cabot,[2] that he and B. are well at Bordeaux. Cabot from Bilboa. Snow.

18. News from Boston of a difference at Ticonderoga between the Western and Southern soldiers and officers, and that some ears had been cut off; that the Newport affair is not true. Cold, and good sledding. Capt. Sullivan returns by leave of Gen'l Howe.

21. *Tuesday.* Wrote to Mr. Burke of Antigua by Mr. Payson, enclosing the condemnation of the " Little Hannah."

23. *Thursday.* Snow storm. Setting chimney on fire nearly burnt [the] keeping room.

24. *Fryday.* Snow and rain. John's proposal to S. Blyth to be a painter.[3]

The current doctrine among the inventors of the New State is that the friends of the Old State may move off with their effects, but have no right to speak here.

29. *Wednesday.* Fast day. Capt. Dodge's house on fire.

---

[1] James Hastie of Salem.

[2] John Cabot, son of Joseph, and grandson of the first John Cabot. He was born on the 13th of January, 1765. His wife was Hannah Dodge, who died on the 17th of February, 1830. He died on the 28th of August, 1821. His daughter Fanny married Judge Charles Jackson.

[3] Samuel Blyth, who at one time kept a boarding-school for young ladies, near St. Peter's Church.

30. *Thursday.* My keeping room chimney on fire again. News that the King of France was cast away with the Fleet at Newfoundland, but that he and a few escaped, and almost starve in a fishing vessel. Walker, Lawson, and others were taken and seized at Piemonts, [and] carried before the Committee, for profaning Fast day by going to Danvers and to the tavern.

31. *Fryday.* Fair, moderate day. The contest between farmers and Salem traders, etc., as to price of meal begins; the former threaten to starve the seaports.

February 1. A beautiful day, clear and serene. News that Gen'l Washington's army had attacked Gen'l Howe's lines at   , and had carried them with the loss of men ; this not true. [It is] said that Colo. Campbell is to be committed to Concord jail this day.

2. *Sunday.* Cloudy, wind S. E. N. B. John Wedderberne, Esq., at Blue Castle in the parish of Westmoreland in Jamaica, agent of W. Vassal's, Esq., plantation.

9. *Sunday.* The Church not opened, Mr. Gilchrist [1] having information of a design, in case he preached any more, to take him by force out of the pulpit, and of a design to prosecute him on the new Province Law. Mr. Dana told me that it was thought to be against the Law for Churchmen to use the common forms of prayer in the Desk. *Tempora !* Cloudy day, but moderate, spring like weather.

10. *Monday.* Went to Boston in the stage with Judge Sargeant, Mr. Wetmore, etc.

11. *Tuesday.* Snowed. Went to Dr. Lloyd's.

12. *Wednesday.* Went up to Cambridge Court ; returned at night.

---

[1] The Rev. William McGilchrist was an English gentleman of much culture. He was educated at Oxford, and was rector of St. Peter's from 1747, until his death in April, 1780.

13. Went to see Mr. Payson at Chelsea, respecting John's living with him.

14. *Fryday.* Set out in an open sleigh for Salem with Mr. Vans and company, and was nearly frozen in passing Winter hill; were met at Medford by Mr. Wetmore, and returned home P. M.

15. *Saturday.* Clear and cold. Good sledding, and much wood brought to market, but very little meat.

19. *Wednesday.* Mr. Dowse [1] as he passed the street had the discipline of snow balling.

20. *Thursday.* Went to Boston with Katy and Sally in Daland's close conveyance.

21. *Fryday.* Dined at Mr. Hitchburn's with Court and Barr.

22. *Saturday.* Hooper and Norwood at Superior Court; in the afternoon set out from Boston, crossed Winnisimet Ferry, and were at home to drink tea.

24. *Monday.* Snow. J. Williams came here.

25. *Tuesday.* Snow deep. Dr. Putnam received the discipline of snow balling as he passed the street.

26. *Wednesday.* Clear and pleasant. Difficult passing to and from Marblehead for depth of snow. Letter from G. Deblois.

27. *Thursday.* Clear and warm. News from B. P. and W. Cabot in England. Colo. Browne and Porter gone to France.

28. *Fryday.* Cloudy and very windy and cold. When at Boston wrote to Eph. Spooner and Thos. Davis by Mr. Lothrop, as to their note to Symonds being lost.

March 1. *Saturday.* Cold and fair. Mr. Wetmore returned from B. News by Mr. Brimmer of Mrs. Sewall's death, and of her child.

2. *Sunday.* Cloudy and very cold. At Mr. Barnard's

---

[1] Joseph Dowse was surveyor of the port of Salem.

meeting.   News of the arrival of a frigate at New York, and of Gen'l Howe's sending a message to the Congress upon it.

13. *Thursday.*   Capt. Leach here, A. M.   Cloudy and some rain.

14. *Fryday.*   The Cartel sailed for Halifax.   Fair and moderate ; wind, N. W.

19. *Wednesday.*   Clear and fair.   Yesterday voted to open and regulate a small pox hospital.

22. *Saturday.*   Fair and moderate.   Fleet of 28 sail ships in Ipswich Bay, Marblehead fishermen, etc.

23. *Sunday.*   Moderate — clear ; wind S. W.   Privateer fired at while going out.

24. *Monday.*   Dark and cloudy ; wind S. E.   The Marblehead fishermen, who bro't news of the 28 sail ships, saw a privateer and heard a gun, and imagined all the vessels by Jas. Mugford's [1] accounts.

25. *Tuesday.*   Fair and exceedingly cold.   Obliged to stop twice to warm us on the road to Ipswich.

29. *Saturday.*   Snow, and very raw and cold wind. At night returned from Ipswich.

30. *Sunday.*   In the morning about 6 o'clock, Mrs. Lowell [2] died, after enduring for a long time, and with

[1] Captain James Mugford commanded the Continental cruiser Franklin.

[2] Mrs. Susannah Lowell was the youngest daughter of Francis Cabot. She was the second wife of John Lowell, whose name appears so often in this diary.   Mr. Lowell was the son of the Rev. John Lowell of Newburyport.   He was born June 17, 1743, and was graduated at Harvard College in 1760.   He was sent to Congress in 1781, was made a judge of the Court of Appeals in 1782, and judge of the U. S. District Court in 1789.   By his first wife, Sarah Higginson, he had John, the father of John Amory Lowell ; by his second, Susan, daughter of Francis Cabot, he had Francis C. Lowell, founder of the city of Lowell, whose sons were John, Francis C., and Edward J. Lowell ; by his third wife, Rebecca Russell, he had Rebecca R., married Samuel P. Gardiner, Rev. Charles, and Elizabeth Cutts, who married Warren Dutton.

uncommon fortitude and patience, great distress and pain. Mr. W. maintains and passionately the doctrine of January.

31. *Monday*. Fair and moderate. By Mr. Waldo heard that B. was well at Bordeaux, and seen by a French gentleman lately arrived from thence into Boston. Mr Seton committed to jail, being, as he says, invited or desired to meet some of the committee at Browne's house ; there he went to meet them, but none were there, and the Jailor confined him.

April 2. *Wednesday*. Cloudy and cold. Mrs. Lowell's funeral.

Bearers —	G. Dodge	T° Lee
	H. Derby	J. Goodhue
	J. Derby	Wm. Pickman

Procession —	Mr. Lowell	Mr. Cabot et ux.
	W. Gardner and	Mrs. Higginson
	J. Barnard et ux.	Dabney et ux.
	The Cabots of Beverly	
	Mr. Jackson et ux.	W. Wetmore et ux.

Mr. Gardner's family, called children of John, preceded the other relations. N. B. Mr. Appleton not in the room with the relations, nor in the procession with them ; objections to Appleton, Orne, Blaney, Brimmer.

3. *Thursday*. Rumours of attacking Philadelphia, Ticonderoga, etc., and that the latter is in a weak state, and in great danger if attacked.

4. *Friday*. Went to Boston in Verry's[1] stage — exceeding cold — on the Ipswich business.

---

[1] Mr. Verry drove a post-chaise from Salem to Boston as early as 1774. The price to Winnisimet Ferry was 3-/4.

5. *Saturday.* Returned in the stage; Mr. G. foretells that a constitution will be made for us in less than 12 months. *Haud credo.*

6. *Sunday.* Fine, moderate, and clear morning; wind, N. W. Mrs. Anderson went in P. Stage for Sewall's Point. Qu. Can any more than a negociation be expected within Mr. Goodale's terms? Confined by a cold.

10. *Thursday.* Warm and pleasant; [wind] S. W. Mr. Barrett lodged here; news [that] Continental bills [are] credited in France.

12. *Saturday.* Morning fair and moderate. J. went with S. Orne to Chelsea to Mr. Payson's school. Wrote Cab. Gerrish[1] by Capt. Emery from Newburyport, inclosed in letter to Mess. Guardogui, in answer to Gerrish's letter this day received; also sent Capt. Pyne's papers.

13. *Sunday.* Cloudy; wind S. Confined by a cold, and a stitch in my side.

14. *Monday.* Fair and windy. Floyd came to work in the garden, which he agreed to take this season to the halves.

15. *Tuesday.* Went to Concord. Very cold and windy.

16. *Wednesday.* Fair and pleasant. Tom Duckerfield returned home.

18. *Fryday.* Rain. Went from Concord to Cambridge.

19. *Saturday.* From Cambridge to Salem. News from Boston that E. Sargent, Esq., Green, Mess. Perkins, W. Jackson, and Cary were taken out of their houses and thrown into a cart and carted out of town and left on the neck, and charged not to return at their peril.[2]

---

[1] Cabot Gerrish was the son of Benjamin Gerrish and Margaret, daughter of the first John Cabot. He died in the summer of 1777, as will be seen below.

[2] See *Boston Gazette*, April 21, 1777.

20. *Sunday.* Rain. Vessel with goods from Bordeaux into Boston.

21. *Monday.* In the paper, Joyce's insolent publication. Sitting, the General Court. Vessel from France into Portsmouth, with powder, goods, cannon, etc., as it is said. Mr. Seton went to Boston in the coach.

25. *Fryday.* Plentiful rain. Commodore Manly and McNeal challenged to go out to [meet] the English Cruisers on the Coast.[1]

26. *Saturday.* Cloudy, but warm and pleasant; wind S.; rained in the afternoon and [a] great part of the night. W. West's store, opposite my house, broken open, and a barrel of sugar stolen out of it. News of troops arriving at New York; some say Russians, others, Hessians. Great numbers of N. Hampshire Bills found to be counterfeit. Warrants issue in this state and N. Hampshire against suspected persons.

28. *Monday.* Fair, N. W. The Marblehead people and Salem people quarrel for bread at the bakers, and a scramble at the wharf in weighing out and selling Capt. Derby's coffee. Query, is it not become a duty to take care for tomorrow?

30. *Wednesday.* Hard frost last night. Water froze in vessels standing exposed. At night Mr. Oliver returned from Boston. News that 1000 regulars had landed at Fairfield, and more were landing; that Ticonderoga was attacked, — this by letter from S. Higginson; [and that] Burgoyne was coming to B. with 10,000 troops. *Credat Apella.*

May 1. *Thursday.* Wind N. E. Cold, and snow in the morning, and rain also the remainder of the day, it being Fast day. News of 3000 or 4000 regulars landing at Fairfield, and marching to Danbury, burning some

----

[1] See *History of Marblehead*, p. 177.

houses and taking magazine and stores without opposition ; that H. Higginson and vessel probably were taken.

3. *Saturday.* John came home with Mr. Payson from Chelsea.

4. *Sunday.* Warm. P. M., Mr. Payson preached at Mr. Dunbar's [1] meeting house.

5. *Monday.* Mr. Mellen,[2] with [the] Club, in the evening at my house.

6. *Tuesday.* Mr. Alcock[3] presents to the committee a list of people to be carted out of town.

7. *Wednesday.* John returns to Chelsea with Joe. Daland, who is going for Brookline in an empty carriage. Rain, P. M.

8. *Thursday.* Cloudy day. News of a skirmish at Brunswick, and that we lost 100 men. Rain, P. M.

10. *Saturday.* Cloudy and some rain, A. M., wind E. Whiting taken out for examination, and committed again for further examination.

11. *Sunday.* A fine, clear morning ; cold and frost last night ; A. M., the wind south, and warm. News that 40 transports were on the coast, and that 6 of them were taken ; no convoy with them. Cloudy and cold, P. M. ; wind N. E.

15. *Thursday.* Fair and warm. Drums beat at 5 in the morning for draughting men for the Continental army, pursuant (as said), to an Act of the General Court ; on enquiry it was found that only 3 or 4 had seen the Act, which was in a handbill sent to the Committee or officers of militia. The alarm list, as well as train band, were warned and attended, and nothing [was] at-

---

[1] Mr. Dunbar was the minister of the First Church from 1772 to 1779. He was graduated at H. C. 1767.

[2] Rev. John Mellen, of Hopkinton, H. C. 1741.

[3] Mansel Alcock, a public crier.

tempted in the morning ; and in the afternoon attended again, and nothing was done further. *Libertas !*

16. *Fryday.* Wind south, and rain. Bought half a cord of wood, and am now richer in wood than 39/40 of the whole town, having part of 2 loads by me! We crawl about and exist, but cannot be said truly to live. It is said we have full enjoyment of our liberty, but where is the proof of it?

17. *Saturday.* Fair and pleasant ; wind N. W. News that Col. Holland is taken in Connecticut; a parson committed in Boston for treason ; and that politics begin to wear a new face. W. Cooper[1] *et alii* likely to go astern.

18. *Sunday.* Fair and warm ; wind south. Went to Salem hospital.

19. *Monday.* Rain, P. M. The representatives for Salem accept.

20. *Tuesday.* Fair ; wind south. Good news from Ipswich that the town would choose but 2 representatives at most, and Story was left out.

24. *Saturday.* Clear and warm. Floyd plants the beans, squashes, etc. News that Maj. Hawley is not well enough to come to Court ; that W. Cooper is not chosen representative of Boston.

27. *Tuesday.* Small pox broke out in many places in Beverly.

28. *Wednesday.* Began to inoculate at Beverly, but the town meeting votes were against their proceeding further. A fair day and pleasant.

30. *Fryday.* Clear and very warm day. News that

---

[1] William Cooper was son of the Rev. William Cooper, H. C. 1712, who was a colleague with Dr. Colman at Brattle Street Church, and a brother of Rev. Samuel Cooper, H. C. 1743, a classmate of Mr. Pynchon. He was town clerk of Boston for fifty years.

Gen'l Howe had sent to Gen'l Carlton for 4000 of his troops, and he to act on the defensive ; and that no more than 2000 foreign troops are expected from Europe this spring to America.

31. *Saturday.*   By Mr. Wr that the great and vociferous W. Cooper had no votes either for representative or councillor.   Warm day.   News that very few troops, and no foreign troops, are to come this season from Europe.

June 1. *Sunday.*   Clear and warm ; wind south.   At Mr. Oliver's in the evening.

2. *Monday.*   Town meeting as to inoculating for small pox.   Rain in the morning ; clearing off warm.   John with Warner went to Malden.

6. *Fryday.*   Went to D. Marshes.   Warm weather.

7. *Saturday.*   Very warm ; wind south.   The news of the battle in the Jerseys comes to nothing.

20. *Fryday.*   Fair and pleasant.   Returned from Court.

21. *Saturday.*   Fair.   J. Prince, from Newport, [says] that the regulars were proceeding towards Delaware.

22. *Sunday.*   Cloudy ; wind N. E.   At Mr. Barnard's meeting.

27. *Fryday.*   Very warm A. M. ; cloudy P. M.   News that the Americans were skirmishing with Gen'l Howe's troops on their march in the Jerseys ; that part of Gen'l Carlton's regulars had joined Gen'l Howe's troops at New York ; that the northern portion of the American army were in want of clothes and supplies, and not in so good spirits as we had heard, and not in a condition to oppose Howe directly.   A plentiful rain with thunder in the afternoon and night.

28. *Saturday.*   Warm and cloudy.   News that the monopoly act is suspended ; that Gen'l Howe is returned to Brunswick, and is intrenching ; that 12 or 15 wood

sloops at [the] eastward were taken and burnt; Tom Bufton in one of them.

30. *Monday.* News that Gen'l Howe left Brunswick hastily, embarked his whole army, and went to Staten Island; was closely pursued by some riflemen, and lost many men in skirmishes.

The Acts of the State absolutely prohibit every kind of depreciation of the paper currency, either by words or actions; yet every trader, huckster, marketman, and peddler, with open mouths, unitedly declare and publickly say it is of little or no value; offer to take anything in payment for their wares or for their debts except paper. Broadcloth said to be £6. 3. 4. per yard, and scarcely any to be had. B. Tea at 7 and 8 dollars per pound.

July 1, 2, 3. *Tuesday, Wednesday, and Thursday.* News that Gen'l Carlton, with an army of considerable numbers, had arrived at Crown Point, which came in several ways, and in a letter from Gen'l Schuyler.

4. *Fryday.* Hen. Higginson at Boston in a Flagg from Halifax. Cloudy at night and signs of rain.

5. *Saturday.* Very warm and clear. Mr. O. set out for Danvers between 9 and 10 in the evening.

6. *Sunday.* Fair and pleasant. Mr. and Mrs. O. here. At Mr. Barnard's meeting. Mons. Charier came to Salem yesterday.

7. *Monday.* Fair and pleasant; wind N. E. Letters from B. at Bordeaux per Capt. Higginson; Harry Higginson returned to Salem in the hour of his brother's return.

8. *Tuesday.* Inferior Court sits.

12. *Saturday.* Capt. Wms. from General Court [says] that Gen'l Prescott was taken by a party from Providence, and carried off from his bed in the night, and obliged to march without hat, etc., much as Gen'l Lee had been before him; and that Ticonderoga was evacu-

ated by   and his army of about 5000 men in a disgraceful manner, very little being brought off with them more than their muskets and swords. Can this be true, when in all the late publications we find the army in high spirits and eager to meet the Regulars, and some longing to rap them over the knuckles ?

13. *Sunday.* Cloudy and cold ; rain in the evening. At Mr. Barnard's meeting. Betty Whitworth went to Salem Hospital.

14. *Monday.* Cloudy; wind N. News that Manly had sent to the eastward an English frigate of 32 guns.

15. *Tuesday.* News of Ticonderoga evacuated.

16. *Wednesday.* News that many were ambushed and killed at retreating from Ticonderoga.

17. *Thursday.* Clear and warm. The Fox frigate said to be taken and carried into Halifax.

19. Sent to Asa Upton, by his wife, two original deeds: *Jos. Pope* to *Benj. Upton*, and *Benj. Upton* to *Asa Upton*. By Parson Hitchcock's letter, there were, two days before Ticonderoga was deserted, 4000 continental soldiers and 1000 militia.

21. *Monday.* News of 40 transports at Newport, bound westward.

22. *Tuesday.* Fair and clear. Hastie and Capt. Lee go to Boston. Rained all night. Mob at Salem demand sugar, and the stores are opened.

23. *Wednesday.* Warm, fine growing weather. The ladies rise and mob for coffee ; cart it and the owner, Boylston.

24. *Thursday.* Fair, with northwest wind. News is confirmed that Manly is taken by the Cabot and Rainbow frigates, and carried into Halifax ;[1] Capt. Stanley commander of the Rainbow. Ladies mob again on Copp's Hill.

[1] See *History of Marblehead*, p. 178 ; *Hutchinson's Diary*, ii. p. 157.

26. *Saturday.* A countryman beat for not taking paper for his meat, which (he says) he had sold before.

28. *Monday.* Went to Chelsea with John, and to Boston. Bad news from Ticonderoga, [the] Regulars advancing and 14 towns submitting to them.

29. *Tuesday.* Returned from Boston. The story of Manly's being taken not credited, he having been seen a few days past at the eastward.

31. *Thursday.* Fair and pleasant. It is said again that Manly is at Halifax, and ill treated ; also that a fleet of 100 sail was seen this afternoon off Gloucester, standing northward ; expresses were sent to Boston and greatly alarmed the inhabitants ; Friday evening an express was sent from Salem to Boston to contradict the story.

August 1. *Fryday.* Warm ; some rain in the afternoon. Nothing further from the fleet.

2. *Saturday.* Cloudy, and some rain. No confirmation of the rumour as to the fleet. Mr. Lewis in Salem in the evening. By Colo. Glover's letters, received at Boston, it seems that the fleet was going for Delaware. People of middle station and others say that if the fleet came here they would not oppose them, having to fight for   .

4. *Monday.* News that Gen'l Howe had landed at Newcastle, within 18 miles of Philadelphia, some say within 40 miles ; that there had been a battle near Ticonderoga, and the Provincials had driven the Regulars from all their posts into Ticonderoga, and had killed or taken 900 or 1000 men ; this comes 2 or 3 ways, into Boston and from New Hampshire.

5. *Tuesday.* Rumoured that the fleet does not appear at Philadelphia, and it is supposed that it is gone off. Rain.

6. *Wednesday.* Cloudy, with N. E. wind. Mrs. Wet-

more [1] taken ill at 12 o'clock last night, and on Wednesday night, past 12, was delivered of a fine boy; Dr. Holyoke in attendance.

9. *Saturday.* Very warm; some rain in the evening. News that Gen'l Washington passed the Delaware, and that Howe returned to the Hook.

10. *Sunday.* Mr. Diman preached at Mr. Dunbar's.

13. *Wednesday.* Warning for draughting men — each sixth able bodied man; a cloudy day in two senses. I offered 10 dollars a cord for wood, and could get none.

14. *Thursday.* Berry's cord of wood received. Training day; Mr. Lewis and Lamb. Very warm day; rained in the night.

16. *Saturday.* Fair and cool. Mr. and Mrs. Phillips here from Middletown.

18. *Monday.* Some rain in the morning; cloudy in the evening. Mr. and Mrs. Phillips, with Mr. Wetmore, go to Boston in the stage. News that the Regulars, Indians, etc., who attacked a party of Americans going to Fort Stanwix, were defeated and lost 200.

19. *Tuesday.* In the evening Dr. Eliot here. Fair. At Mr. Orne's.

20. *Wednesday.* Mr. and Mrs. Orne: he ill; his memory affected. News of an engagement at Bennington; that the lines of the Regulars were forced and carried, and 400 prisoners and 4 pieces of brass cannon taken from them. Very hot.

21. *Thursday.* Very warm. Mr. Parker here.

22. *Fryday.* Very hot. News in a handbill of the victory at Bennington. Mrs. Sargent's deed from W. B. Browne, of house, etc., by Lillys, dated Oct. 28, 1768, for £400, paid by her.

---

[1] Katharine, second daughter of William Pynchon, was married to William Wetmore November 5, 1776. She was born February 25, 1754.

23. *Saturday.* News confirmed as to the Bennington affair. Very hot day.

24. *Sunday.* 'Fair. Mr. and Mrs. Orne.

25. *Monday.* Some rain. S. Sewall here.

26. *Tuesday.* Mr. and Mrs. Orne went home just before the rain, which was heavy. Mr. Wetmore went to Boston.

27. *Wednesday.* Fair. News that Fort Stanwix is besieged by 3000 men. What, this too? Are we to lose this also?

28. *Thursday.* Fast day ; fair. Chas. Phelps here. Capt. Haraden [1] arrived with his privateer ; says, by news from Bilboa at Bordeaux, that C. Gerrish's life was despaired of, and his vessel ordered to Salem from thence ; that Capt. Cleaveland was to sail with Haraden, and it is supposed that he sailed the day after him, about July 10th.

30. *Saturday.* Fair and cool. Capt. Gerrish's [vessel] into Marblehead from Bilboa, with rigging, etc., for a 74 gun ship to be built. Gerrish was left ill at Bilboa, and his life nearly despaired of. The news of the defeat and raising the siege at Fort Stanwix contradicted. John came home from Chelsea.

31. *Sunday.* Fair and pleasant. At Mr. Barnard's meeting. After service in the morning, he, from the pulpit, invited all of other communions in other of the neighboring churches to tarry and partake with the communicants of the church, which was new to me.

September 1. *Monday.* Fair and moderate. News

---

[1] Captain Jonathan Haraden. Mr. Haraden, a recent writer says, " was one of the bravest officers and best seamen who sailed from Salem in a privateer. His desperate actions and wonderful triumphs, his consummate courage and severe intrepidity, entitle him to a place in history by the side of Paul Jones, Decatur, and Farragut." (*History of Essex County,* p. 388.)

that Admiral Howe's fleet is gone up Chesapeake Bay, and is about landing near Baltimore. Mr. Sewall bought a house and land at Manchester, with 3 good rooms on the floor, last month, and this day bought a hhd. of W. I. Rum at Salem of 113 gallons, @ 36/, which is deemed a low price, and the house and land cost but 4/ more than the hhd. of rum.

3. *Wednesday.* Very fine day. News of Cabot Gerrish's death at Bilboa.

4. *Thursday.* Fine day. Mr. Wetmore returned from Boston. Went to Mr. O.'s farm.

5. *Fryday.* Very fine day. Gen'l Howe said to be within 50 miles of Philadelphia ; news that Colo. Frye was shot at the eastward.

6. *Saturday.* Mr. Lowell in town ; 1400 prisoners from Bennington to Boston.

7. *Sunday.* News of the taking of an admiral, said to be Gayton.

8. *Monday.* Club here.

9. *Tuesday.* Heavy guns at Boston. Cloudy ; plentiful rain at night.

10. *Wednesday.* Bro. Mitchel in town ; Dr. Putnam, D. Lamb, Orne.

11. *Thursday.* At Mr. Orne's. Bro. Mitchel went to Manchester. Peter Frye, Junr.,[1] was bro't out to be shot in the Common, Boston ; his coffin was bro't with him, and the dead body of one[2] who was shot for desertion was shewn to him ; then he was blinded and re-

---

[1] Peter Frye was the son of Colonel Peter Frye, who married Love Pickman. He entered the Provincial army, and was sentenced to be shot for desertion, but through the intercession of his grandmother, Madam Pickman (Love Rawlins), with Washington, he was reprieved.

[2] Elijah Woodward was shot on the Common for desertion, on Thursday, September 11th, and Peter Frye was reprieved, as above stated. See *Boston Gazette*, September 15, 1777.

quired to kneel, and the soldiers made ready ; but Peter was reprieved, being deemed a lunatic (as he was all his days).

12. *Fryday.* Rain. Yesterday James Lawrence confessed the stealing 12/ from B. Whitworth, and his putting it into John's pocket for fear of the conjurer. Mrs. Lawrence had notice to provide for her son, as we could not keep him the fall and winter. She came and said she would take him. Mr. Wetmore.

15. *Monday.* Katy Wetmore rode out ; Mr. W. went to Boston in the evening.

17. *Wednesday.* Cloudy, with fine rain ; wind N. E. Pd. Warner for John's passage to Chelsea.

18. *Thursday.* Rain. About noon Capt. Cleaveland came into Beverly. Wm. came home.

22. *Monday.* Rain. Gen'l Howe at Chads Ford, [30] miles from Philadelphia, with part of his army.

23. *Tuesday.* Cloudy. John set out for Chelsea with Wm. and S. Orne in Daland's chaise. New demand for men on account of some advantages gained by Gen'l Burgoyne. Rain.

26, 27. *Fryday and Saturday.* Rumours that Fort Edward and Ticonderoga are in the hands of the Americans, and Gen'l Burgoyne's army worsted, many being killed and taken prisoners, and he badly, some say mortally, wounded ; by Mr. Lowell that Gen'l Gates writes that he has the greatest encouragement to think he shall soon rout the whole army and disperse them.

29. *Monday.* Cloudy and cold, with N. E. wind. B. went to Cambridge with S. O., and returned at night.

30. *Tuesday.* Cold in the morning, warm in the afternoon. Went to Newburyport Court, and no storm the whole week. Saturday a fine day, and I returned from Ipswich to Salem, being the 4th of October. There

the news was that there had been a battle at Schuylkill, and that Gen'l Howe lost, in passing the river, 3000 men or more, Washington but 1200, and that Howe had retreated ; others suppose Howe to be in possession of Philadelphia ; Parson G., news that lately 4000 militia in the rear of Howe's army were all to 11 men killed and taken prisoners, which he says may be depended upon. *Quære.*

October 5. *Sunday.* Fair, pleasant ; wind S. W. The late news of Howe's defeat said to be groundless, and the reporter [to have] run off.

7. *Tuesday.* Marit. Court here. News confirming the great slaughter of Gen'l Howe's troops. Very warm day.

9. *Thursday.* Cloudy, with some rain. Rumour that Philadelphia was taken by Gen'l Tryon, and 3000 troops from New York, who marched thro' the Jerseys and crossed the Delaware, said to come by last post, and that Gen'l Burgoyne was entrenching and building barracks at   , and was advantageously situated.

10, 11. *Fryday and Saturday.* That Gen'l Gates could not attack his troops with a prospect of success.

12. *Sunday.* Rain last evening. The news of Philadelphia contradicted, and it is said that Gen'l Mifflin was in the city with 5 or 6000 American troops, and that all the inhabitants who would not take arms were removed with their effects out of the city ; that Gen'l Howe's army was between Gen'l Washington and the city, and that Gen'l Mifflin was to set fire to the city, if he could not hold it against Gen'l Howe.

14, 15. *Tuesday and Wednesday.* Gen'l Burgoyne's army, in part worsted, and Gen'l Fraser killed, are forced to retreat.

17. *Fryday.* Cloudy. Capt. Fiske came in. News

from Washington's army, and from Gen'l Gates, of a battle at the westward and one at the southward, each greatly in favour of the Americans ; 1000 of Burgoyne's troops killed and taken, and the rest surrounded ; and of great slaughter among Howe's army; Gen'l Sullivan and many Americans killed or taken, and Howe retreating above 9 miles back from his encampment.

18. *Saturday.* Some rain, and cloudy ; wind N. E. W. Gray returned from his journey for Virginia. Rumours come from Boston that the last accounts of the advantages gained over the Regulars want confirmation, some say are very far from truth ; and that the advantages gained at the northward are far less than reported to have been.

21. *Tuesday.* Court for trial of Marblehead Tories. News that Gen'l Burgoyne and his army have surrendered themselves, arms, baggage, and 50 brass cannon, to Gen'l Gates.

22. *Wednesday.* The Court of Special Sessions adjourned without day, the respondents being all acquitted who were tried, and *nolle prosequi* entered against Bowen and Wormsted.

23. *Thursday.* Clear and cold. News that an express has come to Boston from the army, confirming the account that Gen'l Burgoyne and his army are all prisoners, and to be sent home to England. Rejoicings at Boston, Salem, Marblehead, Portsmouth, Newbury, and at Gloucester. Went to Boxford, and returned on Fryday.

24. *Fryday.* On my return from Boxford, after the rejoicing for victory over [the] army, I found my windows broken, as well as my neighbours'. Upon enquiring whom I was to thank for it, I was told, myself, for not being at home. On observing that those who were at

home fared no better than the absent, I was answered
that all Tories should be served alike ; others said it was
only an accident, and the effect only of extravagant rejoicing, and must not be noticed while I had any windows
left.   The last was a needless caution to me, so I con-
tentedly boarded up my windows.[1]

[1] The following extract from a letter, written at a somewhat earlier date,
April 16, 1775, illustrates the trials to which suspected persons were subjected : —

"Mr. Cabot, Dr. Putnam, Mr. Goodale, and many others talk of removing, some of them out of Salem, others out of the Province.   The threats
and insults of the rabble have been insupportable to many.   Col. Pickman, Capt. Poynton, Mr. Paine, and several from other towns are gone
to England.   Col. Browne's tenant, Vining, and Mr. Hooper's tenant, at
Danvers, are ordered by the committemen to depart with their stock and
effects, and to leave the farms to lie unimproved.   None dares to build on
Col. Browne's land where the fire was, viz : where Mansfield's shop stood.
The church windows and Col. Browne's have repeatedly been broken by
the rabble.   People of property had been so often threatened and insulted
that at length several more proposed to leave the town of Salem.   The
merchants began to be alarmed at it, and at the March meeting obtained
a committee of 30 persons, some of them friends of the government, to
make inquiry and prosecute window breakers and other offenders.   The
committee exerted themselves so far as to cause the windows to be mended
by the offenders, and reduced the bawling and other insults of the boys
and rabble to sneering and hissing at people in the streets, and other
more secret abuses, as daubing and painting doors and windows, tarring
houses, etc., etc.   Soon after Dr. Warren's oration on the 5th of March,
in the Old South meeting-house, one, Dr. Bolton, a lame, droll body, at the
instance of some of the army who were affronted at Dr. Warren and party,
pronounced a mock oration from Cordis' balcony, grossly reflecting on
Warren, Cooper, Hancock, and other Whiggs, and rendering them as
ridiculous as he could.   The gentlemen of the army have established a
Congress here for taking in hand the prinkers and other abusive persons ;
the Congress meets weekly ; the punishment will be tar and feathers,
it is supposed.   The inhabitants here are more and more insulted by
the soldiers, who in excuse say that no other conduct can now secure
themselves against the people ; many of them are daily moving out of
Boston to live in the country, some also from Charlestown and Roxbury.
On the other hand, all friends of the government are insulted in the country : some have been seized, yoked, and driven like cattle ; one or more
hath been bound out to hard labour.   One respectable householder, in

25, 26. *Saturday and Sunday.*   The talk is of calling a town meeting, relating to the windows broken.

particular, was bound and let out to several masters at different days, and was sent or carried to meeting on Sundays as a criminal, and at length was forced to attend to a sermon preached principally for him, as an enemy of his country, till, weary of insults, he subscribed a confession prepared for him, and was gazetted.

"The Provincial Congress now sitting keep all their councils and doings a profound secret; part, however, hath leaked out. It is said they have been endeavoring to raise an army of 20 or 25,000 men, to assemble at Worcester, where they have a magazine of stores and provisions for such an army, and sufficient to support it 12 months; but in Essex County so many delegates dissented that the project, as is supposed, must be laid aside, or referred to the Continental Congress. T. Pickering is chosen Colonel of Salem minute men, and at the muster of the alarm list there, the ministers (excepting only Mr. Gilchrist and old Mr. Barnard) appeared with carnal weapons and accoutrements, and were viewed and examined by the Colo. and officers. This appeared very droll to many, as not a soul of those officers had ventured to subscribe to the warning given in the newspapers and other notifications for the muster. Many of the people, however, refused to follow the example of their ministers in submitting to be examined by such officers. Threats were given out by the rabble against all who neglected to appear, but their threats were not put into execution. The fishermen of Marblehead are excessively high and outrageous, and some of their shoremen declare publickly that as soon as Gen'l Gage shall begin to execute any of his orders, that every friend of government there is to be immediately seized and destroyed ; that neither parents nor children shall be spared. A deacon of note declares that he would kill his own children if he should find them to be tories, and that none will be allowed to be neuters. But those who talk the loudest generally do least. Parson Nichols is removed to Boston, and left the church here. Mr. Fisher's family are gone to Portsmouth; he continues at Salem, at the earnest desire of the merchants ; they cannot do business without aid of his office. Mr. Fayerweather hath purchased a seat at Cambridge, and Colo. Williams could now dispose of both farms, but the difficulty of the times prevents it.

"By the Nautilus and Falcon, men-of-war, just arrived here, we hear that the General and Admiral have received their orders ; that seven regiments, each of 750, rank and file, 600 marines, 500 light horse, Major-Generals Howe, Clinton, and Burgoyne, are embarked in 33 transports, and are daily expected here ; a number of frigates, with £220,000 sterling. attending, and coming with the fleet ; some of them sailed the 4th of March ; the troops not to act till the colony assemblies have time to con-

29. *Wednesday.*   N. E. storm ; cold.   The town meeting vote their disapprobation of breaking the windows, and recommend to the rioters to repair them and make satisfaction for the damage done on that day of rejoicing.   News that 17 ships were greatly damaged, and were driven back from *chev. de frise*, and 1700 men made prisoners ; that Gen'l Howe was taking off the roofs of the houses to make boats for his army to retreat on from the city over the river.

31. *Fryday.*   Clouds go off, and it is clear at noon.

Judges and rulers, as at the beginning, of our own choosing, learned men.   The clerk of the Superior Court, in his account on file, puts 20 in the column of shillings. The clerk of the Superior Court spells well, as Mr. Peirce says — thus, the word ———.

November 1. *Saturday.*   Very cold last night, and the ice this morning would almost bear.   B. went to Chelsea for Mr. Wetmore.

4. *Tuesday.*   Superior Court sat.

6 and 7. *Thursday and Fryday.*   Fair. Gen'l Burgoyne's army arrive in Charlestown in part.[1]

sider and answer the parliament's proposals as to taxation.   Mr. Paxton, we hear, hath been very sick, and 't is said is dying.   Mr. Hancock at length is married to Miss Quincy; he with the Adams's, Church, Warren, Kent, etc., etc., live in the country with their families.   Dr. Whittaker hath, at his own risque, begun to build a meeting-house on Hunt's land, near the school-house, for his party ; the other part of his congregation have purchased the Assembly House, and [have] Mr. Hopkins for their minister.   If Salem goes on thus increasing in meeting-houses and ministers, will they not be the most religious people on the face of the whole earth?   Thus far our good friend hath ventured in politics and anecdotes, but as neither he nor I can say that $\frac{1}{3}$ part is true, you will doubtless keep all to yourself and family."

[1] The duty of guarding and conducting General Burgoyne and his army to Cambridge was assigned to General Glover, whose name appears so often in this Diary, and whose brilliant career during the war of the Revolution had made him famous throughout the country.   He was the officer of the day at the execution of the unfortunate André.

14 and 15. *Fryday and Saturday.* Cold. John came home from Chelsea with Mr. Fox.

17. *Monday.* Snow. On news of Gen'l Howe being taken at Marblehead, the people break Mr. Hooper's and others' windows, to prove their true joy.

20. *Thursday.* Thanksgiving. At Mr. Dunbar's meeting.

21. *Fryday.* Mr. Lowell and Brimmer in town.

22. *Saturday.* At Marblehead ; hear cannon from Boston.

24. *Monday.* Rain. I went to Boston, and returned on Thursday ; went to Cambridge on Tuesday night, and returned to Boston.

30. *Sunday.* Cloudy. The stage returned from Boston, the weather being very bad yesterday.

December 4. *Thursday.* At Cambridge with Mr. Cabot. Excessively cold. The Superior Court there. Mess. Paine and Parsons, — rumpus, — and Mess. Paine and Lowell. We returned on Saturday.

9. *Tuesday.* John Bonnet went away.

11. *Thursday.* News that Gen'l Howe had taken Red bank Fort, which was evacuated by the American troops, and some of his ships had gone up to the city of Philadelphia.

13. *Saturday.* Rain ; moderate air. Mr. Wetmore from Boston. Cato came and lodged here. Mrs. Orne came, also cousin Jno. Williams.

16. *Tuesday.* Snow. J. Williams left us.

17. *Wednesday.* G. Dodge from southward says Gen'l Washington's army remains near Gen'l Howe's, and frequent skirmishing between parties of each. John came home from Chelsea. Mr. Lewis took leave of his friends here.

18. *Thursday.* Thanksgiving for late successes ordered by Congress. At Mr. Dunbar's meeting.

19. *Fryday.*   Bro. Stephen here, and went to Marblehead on Saturday.

20. *Saturday.*   B. and J. at Mrs. Orne's farm.   News that Howe went out of Philadelphia, and a fleet went out for New York and Rhode Island.

25. *Thursday.*   Marit. Court here from Tuesday last to Thursday.

27. *Saturday.*   Mr. and Mrs. Carpenter return to Salem from London and Bilboa, and bring letters of the 17th of September from Mr. Curwen at Bristol.

30. *Tuesday.*   The court meets at the school-house ; the weather very cold.   New plan of a Constitution appears for this State.

1778. *January* 1. *Thursday.*   Very cold.   The court sit.

2. *Fryday.*   Some rain, and the warm weather carries off the snow.   Threats to set fire to the houses of those who were witnesses and prosecutors of the women's mob which seized the   there ; some coals were placed at the front doors of several of the houses there.

4. *Sunday.*   Cold.   At Mr. Barnard's.   The church at Marblehead shut up,[1] and the G. Jury present the members for not going to meeting on Sundays.   Mr. Carpenter and wife here.

11. *Sunday.*   Cloudy, moderate.   Capt. Leach here. He says that Lewis, Mr. Baron, and others are gone to Halifax.   Snow in the afternoon.

12. *Monday.*   Snow.   News that Colo. Hendley stabbed a regular soldier for hissing as he passed by him.

13. *Tuesday.*   Clear and some sledding.   News that some light horsemen were killed in cold blood by Britons and by Americans.

---

[1] St. Michael's Church was closed at this time, many of its members being loyalists.

14. *Wednesday.* Warm, and much wood brought in from the country ; the sledding good.

15. *Thursday.* Clear and cold ; good sledding. Mr. Parsons from Boston. News of a transport with army clothing, etc., taken at the southward, worth £   .

16. *Fryday.* Very cold ; good sledding, and wood at 14 dollars a cord.

17. *Saturday.* Mr. Wetmore returned from Boston. I settled B.'s affairs with Mr. Cabot on behalf of his son, now in London. B. begins to droop ; Dr. P. concerned about him.

18. *Sunday.* Rain all last night, which carried off much snow ; moderate and cloudy weather this morning ; windy and cold in the evening.

19. *Monday.* Moderate ; rough carting ; very little wood brought in.

20. *Tuesday.* Cloudy, but moderate. Wood now at 20 dollars a cord ; last week from 12 to 16.

21. *Wednesday.* Cloudy, moderate. Sent examination of *Orne v. Hooper* by Diman to Mr. Winthrop [1] to be recorded.

22. *Thursday.* Mr. Williams here. A very cold night. A. Cabot went to view the house and consider and report. Set out for Congress. Williams went only to Medford, and returned at night.

25. *Sunday.* Snow. Mr. Williams returned to Boston.

26. *Monday.* Cold ; some snow ; a very cold night. Saw Durkee's letter to Gen'l Washington ; Andover rejects the confederation scheme, instructing their representatives to vote for a reconciliation with G[reat] B.[ritain].[2]

[1] Adam Winthrop was the brother of Professor John Winthrop, and son of Adam, great-grandson of Governor John Winthrop. He was clerk of the court in Suffolk.

[2] This statement, which we may suppose was contained in the letter of

27. *Tuesday.* Very cold and clear. Katy Wetmore came with B. and maid.

28. *Wednesday.* Cloudy, with So. wind. Wms. came with flour.

29. *Thursday.* Rain in the morning ; clearing in the afternoon ; muddy. Mr. A. Cabot decides to take the house ; offers no price.

31. *Saturday.* Many, as in the year past, are grown and are growing less by elevation, like *little statues* placed on *high pedestals,* and yet these little lofty animals may do us a world of mischief. But if we are on our guard, and avoid them, and bear the effects of their insolence with stability and dignity, their insults will prove harmless to us, their stings hurt none but themselves. Their malevolence can neither add to nor diminish our real enjoyment, but like the good or ill accidents of life will be felt, not according to their, but to our own qualities.

February 2. *Monday.* Gave deed to Cabot for my house, etc.

3. *Tuesday.* Shelton and Johnson went to Just. Ward's.

4. *Wednesday.* Clear and moderate. Mr. Jones and ux. and Mr. Dunbar here.

5. *Thursday.* Mr. Jones and Wms. here. Shelton and Johnson's affair at Just. Ward's. Cloudy, but moderate.

Major Durkee, is erroneous, and was based upon the vote passed by the town January 15th, to instruct its representatives respecting the confederation, and the probable report of the committee appointed to draft an instruction for its consideration. The well-known views of this committee, and the consequent character of their report, which was not presented until February 9th, naturally led to the inference that the town would coincide with its recommendations. The report was, however, rejected, and the town voted that their representatives use their influence that the plan of confederation be ratified.

6. *Fryday*. New oath of allegiance in the newspapers.

7. *Saturday*. Mr. Dunbar, Jones, Wms., and self dine at Mr. Orne's farm ; in the evening they at my house.

8. *Sunday*. Cloudy and cold. Floyd went to Chelsea, and Jones to Roxbury.

10. *Tuesday*. Fair and moderate. B. starts with Mr. Williams and ux. for Deerfield. Floyd returns from Chelsea. At Colo. Sargent's[1] in the evening.

11. *Wednesday*. Snow and rain. Mr. Smith of Boston here, and gives an account of the prosecution and imprisonment of persons averse to the independence of the colonies on Great Britain, especially as to Dr. Lloyd.

12. *Thursday*. Snow and rain. Wood, 19 dollars for a 6 to 7 feet load.

13. *Fryday*. Cloudy, and freezes. Sent letters by Lieut. Hooper to Marblehead, to be forwarded to Colo. Gerry or put on board Capt. Hodges', for Capt. Emery, Bilboa, and for W. Cabot.[2]

14. *Saturday*. Clear and cold. Wood sold at 30 dollars the cord; pork 1/8 and 1/6. Jno. came home from Chelsea on foot. Dr. Whitaker from Boston, and [says] that the negroes would soon be made free by the Gen'l Court.

17. *Tuesday*. Superior Court in Boston. Clear.

18. *Wednesday*. I went with Verry to Boston, and attended at the Treasury for exchange of bills.

19. *Thursday*. Attended at the Treasury for the exchange of bills for State notes ; came home in the evening, having promises of the notes to be sent.

---

[1] Colonel Epes Sargent.

[2] William Cabot was the son of Francis, son of the first John Cabot. He was born 27th April, 1752, and died unmarried in 1828.

20. *Fryday.* Cloudy, but moderate. By this day the oath of allegiance was by law to have been taken by lawyers.

21. *Saturday.* Cloudy and very cold. News that Dr. Holten is chosen a member of the Continental Congress instead of John Adams, Esq., who sailed for England last Wednesday.[1]

22. *Sunday.* Cloudy and cold. At Mr. Dunbar's meeting.

23. *Monday.* Snow. Sent word to Mr. Payson by Bartlet that I should be in Boston soon.

24. *Tuesday.* Fair and pleasant. Fowler and Jno. here.

25. *Wednesday.* Fair. Sent a letter to Mr. Emery, Bilboa, by a Marblehead vessel.

26. *Thursday.* Cloudy and foggy, with some rain. Went with Jno. to Chelsea, and lodged there. Account of parliamentary debates ; Dr. Franklin's assassination,[2] and new levies coming. Note debates on the new constitution.

28. *Saturday.* Returned from Boston, where it was proposed in the Assembly that the governor should hold his place certain but for 3 years ; that civil officers hold during good behaviour ; small districts, corporations, etc., might join and choose representatives.

March 2. Monday. Cold. Club in the evening.

3. *Tuesday.* Cold and cloudy. Letters from Mr. Payson.

4. *Wednesday.* Cold and clear. Warrant issues

---

[1] John Adams was appointed Commissioner to France on the 14th of February, superseding Silas Deane.

[2] This entry is from a letter from Bordeaux, dated December 12, 1777, which stated that Franklin was assassinated in his bed-chamber at the instance of Lord Stormont. See the *Continental Journal* of February 26, 1778.

against Mr. Hooper[1] [that he] take the oath of fidelity and allegiance to the State before Justice Ward.

5. *Thursday*. Clear and cold. Mr. Browne goes to Marblehead with warrants against persons to take the oath of allegiance.

9. *Monday*. Cloudy and moderate. Town meeting. Norwood sues Peirce and Vincent in replevin. Peirce shuts his doors and opposes the officer Browne with gun and bayonet, and threatens to kill him if he should enter the house ; Peirce had lately been bound to his good behaviour.

10. *Tuesday*.   Cloudy ; some rain, but good sledding. Wood at 18 and 20 dollars the cord.

11. *Wednesday*. Cloudy, and thaws. The morning lours, and heavily brings on the day — important to the gentry of Marblehead who are to appear before Justice Ward, Esquire, tanner and deacon, to take the oath of allegiance, etc., or accept of a room in jail, to which he, for some time past, has declared they shall be committed on refusal of the oaths. The charge against them is that they are inimical to the grand cause of America. The proof is that they keep bad company and are Tories. Parson Weeks[2] is charged with dining on board of a Flag of Truce at several times. The Justice refused to give them a copy of the complaint against them, saying it was private, and not to be sent about the world, but he shew them the clerk's list ; but trial being denied them, they refused to take the oath without further consideration, and time was allowed them until Monday, 23d inst.

[1] Robert Hooper, known as King Hooper, was the wealthiest merchant of Marblehead, and one of the wealthiest in New England before the Revolution.

[2] Rev. Joshua Wingate Weeks, rector of St. Michael's. The church was closed from 1776 until 1780, and he was driven to Nova Scotia.

16. *Monday.*   Cloudy ; snow and N. E. wind.   Oaths deferred by act of Assembly.

17. *Tuesday.*   Cloudy, with some rain.   News that more than 100 fat oxen and a quantity of clothing were taken on the way to Gen'l Washington's camp.

18. *Wednesday.*   Tradesmen and salary-men grumble at the countrymen's extortion, and threaten to join the Regulars against them.

20. *Fryday.*   Fair and pleasant.   Went with Dr. Holyoke's horse to Peabody's, Middleton, and saw D. Balch.

21. *Saturday.*   By Mr. Oliver returned Lord Bolingbroke to the library.

22. *Sunday.*   Fair, and very windy and cold.   Sent John's bundle by Diman.

23. *Monday.*   Fine, clear day, and the high wind begins to abate.   Two of the Marblehead gentry take the oath of abjuration, Mr. Abram and Mr. Foster ; the others do not appear.   Cæsar's Commentaries, Warburton, and Tacitus out of the library.

24. *Tuesday.*   Cloudy and moderate.   Grumbling at the extortion of the farmers, the blunders of politicians and legislators, the ambition and selfishness of the ministry and of the demagogues, badness of the times, etc., etc.

25. At Wenham, Colo. Browne's.

26. *Thursday.*   Snow.   News of 32,000 troops to come to America this Spring.

27. *Fryday.*   I wrote to Dr. Smith to thank him and Mr. Upham as to the bills.

28. *Saturday.*   I dined at Mr. Orne's.   Heard by Mr. Dunbar from B. that he was well at Deerfield, and would return in a fortnight.

31. *Tuesday.*   N. E. snow storm ; excessively heavy riding to Ipswich Court.

April 1. *Wednesday.* Fair. It is said that 8000 troops are to be raised in this State, and that Gen'l Howe's troops are preparing for some expedition.

4. *Saturday.* Cloudy. Smith and Cato about opening the drain, but the water prevented them. Snowstorm in the evening. The privateer crews all hurrying away to get their vessels from the wharves, thro' fear of the embargo. In the newspapers, the new constitution ridiculed in a number of articles, and parson Gordon attacks and objects to it.

5. *Sunday.* Mr. Brimmer and Miss Watson;[1] by him I wrote to W. Cabot by a vessel *via* Holland, enclosing one of the bills of exchange from Mr. Cabot of £25 sterling, and a letter to S. Curwen, Esq., of Dec. 31st.

6. *Monday.* A fine, fair day. Mrs. Wetmore rode out.

7. *Tuesday.* A very fine and clear day. Mrs. W. rode out again; grows better. Mr. W. went to Boston.

16. *Thursday.* Floyd at work in the garden.

18. *Saturday.* Fair and clear, but windy. Mrs. Orne came. Jno. and little B. went to Danvers.

19. *Sunday.* Cloudy. News of France and Spain's declaration in favour of American independence and of a free trade with us. Dean returns.

20. *Monday.* News that France had entered into a treaty of alliance with the American States, and that almost all of the other powers of Europe would soon [do the same].

25. *Saturday.* Mr. and Mrs. Wetmore went home.

26. *Sunday.* News that some of the English commissioners had arrived at New York.

---

[1] Miss Watson was a daughter of Major George Watson, and granddaughter of Judge Peter Oliver. She afterward married Martin Brimmer.

27. Mr. Oliver set out for Connecticut.

May 2. *Saturday.* Received a letter from J. Emery, Bilboa, and Mr. Cabot received letters from England, his son, etc.

3. *Sunday.* News that the English and French ambassadors had withdrawn from their respective courts, and that the French minister had seized on divers English vessels in the harbour for security until the ships taken by the English from the French should be restored. Qu. : Will a French war commence now ?

5. *Tuesday.* Mr. Wetmore and I went to Boston. Nath'l Browne died.

7. *Thursday.* B. came home this afternoon. Rode from Worcester this day.

17. *Sunday.* Mrs. Orne's child baptized.

24. *Sunday.* At Mr. Barnard's.

25. *Monday.* Mrs. Orne and two children go into the hospital for the inoculation of the children.

June 9. *Tuesday.* Rumours that the Indians at the westward are in motion, and that Philadelphia was evacuated and burnt. John went with me to Chelsea.

12. *Fryday.* Fine, warm day. Mrs. Lynde and Mrs. Oliver here.

24. *Wednesday.* Went with Mrs. Orne to visit Mr. Sewall and lady at Manchester, and returned on Thursday.

25. *Thursday.* Mr. Lafitte and Mr. Kate and co. here.

Mr. Hancock calls on his debtors, and desires payment in paper currency, preferring that to silver money — the difference in the exchange being at $3\frac{1}{2}$, and from that to 5 paper dollars for one of silver. Does Mr. H., in fact, mean to give his debtors the difference ; or to induce his own creditors to take of him their dues at that rate because he takes his dues at that rate ; or to become popular, and obtain votes at the choice of governor next May?   See the newspapers.

July 5. *Sunday.*   At Mr. Dunbar's.   Mr. and Mrs. Orne here in the evening.

6. *Monday.*   John went to school with Eben. Putnam to the Rev. Mr. Dunbar.   Military muster in School Street.

8. *Wednesday.*   B. sets out for Portsmouth ; very hot weather.

11. *Saturday.*   Hot.   News that Gen'l Clinton's army is surrounded, the communication with their ships cut off, and, in an engagement, had lost 1200 men, killed and taken.   This intelligence said to come in a letter from Gen'l Washington.

15. *Wednesday.*   Moderate.   Inferior Court sat.

18. *Saturday.*   By handbill we hear of the arrival of Mons'r D'Estaing and French fleet in the Delaware, with troops to coöperate with Americans against Britons, etc., etc.

19. *Sunday.*   Rain in the evening.   Mr. Oliver returned from Commencement.

25. *Saturday.*   C. W. rested well last night, and this morning seemed greatly relieved, but about 12 she grew worse and delirious.   The Lord be merciful to her.

28. *Tuesday.*   Caty Wetmore dies, and is buried on Thursday.

August 4. *Tuesday.*   The Salem volunteers march about 7 o'clock, A. M., to Flynt's tavern, where they mount their horses and carriages for R. Island, to return in 3 weeks.   Query, if so soon.   Marblehead committee, Orne *et al. v.* Martin.   In the afternoon a fine shower of rain.

6. *Thursday*.   Mrs. Mascarene [1] came to see us last evening ; goes to Boston to-day.

9. Mr. Oliver has a letter from Mr. Walter.   It rains plentifully.

10. *Monday*.   It rains this morning.   [The] confirmation of the arrival of a part of the English fleet at New York.   This day bung up the currant wine, having added of sugar.

12 and 13. *Wednesday and Thursday*.   Rains, and blows down corn, etc., [and] drives 27 vessels ashore at Marblehead.   B. went to Boston on Wednesday morning. Query, the event of the expedition to R. Island, the soldiers being without tents, etc.

28. *Fryday*.   The French fleet of [14] sail of ships of war go into Boston.[2]   News from Gen'l Washington by express to Gen'l Sullivan at Rhode Island that the troops must quit the Island, as troops are embarking at New York for Rhode Island to raise the siege.   We hear that the soldiers are coming off R. Island, and it is said that some of Admiral Byron's fleet are arrived at New York. At night Mr. Wetmore moved into Mr. Ropes' house.

29. *Saturday*.   The Salem volunteers return home from Rhode Island — *quibus gravis infamia læsit.*

September 1. *Tuesday*.   English fleet standing off, this morning, from Boston.   News that New York is evacuated.

3. *Thursday*.   None of the fleet to be seen ; horse race at Flynt's.

5. *Saturday*.   Mr. Derby sent word that he should this Fall move into this house.   By Mr. Oliver news from

---

[1] Mrs. Mascarene was the wife of John Mascarene, the comptroller of the port of Salem.   She was a daughter of President Holyoke, and a fourth cousin of William Pynchon.

[2] Eleven ships of the line and three frigates.

Boston of an express from Gen'l Washington that Admiral Byron's fleet had arrived at New York, 12 sail of the line ; 19, as some say.

7. *Monday.* News in the paper that Bedford is burned by the Regulars. Is this the way for reconciliation ?

9. *Wednesday.* Rain. Mr. Jones in town. Rumour of a mob at Boston, and a riot between the sailors and Frenchmen, and of burning the whole of Dartmouth and Bedford.

10. *Thursday.* [The] account of the burning of a part of Bedford in the paper, and the former account in great part contradicted.

11. *Fryday.* B. went to Boston. A fair and moderate day. Mr. Jones, Mrs. Dunbar, myself, and wife [went] to see Mrs. Orne at Danvers.

13. *Sunday.* Cloudy and cool. News that the Spanish fleet on the coast has been spoken with, and that Congress has notified R. Island State to provide for them, viz., for about 20,000 men.

18. *Fryday.* Cloudy ; wind So. B. went to Marblehead, and carried Mrs. F. Bourn to Mrs. Orne's, Danvers.

28. *Monday.* The drummers and trumpeters of faction have for a long time drowned the voice of truth and reason, but begin to be more moderate. Their pay is in paper and promises, and if the credit of these continue declining it is likely that a cart-load of them may, 12 months hence, purchase a bushel of turnips, if not more.

October 2. *Fryday.* The prizes came in ; also the Black Prince. Gilbert's death reported in Salem.

4. *Sunday.* Mr. Perry preached at Mr. Dunbar's.

8. *Thursday.* Dr. Orne's wife was buried.[1]

13. *Tuesday eve.* Miss T. Bourn and Miss Gallison here.

---

[1] Mrs. Orne was a daughter of Rev. Dudley Leavitt.

14. *Wednesday.*   Began to move my house furniture and goods to Mr. Orne's store, while Mr. White was moving his out of the house.[1]

15. *Thursday.*   Put up the beds, and so forth, and moved most of the furniture.

16. *Fryday.*   We lodged at Mr. Orne's house, all but the maids.[2]

17. *Saturday.*   The maids came there also, but B. lodged at Mr. Derby's house, to take care of it.

20. *Tuesday.*   I went with Mr. Wetmore to Newbury-port Court adjournment, and we returned on Friday, P. M.   Cook's horse was tired, and we hired Kimball's at the Hamblet.

24. *Saturday.*   Cato took the old chest of drawers away.

31. *Saturday.*   Mr. Luscom came to mend the floor.

November 1.   *Sunday.*   Dined at Mr. Pickman's.   The weather cloudy ; wind N. E. and cold.

5. *Thursday.*   Mr. and Mrs. Newhall came to town. News that the Somerset was cast away on Cape Cod.

6. *Fryday.*   They called on us.   Mr. Mansfield left Judge L.'s house.

7. *Saturday.*   It rained.   At evening Judge Sewall called to see us, and spent the evening.

8. *Sunday.*   He came and spent the day till evening. I went to Mr. Higginson's.

---

[1] The house in Summer Street from which Mr. Pynchon now removed, and lately occupied by Dr. Emmerton, was built by him somewhere about 1760, and sold in 1778 to Mr. John Derby, who, it appears by a letter from Mr. Pynchon, dated August 3, 1784, added to it a story, with a flat roof and balustrade.

[2] Timothy Orne, who married Elizabeth, the daughter of William Pynchon, was the son of Timothy, who was the son of Timothy Orne and Lois Pickering.   He was born April 30, 1750.   His house was in Essex Street, between North and Court streets, and was occupied by Mr. Pynchon from this time until 1784.

9. *Monday.*   Rain.   Judge Sewall set out for York.

12. *Thursday.* Fair and windy.   An exalted character given in Monday's paper is worth notice.   The cotemporaries of the party used to say that in his business he was most rapacious and oppressive ; that in the Assembly he was rarely trusted, was venal, commonly taking presents, fees, etc., for managing business there ; that the severe Act against bribery and corruption was principally aimed at him and his junto, was proposed by his brother members and brothers in profession.   If this be credited, and we turn to the account of Dr. Eliot's death[1] in [the] papers, it is something remarkable that the latter, almost universally agreed to be as proper a pattern for imitation as any in the State, should pass unnoticed by certain brethren of his persuasion in religious matters, while the former is set up on high as excelling in piety, goodness, justice, etc., etc. ; while none dares in public, at least in the papers, bewail the great loss by the death of that excellent preacher, that polite, affable, and most agreeable gentleman, that truly good man, Dr. Eliot.   But all wonder vanisheth on considering that the modern question as to character is not whether the party be a person of honor, integrity, learning, piety, etc., but whether he be Whig or Tory. Alas ! party spirit changeth the manners of men, altereth the very genius of a people ; as if it would have the

---

[1] Dr. Andrew Eliot, minister of the New North Church, was a graduate of Harvard College in 1737.   He was a man of irreproachable character, and during the trying times of the Revolutionary struggle was without the bitterness so often engendered by political strife, doing what he could to alleviate the sufferings of those about him, without regard to party or creed.   At the sacking of Governor Hutchinson's house by a vindictive mob, Dr. Eliot saved many valuable manuscripts from destruction, including the second volume of the *History of Massachusetts Bay*.   The presidency of Harvard College, now so ably held by one of his family, was once offered to him, but declined.

civilized turned into barbarians, and charity and benevolence kicked out of the State.

21. Mr. Oliver and wife remove from mine to his house, and lodge there.

25. *Wednesday.*   Mitchell Sewall here.

26. *Thursday.*   Thanksgiving ; cold and fair.   Mr. Wetmore here.

December 4.   *Friday.*   Mr. and Mrs. Mason come ; drink tea at Mr. Wetmore's and lodge at my house.

5. *Saturday.*   Go to see Mr. Bowdoin.

6. *Sunday.*   Mr. and Mrs. Mason here ; at Mr. Orne's in the evening.

7. *Monday.*   Cloudy and cold.   Mr. and Mrs. Mason[1] return to Cambridge.

10. *Thursday.*   High winds and rain.   The Enterprise said to be taken and gone to Halifax.   Snow.

16. *Wednesday.*   Mr. Orne here ; returned at night. Carried to Mr. Gilchrist Miss Gerrish's 96 shillings. Snow much drifted.

20. *Sunday.*   Very cold.   Mr. Dunbar ill.

24. *Thursday.*   Excessive cold.   Wood at £10 a cord. Cold, cold, cold !

25. *Fryday.*   Christmas.   Cold continues.   N. E. storm at night.

26. *Saturday.*   Severe snow-storm ; excessive cold and windy and snow greatly drifted.   Yesterday Messrs. Jones and J. Williams come ; they tarry till Monday, A. M. D. Smith from New York gives an account that it is

---

[1] Thaddeus, son of John Mason, was a graduate of Harvard College in 1728.   He was a Register of Deeds in Middlesex from 1781 to 1784.   His second wife was Elizabeth, a daughter of Jonathan Sewall, of Boston.   One of his daughters married William Harris, from whom descended the late Thaddeus Mason Harris.   He died May 1, 1802, aged 95.   He was the oldest living graduate for 8 years.

not likely the British troops will evacuate it soon ; they being about 10,000 men, and securely fortified.

Politicians and man-slayers, is it your pride or ignorance that prevents your discerning when to have done ? Is it with strife as in feasts, that, however full or weary, men are unwilling to depart ?

27. *Sunday.*   Cloudy, windy, and very cold.   Want of breeches and shoes is surely a tolerable excuse for absence from meeting ; Dr. W. allows it in case the preacher be not orthodox.

29. *Tuesday.*   Still clear and cold ; the snow is so drifted that none of the Court of Common Pleas met. Three of the Court of Sessions meet, and adjourn to March.

30. *Wednesday.*   Cloudy and more moderate weather. It is continental Thanksgiving, but for want of provisions and the necessities of life [it] seems more like a *Fast* here.   We have, however, many reasons for gratitude and cause of thankfulness ; for, though our peace and much of our property are gone, we yet move and have being, and enjoy this comfort : that the miscreants whose ambition and avarice have brought on us distress and want, bloodshed, and much destruction on the country, will not have the whole honor of the invention, theirs being coeval nearly with the creation.

31. *Thursday.*   Fair and moderate.   Mr. Wetmore's brother here.   The newspapers show us the increasing jealousies between the Lees and others and the parties in Congress ; also between Mr. Dean, the ambassador, and them and others.   May their disputes procure peace and reconciliation, if nothing else will.   Does not disappointed ambition often, too often, assume the guise and the looks of publick spirit and of great patriotism ? Let us bear this in mind when reading or hearing the

disputes, pretences, and promises of ambassadors, commissioners, and agents.

May 3, 1780. *Wednesday*. Wind So. and warm ; P. M. comes about to N. W. ; the sun breaks forth. At dinner B. looks sober, eats but little, seems to have no appetite ; is called by the passengers to go on board the brigg, the wind and weather being fair, and all ready for sailing. Mrs. P. sheds tears, Patty makes a long face ; grief is contagious ; John catches it and is in tears ; Mrs. Goodale comes over, and, finding none to speak to her, goes home again. B. goes on board with the company, attended to the boat by John, with his roll of tobacco for an adventure. They come to sail toward night ; have a moderate sea and fine breeze. The Pickering, that was to have sailed with the Fame, ran aground, and did not go out till Thursday morning.

4. *Thursday*. A fine, brisk gale last night and this morning for the brigg. God be merciful to all on board, and give them health and a prosperous voyage.

5. *Friday*. Fine N. W. breeze and clear day. Cato came to gardening.

6. *Saturday*. A fine, warm day. I went with Mrs. Pynchon in Mr. Cabot's chaise to Mr. Orne's to see Mrs. Orne, and missed her on the road.

8. *Monday*. Cloudy and rain. Mr. Sparhawk [1] brings home his new wife. News that South Carolina is closely invested by sea and land.

9. *Tuesday*. Fair and clear. Mr. and Mrs. Orne and their two children come.

10. *Wednesday*. Fair. Mr. Orne goes to Andover ; Salem town meeting ; Mrs. Pynchon and ladies go to Mrs. Prince's. Rains in the night.

---

[1] Nathaniel Sparhawk, grandson of Sir William Pepperill.

12. *Friday.*   Cold ; N. W. wind.   Rumours that Charleston is taken.

13. *Saturday.*   Clear and moderate.   More rumours as to the taking of Charleston.

14. *Sunday.*   A fine, warm day ; wind S. W.   The conversation of all parties now implies more than they dare to express, viz., that Charleston is lost.

18. *Thursday.*   Town meeting upon the constitution.

19. *Friday.*   Rain ; S. W. wind.   A dark morning ; about ten the darkness increased, and at eleven and twelve o'clock it was so great that people used candles to get dinner by and to read ; the cocks began to crow, as in the night ; people in the streets grew melancholy, and fear seized on all except sailors ; they went hallooing and frolicking through the streets, and were reproved in vain ; they cried out to the ladies as they passed, " Now you may take off your rolls and high caps and be d——d."   Dr. Whitaker's people met at the meeting-house, and he preached from Amos vi. 8–9 : " I will darken the earth in the clear day," etc.   He urged that it was owing to the immediate act of God for people's extortion and other sins, and enumerated them.   At four P. M., it grew somewhat lighter ; in the evening, although the moon was up and full, it was, until 12 o'clock, darker than ever was seen by any.

20. *Saturday.*   It was tolerably clear, and the clouds were dispersed in a great measure.

21. *Sunday.*   Moderate weather, somewhat hazy and cloudy.   Mr. Prince preached, but said not a word of the dark of last Friday ; many think it very odd in him to omit it, when Dr. Whitaker thought it clearly pointed at the prevalent sins of this day, extortion in particular. Mr. Prince, after service, warned the town meeting from the pulpit, and all were desired to appear and attend on

affairs of the last importance, viz., of the new constitution.

22. *Monday.* The town meeting was full, and the whole day was spent upon the constitution ; many objections and several amendments were made, but no reasons were prepared for the convention, as they desired, because the convention had no right to require reasons other than the delegates might verbally give them.

23. *Tuesday.* Cloudy ; wind N. E. Rumours by Capt. Stickney from New York that Carolina was safe on the 6th instant, as was said at New York ; also that G. Clinton was killed by a random shot, but that it was hushed up there ; but the New York paper intimates that there are rumours of Carolina being taken.

24. *Wednesday.* Clear, moderate day. Handbill from   , and rumours from So. Carolina, shew the great probability that the siege there will soon be raised, there having been two skirmishes, in which Clinton's troops were worsted and lost 800 men. The messenger is a deserter ; *ideo quære.*

25. *Thursday.* The paper confirms the rumours, and they still are credited in part.

26. *Friday.* Clouds and some rain ; very warm at noon. People grow impatient and somewhat suspicious as to the affair of Carolina.

27. *Saturday.* A fine, warm morning ; wind S. W. Folger from Nantucket says deserters from New York say, some, that Clinton on second attack lost 900 men, and had many wounded ; others, that Charleston hath since surrendered, or is taken.

28. *Sunday.* Warm and pleasant. Mr. Barnard preached P. M. at Mr. Prince's.

30. *Tuesday.* Clear and very warm. People dress in

summer apparel, and are preparing for election to-morrow. This day the new society meet at Cambridge upon a summons from President Bowdoin.[1] This is a day of rumours, viz., that Gen'l Washington writes to G. Trumbull that he must prepare vegetables for the French fleet, daily expected;[2] that Charleston was safe the 4th instant; that the Regulars are about to leave Penobscot.

June 4. *Sunday.* Cloudy; wind N. W. and cool; towards night the wind rises, and a small, fine rain. Rumours of a requisition of General Washington for some recruits to join the French when they come against New York, and of an embargo.

5. *Monday.* Clear and cold. The Council and Court, it is said, sat all Sunday upon the affair of an embargo and of raising men. Charleston is said to have surrendered.

8. *Thursday.* More rumours of the surrender of Charleston. Insurance at 75 per cent. in the office is offered, and actually accepted for insuring it to September next; but see the papers of this day giving a particular account of the surrender and the terms, etc., upon the 12th of May; and see extracts of letters, etc., by the ship Iris into New York; but all being from " Rivington's Gazette," called the " Lying Gazette," the public is ordered in Powers and Wyllys to give no credit.

10. *Saturday.* Mr. Hunt, from Boston, and Mr. Payson say that Rivington's account is by all supposed to be untrue, and yet that Charleston was taken at or about the time he mentions. Mr. Bromfield, in   days from Philadelphia, says it was supposed there by most people to be taken.

[1] The Society here referred to was the American Academy of Arts and Sciences, founded during this year, of which Mr. Bowdoin was one of the founders and its first president.

[2] The letter referred to, dated May 19th, may be found in the tenth volume of the *Massachusetts Historical Collections,* page 164.

14. *Wednesday.* Cloudy and some rain. More rumours of the fate of Charleston ; more insurances made ; the premiums are fallen to 50 per cent. It is said that the Council believe it taken, but we have not yet raised our men for the army.

15. *Thursday.* Fair and moderate. The prize taken by the Pilgrim was sent in here, and two gentlemen from New York came in her, and bring assurances and many confirming circumstances showing South Carolina to have been surrendered to the British troops, adding that Gen'l Cornwallis had reached as far as Georgetown in his way to North Carolina, and that many from both Carolinas flocked to the King's standard ; they aver that Sullivan's Island and Fort Moultrie surrendered the 8th, and the city on the 12th of May, and that Gen'l Cornwallis had with him 3500 regular troops, besides many of the militia ; and on Friday that T. Pickering had written to G. Williams that Carolina was taken. And now the underwriters begin to account together with the assured of the losses and gains by insuring Carolina.

17. *Saturday.* Cloudy and cool. Mr. Greenwood, from Boston, says that he does not believe Charleston to be taken or surrendered to the Regulars, nor that it will be, notwithstanding all the accounts and rumours about it. I go to Danvers, and tarry.

18. *Sunday eve.* I return from Danvers.

20. *Tuesday.* Fair and pleasant. Go with Mr. Wetmore to Ipswich Court, and there hear of rumours as to Gen'l Washington and his little army's difficulties and dangers near New York ; that unless speedily relieved and reinforced they probably must retreat into the country, or be dispersed or surrounded as soon as Gen'l Clinton's forces shall return from South Carolina.

21, 22, 23. *Wednesday to Friday.* Fair and pleasant

weather; and on Friday evening return from Ipswich Court.

24. *Saturday.* Cloudy, and some rain in the afternoon Mr. Higginson and wife and Mr. Gray and wife go eastward.

28. *Wednesday.* Cloudy and some rain. Mr. Wetmore goes to Boston on the affairs of Span. ship; I send my excuse by him to Mr. Tudor. The militia muster; all the gentlemen, a few excepted, follow the drum through the streets; some sneer, and some leer, as they march, but covertly; Bro. G. looks straightforward. A fine and plentiful rain at night.

29. *Thursday.* Clouds and sunshine, alternately, all day. Mr. Wetmore from Boston; he says that Washington hath called for the Connecticut militia to oppose Gen'l Clinton's proceeding up North River with an army of 11,000. Large demands are made on us for men to fill up the army, which costs us from £1000 to £1800 for each man to serve but six months; heavy taxes.

30. *Friday.* A little more rain to-day, reviving the herbage and our spirits, but Gen'l Clinton proceeding up North River fills us all with concern for West Point. We are told that Connecticut and New York militia are crowding that way, and fill the roads, so that it is very difficult for travellers to get along.

July 4. *Tuesday.* Mr. Bell here.

5. *Wednesday.* It rains again. Mrs. Pynchon and Mrs. Oliver visit at J[udge] Lynde's.

6. *Thursday.* Warm, cloudy. Rumours that the Regulars are driven to their ships in North River and beat in the Jersey, and a great number slain.

7. *Friday.* Cloudy; fine growing weather as was ever known; nothing hath suffered much but the grass.

8. *Saturday.* Mr. Vans, in the street by West's cor-

ner, in company with J. Ropes, Mr. Dowse, F. Cabot, and myself, and speaking of the exertions and bad conduct, nonsense and folly, of Great Britain, says, " Mark my words, she is just like a candle blinking and blazing up just before it expires ; her candle by next January will be burnt down to the socket, and her blaze by that time will expire and go out quite, d' ye mind me ? Take my word for it, by next January this will be the case with G. Britain as to her concerns in America." *Nota.*

10. *Monday.* Warm. Mrs. Derby here. Mr. and Mrs. Vans, Mr. and Mrs. Oliver.

11. *Tuesday.* Cloudy, warm, and some rain. The Court sits here.

12. *Wednesday.* Warm day. News of the arrival of the French fleet at Rhode Island.

13. *Thursday.* Cool, fair day. In afternoon Mr. Barnard sets out with B. Pickman [1] and Mr. Steward with Master John Pynchon for Cambridge College, in order to examination. John eats little or no dinner through anxiety; declares that if he is rejected upon examination he never will go again to college, and never will be seen in the town of Cambridge again.

14. *Friday.* At night Master Steward and his pupil return from Cambridge ; joy not to be described was visible in John's countenance, accompanied with his utmost endeavors to suppress its appearance, and to induce his mother to suppose he had been rejected ; his nerves continued to be agitated by it two full days. He was admitted, and, it is said, behaved very agreeably at examination.

15. *Saturday.* John is unwell ; his tender frame

---

[1] Benjamin Pickman, who was in the class after that of John Pynchon, was the son of Benjamin Pickman, who married Mary, daughter of Dr. Bezaliel Tappan.

almost sinks under the effects of yesterday's agitation. Carpenter and Dr. Smith arrive from England.

16. *Sunday.*   Fair and warm.   Mr. Prince preaches. Mr. Wetmore and myself are sent for to Boston to assist at the hearing of counsel upon the question of the Admiralty jurisdiction in the Spanish Cause; we return on Tuesday afternoon, the judge not sustaining the libel; his jurisdiction being most ignobly limited by the State Law, which requires him to hear and determine in several cases (as he says), and yet gives him no marshal or other officer to execute any order or decree he should make !

17. *Monday.*   Cloudy morning; fair and very warm. The Judge of Maritime Court hears counsel as to his jurisdiction; the hearing takes the whole day.   At eve he declines proceeding on the libel for the reasons above, and declares he will not proceed on libels for wages, etc., tho' expressly mentioned, for like reasons.

18. *Tuesday.*   Very hot all day ; the corn suffers.

19. *Wednesday.*   Cloudy and clear by turns ; the gardens fail.

20. *Thursday.*   Fast day ; clear.   Letters by Carpenter from England ; our money is gone.

22. *Saturday.*   News of [the] English fleet at New York equal to that of the monsieurs at Rhode Island. England ! England ! why pursue a shadow ?   America ! America ! thy dreams of greatness ill meet with thy condition ; *vera virtus quum semel excidet curatne reponi deterioribus ?*   Brother Stephen here.

24. *Monday.*   Patty goes to Wenham.   I go to Danvers A. M. with F. G. and W. W., Jr.

25. *Tuesday.*   Cloudy A. M. ; warm and very dry P. M. Mr. Johnson here.

26. *Wednesday.*   Hot and dry.   Mr. Mellen in town. No lights at evening.

27. *Thursday.*   Excessive heat made this a most uncomfortable day.   Messrs. Barnard, Mellen, and Steward dine with me ; no lights in the evening.

29. *Saturday.*   Warm.   Rumours of an embarkation of British troops at New York, destined for Rhode Island.

31. *Monday.*   Fair and cool.   According to Boston prophecies, it will not be in the power of all the fleets and troops that Great Britain can send to save Jamaica, nor raise the siege of Gibraltar, nor secure the English fleet at Rhode Island ; that the English troops at New York dare not venture out ; that the superiority of France and Spain in America is so great as to silence the English [in] this campaign, which would be a very active, if not a bloody one.   Mrs. Orne moves down to Salem, [to] Mrs. Cabot's house.

August 1. *Tuesday.*   Fair and pleasant.   Mr. Steward is applied to as a reader at church, and has no objections which at present occur.

3. *Thursday.*   Cloudy.   Brother Mitchell came, and he and Mrs. Pynchon, Mr. Goodale and wife, go to Marblehead.   He lodges here, having spent the evening at Mrs. Orne's.

4. *Friday.*   [In] morning some rain.   Brother Mitchell gets up at 5 o'clock, and goes to Gloucester to see Bro. Stephen, and does not return.

5. *Saturday.*   Excessively hot and dry on the surface of the earth, [and] things parched to a great degree ; a violent thunder shower at the eastward and in the Bay, and rain at Topsfield and Newbury.

6. *Sunday.*   Pleasant.   We hear that the English troops have returned to New York from Newport. Prizes come in here taken out of the Quebec fleet ; the prisoners say that the English are building ships, and proceeding with great spirit for the war.

8. *Tuesday.* Warm, and excessively dry, that the like of late years has not been known.

9. *Wednesday.* 10. *Thursday.* 11. *Friday.* Daily firing in the harbor by privateers and prizes coming in, and they say this town grows poorer and poorer.

12. *Saturday.* In the morning a fine rain, with thunder and lightning. Among other takings and other doings of the privateers with the persons and properties of the prisoners, we are told by credible persons (Mr. and Mrs. Cabot) that one of the prisoners who cried to the captors for quarter, after his arm was broken, was refused, and in despair jumped overboard and was drowned ; another had a silver spoon (a family spoon), given him by one of the company of the captors, and another of the captors, Carleton, took the spoon from the prisoner, refusing money and everything he offered for redeeming it, and carried it off. From another young lad, who was learning music, was taken his guitar, which had been delivered up to him by others of the captors. A doctor, who valued highly a fine head of hair, and begged it might be saved, had his hair shaved off against his will, and he made a laughing-stock.

13. *Sunday.* Very hot in the morning ; the wind at east P. M., and cool. Mr. Steward read prayers and a sermon at church, and Britton interrupted the reader, and desired him to come to a close ; but the reader took little notice of the caution, and went on.

17. *Thursday.* Cloudy. I went to college with son John, and he is highly pleased with his reception and with the tutors' treatment of him, with his chambermate, room, and his being situated near four of his townsmen ; he assures me of his resolution to attend diligently to his studies, to be observant of the laws of the college and the orders of tutors and all his superiors,

to avoid gaming and bad company, profanity and vice, and, as far as shall be in his power, to govern his hasty temper. God grant he may perform his promise.

18. *Friday.* I leave son John in good spirits and, to appearances, easy and contented, and return to Salem. Cloudy day.

19. *Saturday.* Warm. My family with Mr. Wetmore dine at Mr. Greenwood's.

22. *Tuesday.* Warm. News of the arrival of the Fame at Amsterdam ; passage about five weeks.

23. *Wednesday.* Warm. Maritime Court sits here to-day.

24. *Thursday.* Very warm indeed. Maritime Court breaks up.

25. *Friday.* Cool and pleasant. Judge Trowbridge dines with us, and visits his old acquaintances. He hath not been in Salem since November, 1774, till this day. The earth excessively dry, and wells in town and country begin to fail, and the cattle suffer greatly in the pastures for want of water ; the springs have not been known to be so low before.

September 2. *Saturday.* Cloudy, and a little rain. Dr. Putnam went with me to Mr. Derby's farm, to see him and Judge Trowbridge. Wind E.

3. *Sunday.* A moderate rain, which greatly refresheth the earth, man, and beast.

4. *Monday.* A fine, warm day ; some clouds. Town meeting for election of officers on the new Constitution. Accounts of mob of 50,000 men in London, headed by Lord Gordon, and of abuses to members of the House of Lords, Bishops, and of robberies, burning down ambassadors' chapels, prisons, burglaries, etc. Mr. Flagg takes the store for salt.

5. *Tuesday.* Cool and pleasant. Judge Trowbridge dines at Dr. Putnam's.

6. *Wednesday.* 7. *Thursday.* 8. *Friday.* Rumours of battle between Gen'l Gates and the Regulars at the southward. Some say G. carries all before him ; others, that all are behind, pursuing him.

9. *Saturday.* Judge Trowbridge dines at Dr. Holyoke's ; Dr. Pickman and myself there.

10. *Sunday.* Cloudy and cool. In hourly expectation of news of the Fame.

11. *Monday.* Three privateers carried to Quebec, the Harlequin and Eagle and the Jack.

13. *Wednesday.* Warm, and rains at night plentifully.

14. *Thursday.* Clears away ; wind N. W. News of Gen'l Gates' defeat at N. Carolina, and loss of men, and that the militia deserted from him, and that he narrowly escaped. Can this be true, after the news in the paper?

15. *Friday.* Several have letters from the passengers and the company of the Fame ; none from B. ; the letters say all are well.

16. *Saturday.* Capt. Knight from Amsterdam says that he left.

20. *Wednesday.* The Fame's prize brig comes in, and they say that they left the Fame twelve days ago near   Bank, and all well on board ; and that she sailed finely, and chased all she saw. Now who tells us where she is ? At Halifax, New York, or was she chased in her turn, and gone into some harbor ?

21. *Thursday.* No news of the Fame ; William ! William ! *Animum rege.*

22. *Friday.* Clear ; wind at So. A report that two brigs and a ship are seen in the offing, one much like the Fame.

23. *Saturday.* Clear and warm ; wind northeast. But the brigs, etc., gone into Gloucester, came out this morning, and [have] gone up to Boston.

24. *Sunday.* Cloudy; wind at southwest. No tidings of the Fame yet, — nor yet. Nantucket friends, a sister and wife here, the latter a daughter of William Roche : all polite, sensible, and good people.

25. *Monday.* Mr. Wetmore and I go to Newbury Court, and had a pleasant week, excepting N. E. storm and rain on Thursday ; return on Saturday. There Dr. Holten,[1] one of the Justices, attends and conducts with dignity on the bench, having been two years at Congress, and there caught considerable of the Southern manners. He tells us that Congress has no expectation of any negotiation with Great Britain taking place this year, and that probably the English will continue masters of the sea, and while they do they can maintain the war ; that the revolts, etc., in South America will probably take off the Spanish navy.

October 2. *Monday.* Fair. Returned Shaftsbury, and took Francis' Horace. Rumours that Gen'l Arnold left his post, and is gone off to N. York, having been suspected of conspiring with Gen'l Patterson, an officer of the Regulars, to deliver up to the British forces [our] fort.

5. *Thursday.* Rain ; wind N. E. Salem town meeting for choice of representatives on the new Constitution.

6. *Friday.* Morning fair and pleasant. Joseph Bowditch, Esqr.,[2] dies this morning. Mrs. P. is greatly dejected, having no news of the Fame. She has neither sleep nor rest. The good news brought us by Mr. Sanders of son John's good behaviour at college does

---

[1] See page 4, note.

[2] Joseph Bowditch was the sixth child of William Bowditch, whose wife was Mary Gardner. He was born August 21, 1700, and was the great-grandson of William Bowditch, the emigrant. His brother, Ebenezer, was the grandfather of Nathaniel Bowditch, the distinguished mathematician.

not serve to revive her ; the soul, like the sun, hath its clouds.

7. *Saturday.*   Cloudy, and some rain P. M.   Mr. Wetmore from Boston, and news of depreciation law, but none of the Fame.   A violent storm at night, of wind and rain.

8. *Sunday.*   A fine morning, clear and pleasant. Neighbour Williams prophesies that the Fame and crew are gone to [the] bottom ; it at present seems to be the language of fear ; they may, for any one circumstance to the contrary, be either at New York, Newfoundland, Charleston, Quebec, or Europe, as well as foundered. Why then need they be given up for lost ?   God forbid !

9. *Monday.*   A fine, warm day.   Town meeting for choice of representatives, according to the new Constitution.   Al. Alcock, a bankrupt, who ran away from his creditors in London in 1774, at the beginning of American troubles, now puts up an advertisement at the Town house door on Sunday morning, advising the inhabitants of Salem not to vote for any who had left the place of their nativity in the late troubles, none who had been timid, no lawyers, however good their character, as the profession is dangerous and damnable, to say no worse of it; but to vote for men of clear heads and high spirits.

The town choose 4 representatives, and all refuse but B. Goodale ; he upon condition that J. Ashton will go. The meeting adjourns, and is, as J. Gardner [says], in his speech to the moderator, in a lam-men-tabe-bel condition.

10. *Tuesday.*   Fair day.   Dr. Lloyd calls to see us. Mr. Williams here in the evening.

11. *Wednesday.*   Wrote to Jno. by Mr. Williams that

he should send word as to conveyance from Cambridge to Salem next week ; at evening Jno. comes home with Mr. and Miss Sanders in their chaise.

12. *Thursday.*   Fair.   At adjournment of town meeting H. Higginson is chosen representative, and 't is now hoped that Mr. Ashton will be induced to go to Court with Higginson, Goodhue, and Ward.   Mr. Dowst, Dr. Lloyd, Mrs. and Miss Lloyd, and Misses Dowst are here at tea.   Major André is executed according to sentence in the papers, and the infamous Arnold is secured at New York with the Regulars.

13. *Friday.*   Cloudy ; wind S. E.   A white flag is in the offing, said to be a flag of truce from Halifax.   God grant us good news of the Fame.

14. *Saturday.*   Fair weather.   Dr. Lloyd and family go to Andover from Salem ; they came here on Tuesday last.

15. *Sunday.*   Fair and moderate.   Reports from N. York that the Fame has not been there, nor at Carolina ; *æquam, difficile, rebus in arduis servare mentem !*

N. B.   At Mr. Prince's meeting, and heard nothing said of the upright Capt. Bowditch, deceased ; look into the newspapers, and with indignation behold a pompous account of the piety and merits of the almost infamous Colo. O., and little, very little, said of the good Dr. Eliot.

16. *Monday.*   Cloudy ; W. wind.   Combined fleet join.

19. *Thursday.*   Fair.   News that the combined fleet take a large fleet of merchantmen, and some men bound to Jamaica.   Capt. Howland returns.

20. *Friday.*   Fair.   No Flag from Halifax, and hear nothing of the Fame.

21. *Saturday.*   Fair.   Jno. sets out for Cambridge on Mr. Steward's business, and returns P. M.   J. Russell, Esqr., and Mrs. Henly at Mrs. Curwen's ; Dr. P. and I

spend the evening with them. It is now said that Rowland, on his return from Halifax, spake with a Bermudian, and heard nothing of the Fame being carried in there, tho' several vessels had been carried in there.

22. *Sunday*. Hazy, but pleasant. Tea at Dr. Putnam's with J. Russell, Esqr., one of the worthiest of men ; he was appointed a Mandamus Councillor, and for a while detested by the rabble, and yet had this summer a great many votes for Lt. Governor under the new Constitution ; and Mr. Paine, another Mandamus Councillor, wanted but one vote for representative of Worcester. Remember, ye Whiggs, what was formerly done ! We spend the evening at Mr. Cabot's with Mr. Russell, Mr. Cary, and Mr. Prince.

23. *Monday*. Foggy ; moderate day. A sailor from Newfoundland says that the Fame has not been carried in there ; he left it 14 days ago. O William ! William ! our fears increase, and the circle of our hopes lesseneth daily ; where art thou, my son ! my son !

24. *Tuesday*. The sailor's account is by many discredited ; has been found in part untrue, and the other part is hoped to be false. Jno. sets out with Mr. Wetmore for Boston election.

25. *Wednesday*. Remarkably fair and pleasant. Well ! this is the day for election of Governor, Senate, etc., according to the new Constitution ; but at noon no cannon is heard, no 42 pounders, as formerly on Election Days. News of Indians burning houses and doing much mischief at the westward.

26. *Thursday*. Fair and very pleasant. Mr. Wetmore and Jno. return from Boston, where Governor Hancock, in a suit of crimson velvet, plain, was yesterday escorted from his house to the Council Chamber, and declared to be Governor elect before a great concourse of people.

The committee of the House of Representatives were the Boston members, and S. Ward of Salem, who waited on him and addressed him for his acceptance ; which ceremony, with divers other ceremonials, etc., etc., took up all the afternoon, and dinner was about sunset.   No Lt. Governor or Senate yet chosen.

27. *Friday.*   Fair.   Capt. Cook arrives from Bilbao ; says that he saw the B. Fame off N. F. L. banks 14 days agone, standing westward ; yet Cook and Brewer knew her well, as did others of the crew.

28. *Saturday.*   Clouds, and some rain ; an appearance of a storm upon the [late] eclipse.[1]

30. *Monday.*   Wrote to Nat. Sargent of Malden for my due.

31. *Tuesday.*   Cloudy and rain ; cold.   J. Sargeant in town.   Behold Governor Hancock's speech ; 't is said he is ill, and was so when he composed it.   See Dr. Cooper's sermon and address, and behold the man — *ecce homo !* *ecce vir !* *en* and *ecce !*   Oh, dear !   Pitcher is dead !   Oh, dear !   Indians !   Indians !   Tories !   Tories !

November 1.   *Wednesday.*   High wind and N. E. storm from 3 o'clock in the morning, and snow, rain, and high wind.

4. *Saturday.*   Clear and cold.   At evening Mr. Parsons here from Cambridge.

5. *Sunday.*   Clear and fair.   See Mr. Bowdoin's resignation of seat in the Senate, and Governor Hancock's speech, or (as some insist) Dr. Cooper's oration.

6. *Monday.*   Clear and cold.   John sets out with S. Orne in B. Daland's carriage, the horse, driven by little Scipio, to Cambridge.   Put into the post-office a letter for Mr. Browne, Virginia.

7. *Tuesday.*   Supr. Court here ; cold weather all the

---

[1] This eclipse, which occurred on the 27th, was almost total.

week.   Sargt. Daniel convicted of manslaughter — between 12 and 13 years old when he committed the crime ; upon motion on his behalf, judgment was staid, and he bailed.   Query, as he is of a violent temper, whether this indulgence be for his benefit finally.

8. *Wednesday.*   Mr. Van   from New Haven, with a letter from Mr. Whittlesey, here, and went back on Friday.

10. *Friday.*   The Court adjourns without day.

17. *Friday.*   Cloudy and cold.   John comes from Cambridge, and brings a rumour from J. Amory of the Fame being at N. F. Land.

18. *Saturday.*   Cold N. E. storm ; rain.   Mr. Wetmore returns from Cambridge and brings news of choice of a committee to revise the State Laws, and reduce them to a new system or code.   Who can be the committee ?   Of the house, doubtless.

19. *Sunday.*   Rain.   Upon enquiry, Mr. Wetmore finds no dependence on the news of the Fame being at N. F. Land.   The proprietors of the church were desired to meet after service, P. M., and they conferred with Mr. Potter from Annapolis as to the Rev. Mr. Fisher[1] being invited to come to preach at church, and the committee for procuring a minister were desired to write to Mr. Fisher, and give him a state[ment] of church matters here, and of the occasion we have of a minister.   John sets out for Cambridge.

21. *Tuesday.*   Mr. Wetmore goes to Admiralty Court at Boston.

22. *Wednesday.*   Write to Mr. Fisher.   Mr. Potter gives us a good account of his moral character and as a preacher ; people are on tiptoe to meet him and to hear

---

[1] Nathaniel Fisher, H. C. 1763, who was settled at St. Peter's two years later.   He died in 1812.

him at church; one will give this and another that. Poor Steward! 't is all bitterness to thee! We are grieved for thee!

23. *Thursday.* Letters from Mr. Hodgson, and an account of B.'s leaving his for another house. In the papers news of a French fleet at Georgia, and of their taking some English ships, and landing part of 6000 troops, and taking forts.

24. *Friday.* J. Parker brought to jail by *mittimus.*

25. *Saturday.* Rains all day; at night wind at N. W., and clears away. Another week ends, and no news of the Fame!

30. *Thursday.* Col. Gridley here.

December 4. *Monday.* Fair and very pleasant. Good news from General Court that the Committee of Ways and Means have agreed to report that they can't proceed with any prospect of success until the iniquitous Tender Law be repealed.

5. *Tuesday.* Cloudy morn, but fair, cool day. Went to Ipswich with Mr. Bowditch's daughter, [Mrs.] Jeffry, and J. Gardner, to prove his will. John comes from Cambridge; could not have leave of absence for more than the vacancy of a week.

6. *Wednesday.* Cool day. Dr. Putnam, Blaney, and self spend the evening at Mrs. Sargent's.

7. *Thursday.* Mist and rain part of day. Mr. Wetmore, John, little Billy, and myself go to Mr. Orne's, Danvers, and dine and keep Thanksgiving; S. Orne there also.

8. *Friday.* Cloudy, and some wet, drifty weather. Account is in papers of a horrible hurricane in the West Indies, exceeding any hitherto known. Spent the evening at Mr. Sparhawk's; present, Professor Williams, Dr. Putnam, Dr. Holyoke; had an account of the professor's

and co. view of the Eclipse at Penobscot ; of Colo. Campbell's disobliging treatment of them, and of Captain Mowat's polite behaviour and obliging conduct on the occasion ; also heard of W.'s and others' ill-treatment of Dr. Calef's son, a passenger.

11. *Monday.*   Town meeting to raise men ; do nothing.

12. *Tuesday.*   Clear and cold.   The drum is beat to raise a martial spirit for town meeting to-day, at which 73 men are to be raised for the Continental army ; the inhabitants meet and vote the sum of £   .

14. *Thursday.*   Fair.   Shocking news as to [the] hurricane in [the] W. Indies by the papers ; as to Jamaica, scarce credible.   Mark this account — 12 men-of-war and crews destroyed.

15. *Friday.*   Cloudy, and some snow.   Mr. and Mrs. Orne here, and return at night by moonlight.

16. *Saturday.*   Cloudy, part of the day.   Mr. Oliver from Boston with a very complaisant letter from Mr. Henshaw, Clerk of Sup. Court.   Mr. Vans [brings] news of [the] appointment of a Judge of Sup. Court.

21. *Thursday.*   Clear and cold.   Sad news from England as to election of members for Parliament ; Burke, Howe, and others fail ; 20,000 men coming to America ; another campaign expected.   State of Vermont seems to be going off.   Mess. . . . and Sumner, Church clergymen, here.

22. *Friday.*   Clear and very cold A. M. ; cloudy P. M. Mr. and Mrs. Greenwood here.

23. *Saturday.*   Cloudy and snow.   Returned Francis' Horace.

25. *Monday.*   Christmas, and rainy.   Dined at Mr. Wetmore's with Mr. Goodale and family, John, and Patty.   Mr. Barnard and Prince at church ; the music good, and Dr. Steward's voice above all.

26. *Tuesday.*   The Globe from Mr. Goodale.

27. *Wednesday.*   St. John's Day.   The Freemasons meet at church; have anthems, etc., to Hancock and Washington, repeating and reciting their names as they proceeded with the musick; the organ and a bass viol by turns were heard.   That done, Mr. Hiller in the pulpit rose and delivered a kind of 5th of March oration, with a mixture of blank verse, on the subject and origin of Masonry and on brotherly love; few mountebanks possess themselves better than he did; he interwove his web with a prayer to God, as founder and Grand Master of Masonry.

28. *Thursday.*   Dined at Dr. Holyoke's with brother Blaney.

30. *Saturday.*   Fair and moderate.   Wrote to J. Smith, Esqr., and inclosed Peter's receipt, by Mr. Wetmore.

January 1.   1781.   A very fine, warm day.   Mr. Orne here.

2. *Tuesday.*   Cloudy, but warm.   The price of wood falls; it is now from £130 to £145 a cord.   A smart firing is heard to-day (Mr. Brooks is married to Miss Hathorne, a daughter of Mr. Estey), and was as loud, and the rejoicing near as great, as on the marriage of Robt. Peas, celebrated last year; the fiddling, dancing, etc., about equal in each.

3. *Wednesday.*   Snow and cloudy.   At evening Mr. Parker came to town.

4. *Thursday.*   Mr. Parker preached morning and afternoon at the church, and in the afternoon baptized 11 children.   It rained hard in the night.   At Mr. Barnard's at supper.

5. *Friday.*   A fine, moderate day, like April weather. Mr. Parker goes home.

6. *Saturday.*   A fine day, like May; a robin appears in neighbour Rand's garden.

9. *Tuesday.* Cloudy and cold. Mr. Wetmore comes home from Boston. Mr. Parsons here ; Mr. Osgood here also.

10. *Wednesday.* Snow, and wind S. E., and raw. We hear the debt of this State is in silver money £1,200,600, the half to be paid in August next. This, 't is said, will easily be done, it being no more than was done the year past.

11. *Thursday.* A fine, warm day. Mrs. Sargent died to-day. Mr. Greenwood informs of Capt. Babson's story, told him at . . . . by a Capt. of man-of-war, who says the brig Fame was taken by a fleet and carried to England, and he saw her and described her.

12. *Friday.* A fine, clear day. The selectmen commit to jail as a prisoner of war . . . who came in here as a passenger in order to settle in the country as a subject of the United States. Query, their power — 1, to commit ; 2, to do it without *mittimus.* Note, he is an Irishman, but had not been taken.

14. *Sunday.* Snow. Mrs. Sargent [1] was buried after church. Bearers, Mr. Nutting and Capt. Derby, Mr. Cabot and Dr. Putnam, Dr. Holyoke and Pynchon. Mrs. Cotnam's letter to Mrs. Pynchon was brought from Halifax in the Cartel, and forwarded by express order of Gov. Hancock ; *est-il possible ?* A rumpus is brewing. The selectmen commit to jail Mr. . . . . as a prisoner, and refuse admittance to his *fils ;* complaints are made to G. and Council.

15. *Monday.* Clear and pleasant. Mr. Brian taken

[1] Mrs. Catherine Sargent was the second wife of Colonel Epes Sargent, and a former wife of Samuel Browne. She was the daughter of John Winthrop and Anna, daughter of Governor Joseph Dudley. Colonel Sargent was the son of William Sargent, of Gloucester. After his marriage with his first wife, Esther MacCarty, he removed to Salem, and die in 1762.

up as prisoner, and ordered to go to Boston with his wife and young infant child.

17. *Wednesday.* Clear and cold. News that some of the Continental army have left it for want of clothes and pay ; two brigades gone to Trenton.

18. *Thursday.* Raw and cold. Dr. Anderson married Miss D. Clarke last evening.[1] Sent to R. Rogers, goldsmith, at Ipswich, a pattern for 6 teaspoons, and tea-tongs, by Mr. Dennis, the tongs to be 33 pwt. Mr. and Mrs. Sparhawk and daughter spend the afternoon with us.

19. *Friday.* A very fine, clear morning, as calm as May.

20. *Saturday.* A like morning ; cloudy in afternoon. Great quantity of wood.

21. *Sunday.* Rain and some snow, but a warm air. Mr. and Mrs. Lowell in town ; he tells us of the bill for repealing the Tender Law having passed the House last Friday, and with some small amendment probably would pass the Senate.

22. *Monday.* An exceeding fine day, like May more than January ; at night a storm of rain, snow, wind, etc. Messrs. Barnard and Prince both now meet with our Club.[2] Mr. Hitchburn in town, and returns to Boston ; also Mr. and Mrs. Lowell.

---

[1] Dr. John Hartley Anderson, brother of Mrs. Hoyland and Mrs. Allen, was born at Knottingly. He studied physic in London, and afterward studied surgery with the celebrated Dr. Barrow, of London, for four years. He was a surgeon in the British navy. Soon after his marriage he went on a cruise, and returned to Salem, too ill to be removed from his ship, where he died in Salem harbor, November 16, 1781. Miss Clarke was a daughter of Captain John and Ann (Furness) Clarke. Her only child, Mary, was born on the day after her father's death. Mrs. Anderson died on the 23d of March, 1841.

[2] The Club here mentioned was composed of the leading gentlemen of Salem, the more prominent of whom were Dr. Holyoke, William Pynchon,

23. *Tuesday.*   Northeast storm, snow, hail, wind, and rain ; Dame and I sit quiet and hear it by her shop stove.

24. *Wednesday.* Cloudy, but moderate weather. Spent the evening at Dr. Anderson's ; two ministers and large merry company.

26. *Friday.* A cold morning, and the streets before breakfast are full of wood, the sledding being excellent.

28. *Sunday.* A fine, pleasant day ; no lights at night.

29. *Monday.* An exceeding fine day ; no wind. Rumour that Sir W. Pepperell [is to be] governor.

30. *Tuesday.* A cloudy morning ; little wind ; April weather. Sir Wm. Pepperell, it is said, is to be governor of a province extending from Nova Scotia to Casco Bay, and that the country is to be reduced for that purpose

Dr. Putnam, Judge Andrew Oliver, Judge Benjamin Lynde, Judge Nathaniel Ropes, Rev. William McGilchrist, Rev. Thomas Barnard, Dr. Joshua Plummer, Colonel Pickman, Colonel Frye, Colonel Epes Sargent, Stephen Higginson, Mr. Thomas Robie, and Mr. Samuel Curwen, men for the most part, as has been said, of literary attainment, great critical acumen, and of considerable research in theology. As the war drew on, and political feeling became more bitter, the meetings of the Club, many of whose members were Tories, were more and more thinly attended, and at last, during the first years of the war, were for a time wholly suspended. In a letter to Colonel Browne, at this time, Mr. Pynchon thus alludes to the waning strength of the Club : " You may easily imagine what a figure our solitary clubb now makes. We are at considerable pains to keep the small remains of it together, weekly notifying the time and place of meeting. When met (the waggs say) we sit looking at one another speechless, as the cats in cloudy weather ; and if a word of news, the times, mobs, recantations, troops, or congresses, etc., etc., pops out thro' inadvertence or impatience, two or three forefingers are instantly pointed at the doors and windows of the room, so that a stranger, from the silence, forefingers, and long faces, would suppose a funeral at each door. But the Clubb, regardless of waggs, etc., goes on. However, it would really give us much pleasure and no disagreeable surprise if without previous notice you would bolt in upon us one of these gloomy evenings."

as far north as the Bay.   The sun broke out to-day ; in the afternoon the sky was again covered with clouds. Messrs. Lowell, Higginson, and Clark in town.

31. *Wednesday.*   Cloudy and cold.   Mr. Greenwood and I went yesterday evening to Mr. Orne's ; drank tea and supped there, and returned at about 12 at night.

February 1.   *Thursday.*   Cloudy and somewhat warm. Mr. Wetmore moves to Colo. Sargent's house.   [An] English 74, the Culloden, cast away at R. Island.

3. *Saturday.*   Fine weather.   A prize comes into Manchester, taken by the Essex ; [many] of the people died ; the rest with great difficulty got in.

4. *Sunday.*   A snow-storm ; wind S. E., with hail and rain.

5. *Monday.*   A fine, moderate morning ; the snow not deep.   News that Deerfield, at a town meeting, instructed their representative to use his endeavours to compound with Great Britain ; and it has raised a fog and a flame, and a fuss at the General Court and in the political world ; J. Williams ! what is thy portion ?

6. *Tuesday.*   Morning an exceedingly fine one, like a morning in May, excepting the snow on the ground.

8. *Thursday.*   A fine day, like yesterday.   The countrymen, farmers, etc., now groan out aloud about taxes, and about the burthen of raising men for the Continental army, and about an army to be sent to the eastward to secure Casco Bay, parts of which, as is said, are to be attacked by the English in the spring.

9. *Friday.*   Clear and very cold.   Wood is coming down to £80 to £90 a cord.

11. *Sunday.*   The snow pretty deep, and the weather cold.   At Mr. Cabot's at night.

12. *Monday.*   Fair and cold.   Evening, Club at Mr. Blaney's lodgings at Colo Sargent's.

13. *Tuesday.*   A very fine day ; good sledding ; plenty of wood.   Mr. Greenwood, Ward and co. set out in Walker's sleigh for Boston ; J. P., coachman, on the box, as happy as a lord.   Mrs. Newhall and daughter come to town.   Mrs. Orne very ill.

16. *Friday.*   A fine, warm day ; no wood comes ; the sledding and snow are going off.   John sets out again with Count Walker for Boston.

17. *Saturday.*   News confirmed that Count D'Estaing fell in with the English fleet, and took or destroyed 7 of the Line, with Transports.   A fine, fair day ; wind comes in to N. W.

18. *Sunday.*   A cold day.   I went with Dr. Putnam to Mr. Orne's ; find Mrs. Pynchon, Mr. and Mrs. Orne, all ill.   Mr. Sanders, from Albany, says that Vermont is to be a separate State, allowed by Congress ; that State to defend the frontiers and to be in confederation with the other American States against their enemies.

19. *Monday.*   Rain and snow ; wind S. E.   Mr. Wetmore goes to Boston with Mr. Hill.   The English papers give an account of Mrs. Ab. Gardiner's death at Pool, near Bristol.   She was the wife of Dr. Sylvester Gardiner of Boston,[1] daughter of the late Colo. Pickman, widow of W. Epes, Esq., a gentleman of great worth and deserved esteem, a Virginian.

21. *Wednesday.*   A very fine but cool morning.   Rumours that several towns meet and decline raising more men for the war, by reason of inability to pay them.

---

[1] Dr. Sylvester Gardiner was the great-grandson of Joseph, one of the first settlers of Narragansett.   He was born in 1717, and was educated as a physician.   He was a determined loyalist, and left Boston with the British troops.   He returned to Newport, however, and there died in 1786.   His second wife, here mentioned, was Abigail Epes, of Virginia.   He was a man of large estate, much of which was confiscated.   His grandson was the Rev. Dr. Gardiner, rector of Trinity Church, Boston, from 1805 until 1830.

22. *Thursday.* Snow and rain. News that Gen'l Green obtains a victory at . . . . , and that the account of the capture of the English ships by D'Estaing is groundless ; but it probably had been held much longer as true had it not been for Green's affair.

24. *Saturday.* Fine, clear, and warm morning. News that the owners, etc., of the Rhodes privateer are adjudged trespassers for taking the Rhode Island ship, and have to pay £2000 silver money and upwards, damages ; that certain Justices in each county are empowered by Act of the General Court to suspend the Habeas Corpus Act, in case (as it is said) that any towns or persons shall dare instruct their representatives as Deerfield hath done, or be guilty of speaking or [think]ing too loud against either wind or tide of politics ; . . . . for Essex are appointed.

26. *Monday.* Fair and blustering. I go with Daniel Oliver to Danvers in Mr. Cabot's chaise ; find Mrs. Pynchon and all of them growing better of the throat distemper ; we return at tea-time.

27. *Tuesday.* Clear and moderate. Some wood, but very little provisions. Friend Hussey denies his telling me insolently that he had work'd or jockeyed me, but P. Pynchon and J. Osgood were present. News that Arnold's fleet is taken and sail to Newport.

28. *Wednesday.* Went with Dr. Putnam to Mr. Orne's farm. Mr. Wetmore returns from Boston ; speaks of certain proposals of consequence *pro vitâ.* Mr. Pulling [1] comes to town to live.

March 1. *Thursday.* Cloudy. Mr. Goodale with Mr. Wetmore goes to Danvers. Dr. Putnam is some-

---

[1] Edward Pulling, H. C. 1775, was a son of John Pulling and Jerusha Bradbury, his second wife. He became a distinguished barrister of Salem, and died prematurely in 1799, at the age of forty-three.

what better. R. Derby, Esq., taken ill, voiding blood from his stomach, and accounted dangerous.

2. *Friday.* Cloudy, and at night rain. Mr. Pullen and clerk Osgood at my house. Mrs. Pynchon grows better.

4. *Sunday.* Clear and windy. I go against the wind to Mr. Orne's, and find little benefit from oiling my face. Find the sick recovering, and return and drink tea at Dr. Putnam's.

5. *Monday.* Cloudy, and snows. Club. Mr. Cabot dangerously ill.

6. *Tuesday.* Cloudy and moderate. Mr. Dunbar in town ; he appears to be distressed, and to think he is oppressed by tyrannical creditors.

7. *Wednesday.* N. E. storm and some snow ; at 12 the wind high, and snows. At 2 John sets out for Boston with F. Cabot, thence to walk to college ; Mr. Winthrop carried his bundles in his sulky to Cambridge ; they lodge at Chelsea.

8. *Thursday.* News of Admiral Rodney's attack upon merchant ships at St. Eustatius.

9. *Friday.* Mr. Dunbar very ill at Dr. Putnam's.

10. *Saturday.* Fair and cool. Plenty of wood brought in sleds. I go to Danvers and lodge.

12. *Monday.* A fine, fair day. Wrote to John by Mr. Jennison. Town meeting.

13. *Tuesday.* A fine, clear, windy day. Dr. Lloyd in town.

14. *Wednesday.* Some rain and some snow. Mr. Vans informs of the imprisonment of Catlin, Williams, and Ashley of Deerfield, by Governor and Council, as seditious and dangerous persons ; proof was by [their] conduct at Town meeting, and instructions to the representative of the town as to a speedy peace, and as to the

sentiments and expressions about taxes being insupportable by many of the people.

16. *Friday.*   Mr. Wetmore returns from Boston; while
there went twice to see Williams, but could not see him,
he being committed to close confinement in a low, dark
room ; denied pen, ink, etc., and all conversation with
any but jailer. A physician, Dr. Williams, went twice to
see him and was not admitted.

20. *Tuesday.* The last of arresting for the April
Court.

21. *Wednesday.*   Went to Boston on Dr. Orne's horse
to see Williams ; no *mittimus* nor cause of commitment
to be seen ; then I went to Sheriff Henderson, and with
him to Gov. Hancock, who humanely ordered that the
prisoners should have a physician and all necessaries and
conveniences.

22. *Thursday.*   [In] morning returned from Dr. Williams of Roxbury, where I lodged last night.   Saw Mr.
Powell, Mr. Rowe, and Lt. Gov. Cushing, and finding
no prospect of their being admitted to bail was returning
home, and found the sheriff had orders from the governor
that the prisoners might have pen, ink, etc., and petition
for enlargement, etc., but the petition was rejected ;
Mr. Cushing and Dr. Holten, committee.

24. *Saturday.* Fair.   Mrs. Pynchon and Mr. Wetmore go to Cambridge, and return home from Boston at
night.

25. *Sunday.* News that the British fleet had returned
to New York.

26. *Monday.* Cloudy, and some rain.   Mr. Lowell
here, and says that the fleet of Transports only returned.

28. *Wednesday.* Cloudy and cold.   Dr. Orne went
to Boston to see J. Williams in jail, and returns, and
says that he hath a bad cough and hath spit blood.

29. *Thursday.*   Snow; wind N. E., and cold.   News that St. Eustatius is taken by the British fleet, and 2000 troops landed, and it surrendered without opposition ; and all the shipping was taken, a Dutch man-of-war, and frigates ; that St. Martin's also was taken ; that the French fleet was returned to R. Island, having had a bloody engagement with the English.

31. *Saturday.*   A fine, pleasant day.   At night visit Mr. Cabot, and find him in good spirits.

April 1. *Sunday.*   A fine, fair day.   The Brutus brings in a privateer sloop taken near Cape Cod.   The prisoners, as soon as the jail door was shut upon them, gave 3 cheers, making the house to ring: much better this than either snivelling or being sulky.   Mr. Cabot worse.

2. *Monday.*   Rain and cold N. E. wind.   Town meeting for choice of State officers.

3. *Tuesday.*   Rain.   Court at Ipswich.

4. *Wednesday.*   I went to Ipswich with young Mr. Hodges ; the Court did very little business till this morning.

5. *Thursday.*   Mrs. Pynchon returned from Boston.

7. *Saturday.*   At night I returned from Ipswich with Mr. Osgood and Oliver.   Drank tea at Mr. Browne's, Wenham.

8. *Sunday.*   We hear from Philadelphia that the Exchange is at 120 dollars for one.

10. *Tuesday.*   And here hath risen from 75 to 80.

11. *Wednesday.*   Goods grow scarce.

14. *Saturday.*   Wrote to J. Williams by Mr. Flagg not to hurry on a petition to the General Court.

15. *Sunday.*   A fine, clear day.   Several vessels came in from the W. Indies to Boston, Beverly, and Salem. Mrs. Orne came alone, and went to church with us, and returned at night.

17. *Tuesday.*   Fair.   Dine at Mr. Goodale's.

18. *Wednesday.*   Fair and moderate.   What are the troops about [at the] southward ?   S. G. says they have had a bloody [battle].   Mr. Sanders and B. Pickman dine with us.

19. *Thursday.*   Mr. Wetmore returns from Boston. Williams is not worse, but rather firm and cheerful, and the prisoners choose to bear the inconvenience of the damp room in which they are rather than turn out a stranger from a better, for accommodating them.   Parker puts Riddon in jail.   Mr. Sewall dines with us.

20. *Friday.*   Cloudy, and rain.   Mr. Sewall explains the mysterious conduct of the Councillors as to Gov. Hancock and the prisoners' petition, and as to Dr. Holten.   Some thunder and lightning at night.

23. *Monday.*   A fine, warm morning.   Rumours that Cornwallis fled after the battle, and left his wounded on the field.

24. *Tuesday.*   Cloudy, and fine rain.   See new Act prohibiting all correspondence with Britons.[1]

26. *Thursday.*   Cloudy and cold.   Baldwin and his brother come and lodge here.

27. *Friday.*   John goes to Cambridge with Baldwin. Mr. Wetmore returns from Boston, and says that Williams and co. are enlarged and gone home ; that they petitioned for it to the whole Court ; and that he himself is dismissed by Madam D.

28. *Saturday.*   A fine, fair day.   Bottled 34 bottles of spirit and 10 case bottles, in all about 11 gallons.

---

[1] The Act here referred to is probably that passed on the 3d of March, requiring all vessels arriving at any port in the Commonwealth from any port in possession of the enemy to be searched, and any private letter or packet belonging to any passenger to be examined and detained, if thought necessary. See Acts and Resolutions, Massachusetts Records for the year 1781.

May 1. *Tuesday.* A fine, warm day. Put into the ground some dwarf peas, radish seeds, and, last, planted early beans. Judge Lynde kicked by a horse.

2. *Wednesday.* Planted large marrowfat peas in two rows east of the cherry-trees, and white beans west of the main alley, and speckled beans on the east side half, and the northern part the white sort ; Mr. Flagg's beans on the left hand turning to the garden ; peppergrass in short bed by *sparrowgrass.* Yesterday Judge Lynde's leg was broken by kick of his horse, and it is thought he cannot recover.

3. *Thursday.* This is Fast day, and should be (as it proveth to be) somewhat cloudy and gloomy. Mrs. F. Cabot taken ill of a pleurisy.

4. *Friday.* Mr. Dowst comes from Boston ill. Mrs. Cabot delirious.

5. *Saturday.* Fine, moderate weather. Barker in jail as [a] dangerous person. Mrs. Cabot grows worse.

6. *Sunday.* A fine, warm day. Mr. Eliot preacheth at Mr. Barnard's meeting-house. Mrs. Cabot has had no sleep since Friday until this night.

7. *Monday.* Cloudy. Mrs. Cabot was raving most of the night, but sleeps a little ; little hopes of her recovery. Mess. Eliot and Prince dine here. Mrs. Cabot sleeps, and there seems now some hope.

8. *Tuesday.* Rain, and northeast wind and raw cold. Mrs. Cabot rested finely and seems to be in a hopeful way, which has cheered up Mr. C. and the whole family. Mr. Lowell comes to see Mrs. Cabot.

9. *Wednesday.* Rains so that we can't go to Ipswich Court, the adjournment being to this day.

10 *Thursday.* Cold N. E. wind, and cloudy. We go to Ipswich and find the Court did not meet, so that all the business of the Court continued over is dead and gone, null and void, and we return E. D.

11. *Friday.*   Fine, fair day ; and I plant corn in the garden, and find the beans are coming up.   Mr. Oliver returns from Boston ; Mr. Winthrop of New London in town.

12. *Saturday.*   Cloudy, and small rain.   It is said the *wicked and abandoned* Colo. Browne,[1] formerly of this town, is made governor of Bermuda.   I dine at Mr. Wetmore's with Colo. Sargent, Mr. Blaney, Mr. Winthrop, Forbes, and co.

14. *Monday.*   Very pleasant.   Town meeting, and Mr. Goodale chosen a Representative.   Mr. Wetmore had one vote, H. Derby one, I none.   Spent the evening with the Club at Mr. Sparhawk's ; four clergymen present.

[1] Colonel William Browne, here alluded to, was the son of Samuel Browne, who married Catharine, a daughter of John Winthrop, Esq., and great-grandson of Major William Browne.   He was born on the 5th of of March, 1736, was graduated at Harvard College in 1755, was appointed a judge of the Superior Court in 1774, and left Salem in 1775.   He married Ruth, a daughter of Governor Wanton of Rhode Island, and was made governor of the Bermudas in 1782.   He died in London.   "The family to which Colonel Browne belonged," says Colonel Pickman, was "the most respectable that has ever lived in the town of Salem, holding places of the highest trust in the town, county, and State, and possessing great riches."   In a memorandum made by Mr. George A. Ward, and now in the possession of his nephew, George R. Curwen, of Salem, it appears that the appointment of Colonel Browne to the governorship of Bermuda was partly due to the influence of Mr. Thompson, afterward Count Rumford, who, when young, took passage in the same vessel with Colonel and Mrs. Browne.   Young Thompson, who from motives of economy occupied a place in the steerage, was especially noticed by the Brownes, who often sent him meals from the cabin table.   On their arrival in England, Mr. Thompson, having letters to Lord George Germain, then at the head of the war department, whose wife was an American lady, and a supposed connection of Thompson, was taken into the family and friendship of his lordship, to whom he was much indebted for his rapid elevation and subsequent success.   On the unexpected appointment of Colonel Browne to the government of the Bermudas, he inquired at the war office to whom he was indebted for this interest in his behalf, and was informed that it was Mr. Thompson.

15. *Tuesday*. Fair and moderate. Mrs. Vans and Mrs. Pynchon set out for Medford and Cambridge. Harry Gardner and his family come in to-day from the West Indies, having a brief of his admission as Burgher of St. Eustatius, now in [the] hands of the English, our enemies.

17. *Thursday*. Cloudy ; N. E. wind. Mrs. Pynchon and Mrs. Vans returned.

18. *Friday*. Cloudy. The continental currency, old emission, passeth no more here.

19. *Saturday*. Some take the old emission on pretence of patriotism.

20. *Sunday*. A fine, fair day. Dr. Woodbury, who succoured many American prisoners, [and] assisted them in escaping at Nova Scotia from British men-of-war, is now threatened with imprisonment for claiming his property.

22. *Tuesday*. A fine day. The Admiralty Court sits here. Dr. Woodbury and another Nova Scotian are thrown into jail as prisoners of war, after going about Salem and Boston for a month or more without interruption. Shame to those who imprison him.

23. *Wednesday*. Cold and cloudy. The Maritime Court ends. Mr. Lowell and Parsons call to see me. Dr. Woodbury is let out of jail by those who put him in, — this at Mr. Parsons' desire ; the Dr. being a Son of Liberty.

24. *Thursday*. Fair and cool. Exchange between old emission and silver is at 150 for one ; at Boston at 120 to 140 for one. The jurymen in the Maritime Court here yesterday refused to give in any more verdicts to the Court without an assurance that they shall be paid in new emission. So ! so ! so ! members of Congress, whither is your credit going ? Down hill surely ; but they will bring it up with a heavy tax.

26. *Saturday.*   Cloudy, but less cold than yesterday. It is said that Morris, the financier, hath reported to Congress in favour of hard-money currency.

27. *Sunday.*   Clear, and wind S. and moderate.   Soh! soh!   The register, Pickering, says he is not at liberty to record Mr. Robie's[1] mortgage deeds of his house and land, which he made for securing his creditors in England.   Johnson comes in and says that Gibraltar is relieved by the English fleet.   What ailed ye Powers and ye Fleets of the House of Bourbon that ye have been so often driven back by the English, — that all your attempts against Gibraltar have hitherto failed ?

28. *Monday.*   Fine, clear, and warm day.   Exchange is now at 3 for one between hard money and new emission, and at . . . . for one between hard money and old emission.

29. *Tuesday.*   A fine, warm day ; So. W. wind.   Trade in Boston in great confusion, almost stagnated ; the credit of the new emission sunk 30 per ct. upon failure of the old in its credit; all growl ; some rave and stamp ; others curse and swear, some at Congress, some at the General Court, some at Whiggs, others at Tories, — all at the French.   The moderate Whiggs express their joy that Gibraltar is relieved and the siege raised ; they who trouble the waters first have seldom the benefit of fishing.

30. *Wednesday.*   Election Day ; very dark and cloudy ; wind S. W.   No public dinner, no parade ; the most miserable procession ever seen.

31. *Thursday.*   Went to [Cambridge] with Patty ; saw the library, philosophical rooms, and museum ; visited all my acquaintances ; dined at Mr. Mason's.   It is said

---

[1] Mr. Thomas Robie, who married Mehitable, daughter of Major Stephen Sewall.

that the new house is in looks meaner than the old ; if so, mercy on us !

June 2. *Saturday.* Cloudy and moderate. The marketmen refuse bills of the old emission for provisions; the jurymen refused it at the Maritime Court, here in open Court ; the Judge declined to take it : and yet this is our established currency, established by law ! O Congress ! O legislators ! O money-makers all ! what ails ye ? This day Sheriff Chandler took Carlton on a warrant from the Inferior Court against him for a riot in breaking windows, etc., at the rejoicings at the taking of Burgoyne ; he was carried to the town house, and a justice was sent for to bail him, but he departed, and left justice, sheriff, and all in the lurch ; threats were given out at the jail that if he was to be committed the jail would not stand long. Mark the end !

5. *Tuesday.* Fine, moderate weather. Mr. Forbes spends the evening with me ; comes from Boston, and says Fort Camden is taken by Gen'l Greene.

8. *Friday.* Rain and cold. The French fleet get into Boston and other ports.

9. *Saturday.* A fine, pleasant day. We have a letter from Jno. at Cambridge ; his chum ill, and he unwell. Mr. Goodale and [Mr.] Ward from the G. Court. The Court had written to the Congress respecting the currency, and can do nothing about it before they have an answer. A few weeks ago, who even held paper money not to be as good as silver were called Tories, enemies to the country.

12. *Tuesday.* A fine, pleasant day. Mrs. Waldo [1] is buried ; her funeral is attended by a great number of people of condition and others. She was an only child,

---

[1] Mrs. Mary Waldo was the first wife of Major Jonathan Waldo, and the daughter of Jonathan and Mary (Coffin) Ropes.

and they lived with her father most happily; she was very young, [and] had lately been delivered of a fine child, and at the time when nothing seemed wanting to complete the happiness of this little family she was taken from them, and left them almost distracted with grief.

14. *Thursday.* Capt. H. Williams comes home from New York. Mr. Winthrop and co. come from New London; [they] say the paper currency is in very low credit there. Dr. Woodbury is with difficulty allowed to return home to Annapolis; his treatment here hath nearly converted him to Toryism.

15. *Friday.* Cloudy, and some rain. John comes from college with Mr. Bartlett of Plymouth. In the N. York papers brought by H. Williams, it seems a congress is to be held at Vienna for examining the pretensions of France, Spain, and England, etc., for making war and offering terms of reconciliation not to consider the American Independence; and the papers show the progress made by British troops at Virginia. England seems determined not to give up America.

16. *Saturday.* A fine, fair day. Mr. Winthrop and Mr. Stewart of New London, Colo. Sargent and family, here P. M.

18. *Monday.* Rumours that through the influence of the congress at Vienna matters begin to wear a more peaceable face. Shepard of Amherst here, and speaks of Hale's going *incog.* to Penobscot in March last, and heard of an intended expedition to Casco Bay.

19. *Tuesday.* A fine, fair morning. Mr. Wetmore and I set out for Ipswich; there I hear that Vermont hath entered into a contract of neutrality with Canada; that D. Jones is appointed Ch. Justice of the State of Vermont.

20. *Wednesday.* A very fair day. I return from Ipswich, having done the very little business I had to do there ; I entered not one action : so much for politicks ! Wright here.

21. *Thursday.* A fine, fair day. By the papers, Camden is taken and the army in Virginia increasing, and things begin to look more favorable for America at the southward.

23. *Saturday.* A fine, clear morning. Mr. Cosset of Claremont, in Vermont [sic], comes, and brings letters to Mr. Dowse from Mr. Parker, and an account that Mr. Bass will probably be allowed his salary from the society. Last night the noted John Long escaped out of Salem jail, and two prisoners of war went off the same night, and with him, as supposed. Long is he who took Gen'l Wadsworth and carried him to Penobscot ; it is said that soon after Long was taken, ten guineas were sent for his use to the commissary of prisoners, and a letter from Capt. Mowat was delivered to him in jail.

24. *Sunday.* Cloudy, but moderate. Gen'l Farley from Ipswich to seek for the breakers of jail, and advertise the brig. Mr. and Mrs. Lowell call to see us.

25. *Monday.* A cool morning, but clear. Mr. Winthrop and co. return from Portsmouth. Rumours that Arnold is arrested and sent to New York, on a suspicion of having poisoned or otherwise destroyed G. Philips.

28. *Thursday.* Rain and cloudy by turns. Spent the evening with Colo. Sargent's family. Mr. Winthrop and Stewart at Mr. Wetmore's. More signs of peace by the papers.

30. *Saturday.* Clear and warm. Mr. and Miss Winthrop and Mr. Stewart here.

July 1. *Sunday.* A fine, warm day. Mr. Winthrop

and Stewart and co. here. The General Court sit all this day, as we hear, upon matters of great importance, and relating to congress at Vienna, proceedings as to peace, etc. Last evening Mr. Ford was buried in the churchyard. Mr. Barnard prayed at his house and attended at the funeral; the bearers were all dissenters, as I remember.

2. *Monday.* A fine, pleasant day. Spend the evening at Mr. Goodale's, with Mr. Winthrop, Stewart and co., and Colo. Sargent and co.

6. *Friday.* A warm day. Mr. Wetmore goes to Boston. Expectations of peace.

8. *Sunday.* Very hot last night; slept all hands with windows open, my honoured self on the floor. Mr. Higginson from Boston says that the bills of the new emission are to pass in payment of taxes at $1\frac{7}{8}$ paper for one silver dollar, or 11*s.* 3*d.* paper for six shillings in silver, and that the old emission passeth no more, not even for payment of taxes.

10. *Tuesday.* Judge Trowbridge called at the door, being bound to Mr. Derby's, at Beverly.

14. *Saturday.* Cloudy and warm ; wind S. W. Mr. Wetmore and H. Higginson dine with me. Rumours of an English expedition in favour of the Corsicans.

16. *Monday.* Town meeting to raise more men, about ninety in all. Rumour that Gen'l Lee of Virginia is gone over to the Regulars. Church meeting adjourned to September 17th.

18. *Wednesday.* Commencement; a fine day.

19. *Thursday.* Rain ; gloomy day for all concerned in Colo. Doane's ball.

20. *Friday.* We return to Salem with Mrs. Mason, and find neighbour Satchel greatly disturbed about his new chaise, which he lent me, Foster not having procured

him one to ride with in my absence; neither money nor concessions appease his piratical ire. From purse-pride, good Lord, deliver me, — and my prayer is answered.

21. *Saturday.* Fair day. A wine prize to Grand Turk comes in; paper money, new emission, goes fast down hill.

22. *Sunday.* A fine day. Mr. Eliot at Mr. Prince's meeting.

24. *Tuesday.* A fine day. The market people will not take any paper money for provisions.

25. *Wednesday.* Judge Trowbridge, Mr. Parsons, and Mrs. Parsons dine with me and Mrs. Mason.

26. *Thursday.* A fine day. Mr. Wetmore and son, Mrs. Mason and self, Mrs. Pynchon and son John, dine at Mr. Orne's, Danvers.

27. *Friday.* A very fine, cool day. Dine at Mr. Greenwood's with Mrs. Mason, and go up to see Mr. Derby and Judge Trowbridge.

28. *Saturday.* A fine day. Last evening wrote to Mr. Walter, New York, in favor of Mr. White and Mrs. Fairfield's son, prisoners there. Dine at Dr. Putnam's with Judge Trowbridge, Mr. Nutting, and Dr. Holyoke.

29. *Sunday.* A fine day. Go with Mrs. Mason to Mr. Barnard's meeting all day.

30. *Monday.* Cloudy in the morning; clears away and very hot before noon. I go with Mrs. Mason to Cambridge with Mr. Goodale's horse and chaise.

31. *Tuesday.* Cloudy morning. I return by half past eight o'clock from Malden, and breakfast at Salem. Continental bills, whither is your credit flown? And where the credit of your makers and creators? "Oh!" says Dr. C., " they have answered well the purposes of their creation : they have *supported the army* for some years, and it is time for them to rest, being of no more

service." O pious doctor, rare Dr. C.! when fraud and deceit can no longer prevail, let them be laid aside as useless.

August 1. *Wednesday.* Judge Trowbridge dines in town at Mr. Derby's.

2. *Thursday.* Fair. Mr. Gannet and Mrs. Gannet come P. M.

3. *Friday.* Trowbridge Ellery [1] comes, and dines at Mr. Derby's. Mr. Gannet and co. drink tea at Dr. Putnam's and sup at Mr. Oliver's ; dine with me.

4. *Saturday.* We dine at home; Mr. Gannet at Mr. Prince's.

5. *Sunday.* Mr. Gannet and co. dine at Dr. Putnam's ; at night sup at Mr. Goodale's.

6. *Monday.* Clear and very warm. Mr. Gannet and Mr. Barnard go to Beverly and spend the day ; Mrs. Gannet with us.

7. *Tuesday.* Warm. I go with Mrs. Gannet, Mrs. Pynchon, and son John to Marblehead, and have tea at Brother Sewall's.

8. *Wednesday.* Clear and warm. Mr. and Mrs. Gannet set out for Cambridge late, and at noon the weather is very hot ; at evening, aurora borealis.

9. *Thursday.* A fine, cool morning; very warm at noon. Dine at the Fort on turtle, — about four persons ; Professor Williams, Mr. Barnard, Mr. Hopkins, and Dr. Whitaker, the latter by far the strongest man ; he seized Esquire Blaney and took him up on his shoulders and laid him flat on his back in a masterly manner, to the entertainment of his parishioners. "Aye," says T. Mason, "the doctor is fit for anything; he would have made as stout a sailor as any in the town of Salem ;

---

[1] Edmund Trowbridge Ellery was a son of the Hon. William Ellery, one of the signers of the Declaration of Independence.

he is a smart man, and fit for any business ; he made as good an agent for the privateers as ever was." At about five o'clock we sit down to dinner.

10. *Friday.* A fine, cool morning. I returned to Mr. Oliver the dollar which I borrowed of him at the Fort.

12. *Sunday.* Fair and warm. Mrs. Orne and her maid Landor come.

13. *Monday.* Fair and cool. News that Mrs. Fairfield's son died in the prison ship at New York. Three more privateers are taken and carried to Halifax. Mrs. Cabot makes her will ; in it gives Titus, her negro, £40 and his freedom in case he shall continue in her service henceforth till her death. Titus cares not, as he gets money apace, being one of the agents for some of the privateersmen, and wears cloth shoes, ruffled shirts, silk breeches and stockings, and dances minuets at Commencement ; it is said he has made more profits as agent than Mr. Ansil Alcock or Dr. Whitaker by their agencies. A plentiful rain last night.

14. *Tuesday.* A fine, cool day. Mr. Greenwood dines here. Mrs. Frye calls after dinner, and diverts us on the new law of Congress that the wives of Tories might marry within a year after their husbands left them, and she determines to wait but one year longer for the Colo., and sends word to R. W. that she is sorry he is sick.

16. *Thursday.* A fine, cool day. See Salem papers of Monday last, in which our paper money-makers are aspersed for their frauds, deceipts, meanness, and many of their tricks, by which honest people have been defrauded.

17. *Friday.* Cloudy and cool. Prizes daily come in : Dr. Whitaker agent for one of them ; Titus Cabot for another, as we hear.

18. *Saturday.* Mr. Baldwin called here with Mrs. Eliot.

19. *Sunday*. Cloudy and a little rain. Mrs. Orne and little Kate come, and return at night with Mrs. Brewer. Mr. Lowell here. [It] rains plentifully in the night.

20. *Monday*. Cloudy and some rain. Judge Trowbridge here. More rumours as to the Fame.

21. *Tuesday*. A fine morning. Mrs. Dana spends the day here. Mrs. Gridley here, being brought in by one of our privateers to the eastward.

22. *Wednesday*. Cloudy ; S. E. wind. More rumours as to the Fame.

23. *Thursday*. N. E. wind. Buffinton writes to his wife that some people in the Roads tell him that they saw my son and others.

25. *Saturday*. A fine, clear day. Mr. Gridley and Mr. Goodale here. News of Mr. Browne at Virginia by Colo. Griffin.

27. *Monday*. Cloudy and moderate. Miss Dana here, and I send money by her to John at Cambridge.

28. *Tuesday*. A fine day. Mrs. Marston and Mr. and Mrs. Greenwood here ; also Mr. and Mrs. Prince in the evening.

29. *Wednesday*. A very fine day. News that Capt. Carnes in the Porus, and Dr. Anderson in the Essex, are taken.

September 1. *Saturday*. A fine, clear morning. At . . . o'clock was seen from the steeple a severe engagement between an English gunship and a French frigate of [32] guns off Marblehead. It lasted . . . hours ; the French [vessel] was torn to pieces.[1]

---

[1] This was an action off Boston harbor between an English frigate of 44 guns, said to be the Assurance from Halifax, and the French frigate, Magicienne, of 32 guns, coming round from Piscataqua. The Magicienne was, after a short conflict, finally obliged to strike. See *Continental Journal* of September 6, 1781.

3. *Monday.* I send by Dr. Rice, to the care of Mr. Barnard of Cape Pursue, a letter from Mrs. P. to Mrs. Cotnam, enclosing one to Mr. Robie, and his enclosing one to Wm. Cabot, London. Colo. Griffin comes to Salem, and goes out of town P. M. I carry Mrs. Pynchon to Marblehead.

4. *Tuesday.* A very warm day. Went with Mrs. Mason to Marblehead in Mrs. Orne's chaise.

6. *Thursday.* A very fine day. Patty and Mrs. Mason go out to Miss Diamond's.

7. *Friday.* Cloudy. I went to Marblehead for Mrs. Pynchon, and brought her home.

8. *Saturday.* A fine, pleasant day. Jno. Williams and wife and son come to Salem ; he with us on Sunday.

9. *Sunday.* News that H. Derby's . . . is taken and carried to Penobscot.

10. *Monday.* Clear and cold. Mrs. Browne of Wenham dies.

11. *Tuesday.* Cloudy, and rain at night. Mr. Parker and Stephen Greenleaf come to town.

12. *Wednesday.* Cloudy. Mr. Parker, Greenleaf, and Dowse at tea at my house.

13. *Thursday.* Cloudy. F. Cabot tells us of the horrid destruction and massacre at New London by Arnold and co. ; the commander of the Fort was stabbed upon resigning his sword, and nearly all the garrison put to the sword. *Query.*

14. *Friday.* Cool and cloudy. Town meeting here, and committee chose to prepare matters for defence of the town against Arnold and crew, who burnt [the] N. London privateers, and are said to be inveterate against Salem and Beverly rovers and plunderers ; a handbill comes from Boston giving an account.

15. *Saturday.* A fine, warm morning. The town

seems almost distracted with joy at the news in the handbill. God bless Gen'l Greene, the Baron and Marquis, and all our generous allies, is the word, and damn the Britons ; Charleston is to be in our hands in a few weeks ! The British fleet is beat all to pieces, and returned to New York.

16. *Sunday.* A fine day; very warm. Rumour that Mr. Stewart of N. London is killed ; false.

17. *Monday.* Cool and S. wind. Mr. and Mrs. Cutts in town. Rumours of two spy boats taken off Marblehead prove false.

19. *Wednesday.* Fair and pleasant. The return of the British fleet to N. York is doubted.

20. *Thursday.* Cloudy and some rain. Rumours of the engagement of the fleets confirmed ; in the afternoon contradicted.

22. *Saturday.* A cold day. Went to Cambridge with Miss Mason, [with] Stevens' horse and Daland's chaise.

23. *Sunday.* Pleasant and warm. Returned from Cambridge. Mr. Lowell in town.

25. *Tuesday.* Very warm. Mr. Wetmore and I set out for Newbury Court ; dine at Beverly ; get to our lodgings at Mrs. Leather's at 8 o'clock.

26. *Wednesday.* The Court (newly vamped and sworn) proceed to business ; the Ch. Justice magnifies his office, feels his importance, and grows severe.

27. *Thursday.* Clear, fine weather. Dr. Shepard's trial with Wayland on a charge of being put. father of her b. child comes on ; every possible art used for acquitting him, but the truth at length prevailed, and he was convicted, and ordered to pay 5 shillings a week. He threatens a *certiorari*, and fumes and smokes, all to little purpose. *Hæret lateri*, etc.

29. *Saturday.* All is confusion and hubbub about

dismissing the Jury and adjourning the Court, not one of the new entries being called yet. Mr. Hooper's is No. 1, and issue joined in it, and he insists that it be called (being on a plain note of hand), although the *continues* not finished, because, as the Court must go against law in dismissing the Jury without trial of his, they ought to pass over the continued actions for his, being of importance : *sed non allocat.* Up starts Mr. Hooper and leaves the Court ; so do Wetmore and I, being debarred of our clients' rights. Whieu ! !

30. *Sunday.* We came this morning from Ipswich ; a fine day, though somewhat cloudy and wet at setting out. Various are the rumours concerning the English and French fleets at the southward, and of their engagements, and of the return of part of the English fleet into N. York, all tattered and torn ; others say that there was an engagement, but both sides were mauled much and parted, but continued in sight of each other without offering to engage again.

October 1. *Monday.* A fine, clear morning. More rumours as to the battle of the ships.

2. *Tuesday.* Mr. Wetmore carried Mrs. Pynchon to Boston around by Cambridge.

3. *Wednesday.* Mr. Parsons here. Mr. Cabot from Boston says Mrs. Goodale and Mrs. Pynchon are at Mr. Higginson's, in good spirits.

4. *Thursday.* A cool morning. Mr. Parsons breakfasts with us. At night we hear from Boston ; Mrs. Pynchon and Salem people there, all well. A very cold night.

5. *Friday.* A fine, cool day. Esquire Batchelor and Butler here about the affairs of N. Fairfield. Last night Judge Lynde dies, 81 years of age. I spend the evening with Judge Oliver, he being alone ; on my return I

find Mrs. Pynchon and Mr. Wetmore returned from Boston.

6. *Saturday.* A fine, fair day. Mrs. Pynchon and I drink tea at Mrs. Lynde's. At night a billet is prepared for requesting Judge Trowbridge's attendance as a bearer to Judge Lynde, to be forwarded on Sunday morning to Cambridge by Primus.

7. *Sunday.* Cloudy, and wind N. E. At Mr. Cabot's in the evening.

8. *Monday.* A clear morning, and cool. About 10 A. M. Mr. Barnard and I set out in his chaise for Woburn, where we dined about 4 P. M., and returned to Mr. Haven's at evening ; lodged and were most agreeably entertained there, and returned on Tuesday noon. See N. Coffin's jolly letter in Boston paper.

9. *Tuesday.* A fine, fair day. Judge Lynde's funeral was at 5 o'clock, P. M. Bearers, Mr. Hooper, Mr. Nutting, Mr. Dowst, Dr. Turner, Mr. Cabot, and Dr. Putnam ; Mrs. Pynchon and I, Mr. Wetmore and Patty, next the children of Mr. Oliver; Mr. Russell and Mrs. Curwen in the procession next Mr. Wetmore.

10. *Wednesday.* A fine, fair day. Mr. and Mrs. Russell go out of town.

13. *Saturday.* Cloudy, and rain at night. Jno. and Bartlett come from college, and dine with us, and return in the afternoon, and are caught in the rain. J. Higginson and wife come to Salem at night ; John Williams also, and tells us that he was not called on his bonds at Springfield.

14. *Sunday.* A fine, clear day, tho' windy. J. Williams and wife here.

15. *Monday.* Fair day. Mr. Sears here from Boston.

16. *Tuesday.* Mrs. Pynchon not well, and keeps her chamber.

19. *Friday.* Mowat's brig Swift brought in 60 persons.

20. *Saturday.* Cloudy ; thunder and rain in the night. English fleet gone from New York.

23. *Tuesday.* Cool and clear. Lord Cornwallis in trib[ulation] ; 130 heavy cannon are playing upon his encampment, some of his redoubts taken, and the insurance offices have waged that he and his army were taken the 4th instant ; others, that they will surrender this month ; others, that it will be early in next month ; a few, that he will get clear, — some say by his own, others, by the help of the English fleet and troops gone from New York. P. M., set out for Boston.

24. *Wednesday.* Fair day at Boston. Luckily meet brother Stephen Sewall, a punctual, honest, humane, benevolent, good soul, and he performs all in his power for the relief of his friends in tribulation.

25. *Thursday.* I set out from Boston for Salem (Winnisimet way). News of Lord Cornwallis and his whole army's surrender, amounting, with sailors and all, to 9000 men, several frigates, and 100 transports, etc., etc ; a handbill comes signed by Na. Goodale.

26. *Friday.* Cloudy and some rain. Cannon, small arms, mortars, bells, and all kind of arms, sounds, reports, clamours, noises, and rumours through the town make the diversions and employments of this day ; the surrender was on the 20th instant.

28. *Sunday.* Cold N. E. wind, but clear. Widow Cabot[1] buried here.

29. *Monday.* Wet day, and cold. Expresses come, and no confirmation of Cornwallis' surrender ; some begin to doubt of the matter.

---

[1] Mrs. Elizabeth Cabot, *née* Higginson, relict of Joseph Cabot of Beverly.

31. *Wednesday.*   Clear and moderate.   Handbill comes of Greene's victory near Charleston.   Havock, havock!   Parson Fisher comes to town in the evening, on his way from Portsmouth to Boston, under guard ; he, with 3 other gentlemen as prisoners of war, carried into Portsmouth, where they were coarsely treated ; he not allowed to preach or baptize, nor to dine abroad upon an invitation of his friends.   Mr. Fisher went and settled in Nova Scotia in a school before 1775, and, being a friend to the American cause, could not continue there in peace, [and] comes up to reside in this State, the place of his nativity, and to settle here.

November 1.   *Thursday.*   Mr. Fisher and Williams set out for Boston.

2. *Friday.*   Zech. Foot calls on me, with Mr. Fisher's desire to acquaint me that he is not allowed his parole, but is to be sent to the Island with other prisoners. Windy and cloudy ; rains at night.

3. *Saturday.*   Very stormy, rain, and N. E. wind. Yesterday the Gen'l Court adjourned to January.

4. *Sunday.*   Cloudy and N. E. wind.   Capt. Haraden and Jona. Gardner, Jr., come home from England through France, thence to Chesapeake, and thence to Salem.

6. *Tuesday.*   Cold and cloudy, N. E. wind.   Supreme Court at Salem.

7. *Wednesday.*   See the newspapers for Adams' letter to Cushing [1] to encourage whipping, hanging, etc., for Tories.

9. *Friday.*   Windy and very cold.   At night Mr. Sewall, Sullivan, Paine, Lowell, and Wetmore.

---

[1] This letter is addressed to Lieutenant-Governor Cushing, and is dated Amsterdam, December 15, 1780 ; its authenticity seems to have been doubted.   It is quoted in the *Continental Journal* of November 8, 1781.

11. *Sunday.* Cloudy and cool. Mr. Bromfield at Mr. Cabot's, and Mrs. Bromfield.

12. *Monday.* Cloudy and some rain. See Mr. Adams' letter for hanging his brother if a Tory ; but the letter is denied.

13. *Tuesday.* A cloudy, cool morning. Money is so scarce that I can't get enough for cyder and wood.

14. *Wednesday.* Cloudy and cold. Dr. Holyoke and Mrs. Holyoke and co. here in the evening. Blyth and Williams' fireworks — thirteen rockets prepared for the 13 States; 5 of them rose about 8 feet, 4 only a tolerable height, and 4 only so-so, and 2 bad.

17. *Saturday.* Mr. Dowst from Boston gives an account of Mr. Fisher's confinement at N[oddle's] Island, as prisoner, being sent there to pasture, as the Attorney-General *politely* says.

18. *Sunday.* Cloudy A. M. ; clears up at night. The English fleet and troops are said to have returned again to N. York without either engagement or disaster. Britons ! Britons ! who now are masters of the ocean ? Negatively, not Britons ; are ye not afraid even of Paul Jones ?

19. *Monday.* Warm morning. Drs. P. and Holyoke only at Clubb, at my house.

20. *Tuesday.* Mr. Walter's answer to my letter as to Capt. White's son and other prisoners ; Fairfield, etc., dead [sic], N. York guardship.

23. *Friday.* A fine, clear day, and cool. Mr. Butler from Boston with a letter from Mr. Fisher at Noddle's Island.

24. *Saturday.* Cool and clear. By Mr. Wetmore I find that the Church Committee, B. and A., have bustled about at Boston among the great, without magnifying themselves or benefitting Mr. F. ; they have made a fuss

and noise, and have paid for it ; they have spent about 100 dollars, and Mr. F. is parolled to D., but can't preach ; they have spent the proprietors' money, raised to pay the proprietors' debts.

30. *Friday.*   Clark Gayton Pickman died.[1]

December 4. *Tuesday*, P. M.   C. Gayton Pickman's funeral attended by all of station in town.

8. *Saturday.*   Clear and cold.   Ri. Derby, Jr., Esq.,[2] dies to-day about 3 o'clock, another sacrifice to the malevolence of the times !   God preserve us all from the effects of future malevolence !   Rumours that R. T. Paine means to succeed C. J. Cushing, who, it is said, cannot continue much longer in health sufficient for the duties of C. Justice.

12. *Wednesday.*   Cloudy and some wet.   Mr. Bartlett comes at evening and tarries.

13. *Thursday.*   Capt. Derby's funeral.   Mr. Sewall marries Miss Devereux.[3]

15. *Saturday.*   Clear and cold.   Mr. Wetmore returns ; Mercy Beadle comes and goes.

16. *Sunday.*   John sets out with Eben. Putnam in his father's carriage for Cambridge.   Mr. Sewall and bride appear at meeting.

17. *Monday.*   Fine, cool, clear morning.   Dr. Lloyd here.

19. *Wednesday.*   S. O. delivered of a daughter.[4]

[1] Clark Gayton Pickman was the son of the fourth Benjamin Pickman, who married Love Rawlins ; he married Sarah, a sister of Timothy Orne. Rebecca, another sister of Mr. Orne, married Joseph Cabot.

[2] Captain Richard Derby was a son of Richard, and brother of the first Elias Haskett Derby ; he was born in 1736.

[3] Samuel Sewall, born December 11, 1757, was the great-grandson of Chief Justice Samuel Sewall.   He began the practice of law in Marblehead in 1781, and married Abigail, daughter of Dr. Humphrey Devereux.   He was made Chief Justice in 1813, the third chief justice of the name.

[4] Mary Lynde Fitch Oliver.   She married Joseph, afterwards Mr. Justice Story, and died without issue 22d June, 1805.

22. *Saturday.* Cloudy and cold. Mr. Greenwood and Dr. Putnam with me in the evening; also Mr. Wetmore.

23. *Sunday.* Cold. Butler and Atkins make report at church of their engaging Mr. Fisher for our preacher.

25. *Tuesday.* Christmas Day. In evening Dr. Holyoke here.

28. *Friday.* Rain and N. E. wind. By Mr. Jones of Boston I receive a letter from Mr. Curwen of 31st of August, shewing great concern for the affairs of America and her doubtful fate. Brother Porter's [1] letter from London of August 8th to Bro. Blaney diverts us; two long pages, folio, and two ideas, — at least more than one; the exordium, or preface, is rhetorical, the conclusion sympathetic toward the widow Dabney. Ah! Brother P. begins to think of the widows.

31. *Monday.* Clouds and snow; very well now for some sledding. This day I venture out, having been confined to my room from the 19th instant.

1782. *January* 2. *Wednesday.* A beautiful day. A greater quantity of wood than usual brought in.

3. *Thursday.* Small rain carries off the snow, but wood comes down to 4 dollars a cord.

4. *Friday.* Cloudy, wind S. E., sloppy ways. Search in vain for Sawyer's bond given Mr. Cabot by him and A. Putnam, and left with me.

5. *Saturday.* J. M. Sewall at Mr. Goodale's in the evening.

6. *Sunday.* Fine day. Mitchell at Mr. Wetmore's at tea.

8. *Tuesday.* Cloudy and warm. Mr. Goodale comes in with A. Putnam's bond, which he found among those he took of me, one of them being the same Putnam's.

---

[1] Jabez Porter, a classmate of Mr. Pynchon, who died in 1792.

Billy Wetmore grows better and comes below. More squibs in the papers at the Justices emitted.

9. *Wednesday.* Fair and cold. S. Sewall and ux. and Mitchell come from Marblehead and dine with us. We spend a very merry evening at Mr. Goodale's with Mr. Prince, and have musick and diversions the whole of the evening. Sam'l Sewall was there also before 9. Stephen and ux. go home to Marblehead.

10. *Thursday.* Cloudy and cold. The evening at Mr. Goodale's with Mr. Barnard and Haven and Mr. Sewall ; all grave ; church meeting.

11, 14. *Monday.* Clear and fair. Town meeting for instructing Congress as to the fisheries. Colo. ill treated at meeting, and left it.

17. *Thursday.* Clear and cold. Mr. Parsons here from Cambridge ; he says that the government is determined to effectually support the new President, and to see that the dignity of the president's office be kept up against all opposition.

18. *Friday.* Cool, but wind S. W. Dine at Mr. Goodale's with Colo. Sargent, Blaney, Dr. Holyoke, Wetmore.

21. *Monday.* Cloudy and cold. Mr. Bartlett comes from college.

22. *Tuesday.* Snow. Dined at Mr. Cabot's. Bartlett returns to Cambridge.

23. *Wednesday.* Cloudy and cold, and snow P. M. ; N. E. storm.

24. *Thursday.* The storm continues ; the snow deep, and much drifted.

25. *Friday.* Cloudy, cold, and more snow seems at hand. Mr. Lee[1] of Concord, Jack's classmate, lodges here.

---

[1] Silas Lee, afterwards member of Congress.

26. *Saturday*. Clear and cold. Mr. Goodale comes from Boston; Mr. Fisher soon to be liberated, as it is said.

29. *Tuesday*. Fair and clear. The church vote to offer Mr. Fisher £150 a year to be their minister, unseen, and not yet heard; and desire the Church wardens and vestry to sign a letter prepared for engaging the sum, and such further sums as they should be able. Mr. N. Barrett and Mr. Lafitte spend the evening here, and tell us of Mr. Platts's being in town.

31. *Thursday*. Clear and cold. Mr. Blaney, Dr. Putnam, and Mr. Oliver spend the evening with me; all very cheerful. At 12 Mr. Platts of Hartford and Mr. Barrett of Boston call to see me, and Mr. Platts agrees to bring Mrs. Platts next week to see us, from Boston, in case his business and the weather shall permit.

February 2. *Saturday*. Cloudy and some snow. [The] Church Committee return without Mr. Fisher.

4. *Monday*. Clear and moderate; very fine sledding. Taxes, taxes ! !

5. *Tuesday*. A fine, moderate day; thaws. Mr. and Mrs. Platts and my family dine at Mr. Goodale's, and spend the evening at Mr. Wetmore's. Mrs. Hathorn and co. go to Lynn to bring home the minister, Mr. Fisher.

6. *Wednesday*. S. W. wind. Mr. and Mrs. Platts set out for Boston.

7. *Thursday*. Cloudy; N. E. wind. No Mr. Fisher yet. Mrs. Hathorn and co. return. Clears up pleasant.

8. *Friday*. Cloudy again, and wind N. E. Mr. Jones (who went with poor B. in the Fame) spent the afternoon and evening with us, and gave us a particular account of their voyage to Amsterdam, and of the transactions and reception there; also of the Americans he saw

in London, and of their great anxiety about returning to America.

12. *Tuesday.* Early this morning the wind at N. W.; was very high and blew violently, and it was extremely cold. Mr. Wetmore sets out for Boston.

14. *Thursday.* Pleasant and clear. Mr. Fisher and Mr. Dowst dine at my house; more church affairs.

15. *Friday.* Cloudy, but pleasant. Mr. Fisher, Oliver, and myself dine to-day at Mr. Dowst's elegantly. Mr. Wetmore returns from Boston.

16. *Saturday.* Moderate weather and thaws. Mr. Fisher and Butler set out for Portsmouth.

24. *Sunday.* Clear and cold. Mr. Fisher for the first time preacheth at church [and] gives great satisfaction. Mrs. H.'s family are in raptures; Mr. Orne goes to church all day.

25. *Monday.* Cold and clear. Proprietors of the church adjourn to my house, and conclude on ways and means as to Mr. Fisher's settlement.

26. *Tuesday.* Clear day and cold. Mr. Barrett and co. and Dr. Loring at Mr. Goodale's.

27. *Wednesday.* Evening at Mr. Goodale's with Dr. Loring, etc.

28. *Thursday.* Mr. and Mrs. Barrett and Dr. Loring here, and Mr. Lafitte and Miss Sanders.

March 2. *Saturday.* Fair day. The proprietors' committee present Mr. Fisher with proceedings of the church in the choice of him for minister.

3. *Sunday.* Sacrament at church; the audience before and after noon pretty full; contributions for Mr. F., unmarked money 54/; last Sunday about 68/. Judge Sullivan resigns for want of support.

4. *Monday.* Fair and moderate. Mr. Hooper here, roaring about the Court's neglect of his cause. Clubb

at Colo. Sargent's in the evening ; Mr. N. Barrett there. Andrew Putnam taken up for deceipt and cheating of his neighbour and brother physician, Endicot. Sullivan and Lowell are chosen.[1]

5. *Tuesday.* Fair morning and moderate. Hunt, Mr. Barrett, and Mrs. Loring come from Boston ; we all sup at Mr. Goodale's.

6. *Wednesday.* Cloudy and rain. At evening Mr. Barrett, Mrs. Barrett, Mrs. Loring, Goodale, and Mr. Osgood spend the evening here.

8. *Friday.* Cloudy and some rain. In the evening at Mr. Goodale's with Mr. Barrett and co.

9. *Saturday.* Cloudy. Old Capt. Derby complains of his taxes ; has 100 dollars abatement. A comfortable letter from Bro. Stephen.

10. *Sunday.* Clear and cool ; N. W. wind. Mr. Prince preacheth at Marblehead.

12. *Tuesday.* Mr. Barrett goes to sea.

14. *Thursday.* A fine, moderate morning. Mr. Derby goes to sea.

15. *Friday.* A fine, pleasant day. This week Mr. B. asks Mr. F. to dine. It being wet, Mr. F., having set out to go, returns, and sends word, but not a card, and Salem is in an uproar.

16. *Saturday.* Cloudy ; S. E. wind. *Litigatio civilis* minds one of the times of peace.

19. *Tuesday.* Clear ; N. W. wind. The last of arresting for April Court.

20. *Wednesday.* A fair and cool, windy morning. I spent last evening at Dr. Holyoke's, with Mr. Fisher, Colo. Sargent, Dowst, Blaney, Goodale, and Mr. Bar-

---

[1] John Lowell and James Sullivan were elected delegates to the Continental Congress in place of S. Adams and A. Ward. They presented their credentials May 20, 1782.

nard ; so much respect to a clergyman of [the] Church of England !! Mr. Prentice here on his way to Derry. A large company, filling two rooms, at Mr. Haraden's, the wedding house ; Mr. F. not there, being yet a stranger in town.

21. *Thursday.* A fine, clear day. In the papers an account from England of the intention of the English to carry on the war with vigour, in which they seem more unanimous than ever, all parties agreeing in that opinion ! Clerk Osgood here.

22. *Friday.* A fine, moderate day. Mr. O. goes to Cambridge and Boston.

23. *Saturday.* Fine, clear day. Ill of a cold, and could not dine at Mr. Goodale's with Messrs. Fisher, Barnard and company. Mr. Bartlett from Cambridge ; but our long-expected daughter at Danvers comes not.

24. *Sunday.* A fine day. All go to church but myself ; my cold grows better.

25. *Monday.* Cool and cloudy. Mr. Bartlett returns to Cambridge at eve. Mr. Fisher, Barnard, Prince, here with the Club.

26. *Tuesday.* Fair and cool. Dr. Holyoke and Mr. Fisher here about the Church books, etc., given in Mr. Gil[christ's] will.

27. *Wednesday.* Cloudy morning. Rep. Belknap, by insolence as to the matter of att'y fees, gave my nerves no small irritation. At evening S. Gerrish and Wetmore and company play at Pope Joan.[1]

30. *Saturday.* [The] Julius Cæsar launched.

April 2. *Tuesday.* Fine, fair day. Mr. Wetmore and I set out for Ipswich Court.

---

[1] A game of cards, in which a board having five compartments is used to hold the pool. The first of these compartments is called Pope Joan ; hence the name.

6. *Saturday.* A very fine day. I return from Court with Mr. Wetmore, Sewall and company.

12. *Friday.* A fine day. Mr. Sewall here ; Gen'l Farley in town.

13. *Saturday.* A fine, pleasant day. I sent Mr. Gilchrist's sermons to Mr. Fisher. Mr. Lafitte, thou art too polite ; I fear more polite than sincere.

14. *Sunday.* A fine, pleasant morning. Mr. Fisher preacheth. Thou saidst that I might not depend on thy dining with me yesterday, accordingly didst not come. Mr. Lafitte said with a smile, and politely, I might expect him, but he came not. Why ? Perhaps because he was not asked the evening preceding. If for that reason, why did he bid me expect him ? Perhaps because the disappointment might operate as a punishment for my unpoliteness. If this be true politeness, query whether the French do not far exceed the whole world in true politeness.

15. *Monday.* The Club at Mr. Blaney's lodgings. Tea at Madam Lynde's.

16. *Tuesday.* A fine, pleasant day. Mr. W. Winthrop from N. London, and gives an account of people at New York.

17. *Wednesday.* Cloudy and cool. Yesterday Gray here from college. Mr. Cockle[1] comes to town from Mount Desert, lodges at Adams', diets at Mr. Vans' ; is all in rags, having been plundered, robbed, abused, and barbarously beat by Britons and Americans by turns.

19. *Friday.* Some rain. A concert at night ; musicians from Boston, and dancing.

20. *Saturday.* Rain. Last night Mr. Oliver returned from Boston with a polite letter from Mr. Parker to Mr.

---

[1] James Cockle, at one time collector of the port of Salem, his commission dating 1762.

Dowse and others, proprietors' committee, and with a gown for the parish clerk. *Quod nota!* Mr. Cockle begins to prosecute the plunderers.   Mark the event!

21. *Sunday.* The day appointed for clerk Atkins to assume the *toga clericalis.* Some think he will defer it until the former clerk Ward has notice, and leaves the seat ; others, that he will in person give Ward notice, etc. A cloudy morning, and wet. Mr. Cockle is to appear at church to-day in his preposterous breeches.

Vans. Qu. Mr. C., why do you forbid your poor neighbour Bunker and others to dig clams on the flats, as they are everywhere common?

C. Mr. V., it is plain you understand nothing of the English Constitution.

Vans. Why don't you forbid people to fish near the flats?

C. Why, don't you know, sir, that fish are itinerant, *feræ naturæ,* sir, and clams are located? Every man who reads the English law knows that.

V. Why, do you read the laws of England?

C. No, sir ; but I used to read them before the rascals stole my books, and you might learn as much in your Bible at your leisure.

V. Why, do you read the Bible, then?

C. I used to read it before the rascals stole my spectacles. Mr. V., no man ought to give up his Prince; by the laws of England and by the Bible, no man ought to give up his bread without an acknowledgment, an equivalent, sir.

V. But you don't call clams your bread and your right and all that?

C. But I do, though, both by the law-book and Bible, as I could show you if I could once get my spectacles.

25. *Thursday.* Fast Day. Service at church, A. M. ; none, P. M. Mr. Cockle breakfasts here.

26. *Friday.* Cloudy. Mr. Mansfield comes to agree on another day for the arbitration at Andover ; proposeth early the week after next.

27. *Saturday.* I dine at Mr. Wetmore's with Mr. Winthrop and Mr. Cockle.

28. *Sunday.* Mr. Fisher goes to Marblehead. Mr. Steward reads, and tries to read. Mr. Winthrop and Wetmore here at tea.

29. *Monday.* A fine, fair morning. At 7 John sets out for Cambridge in Dr. Putnam's chaise with Master Eben'r.

30. *Tuesday.* Mr. Cockle breakfasts with me. Mr. Ward and Ives call to speak with Mr. Cockle, and to confer with him about the robbery which he charged to this Ives' brother Wm., but nothing comes of this conference.

May 2. *Thursday.* Early, Mr. Blaney and I set out for Boston. I catch cold dining at Colo. Sargent's, in his large, cold, and damp room ; add to my cold, and at night go to bed ill, but resting till Friday, 10 o'clock, recover. Mr. Kollock, Dunbar, and Danforth meet and choose arbitrators.

3. *Friday.* Wet day. The arbitrators meet, [and] hear the parties, who behave with much decency and propriety, — how rare a sight where a large estate is the subject of inquiry !

4. *Saturday.* Cloudy, cold, and rain. Mr. Blaney and I set out for Salem ; arrive by 5 o'clock, accompanied by Mr. Bentley from Newhall's. News from Connecticut that Parliament resolves to withdraw the British troops from America, and bend all their force against France, and declare America independent. *Credat Judæus.*

6. *Monday.*   A fair, clear day.   More rumours of independence.

7. *Tuesday.*   A very fine morning.   Mr. Mansfield, Pickering, and myself set out for Andover, on Peabody arbitration.

8. *Wednesday.*   A wet day ; proper for arbitration business.

9. *Thursday.*   Cloudy and rain.   We leave Andover, where we were lodged and treated with great civility by S. Phillips, Sr., and arrive at Salem in season.   On the road we meet T. F., who tells us of a severe firing he heard in the Bay, and that Cabot's mast-ship and some other vessels were taken by a British man-of-war.   On coming to Salem we find nobody had heard of any firing. News from the West Indies of Independence.

10. *Friday.*   Cloudy morning.   More and more of Independence [and] of withdrawing the British troops, etc.

11. *Saturday.*   Cloudy and some rain ; P. M., fine, warm air.   A fiddler goes through the streets fiddling of Independence ; the boys throw dirt at him for joy. Last evening some of the young gentlemen of the town manifest their joy by vomiting along the streets, as though intoxicated by strong drink ; then with brick-bats, etc., attack a poor woman's house, disturb her family, keeping them awake by repeated noises at her doors, and affright her and her six children, crying Liberty and Property.   Mr. Shimmin from Boston says few there fully credit the reports of Independence, etc.

13. *Monday.*   Rain ; at night, thunder, lightning, and rain.   Mr. Hooper offers to lay two against one that, in the sea engagement in the West Indies, the French had a smart drubbing, and lost 4 or 5 ships.   At town meeting, none chosen Representatives will serve for Salem, so the meeting is adjourned.

15. *Wednesday.* Cloudy and rain. Mr. Cockle is detained by the weather. Mess. Cabot, Pullen, and comp. spend the evening here.

16. *Thursday.* Cloudy and rain. Mr. Cockle goes to Marblehead, and thence for Mt. Desert.

18. *Saturday.* Clear and fair day. Mr. Winthrop comes to town with Mr. Wetmore.

19. *Sunday.* A fair day. Mr. Winthrop and Mr. Wetmore dine here.

20. *Monday.* Mrs. and Miss Higginson.

22. *Wednesday.* Moderate, cloudy morning. Mrs. and Miss Higginson,[1] with F. Cabot and F. Oliver, set out for Boston. At night the Commissary Hopkins comes to town to search for stores of goods brought from Halifax by Mrs. Higginson; he behaves with much humanity and politeness, takes an account of trunks, packages, etc., and hath them opened and inspected, but with the eyes, *more humano.*

23. *Thursday.* Cloudy and cool. Mr. Peabody and Mrs. Beck here, but would not dine.

25. *Saturday.* Mr. Fisher calls on us; is rejoiced that he can have Capt. Briton's house. The jealousies and malevolent disposition against Mrs. H. and daughter continue; nay, increase. Thus do the heathen and barbarians rage, and the people imagine a vain thing, the kings of the earth and the Congress. By Mrs. Cotnam's and other letters from Halifax, as well as from his own, we learn that our friend P. Marston continues still in the course of heinous sins and offences, especially those of humanity and adversity. At evening Mr. F. Cabot and Mrs. Higginson return from Boston with-

---

[1] Mrs. Higginson was a sister of Thomas Robie, whose loyalty made it necessary for him and his family to leave the country. She sailed with her brother for Halifax, and was now on a visit to her native town.

out any prospect of success, or of any treatment from government but what is rough and revengeful, except [from] some who feel for the calamities of their neighbours. Mr. Wetmore, Winthrop, Oliver and ux., and Mrs. Orne dine with us.

26. *Sunday.* Cloudy morning. Mrs. Higginson and daughter go to Beverly. News that Rodney took 14 sail, — French ships.

28. *Tuesday.* Some rain. I get 9 gallons of red wine at Story's.

29. *Wednesday.* Cloudy. All election matters go on with languor ; everything seems to be upon a small scale. The clergy allowed no public dinners ; they shrug and look gloomy [when] met together, and seem to whisper their discontent and dislike. Tom bottles off my wine.

31. *Friday.* A cool day. Mr. Fisher and I purchase a pipe of madeira of Smithhurst, at 5/6 a gallon. So here ends May, which has proved cloudy, cold, and pretty wet, but exhibits a fine prospect as to the grass.

June 1. *Saturday.* A fine, pleasant morning. Jona. Rich from Mt. Desert informs of Mr. Cockle's and of Stanley's safe arrival ; also of more plundering by privateers. Sweep on, sweep on, barbarians, 't is all the fashion ! 't is part of the liberty purchased with American blood ! I received a letter of Feb. 7 from Bro. Pynchon, N. York.

2. *Sunday.* A fine day. I saw Mr. Bentley, one of the tutors, at Mr. Barnard's.

3. *Monday.* A very fine morning. Rumours of British troops leaving N. York.

4. *Tuesday.* A fine day. Mr. Wetmore and Mr. Cabot return from Boston. Cartel said not to have sailed.

5. *Wednesday.* A very clear, fine day. Rich and Mrs. Moore go for Mt. Desert; by them I write to Cockle. Tom Duchfield bottles my madeira.

7. *Friday.* Cloudy and some rain. A 2d conversation with Neib. Glover on behalf of a friend, Mrs. Mascarene, concerning her son John's apprenticeship; her years and misfortunes open to her many veins of reflection. Mrs. Pynchon goes to Boston with Capt. Lee, Patty, and Mrs. Orne in the stage; a fine afternoon for them, but the wind somewhat brisk. *Qu.*, whether Mrs. P. will venture over Charlestown ferry.

8. *Saturday.* A fine day. Dr. Putnam and I go to see Judge Trowbridge, and dine with him at Mr. Derby's farm; on return we find that Mrs. P. went from Cambridge to Boston with John, and from Medford to Cambridge with Mr. Fitch. By Capt. Derby and others' accounts, we find that Count de Grasse, F. Admiral, and his ship of 11 guns were taken, and that he lost 7 ships in all; the English, but one. Also hear that Admiral Kempenfelt beat the French and dispersed them in their way to the Texel.

9. *Sunday.* A fine day. More news that Kempenfelt took 4 of the French ships, and drove 3 others of them ashore, as they were proceeding to join the Dutch, so that the French this spring must have lost 18 sail of the Line.

12. *Wednesday.* Invitation to turtle at Webb's on account of the birth of the Dauphin. I go to Boston for Mrs. Pynchon. Mrs. P. and I sup at Dr. Loring's at Cambridge.

14. *Friday.* A fine day. We dine at Mr. Mason's with Mr. Winthrop. I wait on the President and some of the tutors, the steward, etc., Dr. Kneeland and Mrs. Wendell, Mr. Mellen, etc., and find it the prevailing

opinion that taxation will not longer answer the purpose of continuing the war without help by loans, and no prospect of any. Have much satisfaction at hearing of John's behaviour at college.

16. *Sunday.* Mr. J. Lee and lady in town, and go to church. Go on to Cambridge early Monday morning.

17. *Monday.* Clear and very warm. Parson . . . of Dover with the Club at Dr. Holyoke's.

18. *Tuesday.* Very warm. I go to Ipswich. Court opens P. M. I return in the cool of the evening, after Court. I had not an appeal to enter.

19. *Wednesday.* Warm. I tarry at home. News of the rescue of Parson Ely out of N. Hampton jail by a body of armed men, and of another body of armed men pursuing and overtaking them.

20. *Thursday.* Morning cool. Mrs. P. and I go to Ipswich, and return at night. I find Sarah Clough had jumped out of the barn window and sprained her ankle.

21. *Friday.* Warm and clear day. Miss Higginson at Mrs. Goodale's. S. Williams calls and inquires for Mr. G., knowing him to be at Boston ; he stares at Miss Higginson as at an alien ; he came to see *her*, not him.

22. *Saturday.* Warm. G. Williams is for stirring up strife, and making mischief for Colo. Frye's family.

23. *Sunday.* A warm day ; rain P. M. Mr. O. officiates at church to general liking.

24. *Monday.* A clear day and moderate. Grand horse-race to be at Lynn beach. The race was run, but the stakes withdrawn : one of the riders and his horse fell down in the water.

25. *Tuesday.* A fine, pleasant day. The Maritime Court sits here, and it is the last of arresting for July Court at Salem and at Boston. Bro. H. and lady come to town in splendour ; but the Judge came first in an

open chaise, driven by a lad with a flapt hat, sitting at the right hand of the Judge. The latter wore a scarlet coat, his hat not flapt ; he leaned on his cane as he rode. On such occasions every circumstance becomes a matter of importance ; *forma sæpe dat esse.*

26. *Wednesday.* A fine, clear, pleasant morning. Judge N. Cushing, Paine, Emery, Mansfield, and Parsons here, and sup.

27. *Thursday.* A fine, cool day and evening. Sup at Mr. Wetmore's with some of the Bar.

28. *Friday.* Cloudy and cool morning. The Maritime Court ends ; in two causes, having determined that a crew's going ashore and plundering houses of their goods, etc., is a singling, and taking them at sea below low-water mark.

29. *Saturday.* Cloudy and warm. Parsons tells me of J. Cushing's being in nomination for Judge of Superior Court.

July 1. *Monday.* A cloudy morning; a fine shower. The oldest man cannot recollect the time when the face of the earth appeared so finely covered as now with the *green herb for the service of man.*

2. *Tuesday.* A fine, clear morning. Meeting upon Peabody's concerns and arbitration appointed, but Squire Mansfield comes not before 2 o'clock ; then a meeting and hearing of the parties. Mr. and Mrs. Browne come to town, but will not make one visit out of the tavern. Two prizes come in to-day : one with a cargo of fish from N. F. land ; the other with cargo of lumber, etc., from Quebeck. A rumour of 300 men speaking for a dinner at the tavern at Amherst at meeting of the Court there, by way of terror to the justices, as it is surmised. Mr. Lowell writes that Gen'l Washington is offered 3000 men from New York to join his army ; so much for

Huddy's affair. Lippencot, it is said, has had a trial there.

3. *Wednesday.* A fine, cold, and pleasant day. R. Wyer and S. G. walk with me to A. Waters. G. calls at Beck's, but her cake is so dear he buys none, but begs a bit of Wyer and me ; he buys a large lobster, but beats down the poor fisherman 1/4 part of his price. As to the query how he could find it in his heart to take that advantage, " Oh, 't is hard times, partner ; a man must look out sharp, to live now ! "

4. *Thursday.* A very cool morning, — so cool that I can scarce keep myself comfortable with cloth coat and jacket ; the latter, too, lined with flannel. Mrs. Sparhawk died last . . . as appears by the N. papers.

5. *Friday.* A fine day, cool and comfortable. At Mr. Goodale's with Mr. Noyes in the evening. The Gen'l Court is about to rise ; where can they find money for present occasions ? None will trust their promises ; taxation proves inadequate ; none inclined to lend the treasurer ; his accounts in confusion ; an assistant treasurer is chosen.

6. *Saturday.* Cloudy morning ; wind S. E. I spoke to Capt. Derby as to Davis' money in Sheriff Henderson's hands at Boston.

7. *Sunday.* A fine, cool, and clear day ; towards night a fog comes up. We hear that it was proposed at Salem town meeting to choose a committee to wait on Jno. P. and ask him to accept of the office of Judge of Admiralty. Objection that the town could not appoint him at length prevailed, so no committee was chosen.

8. *Monday.* Cloudy morning. In the evening Colo. Sargent was here with the Club.

9. *Tuesday.* The Court met. A fine, pleasant day. Their Honours drove Jehu-like, floundering along thro.

thick and thin ; if a party was but gone to Mingo, " Call him out, call him out," was the cry.

10. *Wednesday.* Worse and worse ; they must go home on Saturday.

11. *Thursday.* Mr. Fisher and lady and goods come.

12. *Friday.* The three judges spend the evening at my house.

13. *Saturday.* The Court about 12 adjourn without day, and three of them dine with me.

17. *Wednesday.* A very cool, fine morning for Commencement. John and Patty, myself and Sally Oliver, set out at 5 o'clock for Cambridge, and arrive at 1/2 past 8 o'clock ; are hospitably and genteelly entertained at Mr. Bartlett's chambers. I dine in the hall, [and] wanted for nothing but elbow-room ; before noon was in the meeting house at the mental feast and entertainment. All eyes, addresses, all compliments, are directed toward thee, Handcocky, O rare Handcocky ! Not a word of thee, stout, first mover, Adams, but all like new year's warm wishes, without meaning or belief ; like "your very humble servant" at the bottom of a challenge. To the President were some bows of affection and sincerity ; to the Lt. Governor and company not a word that could offend their delicacy by way of compliment. What could be said to Adams, who entered the pew as if going to steal a . . . ; to B., who entered as if to beat down a castle ?

18. *Thursday.* A fine day. I go with Miss Orne to Boston, and return to dine at Mr. Mellen's ; at 5 o'clock set out for Salem.

19. *Friday.* A fine day ; warm. Mr. Davis and Bartlett from Cambridge come and lodge.

20. *Saturday.* A fine, cool morning. Mr. Davis returns to Boston.

21. *Sunday.*   A fine, pleasant morning.   Spend the evening at Mr. Cabot's, Dr. Putnam and Holyoke.

22. *Monday.*   Cloudy day.   Sent a jug of white wine, 2 1/2 gallons, to Mr. Fisher, and put 9 bottles do. into the cellar, western wall.

24. *Wednesday.*   President Willard and Mr. Barnard call to see me, Mrs. Pynchon being gone to Danvers with Mrs. Goodale; on their return they were overtaken in a thunder squall.   A fine rain, which rejoiceth the face of the earth and of man.

25. *Thursday.*   News of damage done by lightning at Boston.   Mr. Orne's family endangered by a flash which went down his chimney and passed out at the door.

26. *Friday.*   Clear and cool morning.   At 12 at night Mr. Oliver returns from Boston; gives a partial account of the effects of the lightning upon Judge Oliver's house there, shewing to demonstration the efficacy of points in directing the lightning and preserving buildings, etc. Mr. Fisher and lady and other company spend the evening [here].

27. *Saturday.*   Some rain, cloudy, and wind W.   Mr. Dowse, Atkins, and I at Mr. Fisher's in the evening.

29. *Monday.*   A fine, clear morning.   Mr. Sewall dines with us ; is in much tribulation.

August 1. *Thursday.*   Barber insults Justice Wetmore, and is tried and bound over.

2. *Friday.*   Mr. Atherton and Mr. Dunbar come, and spend the afternoon and evening with Dr. Putnam and Mr. Oliver.

3. *Saturday.*   A fine, cool day ; some rain.   Mr. Sewall here at tea.

4. *Sunday.*   A fine, cool morning.   Mr. Warren at church ; also Mr. Lafitte.

5. *Monday.*   A fine day.   Mr. Warren, Bartlett, and Pickman [1] dine with John.

6. *Tuesday.*   A fine, clear day.   Mr. and Mrs. Fisher, Mr. and Mrs. Carpenter, here in the evening.   Yesterday the young gentlemen and ladies set out at 5 o'clock to breakfast at Danvers.   Every green thing is drying up apace.

7. *Wednesday.*   A fine morning.   Mrs. Cabot sells her house to S. Page for 1500.   Q. If enough.

8. *Thursday.*   A fine, clear, warm morning.   J. Trowbridge and J. Russell at Dr. Putnam's.

9. *Friday.*   A clear, warm morning.   Dodge brings a load of hay ; Mr. Wetmore's and my horse begin upon it.

10. *Saturday.*   Some rain P. M.   Mr. Wetmore with Mr. Waldo come at night.   Jacob moves Mr. Wetmore's hay.

11. *Sunday.*   A fine, cool day.   Prisoners from England, Jno. Higginson *et al.* come home, and say that all the American prisoners are released and sent home at the instance of the new ministry.   Spend the evening till 9 at Mr. Fisher's ; till 11 at Mr. Wetmore's, and large company, Mrs. Waldo, etc.

12. *Monday.*   A fine, cool day.   Evening spent at Mr. Goodale's.   J. Trowbridge in town.

13. *Tuesday.*   A cool, clear morning.   Mr. Dowst calls to see Mrs. Waldo, and she and Mrs. P. go to visit Mrs. Cabot ; she goes to Boston with Mr. Wetmore.

15. *Thursday.*   Dr. Lloyd and company here.   In the papers is Sir G. Carleton's letter to G. Washington as to proposals for exchange of prisoners and for general peace, and American independence is a preliminary !   G. Britain ! and canst thou stoop to the laws of necessity

---

[1] Mr. Benjamin Pickman was the sixth of the name.   He was graduated at Harvard College in 1784, and was afterwards a member of Congress. In 1789 he married Anstis Derby.

only? Why not propose this in 1776; millions of wealth, and thousands of lives, and immense corruption would have been saved! The ambitious is a little man; the ambitious nation must stoop.

16. *Friday*. Clear and warm morning. Miss Wendell and Patty go to Mrs. Greenwood's, and spend the evening with the young company. Circumstances and rumours looking toward peace hourly increase. Mr. King from Portsmouth and Mr. Bartlett are here at tea.

17. *Saturday*. A clear, warm morning. No corn, no 2d crop of grass; dry, terribly dry! Peace, peace is the word; no more taxes now! French 74-gun ship goes ashore and is spoiled.

19. *Monday*. W. S. E., and a fine rain, which prevents John and Bartlett from setting out for Cambridge. Mr. Bentley calls for Miss Wendell's letter. I wrote to the President, etc., for John's learning French at college, upon the terms and conditions required there.

20. *Tuesday*. Sunshine. Mr. Bartlett returns P. M. John and Amory have rooms together.

21. *Wednesday*. Cloudy; a very little rain. Maritime Court sits at Salem.

24. *Saturday*. Clear and warm. By the papers Mr. Sumner is appointed a judge of the Supreme Judicial Court!

26. *Monday*. Clear and warm. The Congress take Carleton's letter as matter of information only, and prepare for a general exchange of prisoners only, but no further for peace.

27. *Tuesday*. A fine, clear morning. Dr. Waldo said to be in earnest as to Miss M.,[1] and L. O. as to Miss C——d. Mark the end of both.

---

[1] This Miss M. was probably Milly Messenger, to whom Dr. W. was married in the following year. She was his second wife, and after his death married Rev. Dr. Prince.

29. *Thursday.*   Mrs. Mellen comes, and we all dine at Mr. Goodale's, and sup, too.   Amory and Parker come and dine with John, and return at night.   Mr. Bartlett also dines with them.   They set out for Cambridge after tea.

30. *Friday.*   A fine, clear morning.   Mrs. Mellen goes to Cambridge.   Parsons and Wetmore come from Boston.   Templeman goes to Boston for good.

31. *Saturday.*   A fine, cool day.   I speak again to Capt. Derby as to Sheriff Henderson's having Davis' debt, and as to suing for it, but he would give no directions in it.

September 1.   *Sunday.*   A cool day; wind S. E.; clear.   Mr. and Mrs. Prince and Miss Messenger, Mrs. Sanders and Miss Harris, here at tea.   Mr. Lowell here. Mr. and Mrs. Fisher spend the evening here.

2. *Monday.*   A fine, cool day.   Mr. Bentley called here in the morning in his way to Cambridge.   Mr. Mellen comes and lodges here.

3. *Tuesday.*   Clear, fine morning.   Mr. Mellen, Mrs. Pynchon, and Mrs. Goodale set out for Cambridge at about 1/2 past eight A. M.   Rumours that negociations at Paris ended abruptly ; these by vessel into Providence. A grand prize of sugar and cotton, the Graftons chief owners.

4. *Wednesday.*   Wind N. E. ; cool and clear.   It is now said that the Dutch demands against England are so high as to break up the negociations for peace.

5. *Thursday.*   Rumoured that the negociation at Paris is proceeding, and that the news to the contrary is not true.

6. *Friday.*   Cool and clear ; wind S. E.   Sol. Davis from Boston says the news is that an English fleet of 31 sail, men-of-war, have arrived at N. York, and troops from England at Halifax ; and that Gen'l Washington

hath sent to the several States to be on their guard, especially at Boston, as their design is probably against the French fleet there ; so all hands, French and Americans, are gone down to the islands a-fortifying.

9. *Monday.*   At Mr. Blaney's in the evening.

10. *Tuesday.*   The last of suing for Newb[ury] Court. Clear and fair.

12. *Thursday.*   Mr. Stacey here from Cambridge.

15. *Sunday.*   A fine, cool morning.   Letters from Mr. Adams, who says that we are to have no more bloody noses in America with the British ; and that the affairs of peace go on still, though slowly yet surely.

20. *Friday.*   Mr. Fitch and ux., Vans, etc., dine at Capt. Lee's.

21. *Saturday.*   A fine, clear day, but continues dry. We hear of Flora's wants ; her husband sick ; also of embarkation at N. York, and of surmises of a design against Boston.   Suspicions are natural to little minds and to the guilty.

23. *Monday.*   I set out for Newbury Court.   Lodge at Ipswich.

26. *Thursday.*   John came from Cambridge unwell.

28. *Saturday.*   We went with Mr. Pullen to see Mrs. Atkins.

29. *Sunday.*   Set out, and at Ipswich heard Mr. Dana.   At sunset arrived at Salem.

October 1. *Tuesday.*   Rain.   Singing - school house goes on heavily ; some withdraw their subscriptions.

2. *Wednesday.*   Fair, clear, and cool.   Bro. Stephen and Mr. Marston here at tea.   John went to Cambridge with Mr. Bartlett.

3. *Thursday.*   Mr. and Mrs. Cranch at Dr. Putnam's.

4. *Friday.*   Mrs. Bourn and Mrs. Lee here at tea. Mr. Walker and Patty exchange goods.

5. *Saturday.* A fine, clear day. Colo. Johonnot stops at the door with horses and servants.

7. *Monday.* Cloudy ; at night some rain. Mr. Bartlett's school fills up apace.

8. *Tuesday.* Rain. Mr. Wetmore married to Miss Waldo.[1]

11. *Friday.* Fine morning. Mr. and Mrs. Fisher return thro. Cambridge.

13. *Sunday.* A. M. at Mr. Prince's meeting, and hear Mr. Eliot. P. M., I go to Cambridge ; lodge at Mr. Gannet's.

14. *Monday.* Return with John.

15. *Tuesday.* Fair and cool. It is said the singing-school will be raised this week, and the 74-gun ship at Portsmouth on Wednesday, next week.

16. *Wednesday.* John sets out for Cambridge, and at night returns with Mr. Dwight. A fair day.

18. *Friday.* Cloudy, and some rain A. M. We sup at Mr. Wetmore's.

19. *Saturday.* Cool and fair. W. Pickman's wife in danger.

20. *Sunday.* Cloudy morning. Mrs. Pickman dies.[2] I go to see Mr. Fisher.

21. *Monday.* At Dr. Holyoke's. Read Jenyns on Evidences of Christianity.

22. *Tuesday.* The singing-school raised.

23. *Wednesday.* Fair. The evening at Mr. Wetmore's, and a large company and an elegant supper.

25. *Friday.* Fair and very pleasant. Evening at Mr. Goodale's ; supper exceeding elegant. Two French gen-

---

[1] Miss Sally Waldo was the eldest daughter of Samuel Waldo of Falmouth.

[2] Mrs. Elizabeth, wife of William Pickman, Esq. She was a daughter of the Rev. Dudley Leavitt.

tlemen there, Mrs. Waldo, Mr. Wetmore and ux.   Band of music there after the company went off at 12 o'clock.

26. *Saturday.*   Clear morning.   Mr. Wetmore and Mrs. Waldo set out for Boston.   Mr. Bromfield and daughter come to town.

27. *Sunday.*   Cloudy, and some rain.   Mr. Wetmore returns with Miss Lucy Waldo from Boston.

28. *Monday.*   Cloudy.   Mr. Upham sets out for Deerfield.

29. *Tuesday.*   Mr. Dwight sets out for Cambridge with Eb. Putnam.

30. *Wednesday.*   Rain.   Eb. Putnam's chaise and my horse return at night.

November 1. *Friday.*   A fine, clear, and cool morning.   Capt. Derby asks about Henderson, whether he has sent the money Davis paid him or not.   I ask him whether he would sue Henderson or not.

5. *Tuesday.*   The Supreme Court sits.

6. *Wednesday.*   Having caught cold, I come home, and go out to Court no more, and suffer in my business.

9. *Saturday.*   The Court and Bar dine with me on fish.   We hear that Jno. Mascarene at length hath a place of business and habitation in the country, to the great relief of the family and friends.

16. *Saturday.*   Mr. Wetmore returns from Boston ; left Mrs. W. and Miss Lucy there. '

17. *Sunday.*   Cool.   What happiness can one of sensibility have in a post, a log, for a companion !   A tree hath life and seems sociable.

18. *Monday.*   I go to Marblehead, and Jeremiah Proctor and Knot Pedrick promise still soon to come and settle.   Soh !   The Spaniards must needs storm Gibraltar, and what have they got by it ?   As much as the Britons have got by invading America.   O brave

Elliot, thy fortune is made at the expense of how many millions, how many lives ! *Carnifices, quo, quo scelesti ruitis.*

19. *Tuesday*. Rain. This the last of arresting for Dec. Court.

20. *Wednesday*. Cloudy and rain. Mr. Wetmore sets out early for Boston.

21. *Thursday*. Snow-storm. How glad that we have wood to carry us through this storm (*lœtus in prœsens quod ultra oderit curare*). It clears up at evening, and I spend it at Mr. Goodale's with Mr. Lafitte.

22. *Friday*. Fair, clear, and cold. In the evening Mess. Noyes, L. Oliver, and Mrs. Higginson here. Mr. Goodale's Old White is sold.

23. *Saturday*. Raw, cold, and cloudy. I give Holt's note of 120/ for the horse to Mr. Goodale.

24. *Sunday*. At church A. M. Cartel from Halifax into Marblehead, informs of the capture of 5 vessels from this town. Mr. Fisher tarries till 10 in the evening, with us, too !

25. *Monday*. Cloudy morning ; rains all day. Thos. Winthrop, Esq., dines here. See the poet. lampoon on his courtship. At the Club this evening we are highly entertained with Savage's Life in Johnson's Lives of the Poets.

26. *Tuesday*. Cloudy and rains ; P. M. clear. Mr. Templeman at tea.

28. *Thursday*. Thanksgiving. We dine at Mr. Goodale's. Extreme cold.

30. *Saturday*. The wind south, and more moderate. S. Sewall of Marblehead here ; Mr. Grafton at tea here ; Hunt from Boston ; also Mr. and Mrs. Wetmore. John and Bartlett ride to Ipswich, and return at night.

December 2. Monday. Clear and pleasant. John, on Mr. Fisher's horse, rides out of town with Mr. Hunt.

3. *Tuesday.* Moderate. Bro. Mitchell comes with his son Stephen, a sweet youth. The Court meet.

7. *Saturday.* Cold. Mess. Pullen and Osgood dine with me.

8. *Sunday.* Mr. Fisher and Mitchell dine with me, and begin upon Murray's plan after dinner.

9. *Monday.* Cloudy and extreme cold. Mitchell at the Club at Mr. Goodale's, and shews Johnson to be wrong as to his criticism on Addison's simile of the Angel.

11. *Wednesday.* I go to Ipswich with Mr. Sewall on John's sorrel horse.

12. *Thursday.* Cloudy and raw cold. I return from Ipswich, and meet Dav. Burnam of Amherst here. What would I not have given to have missed him ! "*O ! te, Bollane, cerebri felicem, aiebam tacitus.*"

13. *Friday.* Clear and cold. Hay from Ipswich. I send the letters to Mr. Cockle by Stanley.

15. *Sunday.* Clear and cold. Mr. O. reads at church ; present Mr. Fisher.

17. *Tuesday.* A fine day. In the evening a *rout* of ladies, etc., at Mrs. Cabot's. Pope Joan.

19. *Thursday.* I carry John to Cambridge with his new horse ; find the weather very cold. Thence I go to Boston ; lodge at Mr. Higginson's ; dined at Newhall's with Commissary Daland.

20. *Friday.* A fine day indeed ! Mr. O. sets out this morning for Providence. I meet Father Kent: tho. 80, he is alert and gay as if but 18. I return by Chelsea ; dine at Newhall's with Capt. Fiske, and am highly entertained with his raptures as to the education of his children at Boston.

21. *Saturday.* A moderate day ; cloudy and a little rain. The family are all invited to dine at Mr. Wet-

more's on the 25th, but are all engaged. Mr. W. expects company from Boston.

22. *Sunday.* Mr. Greenwood and Templeman in my pew at church. We spend the evening at Mr. Wetmore's, with him and lady only.

23. *Monday.* Moderate fair weather. I return the library books save only a volume of plays, and I take out 3 volumes of Shakespeare.

24. *Tuesday.* Fair and pleasant. Mr. Bartlett goes to Danvers for Mrs. Orne ; brings her, and they go to Mrs. Barton's to see the young misses dance.

25. *Wednesday.* A very fine, clear day. The church very much crowded with well - dressed people. Mr. Fisher movingly addressed the people of his church and congregation in the close of his sermon, relating [to] their conduct, their morals and profession as Christians, exhorting them to sobriety and decency of behaviour on the solemn and joyful occasion. In the evening at Mr. Wetmore's, and sup there ; a large company.

26. *Thursday.* Cloudy and rain. Mr. Bartlett's horse is brought to my stable, and Foster tends him. All hands at Mr. Goodale's in the evening. It rains hard and is exceeding dark.

27. *Friday.* Clear and moderate. Mr. and Mrs. Temple return to Boston.

28. *Saturday.* Clear and cold. Brother Stephen Sewall and Major Orne come over, and go to see the new Assembly Room, and admire it (as politeness requires), but can say little in favour of the drawing-rooms, save that they serve as foils to the great room. In the evening Dr. Putnam and Mr. Noyes are here.

29. *Sunday.* Clear, windy, and very cold. Mr. T. is distracted, and runs about [the] streets, and declines going home.

31. *Tuesday.*   Clear and cold.   Mr. Bartlett, with his horse and carriage, brings home son John from college.

1783. *January* 1.   *Wednesday.*   Clear and very cold. A concert in the evening in the new Assembly Room ; a dance for the young gentry at Mrs. Pickman's.   Da. Sears in town, and called on me.

2. *Thursday.*   A fine, pleasant morning.   Musick at the Assembly Room : 2 fiddles, F. horn, and drum. These and the assembly engross the conversation and attention of the young and gay ; the elders shake their heads with, What are we coming to ?   D. Sears calls again ; hopes for 1/2 in Feb'y, as bills may now be had cheap.   A private dance preparatory to the assembly.

7. *Tuesday.*   Cloudy and cold.   Mr. and Mrs. Wetmore, Winthrop, Livingston and co. return to Boston. Fine sledding ; the street is so fill'd with sleds, etc., of wood that there was scarce any passing.   A dance at Bro. Goodale's in the evening.

8. *Wednesday.*   A fine, clear morning, but very cold. Grafton, Jno. and co. go to dance at Endicot's ; return at 12.

9. *Thursday.*   Cloudy and very cold.   A dance at Grafton's.

11. *Saturday.*   Snows all day ; clears up at night, and all go to shovelling paths in order for meeting tomorrow.

12. *Sunday.*   The snow is deep and much drifted in the streets.   Two sleighs come in from Lynn with the help of footmen shovelling, etc., [and] arrive here about 2 P. M.   Mr. Noyes, Bartlett, S. Orne, Oliver and ux., here in the evening.

13. *Monday.*   Ste. Sewall here.   Wind So. all day ; considerable thaw.   I go to Mr. Fisher's at 12.   A dance at H. Derby's ; Bartlett and Jno. both lame, but must

go. The glass chandelier for the Assembly Room comes from Boston.

14. *Tuesday.* A fine morning; pleasant and warm. A dance at Mrs. Pickman's.

15. *Wednesday.* A fine morning ; clear and cold. Music and dancing engross the whole conversation of the town.

16. *Thursday.* Very cold. There are about 90 persons at the assembly : 41 ladies and 28 gentlemen draw for dancing ; the rest repair to [the] gaming-table, and Dr. S.'s partner has no luck, no trumps, yet the Dr. loseth, and he gains.

17. *Friday.* Concert, — 220 tickets. P. Barnard and Prince there till the dancing begins.

18. *Saturday.* Cloudy ; wind So. The sledding grows bad.

19. *Sunday.* Clear. At Mr. Fisher's with Mr. Wetmore and co., Oliver, etc. I go to church all day ; *mirum !*

20. *Monday.* Clear and warm. Dance at S. Blyths'. Maid Hannah grows better. Dr. Manning comes, and is to call again next week and settle.

21. *Tuesday.* The Salisbury parties come to the reference.

22. *Wednesday.* Cold. Meeting of referees at Webb's. I catch cold in his great room. S. Sewall, Esqr., lodged at my house. A dance at the Tradesmen's Hall.

23. *Thursday.* Clear, cool; fine sledding. I write to N. Sparhawk, and send my former letter of the 3d inst. F. Mason's dance at B. store. Sarah goes off in a sleigh with 10 others. On trial, my horse eats swill and does all things that Dr. Barnard's can, except the picking of bones, which his does as well as any dog.

24. *Friday.* Cloudy, cold morning. Most excellent

sledding, but, like other good things, of very short duration. A concert at the assembly house for the poor. Patty and O. go and dance till 12 o'clock.

25. *Saturday.* A fine, pleasant morning ; wind S. W. Jealousies, slanders, envying, among several of the assembly folk. Parties are forming, and a little more tattling and imprudence throw the whole into confusion. Majr. Swasey and D. Spofford sang there ; Mr. Greenwood and Mrs. White dance after the concert. About . . . tickets were purchased at 6/9, chiefly for the benefit of the poor.

28. *Tuesday.* At evening, snow. An exhibition at Bartlett's school ; his scholars rehearsed the Distracted Mother by way of trial for Friday evening. A dance at H. White's.

29. *Wednesday.* Snows. An assembly at night ; about 100 persons of both sexes; but two or three strangers.

30. *Thursday.* Dr. Hill from Cambridge with a letter from Miss Wendell to Patty Pynchon.

31. *Friday.* A clear day, and very cold ; fine sledding again. In the evening several exhibitions at Mr. Bartlett's school ; Distracted Mother was the principal. Musick, 2 fiddles and a drum ; a crowded audience. The performances taken together gave much entertainment to 60 or 70 persons ; it is since said to an 100.

February 1. *Saturday.* Clear and cold ; extraordinary sledding.

2. *Sunday.* Very cold yet. People's faces are nearly frozen in coming from church. Mr. Fisher had both sermons upon Agur's prayer, which appeared to him to shew a very selfish disposition.

3. *Monday.* Clear and exceeding cold still ; cover'd roots and all freeze in the cellar last night. Nothing

done to-day by the privateersmen, sailors, etc., but sleighing and frolicking. Mrs. Wetmore spends [the] evening here; Mr. W. gone to Boston.

4. *Tuesday.* Cloudy, and more moderate than it was. The sledding is good yet. All preparing for frolicking; Grafton and co. and Jno. go P. M. to Endicot's for dancing. No meat in the market to-day.

5. *Wednesday.* Rain; N. E. wind. Mr. Warren and Pickman here at tea.

6. *Thursday.* Cloudy; some rain and a little snow. Mr. Warren breakfasts here; they all dine at G. Williams'; *mirum!* And more so that he treats them civilly. Templeman and Grafton go to Newburyport, and leave Mrs. Lawless in the dumps.

7. *Friday.* A fine, clear morning, and moderate. Mr. O. and family with Mrs. Lawless. Bartlett, etc., dine here on alamode beef.

8. *Saturday.* Clear and moderate. Dr. Holyoke and Mr. Noyes here [in] the evening; Noyes at tea.

9. *Sunday.* Cloudy and moderate. Five children baptized at church. It snows; wind N. E. Mr. Goodale, Mr. O. and family, spend the evening with us.

11. *Tuesday.* Good sledding. Mr. Dunbar and a large company here part of the evening. Capt. Carnes here A. M., having lately returned from N. York, where he was treated with the greatest hospitality and kindness at Mr. Walter's house, who obtained his liberty on promise of returning a prisoner.

12. *Wednesday.* Cloudy and thaws. Assembly and dancing for the night coming engross all the conversation. [Mrs. Wetmore] here at tea, and all but Mr. Orne and I go to the assembly, and return seasonably, some at 11, others by 12 o'clock. Several offences were given by the young misses to the elderly gentlemen. There were

about 80 ladies, and between 40 and 50 gentlemen, several from Boston.

13. *Thursday.*   A fine, moderate morning ; it froze a little.   We spend the evening at Mr. Wetmore's, and sup there with Mr. G. and family.

14. *Friday.*   Cloudy and moderate.   The sledding is nearly gone, but there was a flight of snow last night, and its freezing may revive it.   P. is told by Mr. O. to her face that she is not handsome, which was repeated in presence of his brother S. ; but she bore it with patience and an excellent temper.   Mr. Wetmore returns to-day from Boston.   We are at Dr. Holyoke's in the evening.

17. *Monday.*   Cloudy, and thaw continues still.   Mr. Templeman here.   Jno. sets out for Cambridge on horseback, with letter of excuse to President and tutors, that he was detained by me since the last vacation.   This morning I sent to the library 3 vols. [of] Shakespeare and one of plays.   H. Derby lost his cause.

20. *Thursday.*   A fine, pleasant, spring - like day. Concert and dance at Assembly Room.   Thos. Dwight comes.

21. *Friday.*   A very fine day, and it brings us very fine news, — the King's speech, intimating to the Parliament that the negociations for peace will probably be soon completed (one article only remaining for settlement), and he recommends to his subjects the settling treaties of commerce with the Americans.   Jno. sets out with Eben. Putnam for Cambridge, and the boy returns at night.

22. *Saturday.*   Mr. Dwight sets out for Boston.   Mr. Bartlett complains of consumptive disorders.

23. *Sunday.*   Mr. Bentley at church.   Mr. Bartlett's complaints increase.

24. *Monday.*   Clear, fine morning.   Sent word to Mr. Gannet by B. Pickman.

25. *Tuesday.* A fine, clear morning ; severe flash of lightning with thunder last evening. Mr. Bartlett can't well bear motion of horse or carriage.

26. *Wednesday.* Clear and cold. Mr. and Mrs. Orne came from Danvers, and Sally Higginson from Boston last evening ; all hands for Assembly !

27. *Thursday.* A fine, clear day. Bartlett grows anxious as his illness increases.

March 2. *Sunday.* Very cool, but fair. Parson Fisher preacheth up industry, and tells us St. Paul was a tent maker, a good workman, at least an industrious man, and made tents, when he had leisure, to support himself. Bartlett returns from Cambridge.

3. *Monday.* Fine, cool, clear morning. Bartlett and Mrs. Pynchon go to see Mrs. Dodge at Beverly ; return at night.

4. *Tuesday.* Clear and raw ; cold snow air. Mr. Rogers here. Templeman and P. Fisher are affronted with me. What shall I do? *A.* Hold your tongue.

5. *Wednesday.* Clear and cool. I rose at 5 this morning and made the fires for the servant, who has often made them for me ; I felt gratitude, and she showed it. Mr. Bartlett set out for Cambridge and returned in the evening.

6. *Thursday.* A fine, warm day. A horse-race P. M. at Flint's. Bartlett set out early in the morning for the country.

7. *Friday.* A fine, clear day, and moderate. Mr. Wetmore returns with Mrs. W. and Lucy.

8. *Saturday.* Cloudy, but moderate air. Templeman and Lawless go a-visiting thro' the gardens and over the fences, avoiding the street. Rains P. M. and at night.

9. *Sunday.* Clear. I write to Mr. Hichburn by Diamond as to the Glover affair. With Mr. Williams and

others of the church, spend the evening at Mr. Fisher's, but he says nothing of Templeman's affair, and I am to presume that upon inquiry and reflection matters appear to him in a very different light than before. Capt. Warren there from N. York, where he had been prisoner; he speaks in the highest terms of the humanity of Mr. Walter, [and] of Sir Guy Carleton, [and] of his present of 20 guineas to the prisoners toward their expenses on the road.[1]

10. *Monday.* The wind excessive high last night and this morning, N. W.; we find the pumps frozen very hard this morning.

12. *Wednesday.* Assembly; a great number of gentlemen and ladies; [several] of the latter drew lots for dances; disorders and jealousies increase; Otis, Amory, Pickman, and other collegians at the Assembly; common sense and decency might prevent all the jealousies and disorders; the fiddler told them that he could distinguish an assembly from a frolick.

13. *Thursday.* A very fine day; the air chilly. Otis,[2]

---

[1] The following letter is from Judge Lynde to his son-in-law Dr. Walter, who left the country in 1776: —

SALEM, *Monday, May* 31st, 1779.

REVD. AND DEAR SIR, —

I have the great pleasure of two of yours of the 5th instant; received the first on Saturday, the other about an hour ago by Capt. Hale. . . .

Capt. Hale is full of your praise, and tells us he is greatly obliged to your kind interpositions on his behalf, so is Capt. Ives also.

Suffer me on account of the inhuman treatment our prisoners meet with on board your prison ships to beg that you would use your utmost endeavors that some fresh air be allowed them.

It is a most flagrant instance of cruelty, as well as a reproach to the English nation, that so many are suffered to die in so miserable a state, and will be used as an excuse for all the hard things you suffer.

Your friend Colo. Stoddard died of a feavor some time ago, and his eldest and youngest son lately. God has multiplied his bereavements to that family. May we who are yet spared duly lay it to heart.

[2] Harrison Gray Otis.

Pickman, Amory, and N. Ropes dine with Jno. ; Jno. on Eb'r. Putman's horse sets out with them for Cambridge. Snows at night.

16. *Sunday.* A fine day. I am so fatigued with the business of Saturday last that I cannot go out, and thro' application of divers, pretending necessity and mercy, I have neither rest nor enjoyment at home. The Glover gentlemen I parted with and with their cause ; they grew tedious and indecent, so I offered them their fee, because I would not forward their suit against my judgment, and they think themselves ill-used, yet would not take back the fee ; *tantum religio !*

19. *Wednesday.* Cloudy, and some rain ; [wind] N. W. Mr. Templeman returns.

20. *Thursday.* A fine, clear morning ; wind N. W. More circumstantial and provisional articles of peace published, but mark the letter from Parish intimating that all is with design to lull America, whilst Britain is by sea vigourously carrying on the war, especially by her cruisers, on the trade of the powers at variance ! This day I write to J. M. Sewall and N. Sparhawk, Esqrs.

21. *Friday.* Clear, windy, and cold. Financier Morris proposes to resign, all seem displeased with him ; he tells them that he can't make bricks without straw : they answer that he can as well as any man ; and for years past it surely hath been done in every American State.

23. *Sunday.* Snow-storm ; wind N. E. By Grafton from Boston we hear that 't is thought among the merchants that peace is yet [at] a considerable distance, and that there will be another campaign between France and England, but that New York will be soon evacuated, and no more hostilities in the American field.

24. *Monday.* Cloudy morning. Mr. Bartlett returns from Cambridge ; all seems to go well as to Jno. there.

25. *Tuesday.* A very fine, pleasant morning. I write to Gen'l Warren [1] as to Wingate's matter, and yesterday sent a line of the 20th to Mr. Sears as to Amsterdam affairs. Miss Sewall here, Miss Gallison, and Mrs. Dove and family.

26. *Wednesday.* An exceedingly fine and pleasant day. At eve. I go to Marblehead on Besom's affair with Hawkes. Many strangers go to the Assembly to-night. Stevens goes to Boston.

27. *Thursday.* Mrs. Grafton dangerously ill ; her symptoms hectical. The robins appear on the trees.

28. *Friday.* A fine, spring-like day. Dr. Holyoke and ux. and daughter here in the evening ; Mrs. Pynchon in low spirits and keeps to chamber. Jno. went to Cambridge in the morning and returned at tea, and [was] $3\frac{1}{4}$ hours in coming ; but the poor horse thanks him not for all the fine stories of his exploits.

29. *Saturday.* A cloudy but spring-like morning. Veal in the market ! but very scarce.

31. *Monday.* Cloudy. I ask Capt. Derby whether he would have Henderson wrote to for Davis' money ; yes, says he ; accordingly I write.

April 1. *Tuesday.* I set out for Ipswich Court.

2, 3, 4. Clear and cool.

5. *Saturday*, A. M. The Court adjourns to 4, Tuesday. As we sit down to dine, rejoicing that the Court had adjourned, comes in hand-bill from Salem per Capt. Derby, in 22 days from France, with a confirmation of the news of peace ; *O quanti complexus et gaudia quanta fucre !* Gen'l F.[2] almost shook our arms off with " I give

---

[1] General James Warren was of Plymouth. He was made Paymaster-General in 1775, and afterward Major-General of the militia. He succeeded General Joseph Warren as President of the Provincial Congress. He married Mercy, a sister of James Otis.

[2] General Michael Farley seems to have been a prominent citizen of

you joy! joy! gentlemen, all," etc. *Nunc est bibendum, nunc pede libero pulsanda tellus!* In our return for Salem we all call at Justice Porter's, who treats us with a glass of egg pop upon his taking the oaths of Justice, and we dub him Squire Porter, and almost shake his arms off, in imitation of Gen'l F.

6. *Sunday.* A fine, clear, and cool day. More news. I go to church all day.

8. *Tuesday.* Cool and clear. Mr. Osgood and I go to see Mr. Orne, and return at evening.

9. *Wednesday.* Very fine morning. N. Sparhawk comes to town with his son and lodges here. Gen'l Howe, Mr. Jackson, and a number of strangers at the Assembly this evening.

10. *Thursday.* Very fine morning. Mr. Oliver's [1] waggons come from Providence ; he packs up his goods ; it rains ; his fears and our concern are for Mrs. O. who is ill ; the family come and lodge at my house. Bro. Stephen dines here.

13. *Sunday.* Clear and cold. After meeting, P. M.,

Ipswich, and a very useful one. He held many offices of trust during the Revolution. He was a Representative to the General Court and High Sheriff, and was afterward appointed a Major-General of a brigade.

[1] Thomas Fitch Oliver, so often mentioned in this diary, was a son of Hon. Andrew Oliver, one of the Justices of the Essex Court of Common Pleas. He was graduated at Harvard College in 1775, and commenced the study of law with Mr. Pynchon, but subsequently abandoned it and prepared himself for orders in the Episcopal Church. While awaiting ordination he received a letter from the authorities of King's Chapel, asking him to be their minister. This position he did not accept, and he afterward, in April, 1783, went to Providence and officiated as lay reader at St. John's, until the arrival of Bishop Seabury, by whom he was ordained in September, 1785. In 1786 he went to Marblehead as rector of St. Michael's, remaining there until 1792. He had again no permanent settlement until 1796 at St. Thomas's, Garrison Forest, near Baltimore, where he died in 1797, at 39 years of age. He married a daughter of William Pynchon in 1778.

a little after 3 o'clock, Mr. and Mrs. Oliver and 2 children and the maid, with Mrs. Pynchon, set out in Providence stage, and I following and overtaking them near Newhal's tavern in Lynn, and we stop at Wait's at Malden and have tea. They bear the ride well, considering they go at the rate of 6½ miles an hour ; at sunset they set out for Cambridge, and I lodge at Wait's and confer with the warden on the Sabbath Act till 11 at night.[1]

14. *Monday.* An exceedingly fine day, and, if the coach be not driven too hard, all hands may arrive at Providence to-night.

15. *Tuesday.* The fine weather continues. K. George's proclamation comes from New York — Peace !

16. *Wednesday.* A fine, clear day. Mrs. Orne walks from D[anvers] to Salem to see me in my state.

17. *Thursday.* A fine, clear morning, and moderate. Classmate Porter called to see me and breakfasted with me ; so much altered that I could not recollect a single feature of his former looks.

18. *Friday.* At church, one service only. Mr. Sparhawk in town. Warm and pleasant.

19. *Saturday.* Cloudy and cool. At night I find that I must look out for an house soon.

20. *Sunday.* At church all day. All hands are writing to our friends at Providence. I write to Mr. Robie at Halifax ; I write also to Mrs. Cotnam.

21. *Monday.* [In the] morning, [the] chambers being full of smoke, I get up, and find the office floor burnt through into the cellar, a hole 4 inches in diameter.

22. *Tuesday.* I go with Mr. Wetmore to Ipswich Court.

---

[1] The Sabbath Act passed in October, 1782, was more comprehensive than any that was passed before, allowing the forcible detention of any person suspected of unnecessary travelling on the Lord's Day.

26. *Saturday.* A. M., cloudy but moderate. I return with Mr. Osgood. Rejoicing at Beverly by firing of cannon.

27. *Sunday.* Cool day. New wardens at church, Williams and Bar. I dine at Mr. Goodale's.

28. *Monday.* Mr. Bartlett's scholars, etc., at the Assembly Room, and repeat the plays.

29. *Tuesday.* Rejoicing at Ipswich. Mr. Bartlett's scholars and others exhibit at the Assembly Room ; a great audience.

30. *Wednesday.* Cloudy. Cannon early this morning roar aloud from the wharves of Salem, and probably by night the inhabitants' windows and other property may be broken, plundered, destroyed.

May 4. *Sunday.* A fine, cool, and clear morning. I dine at Mr. Goodale's with Mrs. Higginson ; in the evening at Mr. Fisher's.

5. *Monday.* Fine day ; wind N. E., and very dry yet. I carry home Mrs. Orne, my horse, and Dr. Putnam's chaise.

8. *Thursday.* Fair and cold ; some rain at night. Cato sets out the Pope beans.

9. *Friday.* Cloudy and drizzling weather. Receive a packet from S. Curwen, Esq., London, of English newspapers, via Halifax.

10. *Saturday.* A fine, moderate rain, greatly wanted, comes in good time. I receive a letter from Mr. Oliver of Providence. Deacon Gatchell was yesterday morning brought to jail for the sins of Marblehead, in withholding the schoolmaster's due.

12. *Monday.* Send letters to Providence by W. Vans. Town meeting for Representatives. Adjournment of Church meeting is to 9th June, 10 o'clock, A. M.

13. *Tuesday.* A fine, clear day. Mrs. Goodale and

I go to Mrs. Orne's, Danvers. Bartlett takes leave of his school and leaves them in tears.

15. *Thursday.* Fast day. At night Dr. Whitaker preacheth his old discourse on " *Curse ye Meroz*," with higher colourings than usual.

16. *Friday.* A fine day. S. Osgood returns from Congress, embarrassed there with debt and dissension.

17. *Saturday.* A fine, warm morning. Veal is sold at various prices, from 3d to 6d. Mr. Turner comes about his school.

19. *Monday.* A fine, cool day. Patty and Mrs. Cabot go to Boston ; Jno. escorts them to Medford. Stevens tells me that he has let Deacon Gatchell go home, and has taken the risque on himself.

20. *Tuesday.* Clear, and very cool ; a fire scarce keeps one warm. Stevens says he has received 100 dollars towards exonerating Hawkes of Marblehead, and asks me whether he shall pay my costs out of it ; I decline, and tell him he must settle with Hawkes as well as he can.

22. *Thursday.* I dine at Dr. Putnam's with Mr. Orne. Some rain at night.

23. *Friday.* Cloudy, and little rain only ; thunder and lightning at eve. I go to Flint's P. M. Tea at Mr. Cabot's ; there meet Mrs. Davis and daughter and Mrs. Holyoke. Rains at night.

24. *Saturday.* Cloudy. I send my letter for Bro. Pynchon to Zech. Foot, who is to sail to-morrow for Cape Pursue.[1] Mr. Turner came last evening to town with Miss Greenleafe.

25. *Sunday.* A fine, clear day. No church ; I go to hear Mr. Eliot P. M. Set out for Boston and arrive there at 3 o'clock ; lodge at Mrs. Cotton's.

---

[1] Cape *Fourchu,* or *Fourché,* off Yarmouth, is probably the cape here referred to.

26. *Monday.* A fine day. I go to the Treasurer Ivers, at 7 A. M., to get notes for Clark's money, and return at evening and meet the Clubb at Mr. Blaney's, and hear Beadle's papers read.

27. *Tuesday.* A fine, clear day ; wind N. E., and cool. I send by Mr. Dane my letter to Judge Sewall, one to Sheriff Moulton, and one to Sheriff Porter of Hadley, with execution, Foster *v.* Churchill. At evening Mr. Cunningham came and lodged here. I spend the evening at H. Derby's with wedding company.

28. *Wednesday.* A fine, cool morning. It is Election Day, but every person and every thing one meets or sees hath the appearance rather of gloom than cheerfulness. Mr. Cunningham observes it, [and] sets off for Boston. I sup at Mr. Wetmore's with Mr. Bowdoin and company.

29. *Thursday.* A fine, clear, and warm day. I go with Mrs. Orne to see Mr. and Mrs. Bowdoin. Mr. Bartlett sets out for Boston with Mrs. Cabot, and to bring back Mrs. Pynchon. Mr. Lee returns from Providence, and leaves Mrs. Pynchon at Cambridge, being afraid of passing the ferry to Boston. I spend the evening at Mr. Wetmore's.

30. *Friday.* A warm day. Mr. and Mrs. Bowdoin set out for Boston P. M. Mr. Fisher returns, and at eve Mr. Bartlett, with Mrs. Pynchon, from Cambridge.

June 1. *Sunday.* A cold, N. E. wind, and my new suit does not keep me warm.

2. *Monday.* A fine day. Vessel at Boston from London [with] letters from Mr. Curwen to Mrs. Curwen Ward ; I receive one from Capt. Foster ; Mr. Cabot hath one from his son.

3. *Tuesday.* A fine, clear morning. Mr. Ropes takes the shop and is moving out stove, etc., and I desire him to desist.

4. *Wednesday morning.* He moves in his goods before I get up. Mr. Bartlett was taken ill of the measles.

5. *Thursday.* A fine, cool day. Mr. Bartlett grows worse ; his fever is very high ; has purple spots on his arm.

7. *Saturday.* Cloudy, and fine rain. I send a letter by Mr. Mange and desire an answer, on his return, from Tho. Ruggles Pynchon or Sarah Pynchon, N. York or Guilford. I dine at Mr. Orne's.

8. *Sunday.* A fine, cool day. Capt. West sails for Virginia and Europe ; by him I write to Capt. Foster and to Mr. Curwen. Mr. Bartlett's fever abates, the purple spots are gone off. See Billy Cabot's letter to Mr. Goodale, in which he shows a benevolent and virtuous disposition, rarely found in one so young.

10. *Tuesday.* Mr. and Mrs. Mellen, Mr. Mackey and Mrs. Mackey dine here.

11. *Wednesday.* A fine, warm day. Jo. Jane brings us account that Mr. O. and Sally are on the road hither, and may reach Salem to-night. I have a letter from Colo. Worthington respecting Colo. Browne and Blaney's deeds of lands at Wilbraham. Wheatly tells at Boston that Gov. Hutchinson[1] killed himself in England, having cut his throat ; this account S. Page, the Representative, brings home from Gen. Court, and either is silly enough to believe it (as he says he does), or roguish enough to pretend so, in order to keep up his popularity ; accordingly he is become popular in proportion to this *auto de fe*, or pretence, and having given it out at the barber's shop, present, T. Cabot, Esqr. (whose son is in England for his health), says (A. Richardson there present also), "and *so will all the absentees cut their throats ;*" lo, an emblem

---

[1] Governor Hutchinson died suddenly, June 3, 1780. See *Hutchinson's Diary*, ii. 353.

of patriotic spirits ! an emblem of the times ! Wheatly ! Richardson ! Page ! are popular men, and will become honourable men, so far as . . . and . . . can make them so in such times !

12. *Thursday.* A fine shower of rain this morning [at] 3 o'clock ; the air is close and muggy. Mr. Bartlett's fever returns.

13. *Friday.* Mr. Bartlett slept well, and is refreshed and appears somewhat better, perhaps the effects of anodynes. It rains finely this morning; rains moderately. Mr. Bartlett grows better. Mrs. Richards calls on us to take leave ; she is bound hence with Alcock and family for Philadelphia, he going to Baltimore. I receive letter and catalogue of books from Mr. Curwen, London.

14. *Saturday.* Rain. Mr. Bartlett's brother and sister come and find him better.

15. *Sunday.* Rains P. M. (finely indeed). Mr. Noyes and Dr. A. Putnam here at tea.

16. *Monday.* A fine, cool day. I call with Mr. Pullen to see Mr. Bartlett, and find him weak and feverish. Mr. Wetmore returns from Boston.

17. *Tuesday.* I set out for Ipswich, and am overtaken at the ferry by Mr. Sewall [of] Marblehead.

19. *Thursday.* I return from Ipswich Court, to return again on Saturday morning.

20. *Friday.* Very warm ; P. M., severe thunder and lightning ; W. Luscomb's house is struck.

21. *Saturday.* Cloudy and something wet. At night I return from Court.

27. *Friday.* Mr. Sprague and Lincoln here. Perkins hangs himself at Capt. Mackey's, and is cut down and saved.

29. *Sunday.* Warm. Mr. Fisher preacheth to-day

at Marblehead. Mr. Bentley at Mr. Prince's A. M. I go to Mr. Barnard's P. M. Jno. Williams comes with Mrs. Williams to Salem ; he is Representative from Deerfield.

30. *Monday.* A warm sun, but cool east wind. Jno. Williams dines here with me.

July 1. *Tuesday.* Warm sun, but cool east wind. Jno. Williams dines with me. The soldiers disturb Congress and they decamp.

2. *Wednesday.* J. Williams goes to Boston.

3. *Thursday.* Great expectations of fire-works at Boston ; *partur. montcs.* Mr. Bartlett's brother comes about his affairs.

4. *Friday.* Mr. Bartlett's brother went to Boston ; son John and Mansfield also, and returned P. M.

5. *Saturday.* Cloudy and cool. Sent up my horse to Mr. Orne's by his boy.

12. *Saturday.* Patty dines here with the Court.

13. *Sunday.* Gov'r. Bowen of Providence in Salem, also Mr. Clarke.

15. *Tuesday.* A very fine, cool day. P. M., I set out with Mr. G. Abbot in his carriage for Boston, and thence, on Wednesday morning, I go through Roxbury to Commencement. I do not recollect so fine a day, nor the meeting-house to be filled with a company better dressed ; I see there my classmate Dr. Cooper.[1]

16. *Wednesday.* A very fine day. I breakfast at Boston. I go up to Cambridge in the Governor's troop, and, in getting out of the chaise by Dr. Kneeland, narrowly escape being run down by the horsemen, and had my foot much bruised, and so lost much of the comfort of Commencement. Colo. Worthington is at Boston.

17. *Thursday.* Morning very cool. Get up at half after four in the morning and reach Salem at 11 A. M.

[1] Rev. Samuel Cooper.

18. *Friday.* A fine, clear day. Jno. returns from Cambridge.

20. *Sunday.* A very fine day. I am still confined by my lame foot ; an old man go a-frolicking !

22. *Tuesday.* A warm morning ; thunder, and very warm P. M. Mrs. Hendy was buried ; is carried into church, and a sermon preached.

23. *Wednesday.* Cool and cloudy ; wind N. Mr. Osgood from Congress spends the evening here.

25. *Friday.* Hot in the morning ; P. M., thunder, lightning, and rain, and the air grows cool. Dr. Holyoke and Noyes here in the evening, also Patty.

26. *Saturday.* A cloudy and cool morning. Have a peacock from Mr. Browne of Virginia.

27. *Sunday.* Cool and pleasant day. Our peacock goes off before we are up.

28. *Monday.* A very fine day. The peacock is brought home.

30. *Wednesday.* I set out for Providence ; at Roxbury am overtaken in a shower ; dine at Dr. Williams', and lodge there.

31. *Thursday.* At 9 in the evening I arrive at the glebe of Mr. Oliver.

August 1. *Friday.* Dine at Mr. Oliver's, and P. M. go to Providence, and take tea at Mr. Hitchcock's.

2. *Saturday.* Dine with Mr. Hitchcock at Mr. Oliver's, and in the afternoon go to town and see the college and the President. Drink tea at Mr. Olney's ; call at Mr. Clark's.

3. *Sunday.* Go to church. Dine very genteelly at Mr. Bourn's ; tea at Mr. Hitchcock's ; call at Mr. Mumford's.

4. *Monday.* A fine morning. Mr. Oliver and I go to Providence and ride round to the spring, [from] which

we have a very fine prospect of the college and whole town.

5. *Tuesday*.   A fine, cloudy morning.   At half after 5 in the morning I set out for Salem ; meet Jos. Lee going into Providence on business of creeds ; lodge at Ames', Dedham ; met at Attleboro with the two Holmans going to R. Island for their brother Hastie, who is ill there, and lately returned from N. York with his young child.   Ah, Jammy, is the D. of Argyl yet alive !   Holman took with him a recommendation from the Selectmen of Salem, and from others, certifying Mr. Hastie's conduct as to American matters.   Query, whether it was of avail to save Jammy ?

6. *Wednesday*.   A fine, cool morning ; cloudy till 9. I set out for Ames' at 7 ; get to ferry at twelve, and to Salem at 6 o'clock, and find letters from refugees, and brother Mitchell ill at my house.

7. *Thursday*.   A fine, pleasant morning.   Mrs. Carpenter tells me that the money and gold ring which I left with her for Mr. Carpenter,[1] as the legacy given him, were all right and well, and that he would give me a receipt for them.

8. *Friday*. A fine day. Foster Hutchinson comes to Boston harbour, and at first is not allowed to come into town. Jno. Williams writes that at town meeting at Deerfield Mr. Williams is chosen Representative again by the vote of all but one at the meeting ; thus we act and thus we are.   The dissenter was his good friend, who acted prudentially and not inimically.

9. *Saturday*.   Rain, thunder, and lightning last night, and cloudy and cold this morning. Jno. Williams

---

[1] Benjamin Carpenter married Nabby, a daughter of Benjamin Gerrish and granddaughter of the first John Cabot. She died in Cambridge November 3, 1802, without issue.

comes ; Deerfield resents his expulsion and is for returning the tax bill as the Representative is returned, but Williams dissuades them.

10. *Sunday.*   At church P. M.   Mr. G. Jeffry at church, and sups with us, Mr. and Mrs. Wetmore, and Dr. Holyoke ; he tells us that the news of Foster Hutchinson being at Boston from Halifax is not true.   Yesterday S. Gerrish [1] calls as to Cabot's affairs.

11. *Monday.*   A cloudy but pleasant day.   Jno. Williams and ux. return to Deerfield.   It rains at night. Deerfield instructs the Representative, and show in them some resentment of the treatment from some of the members of the House on the hearing of the Representative.

15. *Friday.*   Cloudy morning.   Mr. Lowell comes to town.

16. *Saturday.*   A fine day.   Jno. goes to Marblehead, and thence with Bro. Stephen, Mitchell and co. to Flax Pond.

17. *Sunday.*   A fine morning.   I go with Mrs. P. up to Mr. Orne's to see them in their illness.   [The] evening spent at Mr. Cabot's with Mr. Lowell.

18. *Monday.*   Cloudy morning.   Dr. Putnam goes up to Danvers with my horse, and [I] send the lemons and oranges, etc., by him.

19. *Tuesday.*   Mr. and Mrs. Lowell go out of town ; a wild horse.

20. *Wednesday.*   Warm.   I go to Danvers with Mrs. Goodale A. M.

23. *Saturday.*   Hot.   Dine with A. Oliver at Mr. Goodale's ; he could eat nothing for the heat.

24. *Sunday.*   So very hot, few go to church.   P. M., I tarry at home thro' the heat.

---

[1] Samuel, son of Benjamin Gerrish and Margaret, daughter of the first John Cabot.

26. *Tuesday.* Cold N. E. wind, and cloudy. Capt. Webb is not gone yet to Boston with Mr. Deblois' goods.

27. *Wednesday.* Received a line from Stephen Deblois. Bro. Mitchell returns in good spirits to Portsmouth by way of Gloucester. Sent Dr. Kast's acct. by Jno. Sparhawk, Esq., to commissioners at Portsmouth.

30. *Saturday.* [In] morning I go to Mr. Turner's D. School.

31. *Sunday.* Fine morning ; P. M., cloudy, and rain after church. Evening at T. Cabot's, and hear of a proposal of [a] college, bishop, etc., for Halifax.

September 1. *Monday.* A cool day. The Club at my house, and we sit by a brisk fire all the evening ; grand account of harbour of Port Roseway, and of the intents of England to encourage [the] settlement of this and other parts of No. Scotia ; of [the] college, etc., to be built there and to be endowed.[1] Jno. goes to Nahant.

2. *Tuesday.* Cloudy, and some rain. N. Sparhawk, Esq.,[2] gone to Boston, and is to call next Thursday and dine with me if he can.

4. *Thursday.* Colo. Gallison here. Mr. Sparhawk passeth on to Portsmouth.

5. *Friday.* Mr. Turner brings his two sons to the dancing-school.

8. *Monday.* Mr. Tucker in town, and by him I send to Mr. Parsons, Newbury, Mr. Wingate's papers.

[1] The plan here referred to, and first suggested by the loyalist clergy of New York to Sir Guy Carleton, resulted in the establishment of the present King's College, at Windsor, the leading university in Nova Scotia.

[2] Nathaniel Sparhawk was the son of Colonel Nathaniel Sparhawk, who married Elizabeth, the daughter of the second Sir William Pepperrell. He was born in August, 1744, was graduated at Harvard College in 1765. He married first his cousin Katy, daughter of Rev. John Sparhawk, and secondly Elizabeth Bartlett of Haverhill, and thirdly a Miss Parker. He died in 1814.

9. *Tuesday.* Rain. Billy Newhall brings home my horse from Mr. Orne, and I send him to pasture at Mr. Phelps's by Zack. Bray. Mrs. Pynchon taken ill.

13. *Saturday.* A fine day. Mr. Wetmore goes to Boston and returns with Mrs. Waldo at night. Mrs. Wetmore spends part of the afternoon with Mrs. Pynchon, who grows a little better. Dr. Loring and I dine at Mr. Goodale's ; he returns with Mr. Turner.

14. *Sunday.* Stevens returned from Andover last evening very ill ; sets out again Monday for Andover, and returns on Tuesday.

15. *Monday.* Mrs. Wetmore taken ill.

17. *Wednesday.* A very fine day. Billy Wetmore taken ill. Town meeting as to petition for removing the Courts.

18. *Thursday.* Wm. Webb calls on Stevens for copies and declares war against me, and threatens to appear at Newbury Court.

23. *Tuesday.* A very fine day. Judge Lee,[1] Capt. Newhall, and Mrs. Newhall come to town.

24. *Wednesday.* Ordination Day. Mr. Bentley and Mr. Parker in town ; Dwight, Amory, Williams, [and] Mr. James. Mr. Parker marks Fr.'s story about Mr. S. as to the visit and misunderstanding.

25. *Thursday.* Mr. Fr. tells Mr. Parker that he designedly went from home to see whether Mr. S. would admit him to be pot or kettle, as he said he was.

27. *Saturday.* Rain. Jona. Mansfield is seen at neighbour Glover's shop, and tells Mr. Goodale that he has been at my office, and that I will not settle with him, and will force him into Court.

29. *Monday.* I went with Stevens to Danvers upon Moriarty's affairs.

---

[1] Judge Joseph Lee, who married Rebecca Phips. He was a moderate loyalist and a brother of Hon. Thomas Lee.

30. *Tuesday.* [In] morning early I set out for New-bury Court, and arrive at noon ; dine at Mrs. Leath-ers', but being lame, remove nearer the court-house to Mr. Browne's, through the friendly interposition of Bro. Parsons.

October 1. *Wednesday.*   Dine at Mr. Browne's.

2. *Thursday.*   I dine at Bro. Parsons's.

3. *Friday.*   Dine at Browne's.

4. *Saturday.*   It rains.   At noon the court adjourned to the 21st instant ; the Bar dine at Mr. Bradbury's.

5. *Sunday.*   I return from Ipswich to Salem with Mr. Sewall, and arrive before the family are up.

6. *Monday.*   I set out with Jno. for Cambridge, and reach Wait's, Malden, and lodge there.

7. *Tuesday.*   Go over to Cambridge, and breakfast at Mr. Mason's.   Go in the procession from chapel to [the] meeting-house, [and] see Dr. Warren and Waterhouse (Dexter absent) installed as professors ;[1] each delivered a Latin oration (both excellent) to Governor, overseers, etc. ; all dine in the Hall ; go from chamber to chamber in the evening, the three colleges[2] being illuminated ; at all the chambers were collations, punch, wine, cheese, cake, etc.

8. *Wednesday.*   [In] morning we set out for Salem and arrive before two o'clock.

11. *Saturday.*   Cloudy, and rain.   Sam. came here. B. Pickman, from Cambridge, tells us of H. D.'s and R'd. D.'s rustication, and of the prospect of several other

---

[1] The design of founding a medical school in connection with Harvard College was first suggested during this year, and the professorship of anatomy was established for John Warren, whose services during the war, and his zeal in surgical and anatomical studies, were preëminent.   The occasion here alluded to was the induction into office of the three gentle-men mentioned, whose names stand first on the list of medical instructors of the Harvard Medical School.

[2] Harvard, Stoughton, and Massachusetts.

scholars being rusticated, expelled, degraded, etc., etc., for riotous conduct at and before the late installations.

12. *Sunday.* Cloudy. Sam'l carries the horse to J. Phelps's pasture, and agrees to tarry on trial, and his wages to commence this day.

13. *Monday.* Mr. Bentley meets the Clubb at my house.

14. *Tuesday.* Messrs. Sewall, Pulling, etc., meet at Robinson's.

15. *Wednesday.* The Assembly opens.

16. *Thursday.* A fine day. Spend the evening at Mr. Wetmore's.

17. *Friday.* Moriarty put into jail yesterday. N. E. storm begins.

18. *Saturday.* Mr. Goodale, Pulling, and Dr. Osgood dine here. Mr. Hodges at tea in the evening.

19. *Sunday.* The storm and rain continue ; the wind very high ; and at night hinges of doors, gates with bolts and bars, give way, etc.

20. *Monday.* Clear and cold. Mr. Sewall and Pulling here on Salisbury reference. Mr. Hastie called to see us in the evening.

21. *Tuesday.* [In the] morning I set out with Mr. Pulling for Newbury Court.

23. *Thursday.* I go to Ipswich on Emerson's business, and Smith, and send to Jno. for Putnam's bond to Mr. O.

24. *Friday.* I return again to Court, and dine at Davenport's ; at night receive John's pocket-book and the bond.

25. *Saturday.* Dine at Mr. Parsons', and go to Ipswich at night with Mr. Pulling, and lodge at Homans'.

26. *Sunday.* I return home by 9 o'clock ; cloudy and cold. News from Jo. Bartlett that he got credit for 2.000 goods.

28. *Tuesday.*   Mrs. Pynchon and Jno. are preparing for their journey to Providence, Mrs. Goodale to go in company.

29. *Wednesday.*   Rain.   Mrs. Derby here in the evening.

30. *Thursday.*   Cloudy, and some rain.   J. Sparhawk, of Portsmouth, in town.

31. *Friday.*   Cloudy morning ; the ground very wet ; the travelling very bad.   I receive a letter from Bro. Pynchon at Port Roseway,[1] where 400 or 500 houses are already erected.

[1] The settlement at Port Roseway, to which allusion is here made, and of which Joseph Pynchon was one of the originators, had now been in existence not far from six months, and at this time bid fair to fulfill the highest hopes of the colonists.   The Revolutionary war was practically ended with the surrender of Cornwallis in 1781, and the Loyalists, with little now to encourage them, had time seriously to consider the question as to their future residence before the formal declaration of peace in 1783.   No less than one hundred and twenty heads of families, we are told, had decided to remove to Nova Scotia so soon as the necessary arrangements could be made; and in the autumn of 1782 a meeting was held in New York, and a committee appointed, of which Mr. Pynchon was one, to proceed to Halifax and make known to the governor the intentions of the company. In accordance with the advice of one familiar with that coast, Port Roseway, or as the French had named it, Port Razoir, was selected as the future home of the colonists, on account of its safe and capacious harbor and, as was thought, its favorable situation as a commercial port.   In the following spring four hundred and twenty heads of families made preparation for their departure ; and on the 27th of April a fleet of eighteen ships, with schooners and sloops, under convoy of two ships of war, sailed from New York for the promised land.

It was believed by many that the new settlement, with its large and beautiful harbor, and its supposed facilities for trade in fish and lumber, would in time become of political importance, and a powerful rival of the Capital.   Indeed, the letters of Mr. Pynchon drew frequent comparisons between Halifax and Port Roseway, invariably in favor of the latter. There were, however, unforeseen obstacles to the final success of this enterprise.   Begun with the utmost enthusiasm, and with the entire approbation of the British government, it became apparent within a few short years after the arrival of the company that it must end in disaster.   The

November 1. *Saturday.* Intention of [the] Assembly co. to ask the Court next week ; the musick is notified to come, but not said when ; *idco quære.*

4. *Tuesday.* Superior Court sits here. Mrs. P., Jno., Mrs. Goodale and company set out for Providence, all sails up. The Court asked to the Assembly to-morrow evening.

5. *Wednesday.* [In the] morning comes on the cause of Fuller *v.* Princeton for Mrs. Salary, and it continues from day to day, and in [the] evening also, to Saturday night.

7. *Friday.* Cloudy, and some rain. We hear of Mrs. P. and company's arrival in good spirits at Dedham on

causes that led to this result are graphically told in an able paper, to which we are largely indebted, recently read by the Rev. T. Watson Smith before the Nova Scotia Historical Society, and published in its Collections. In 1818 the number of inhabitants in what is now Shelburne, which in 1786 was 10,000, had dwindled to 400, a portion of the population having returned to the States, but by far the larger part having sought homes in more congenial places in the British dominions. Mr. Pynchon, yielding to the urgency of his son, who had regained his confiscated property, and troubled by dissensions in the new colony, returned to Connecticut in the autumn of 1784, having been a resident of Shelburne but eighteen months.

The large number of Loyalists who left their native country, not only for the bleak shores of Nova Scotia, but for other parts of British America, the high character they bore, the sufferings they endured, and the influence they have since had in the development of the Canadian Dominion are stated in the paper above referred to. " Two events in the history of Nova Scotia," says the writer, " might of themselves furnish themes for the historians and poets of a great nation, the expulsion of the Acadians and the arrival and settlement of the Loyalists. Longfellow has given immortality to the one, the other has not yet found poet or historian to do it justice. Few records of the wanderings and sufferings of these exiles have been preserved. They left no songs behind them, nor harpers to chant their sorrows. The best writers upon one of the most marvellously sad events in the new world have given us only a comparatively few detached incidents, which serve but to deepen the mysterious interest in the story. Sufficient materials must, however, exist for the preparation of one of the most sadly-dramatic and, for the most part, heroically-dramatic chapters in modern history."

Tuesday night. The musick at Assembly was Prince, a drunken Irishman, and Duane, from the lower parish !

8. *Saturday.* The Superior Court adjourned, the jury having found verdict against Fuller.

9. *Sunday.* Judge Sewall dines with me ; he did not go to the Assembly ; J. Sargeant, Sullivan, Bradbury, King, etc., did go.

13. *Thursday.* Clear and cool ; P. M., the snow thaws, and the ways grow very muddy. I set out for Boston, but am discouraged and return Daland's horse, as by the balling of the snow he stumbles. Jno. and Mrs. Goodale return in pretty good spirits. Ri. Derby, Esq., is buried ;[1] bearers, Mr. Dowse, F. Cabot, D. Britton.

14. *Friday.* Strout from London with English goods, S. Page, owner.

15. *Saturday.* A fine day. I dine with Mr. Noyes and Jack at Mr. Goodale's ; he unwell. Mr. P. Payson there too.

18. *Tuesday.* A clear morning ; very cold. This the last of arresting for Dr's Court, and early in the evening I have leisure to begin a letter for Mad. P. at the Glebe.

19. *Wednesday.* Cloudy, and some wet. Messrs. Mansfield *et al.* meet on the affair of Lynde and Browne. It rains all night. Write to Mr. Dalgleish, Edinburgh.

20. *Thursday.* Storm, and rains furiously. Delivered Sam. Cabot a letter for R. Lechmere, and one for P. Frye, inclosed in a letter to Messrs. Lane, Son, and Fraser, to go in W. Foster's ship, which is to sail to-morrow from Boston.

---

[1] Richard Derby was the son of Richard, who married Martha, daughter of Stephen Haskett, and grandson of Roger Derby, the first settler. He was born in 1712, and died on the 9th of November, 1783. His first wife was Mary Hodges, and his second Sarah, widow of Dr. Ezekiel Hersey of Hingham. His son, Elias Haskett, who became a prominent merchant of Salem, married Elizabeth Crowninshield, and had issue, Elias Haskett, ohn, and Ezekiel Hersey.

24. *Monday*,   Cold.   The Dutch ship's crew reduced to about 30.

25. *Tuesday*.   Present of poems, etc., from J. Bartlett, London, and of [a] box of powdered sugar from the Graftons, Havanna, with a polite letter ; and a great wonder happens : Stevens pays me bill of costs on 2 executions, when I was reduced to the sum of 1/6 only in pocket.   The Dutch 50-gun ship lost in the bay ; about 30 remaining of her crew pass through the town, 270 being lost with the ship ; see the newspapers.

26. *Wednesday*.   Fair day.   Mr. Fitch and Mr. Browne came about the reference suit with Oliver and Lynde. Moriarty gone out of jail yesterday.

27. *Thursday*.   The referees, Mansfield and co., meet at Goodhue's, and have a curious hearing of Oliver and Browne.   It begins to storm and rain in the evening.

28. *Friday*.   Opened the box of powdered sugar, a present from my generous friends, Messrs. J. and J. Grafton at Havanna ; see their polite letter accompanying the present.

29. *Saturday*.   Rain.   Mr. Pulling and Mr. Sewall meet upon Salisbury cause referred.   Dr. Whitaker's people grow uneasy as to his ill conduct, lasciviousness, etc.

30. *Sunday*.   Wet and stormy ; storms and rains at night, and blows briskly ; a great many vessels are supposed to be in hazard in the bay.   Mrs. Orne visits Mrs. Higginson at evening, and comes home in haste, and is taken with shortness of breath, but is relieved before she goes to bed.   Dr. Whitaker confesses to some of his church his imprudence.

December 2.   *Tuesday*.   The Court meet P. M.

3. *Wednesday*.   [The] Court dine at Mr. Pickering's.

4. *Thursday*.   The Court dine at Mr. Wetmore's.

6. *Saturday.*   May is tried, and found not guilty at 9 in the evening.

7. *Sunday.*   A fine, clear morning, cool ; wind S. W. Messrs. Mansfield, Sewall, and Dane dined with me yesterday.   A stranger is buried in the churchyard.

8. *Monday.* Fair.   Mr. Hinckley and lady here.

10. *Wednesday.*   Cloudy and drizzly weather.   Great quantities of provision in the market ; turkeys at 8*d.*, geese 5*d.* and 6*d.*, sausages 10*d.*, eggs 1/2.   Urged Stephens to secure himself in Estey and Lamson's affair of the Exōn.   Wrote letter of thanks to Messrs. Grafton.

11. *Thursday.*   Thanksgiving Day.   Dr. Whitaker preacheth at his meeting to [a] small audience, chiefly of women.   Mr. Fisher gave us a good sermon at church. I and family dine at Mr. Goodale's.

12. *Friday.*   Cloudy and wet all day ; at night clears off.   I bespeak the house of Mrs. Pickman, in case Dr. W. or Mr. Prince shall not have it after the winter ; and this day give notice to Mr. Hunt that the cellar having so much water will not answer for me at all, and he concurs in sentiment with me, and says it will not probably be clear till spring ; so much for the matter.   Mrs. Pickman engages the house to me after Dr. W. leaves it, as she supposes Mr. Prince has engaged one.

13. *Saturday.*   Cold.   Mr. Hastie spent the last evening with me, also Mr. Goodale ; Mr. Hinckley here ; Mr. Noyes and Dr. Putnam here this evening.   Dr. Whitaker and Madam and son Jem. come home, Jem. preceding the company upon a large black stallion ; Madam calls him a fine horse, and is for keeping him for publick use and his own profit.

15. *Monday.*   [At] night, Club at my house, and Mr. Noyes.

16. *Tuesday.*   Stevens in trouble as to Estey's and Lamson's affair. I buy [a] box [of] large candles at 10*d*.

17. *Wednesday.*   Clear and warm. Wrote to Guilford to T. R. Pynchon by post.[1] At the Assembly and spend an agreeable evening. Mr. Templeman there ! Where is she ? where, poor Lawless ? News told there of the loss of Calahan ; Mrs. Wetmore having a brother on board is deeply affected, and at a proper time, when the company was engaged, she retires and goes home.

18. *Thursday.*   Snow-storm. By the post we hear that Calahan by contrary winds is driven back into Pool.

19. *Friday.*   Clears up cold. See the account of Jona. Gardner's death in the paper.

21. *Sunday.*   Fair. Jno. goes up to Mr. Orne's and dines. At sunrise it snowed. Having a cold I tarry and dine at home. Dr. Holyoke and Mr. Wetmore here in the evening.

22. *Monday.*   Cloudy and some snow. We hear of Mrs. Pynchon's coming to Boston from Providence with Mrs. Barrett.

23. *Tuesday.*   Clear and cold. I set out for Boston with T. Sanders in B. Daland's close conveyance. Go over Winnisimet [and] find Mrs. Pynchon at Mr. Higginson's ; set out from thence for Salem at 12, and get in to my house at 6 on Wednesday.

25. *Thursday.*   Christmas Day ; very cold ; some snow. Mrs. P. and I dine at home and have a comfortable Christmas to ourselves, having sufficient elbow-room and a warm fireside. Jno. and Mr. Goodale's family dine at Mr. Wetmore's. Mr. Barnard, Prince,

---

[1] In a letter of this date Mr. Pynchon writes : " I just now hear that Dr. Borland is at last admitted to reside in these States, and he has gone to Portsmouth ; that R. T. Paine is nominated a judge of the Superior Court."

and Bentley at church, and Mr. Fisher delivered an excellent, spirited discourse; Dr. Whitaker was there also.

26. *Friday.* Snow-storm ; N. E. wind. Mr. Noyes here in the evening.

27. *Saturday.* Clear, cold day. Mr. and Mrs. Wetmore here at tea. Mr. Osgood goes to Andover. Mr. Kimball here ; Patty here the day and lodges here.

28. *Sunday.* Cloudy and very cold ; snows. Mr. Fisher here P. M. ; Mr. Wetmore, Mr. Goodale, Mrs. Pickman, and Patty here in the evening.

29. *Monday.* Clouds and rain. Clubb at Dr. Holyoke's ; Mr. Barnard and Prince there, but not Mr. Bentley.

30. *Tuesday.* Cloudy. Mrs. Curwen, Mr. and Mrs. Goodale here, and Susan Higginson here in the evening. Patty goes home this evening to prepare for the Assembly and for the execution of her plan ; query, the event.

31. *Wednesday.* Assembly at night; warm and somewhat sloppy. Billy Cabot writes that he shall attempt to return hither from Britain in the spring.

1784. *January* 2. *Friday.* Write to Mr. Curwen by Mr. Cabot ; send letter for Mr. Dalgleish, written November last.

4. *Sunday.* Cloudy, but seems to be clearing off ; moderate air. At night Dr. Whitaker has a lecture.

5. *Monday.* Some rain and snow, and very wet travelling. See the account of Dr. Cooper's death, and the small number of my surviving classmates.

6. *Tuesday.* Write again to Colo. Frye, and send his and Curwen's letters by Mr. Conant from Boston. Jno. goes on my horse and hears that Calahan is cast away on the shoals.

7. *Wednesday*. Cool and cloudy. Mrs. Higginson and Mrs. Cabot remove to Beverly, having sold the house ; Mrs. Higginson seems much affected at leaving Salem and her old habitation and neighbours.

8. *Thursday*. Clear and cold. The day for Lang and the Doctor ; mark the end of it ; the rabble bear down the Dr. and his cause, and shout at everything said to his prejudice.   I wrote to Mr. N. Sparhawk.

9. *Friday*. [In the] morning [at] 10 o'clock Judge Batcheller gives judgment in a formal manner, and with dignity and decorum, in the cause *v.* Lang, and acquits him, and orders that he go without day ; the audience begin to clap but are discountenanced, and the clapping ceaseth ; the prosecutor is advised not to be present, and therefore does not attend. Thus endeth the cause of great expectation, and with it, as all suppose, the Doctor's clerical character ; and it is supposed he will not attempt to preach again, and if he does he will have no hearers of any character, interest, or influence. I sent my letter to N. Sparhawk, Esqr.

10. *Saturday*. I go to Beverly on reference, Browne *v.* Dodge, and give notice to Mrs. Browne of the prospect of recovery, and caution her to beware of the proposals which may be made to her.

11. *Sunday*. Snow. Dr. Whitaker preacheth at his Tabernacle to about 14 persons, mostly boys and girls.

12. *Monday*. Very cold, and the sledding tolerably good. Mr. and Mrs. Lee and Mrs. Pickman here in the evening ; he speaks of Capt. Stanhope, commissioner at Port Roseway. Club at Mr. Goodale's.

13. *Tuesday*. Snow-storm, and very cold. Wrote to Mr. Walter and brother Joseph.

14. *Wednesday*. Cloudy. Mrs. R. Cabot here and S. Blyth. I go to the Assembly.

15. *Thursday.*   Mr. Bartlett returns to Boston.   Jno. carries him to Newhall's.   I wrote to N. Sparhawk by post, and to Shelburne by Hall, to W. Walter, and Bro. Pynchon.   Clear and cold to-day.   Jno. and Sam'l return with the sleigh, P. M., from Charlestown, whither they carried Mr. Bartlett in Daland's carriage.   The bearers of Mrs. Turner[1] propose to go to see Mr. Turner this evening, but adjourn for to-morrow evening.   Capt. Jno. Gardner dies.[2]

16. *Friday.*   Very cold and clear.   We visit Mr. Turner this evening, and there it was said that Dr. W.'s people would soon shut up the meeting-house and exclude the Dr.

18. *Sunday.*   Cloudy; wind S. E., and warmer than for several days past.   We hear from Halifax of a great concurrence of people at Annapolis and of the arrival of H. Lloyd at Halifax from N. York.

19. *Monday.*   Snow, rain, and thaw; at 9 at night clears away cool.   Mr. Goodale here, the only one of the Club who ventures out.   J. Gardner buried.

20. *Tuesday.*   Clear and cold.   By Dr. Tupper from Shelburne, we hear of 10,000 houses there, all sorts included, and of their having cut the road nearly through to Annapolis.

22. *Thursday.*   Moderate, pleasant day.   Wrote to Mr. Oliver.   I go with Colo. Thorndike to view the

---

[1] Mary, wife of John Turner; at the time of her death, 66 years of age.

[2] John Gardner, a prominent resident of Salem, was the son of John and Elizabeth (Weld) Gardner, and brother of Elizabeth, who married her cousin, Capt. Jonathan Gardner, mentioned above.   He was baptized February 16, 1706–7, and married, first, to Elizabeth Putnam, by whom he had John, who married Elizabeth Pickering, whose son, Samuel P., married Rebecca Russell Lowell, whose son, John Lowell, married Catherine E. Peabody, the parents of George A. and John L. Gardner, of Boston. The second wife of John Gardner was Elizabeth Herbert.   He afterwards married a third wife, Mary Peale.   See *Pickering Genealogy*, 53. v. 20.

great house which he offers to let me [for] 3 months at
£50 per annum. Colo. Pickering and his brother, Clark,
here.

23. *Friday.* Moderate, cloudy, and thaws. Wrote to
N. Sparhawk, Esqr., post. Mr. Story, [of] Marblehead,
dines here. See the newspaper, Salem, announcing the
arrival of the Hon. Colo. Pickering from the southward,
late Qr.-master-gen'l of the army — humph ! See the
Boston paper and character of Dr. S. Cooper ; let all
who have eyes to see and ears to hear turn back to the
papers, and to the time of Dr. Eliot's death, and ob-
serve the truth suppressed by party spirit, envy, and
malevolence.

24. *Saturday.* Wind S. ; the snow is gone, the air
warm. Dr. Putnam and Mr. Noyes here [in] the evening. Mr. and Mrs. Goodale, Dr. P., and Mr. G., T. P.,
and Parson C. dined to-day at widow M. Higginson's.

25. *Sunday.* Moderate, and cloudy. A letter from
J. Atherton,[1] of Amherst, as to Wilkins. At church
P. M., Mr. Dormer and Donatti, the Italians. At eve I
write to Mr. Bartlett as to Mr. Goodhue's affair, and
send his receipt for the note of £48.

26. *Monday.* Cloudy and cold. Club at Mr. Blaney's.

28. *Wednesday.* A fine day ; wind W. John's new
blue comes home for the Assembly. Bro. Mitchell
comes with N. Sparhawk and Jno. Sparhawk in the
stage.

29. *Thursday.* Cold and clear. Brothers Stephen
and Mitchell dine here; Mitchell goes to Mrs. Goodale's.

---

[1] Joshua Atherton was the father of the Hon. Charles H. Atherton, of
Amherst, N. H., and grandfather of the Hon. Charles G. Atherton, both
of whom were members of Congress. Mr. Atherton was a member of the
Convention for ratifying the Constitution of the United States, and a
speech of his is extant against the Constitution, because it sanctioned
slavery and the slave trade.

30. *Friday.*   Stephen comes over again ; is in tribulation ; all strive in his favor, but in vain.

31. *Saturday.*   Fair, pleasant day.   E. Williams comes at evening.   I have a letter from Colo. Thorndike as to the house.

February 4. *Wednesday.*   Ordination day at Lynn of Mr. Parsons ; Mr. Treadwell, the former minister, opposing it.   J. Bartlett dines here.

5. *Thursday.*   A fine, clear morning.   E. Williams sets out for Boston in the stage.   This day Mr. W. came about Richardson's writs, who refused allowing the common price agreed on, viz., 12/, and I told Mr. W. that I refused taking less.   Q. If he drew them for R.

6. *Friday.*   A snow-storm.   Richardson tries to break thro' bar agreement.

7. *Saturday.*   A fine, cold morning.   A letter from S. Gridley as to Moriarty.   Mr. Goodale shows me J. Sewall's cringing and submissive letter, respecting that he wrote to Mr. L. in 77, which was most insolent, and now said by Sewall to have been dictated by the purest friendly motives.   Jno. set out for Boston at 9 this morning about his adventure sent in there from W. Indies.   I drink tea with Caty at Mr. Vans', and sincerely commiserate the family.

9. *Monday.*   Very cold and clear.   Mrs. Higginson, Goodale, and Miss Atkins get "*Curse ye Meroz*" for D. Chapman.   Club at Dr. Putnam's.   Judge Sumner calls on me, but declines to lodge here.   Mr. Reed, from Cambridge, at Clubb.   Writs are issued to a number to take the degree of Barristers ; a small, ordinary seal of somebody's head is affixed to the writ, enclosed in a tin box.

10. *Tuesday.*   Exceedingly cold.   Judge Sewall calls on me.   The Court meet in the Town House, and adjourn to [the] brick School House.   J. Sewall and

Sumner spend the evening, sup, and lodge with us ; Mr. Bartlett comes also in the evening, and lodges here.

11. *Wednesday.* J. Sargeant[1] calls with the other judges, and the sheriffs go with them to Court. J. Sargeant shows me Porter's letter ; truly 't is an original ! The Court go to the Assembly past 9 o'clock.

12. *Thursday.* Cloudy, and snow. Mr. Bartlett and Jno. set out at noon for Boston. J. Sargeant shows me Bro. Porter's extraordinary letter from London.

13. *Friday.* Mrs. Pickman and Mrs. Orne set out for Boston. I write by B. Ely to Colo. Worthington as to Doyle's debt, and as to security for it for 5 or 6 months. I give my account *v.* Hale Ives' estate to Jos. Wood, administrator.

14. *Saturday.* A fine, fair day, but very cold. Judges Sargeant, Sewall, and Sumner dine with me on fish. The Court adjourned without day. J. Sumner sets out for Roxbury. At night Mr. T. Russell, Lowell, and Higginson come to town, and spend the evening at Mr. Goodale's.

15. *Sunday.* Clear, and very cold. Mr. Sewall dines at Mr. Goodale's, and goes to meeting at Mr. Barnard's. Mrs. Barton's[2] funeral to-day ; bearers, Dr. Bickford, Dr. Gray, Dan'l King, Dr. Putnam, Jona. Ropes, myself ; she, 83 yrs old. Last night Mrs. Hathorn's shop broken open, and great quantities of goods stolen out.

16. *Monday.* Cloudy and warmer. J. Sewall set out

---

[1] Nathaniel Peaslee Sargeant was of the class at Harvard College of 1750. He practiced law in Haverhill and held a high rank, says Washburn, in his profession. In 1790 he succeeded Judge Cushing in the office of Chief Justice, which he held at the time of his death, in 1791.

[2] Elizabeth (Marston) Barton was the second wife of Samuel, son of Dr. John Barton, who came to N. E. in the " Hannah and Elizabeth " in 1672, and who died at Barbadoes in 1694. She was the daughter of Benjamin and Patience Marston.

at 10 A. M. to be at Boston seasonably for the uniform and procession to-morrow, the bib and band ! and all to dine at the Governor's.

17. *Tuesday.* Clear, and moderate. A grand procession of Court and Bar at Boston.

18. *Wednesday.* Mrs. Hathorn sets out for Providence to visit the Conjuror to find her goods.

19. *Thursday.* Patty Pynchon here in the evening.

20. *Friday.* Great part of Mrs. Hathorn's goods are found at Marblehead, parts being offered for sale and to exchange, at very low rates ; Jack sets out for Providence to call her home from the Conjuror's; the receivers, etc., of the goods are brought over from Marblehead, examined, and part of the goods found and the persons committed. Spend the evening at Mr. Goodale's, Mr. Dormer, etc., Mr. Vans, etc., present ; and I there received Mr. Sears's letter of the 17th, as to J. Browne's payment.

21. *Saturday.* Morning, fair, and moderate. The Hathorns return from Boston with one of the thieves, and Constable Bickford, from Marblehead, with some more of the goods.

23. *Monday.* Clear day, and cool at eve. The Club at my house, with Hist. of the Jesuits.

24. *Tuesday.* A fine, moderate, clear day. Darrah here, and by him I write to Hollis and Chelmsford. Jno. returns from Providence after 9 in the evening.

25. *Wednesday.* Maj'r Cheever here for witness before the Council against Dr. W. Having caught cold I keep house.

26. *Thursday.* Mr. Story here. The Council meet in Dr. W.'s meeting-house, and Mr. Forbes preacheth a sermon, and the Council's result is published for dissolving the connection between Dr. W. and his congregation, and W. sets off for Newburyport to consult Mr. P.

27. *Friday.*   Very cold.   I write to El. Lynde's widow.

28. *Saturday.*   Clear, and very cold.   Bro. Mitchell sets out in the stage for Portsmouth.   Colo. Mansfield here about his and Norris' account ; Bro. Mansfield here.

March 1.   *Monday.*   Very cold yet ; a more tedious winter hath not been known for twenty years.

2. *Tuesday.*   I write to Mr. Curwen and Colo. Frye.

3. *Wednesday.*   J. Bartlett comes with baggage, etc., to sail in the Pilgrim.   Mrs. Holyoke, Cutts, and company.

4. *Thursday.*   N. wind and snow, and Jno. Peas declares that the Pilgrim will have no good wind before next Wednesday ; see now, says Peas, which knows best, the great folks or Peas.

6. *Saturday.*   Wind continues.   Sam. carries the horse to Sam'l Endicot's.   Little Jos. Flint puts me into a passion with lying and smiling.   In the evening I read Dr. W.'s sermon on cursing.   Mr. Noyes, Bartlett, etc., here.

7. *Sunday.*   The wind continues, and Peas passes for half a prophet.   Mr. Bartlett here, and Mrs. Pickman in the evening.

8. *Monday.*   Cloudy ; N. E. wind.   Bartlett and all the passengers think they could manage the wind much better than Jove, who seems to be prejudiced against them or the Pilgrim.

10. *Wednesday.*   Mr. Bartlett and John go to Danvers and dine ; at night to the Assembly.   Mrs. Lee and George[1] here in the evening.   Mr. Fisher rejoices that he is excused from his proposed journey to Providence.

11. *Thursday.*   Cloudy still, and N. E. wind.   Joshua Grafton returns from Havana.   Mr. Lafitte keeps his

---

[1] The son of Joseph Lee, born in 1776, and who died in 1856.

room. Capt. Haraden's loss of his cause and of his partner's deserting. Mr. Bartlett sets out for Boston and returns to Newhall's at night, and sends Scipio for John.

12. *Friday.* Cloudy; wind south. Bartlett returns from Newhall's, and dines here. Sam'l Gott leaves us, and Peter comes in his room. I am to find Peter his food and clothes so long as I keep him, he being now upon trial only. The roguery of Sam begins to appear. Mr. Smith[1] calls to study here.

13. *Saturday.* Cloudy in the morning ; the sun appears before noon, and the passengers go on board the Pilgrim. Mr. Bartlett returns and dines with us, and they go on board again. In the evening Eb. West comes and speaks of his intimacy with B.

14. *Sunday.* Cloudy, foggy, wind south, and Mr. Bartlett comes on shore ; says all are sick on board the Pilgrim. Rain at 10 o'clock; Mr. Bartlett stays and dines. We find more and more proof of Sam's roguery and deceitful tricks.

15. *Monday.* Cloudy morning, but clears away ; wind southwest, and off goes the Pilgrim with a brisk gale. Mr. Wilds comes to write in my office.

16. *Tuesday.* Cloudy and cold. Messrs. Franklin and Adams recommend moderate measures as to refugees' estates, etc.

19. *Friday.* It snows at night. A concert and dance at the Assembly House.

21. *Sunday.* Clear and pleasant. Mr. Noyes here in the evening. Mr. N. Sparhawk's very friendly letter before me.

23. *Tuesday.* A pleasant day. Brother Stephen goes to Portsmouth, and carries Mitchell Sewall, his nephew.

---

[1] Hon. Jeremiah Smith.

24. *Wednesday.* Miss Atkins spends the day with us, and Mrs. W. and company the evening.

26. *Friday.* Cloudy. I receive a letter from Mr. Sears respecting John Browne's recalling the money paid on my account ; I set out in the afternoon with the money to repay Mr. Sears, and arrive at Boston about 8 in the evening.

27. *Saturday.* Rain. I go to see Mr. Sears, Mr. Lafitte, and T. Fitch ; the latter gives an order on me to pay his money in my hands to Mrs. Lynde ; also go to Mr. Lathrop's as to Knowlton's affair.

28. *Sunday.* Cloudy. Dr. Whitaker's people shut the doors of the Tabernacle against him ; he demands his right to enter and preach as their minister, but is refused.

29. *Monday.* Cloudy, and raw, cold air. Boden *et ux.* call respecting the deacon's objections to their marriage contract, and they are to call for certificate of the deacon's marriage with Dorothy.

30. *Tuesday.* Cloudy, and some rain. Mr. Grafton and a Frenchman here in the morning. My letter, sent for Port Roseway to my brother, is returned to me by Dexter, his vessel being driven off the coast to [the] West Indies.

31. *Wednesday.* Miss Diamond, Atkins, and W. Vans, Jr., here at evening, also N. Barrett ; the latter *et ux.* spend the evening at Mr. Goodale's.

April 1. *Thursday.* A fine, pleasant day. Mrs. Pickman's son, C. Gayton, dies this morning — her only son surviving.

4. *Sunday.* At church. Very cold.

6. *Tuesday.* Rains. I set out with B. Daland in his chaise for Ipswich Court; we go over the ferry, the roads being exceedingly miry.

8. *Thursday.* The Town House thronged on Session trials, wrangles, etc. ; the cats get out of the bag, and are tossed backward and forward from bench to bar ; the Chief Justice is for letting them all out; see memo. of proceedings.

9. *Friday.* About 200 actions to be got over, one way or another, by Saturday night.

10. *Saturday.* Hurry, durry! Call 'em out! call 'em all out! About 5 the Court rises in tolerable good humour.

11. *Sunday morning.* About 5 Mr. Wetmore and I, in his chaise, set out for Salem ; cloudy, and very cold. We get home at 9 o'clock to breakfast. I receive a letter from Mr. Lechmere, Bristol.

12. *Monday.* A fair, cool day. Walker and Capt. Osborn meet at my office about Robinson and his causes.

14. *Wednesday.* A fine, clear day. The ship . . . arrives at Boston from London with some protested bills of S. Page ; to-morrow stand clear, Page the baker! Some begin to-night ; alas, poor Page !

15. *Thursday.* Rain ; wind N. E. Fast Day. Peter goes home with his father for his misconduct and theft, etc., etc.

16. *Friday.* Rain, snow, and blustering winds; the blustering subsides, and Page revives.

17. *Saturday.* Rain and snow all day by turns. Page attacks B. and Thorndike in his turn ; but memo., they were alarmed by reports and only misinformed, but Page's was resentment only; he called them spiteful ; what must they say of him ?

18. *Sunday.* Cloudy. Mr. Fisher at Marblehead all day.

19. *Monday.* Clear and cold. Mr. Bentley here as to Corsican. I agree for Mr. West's house.

20. *Tuesday.*   Gen'l Glover here ; I am to send him a line, when ready, for Sparhawk's securities, whether at Marblehead or here, and take the notes with me from hence.   Mr. Bentley here again.   Mr. Sewall, of Marblehead, dines here ; we go to J. Pickering about the writs not brought forward.

25. *Sunday.*   Cloudy.   I go to church ; Dr. W. there, and behaves with decency, and bows at going in and out.

27. *Tuesday.*   Mrs. Orne takes 3 volumes of Lady Montague's Letters.

28. *Wednesday.*   A fine, fair morning.   Manuel Erskin came to live in my family upon trial, and have his food and clothes.

29. *Thursday.*   Rain, and I buy a glaz'd hat as security against it.

30. *Friday.*   Cloudy, and some rain.   I have much tribulation as to entries of actions ; mark the event, and see if so bad as the present prospect.   I spend the evening at Judge Oliver's.   The Assembly company meet at Bacon's, sup, and have a high go.

May 1. *Saturday.*   Cloudy and cold ; S. E. wind. Capt. Buffinton comes from Providence ; says Mr. Oliver and family are well, and he and Mr. Walter's son are to come to Salem next week.   Mr. Noyes and I ride up to Mr. Orne's.

2. *Sunday.*   A fine, clear, but windy day.   At church all day ; at Mr. Fisher's in the evening with Mr. G. We hear that Miss P. Porter is in Salem at Mrs. Ropes's.

3. *Monday.*   Cloudy morning.   Mr. Wetmore and family move.   I find no house.   Letters from Colo. Frye.

4. *Tuesday.*   A fine, clear day.   My troubles increase ; no house, business fails, enemies multiply, malevolence prevails.

5. *Wednesday.* A fine, fair day. Tea at Mr. Wetmore's ; [in] evening at Capt. Dodge's and at Mr. Goodale's. Mrs. Sparhawk's son in town, and daughter; she a most agreeable lady.

6. *Thursday.* A fine, clear morning. Mr. Cabot a little nettled as to his wife's making offers of his house to A., B., and C. At evening, Mr. Dowse and Fisher and church co. ; high words between F. and W., and seeds were sown for future animosities and jealousies ; F., thou must be less overbearing or depart !

8. *Saturday.* A fine day, moderate and warm. Mr. Cabot condescends to offer me the house where Mr. G. lived, for the present, until his son's return.

9. *Sunday.* A fine, warm day. I first speak with Mr. Cabot as to his house and as to an office.

10. *Monday.* Cloudy and moderate weather. Mr. Vans calls and speaks to me about a house, and about Mr. West's disappointment as to his house.

11. *Tuesday.* I go to Middleton to Eli Curtis' for Mr. Cabot, Mrs. Hunt, etc., as to debts due from him.

12. *Wednesday.* Cloudy and moderate. Vendue of Capt. Webb's goods for Messervy. I have a letter from N. Sparhawk with Bickford's notes.

13. *Thursday.* I write to Mr. Sparhawk. In the afternoon went to Flint's, Danvers. At evening Dr. Holyoke and Mr. Smith, from Andover, here.

14. *Friday.* Cloudy morning. We hear of robberies in Danvers.

15. *Saturday.* Fine, warm day. We go to Mr. Cabot's house and put canvas on the floors and set up the desk.

16. *Sunday.* Cloudy ; wind N. E. [In] evening at Mr. Cabot's ; Mrs. P. at Mrs. Curwen's. More accounts of the robbers in the woods among snakes and the rocks.

J. Hastie in town, and he brings news of the dissolution of Parliament of Britain.

17. *Monday.* Cloudy morning. We begin to move to Mr. Cabot's house.

20. *Thursday.* A fire at midnight ; the house saved.

21. *Friday.* Cloudy. I send to Mr. Sparhawk, Portsmouth, as to lease of his farm.

23. *Sunday.* Morning, rains very moderately. Mr. Dormer sets out for Congress.

24. *Monday.* Cold, N. E. wind, and wet. Mr. Blaney gives us an account of his tour to No. River with G. Lincoln, and that he hears by a vessel from Bermuda that Gov. Browne is not to tarry long there.

26. *Wednesday.* Election Day. John with his horse beat at the horse-race in Danvers. Mr. Haley at Boston.

27. *Thursday.* Cloudy and sunshine by turns ; the wind east all day. I go to Danvers and deliver the key of Mr. Orne's house, with offers to whitewash the rooms, make up the fences, and make good all damages done by my family. I write to N. Sparhawk, Esqr., by Colo. Atkinson. Gov'r Hancock's house, land, etc., are attached by Capt. Erwin.

28. *Friday.* I remove my books and office to Mrs. Curwen's shop.

29. *Saturday.* A fine day, but wind E., and cool. At evening I receive a letter from S. C., Esq., of March last ; Mr. Vans brought it ; C. is a Whig, yet can't trust those here.

30. *Sunday.* Whitsunday. Mrs. Piemont, sister, and daughter at church.

31. *Monday.* Cloudy, but warm and moderate ; wind S. E. Says V. : Why don't you write neighbor C. that he may come directly home without harm or risque ? *A.* Why don't you write so yourself ? *V.* I do, but he

will not believe me. *Q.* Why? *V.* Because I am a Whig. *Q.* Do you wonder at the reason, when the Acts of [the] Assembly subject him to be taken up, etc., etc., on his return? Mr. Wilds comes. See the new face of political matters in the faces of new House and Courts.

June 1. *Tuesday.* Cloudy and cool. I use a stove in the office. Mr. Smith calls.

3. *Thursday.* Fine, warm day; wind W. I go to Danvers, and do not write to N. Sparhawk, Esq., but write to Mr. Curwen, inclosed in [a] letter to Mr. Smith, Boston, by an Ipswich man going for Abr'm Knowlton.

4. *Friday.* Fine, moderate day, warm in the afternoon. Rumours of Mr. Curwen's sailing from England in Emerton, but query.

5. *Saturday.* A fine, warm day. Mr. Amory, Greenleaf, and . . . from college, to dine with John ; Knowlton from Ipswich.

6. *Sunday.* A very warm day. At church all day. In the afternoon Mr. Wetmore's daughter christened, *Waldo ;* Mr. Waldo and Mrs. Orne sponsors, with Mr. Wetmore.

7. *Monday.* A fine, clear, cool day. Walker, the Irish sailor, committed at the suit of Russell for assault.

9. *Wednesday.* A cool, cloudy morning ; wind rises and clouds go off. A dispute between the Selectmen and Rust as to the erecting his house and encroaching on the street.

11. *Friday.* Cloudy, cool morning. Salem Selectmen and ·Rust disputing about the bounds of the street.

12. *Saturday.* Cloudy. James Andrews desires his regards to Colo. Frye, and, if he will come home, he will vote for his being Governor.

13. *Sunday.* Cool day. We have a good fire. English preacher.

15. *Tuesday.* A fine, cool day. I set out for Ipswich Court.

16. *Wednesday.* [In the] evening I return from Ipswich, having judgment affirmed on my complaints.

18. *Friday.* Thieves brought from Marblehead who broke open Roads' shop.

19. *Saturday.* Morning, I return to Ipswich Court, and get there by 9 A. M., as the bell is tolling for the Court.

21. *Monday.* Clear, and very warm. Stevens comes for execution, alias Richardson *v.* Chickering, and says Richardson sent for it and ordered it, and would indemnify me for consenting, if Court denied it; and since, to-day, I find Richardson denies his sending. Richard Manning came and attempted to make a bargain with me to act for the town without pay, that is, without other pay than I could get of the town's debtors ; I told him my circumstances did not admit, at my years, my doing business for nothing, or at such a hazard. Have I in this given the town or Sir Richard just cause of offence?

24. *Thursday.* Cloudy ; wind S. E. Wrote to Mr. Sparhawk by post. Invited to dine at Mr. Goodale's with [the] Governor of Virginia to-morrow.

25. *Friday.* Warm day. A large company dine at Mr. Goodale's; [the] Governor's business requiring him to hasten out of town, he could not stop to dine, and Mr. Blaney was by the company nominated to act [as] Governor for the time, and it being hot he licensed the company to dine in their gowns and caps ; the company accordingly sent for them and dined in them, and a genteel dinner, allowed by all to be quite governmental.

26. *Saturday.* Excessively hot ; Dr. Holyoke's thermometer was at 106 in the shade, Mr. Prince's at 118 in the sun. Most of this hot day is spent in searching

for C. Webb's note, etc., *v.* Fogerty ; never fear, when I 'm not looking for them they 'll be found.

27. *Sunday.* Very warm this morning. Mr. Fisher absent, and we have no church opened to-day ; well ! it 's a day for rest, and rest I want from business for July Court. Mr. Wetmore returns this morning from Boston ; he and Mrs. Wetmore go to Mr. Goodale's ; call at my house as they go ; [they] return on foot and do not call.

July 2. *Friday.* Jos. Grafton returns from the Havanna *via* New York and through Providence, and brings letters from Mr. Oliver.

3. *Saturday.* Cloudy, and rain this morning ; no cleaning and sweeping the streets, though money was raised for the purpose. Mr. Noyes here. Mr. Wilds this morning goes to Topsfield, Mr. Smith for Andover. Mr. Jos. Grafton calls at the window to ask how we do ; he appears exceedingly improved by travelling, and is very polite and easy in his manners and address. Mr. S. Orne taken ill.

4. *Sunday.* Clear and moderate. At church all day ; P. M., Mr. Goodale and Gee sit with me ; the latter a native of Lisbon, educated in England, now lives at Philadelphia. A merchant, well acquainted with Mr. Dormer, spent the evening with me.

5. *Monday.* Cloudy ; wind S. W. Mr. Gee goes to Marblehead with F. Goodale ; he spent the evening with us at the Club at Mr. Blaney's.

6. *Tuesday.* A fine, cool morning ; wind at N. E. Mr. Gee sets out for Boston in the stage with my letter to Mr. O., at Providence, requesting notice to be taken of Mr. Gee as a stranger and traveller.

7. *Wednesday.* A clear, pleasant day. Mr. Smith intimates that John may have a degree at college upon

application for it. Haraden and Smith and Patty seem preparing for a 12-month tattling match. The Topsfield Council at work as to Mr. Breck, and to secure him against the disaffected of his congregation.

8. *Thursday.* Hot and dry ; wind S. W. Mr. Smith, of Boston, here, and gives [an] account of Mr. Curwen, etc., in England.

10. *Saturday.* Cool and clear. L. Oliver returns from Providence ; leaves all well and brings a letter ; Mr. Gee had not been there.

11. *Sunday.* Clear and cold. L. Oliver brings account from Providence of Miss Temple's attempting to destroy herself by [laudanum] repeatedly, and that the potions she took were brought up, being disagreeable to her stomach. The laudanum kept her asleep [so] that she could not be awaked for hours. A. M., at church ; the organist lame and the singing worse than none.

12. *Monday.* Warm and clear. Labourers begin this morning to sweep the paved street.

13. *Tuesday.* The Court meet.

17. *Saturday.* Moderate. The Court and Bar dine with me.

19. *Monday.* Cloudy and wet. Reference — Gallison and Lee meet.

21. *Wednesday.* Commencement ; Mrs. McCauley and Mrs. Haley there. Mr. Smith gives me Mr. Curwen's journal of his tour.

22. *Thursday.* Very warm. We return from Commencement P. M. Rains at night.

23. *Friday.* Cool and clear. A tree struck with lightning by Mackentire's. Rains at night.

24. *Saturday.* The streets are wet this morning ; the weather warm. At night I read Mr. Curwen's journal to Mrs. C., and she is much entertained.

25. *Sunday.* Clear and warm. Mr. Eliot [1] preaches at Mr. Prince's meeting ; I go there to hear so good a rhetorician, so good a preacher, so honest, so good a man.

26. *Monday.* Mr. Wetmore and Stevens set out on their journey for Connecticut. About 11 o'clock a plentiful rain. Mr. Eliot here at tea ; growing grave. [In the] evening at Dr. Putnam's. Mr. Blaney returns from Boston, having been introduced to Mrs. Haley and Mrs. McCauley. I receive a letter from R. Lechmere, Esq., [2] who laments his not disguising his political sentiments, and his not having conducted with more duplicity than he did while in the country. I write to Dr. Thomas Pynchon, [3] at Guilford, by Mr. Wetmore.

27. *Tuesday.* Sessions adjournment. Mr. Sewall, Mrs. Wetmore, and Miss Waldo dine here.

28. *Wednesday.* Cool and cloudy. Sessions proceed. John goes to Flax Pond a-fishing with Major Sprague and company. Letter and sermon from Mr. Bliss, Springfield.

29. *Thursday.* Mrs. Pynchon and company visit at Capt. Haraden's and W. Gray's.

30. *Friday.* A fine, cool, clear day. John goes a-fishing at Spring Pond with J. Nutting and Davenport, and brings home plenty of perch, etc., and they sup here. Mr. Vans and wife, Mr. and Mrs. Sanders here at tea and part of the evening. Nutting and company sup with John on fish in the parlour.

31. *Saturday.* A fine, cool day. I go with Stephen

---

[1] Rev. John Eliot succeeded his father, Andrew, as minister of the New North Church, in 1779.

[2] Richard Lechmere, at one time Collector of Customs, was one of the best bred men in New England. He was a nephew of Nicholas, Lord Lechmere, in the reign of George I.

[3] The son of Joseph Pynchon and nephew of William Pynchon.

Webb to get possession for him on Cook's mortgage, and with forbearance and patience under the reproaches of the woman's tongue, we prevail, and get a release of Cook's right of redemption.   We have a letter from Mr. Oliver, by Mr. Jenkins, of Providence, mentioning Gov. Browne and lady's arrival at Newport.

August 1. *Sunday.*   Cloudy, and So. West wind ; a little rain last night ; warm air this morning.   Mrs. Piemont and fair daughter dine with us.   Sam'l Orne rides out with John twice to-day and bears it well, yet Dr. O. doubts as to his recovery, and thinks it advisable for him to take a trip to Halifax, or a long journey while he can bear either.

4. *Wednesday.*   I, with Mr. Blaney and others, set out in the stage for Boston upon our tour for Newport ; arrive at B., dine there, and engage a passage for Providence in the stage.   I write to Bro. Pynchon from Boston.

5. *Thursday.*   At 4 A. M. we start in the stage with Capt. Carr, breakfast at Gay's, Dedham, dine at Hatch's, and get to Mr. Oliver's at tea ; Mr. B. and I lodge at Mr. Chace's.

6. *Friday.*   After breakfast, Capt. Carr, Mr. B., Patty, and I set out in packet for Newport ; have a pleasant gale and clear skies, and in 4 1/2 hours arrive at the wharf in Newport, and dine at Amie's, where we engage lodgings ; none were sick.

7. *Saturday.*   Dine at Mr. Wickam's with Mrs. Browne and her two daughters.   Patty rides out with Dr. Tupper, who alarms her much by telling her that she is inclined to an hectic habit.   In the afternoon Mrs. Browne and I, the Captain, Blaney, and a number of gentlemen and ladies, ride, and some walk out, some to Malbone's Garden, some to Redwood's, several of us at both ; are

entertained very agreeably at each place ; tea, coffee, cakes, syllabub, and English beer, etc., [and] punch and wine. We return at evening ; hear a song of Mrs. Shaw's and are highly entertained ; the ride, the road, the prospects, the gardens, the company, in short, everything was most agreeable, most entertaining — was admirable.

8. *Sunday.* [In the] morning we go up in a packet for Providence, and arrive in 3 1/2 hours, and dine at Mr. Oliver's ; there being a little rain all went into the cabin, and the wind being high and the passage rough, some began to complain a little of sickness, and all of us, retaining the motion of the vessel, rested ourselves, and did not go out to church.

9. *Monday.* Two stages set out for Boston, and I do not go, being told that several will be ready to go on Tuesday ; so Mr. O. and I go about to visit the Tombs, the Town House, and the Library there, Mr. Carter's bookstore, Mr. Foster, the lawyer, and his brother of the Brookfield family, sons of Judge Foster.

10. *Tuesday.* I went to the funeral of Mrs. Russell, by all agreed to be a most amiable person, and to sustain the best of characters ; she was a Quaker, and was carried into the meeting, where all appeared to be so affected that the speaker and hearers could scarce bear the sight or go on.

11. *Wednesday.* [In the] morning, at 5, we set out in [the] stage for Boston ; I take up the Capt.'s cane and bring it home ; we arrive at Boston in the evening about 8 o'clock ; a French young gentleman was one of our company who came over with the Marquis De La Fayette.

12. *Thursday.* At Boston, I call on Mrs. Waldo, on Mr. Bowdoin, on Mrs. Rea ; dine at Mrs. Mascarene's with Mr. and Mrs. Slater ; set out for Salem in the after-

noon, and arrive at 8 o'clock ; I write to Bro. Pynchon, and hear his family have removed to live at Shelburne.

13. *Friday.* A fine, warm day. Mitchell Sewall, on his return from Boston, calls on us. Wrote in answer to M. Bliss, Esq.

14. *Saturday.* Clear and warm. John Parker here from Boston. Sam'l Orne no better ; he continues yet at Danvers ; he went thither last Tuesday, and little Caty came down to tarry with us. Mr. and Mrs. Lowell, son and daughter, came in the stage to Mr. Cabot's.

15. *Sunday.* A fine, warm day. Mr. Smith preaches all day for Mr. Barnard. John Higginson here on Thursday, Friday, Saturday, and this day several times, and it is supposed that he has left his master's brother and Thorndike.

16. *Monday.* A fine day. In evening at Mr. Wetmore's at tea, and at Mr. Turner's dancing-school — a large collection of young people, two large sets. Mr. Blaney returns from Providence ; at Dr. Holyoke's in the evening with the Club. I finish my letter to Moses Bliss, Esq.

18. *Wednesday.* Cloudy. Mr. Orne dines here. Dr. Prince comes in from Halifax.

19. *Thursday.* Cloudy. Dr. Prince is graciously received here by all ranks, even by the intolerant G. W.'s and T. M-n. I wrote by J. Grafton to Mr. Oliver at Providence, and to Mrs. Browne at Newport. I go to Danvers as to Gridley *v.* Moriarty.

20. *Friday.* A fine, clear day. I go to Mr. Goodhue's at his desire, respecting Mrs. Lynde's affair of the plate, but Mr. Goodhue declines taking it till Mr. Fitch or Mr. Browne shall come.

21. *Saturday.* I write by Capt. Lanjevais to Brother Pynchon. Sent the horse to Phelps' bare pasture.

24. *Tuesday.* Cloudy; wind N. E. Wrote to S. Phillips, Jr., Esq., as to N. Sparhawk. Sent the horse from Phelps' to Waters'.

25. *Wednesday.* A fine, cool day. I go to Mr. Fisher's and to the Assembly Room. In the evening Fra. Cabot came into Beverly in a jolly boat; he left the ship in the bay to pursue his voyage to Boston, having been 60 days on the voyage from Bristol; Mr. Cabot calls to see us in the evening. John's friend, Gatchell, of Marblehead, dines with us to-day. I have a letter from J. Sewall, Esq., and from J. Bartlett; poor Jane Sewall is gone to rest.

26. *Thursday.* A fine day; somewhat cloudy. Wrote to Mr. Oliver by Mr. Swain. I have a letter from Mr. Atherton, and answer it by Mr. Dennis.

28. *Saturday.* Cloudy, but warm. Go to the exhibition at Mr. Noyes' school, and in evening at Mr. Higginson's with Dr. Prince, Dr. Putnam, and Mr. Goodale. Have letters from Providence by Mr. Grafton.

29. *Sunday.* A fine, clear, warm day. Miss Blake and co., of Carolina, at church.

30. *Monday.* A very warm morning. Mr. and Mrs. Fisher here, and Mrs. Gerrish. Billy Wetmore is more than happy with his present of marbles.

31. *Tuesday.* A very warm morning; clear. Mr. Hunt here from Boston, Mr. Orne also. It rains, thunders, and lightens at night. We are at Mr. Goodale's with Mr. Noyes and two Carolina young gentlemen. Mrs. Robie and daughter and Mrs. Johonnot dined at Mr. Goodale's to-day, and Mrs. Higginson and her daughter, Hitty, meet them there; have a cool meeting indeed!

September 1. *Wednesday.* Cloudy. Letter from Mr. Sparhawk.

2. *Thursday.* Cloudy day, and cool. Mrs. Robie comes over with her daughter to go to Halifax. I answer Mr. Sparhawk for orders to take Abbot's land, and that I cannot take it without orders, and cannot compel payment of the money.

3. *Friday.* Mrs. McCauley in town. Dr. Prince sails with Mrs. Robie and daughter for Halifax; Mr. Goodale goes out with them, and his son F. I send Mr. Deblois goods per list. At 3 P. M., John returns from Ipswich with Kimball, glutted with musick, weddings, and frolicking, 't is to be hoped.

4. *Saturday.* Cloudy. I settle with Gen'l Dodge of Ipswich.

5. *Sunday.* Cool morning ; wind E. Mr. Fisher preached two excellent sermons at church to-day ; Mrs. Orne came to church.

9. *Thursday.* A fine, cool day. Dr. Holyoke, Goodale, and co. go to Phillips' beach. Letters from S. Curwen, Esq., and Mr. Lane, etc., by Trecothick's ship. Mr. Cabot is expected to come in Calahan.

10. *Friday.* Warm day. News of Capt. Johnson's arrival from London into Boston, and that Messrs. Curwen, Cabot, Bartlett, Pickman, etc., had sailed for America about the time of Johnson's sailing ; he had about 32 days' passage. Mr. D. Oliver brings John's pistols from Bartlett. Mrs. Curwen puts on her silks, etc., expecting the squire in the stage, but lo, the stage arrives without him !

11. *Saturday.* Cool morning ; wind E. Mr. Orne comes, and Mr. and Mrs. Clark, to see Sam'l O.

12. *Sunday.* A fine, cool morning ; wind S. I go to church in the morning ; strangers in my pew ; I sit in Mr. Wetmore's. Mr. D. Oliver here in the evening ; gives no pleasing account of London, nor of anything in

13

Ireland or England agreeable to him, save the dramatic performances.

13. *Monday.*   Clear and cool.   Very little business in the judicial line to be done.   Bot wrangles and calls names about G. Deblois' affair.

14. *Tuesday.*   Clear and fair and cold.   No money stirring, not enough to go to law with, tho' the last of arresting for September Court.   I had not at sunset received one dollar for the business of the day.   Bot is found in the wrong.

15. *Wednesday.*   Clear and cold.   I go with Stevens to Moriarty's to relieve him and help him out of his distresses ; his creditors and his bail have his body and estate, yet keep their suits going on to his distraction. Haraden and owners are getting together by the ears about the robberies and piracies, and dividing the spoil.

16. *Thursday.*   A cool morning ; wind N. W.   By Patterson we hear that Bartlett's goods have been taken from him, and that he is not coming out ; that B. Pickman's baggage is on board, but he stays behind, is going to France, and what not ; that W. Cabot is not coming. What aileth Patterson that he brings such improbable accounts ?

20. *Monday.*   Cloudy and cold.   Mr. Longfellow dines with me.   John returns from Marblehead.   Turner's scholars' ball at night — above 100 ladies.

21. *Tuesday.*   Cool morning.   A ship from London goes up to Boston ; look out for S. C.   Blaney comes about voyage to Providence.

22. *Wednesday.*   Clear and cold ; a frost last night. We hear of very bad weather in the bay.   Where are Calahan and Ingersoll ?

23. *Thursday.*   Cloudy ; wind S. and warm.   Mr. and Mrs. Cabot, Mr. and Mrs. Carpenter, here at tea.   Letters

from London, and none from Bartlett. Colo. Browne's house is sold at vendue to-day, with store and land. I spend the evening at Mr. Oliver's with Dr. Putnam, Mr. Goodale, and Noyes.

24. *Friday.* Very warm ; at night very foggy. Calahan gets into Boston, and W. Cabot lands there.

25. *Saturday.* Cloudy, foggy morning. At 4 P. M., Capt. Ingersoll gets into Boston, with Mr. Curwen on board ; Mrs. Curwen hath an hysterick fit on hearing the news ; Mr. Cabot, the father, is in high spirits, and offers to dance a minuet on this Saturday, and is satisfied that there is no sin in it. Colo. Pickman's family gloomy at his not returning.

26. *Sunday.* A fine, clear, and warm day. Mr. Boden and wife in town. Mr. Curwen comes home to his house ; Mrs. C. has fits. Mr. W. Cabot returns in the evening, *et gaudia quanta fuere !*

27. *Monday.* Cloudy ; N. E. wind. Mrs. Orne and Blaney defer their tour on account of the weather. John and I set out for Newbury Court, and lodge, Tudor in com[pany], at Piemont's, Ipswich.

28. *Tuesday.* Fine weather. Dine at Mr. Parsons'.

29. *Wednesday.* Fine day. Dine at Mr. Browne's.

30. *Thursday.* Dine at Mr. Bradbury's with the lawyers ; John with us.

October 2. *Saturday.* Clear, fine day. We set out from Newbury and arrived at Ipswich ; lodged at Homan's.

3. *Sunday.* A fine, clear morning. We get home at 9 o'clock to breakfast. W. Cabot, Carpenter, Noyes, etc., here in the evening. Great rejoicings in Salem for Capt. Haraden's success against Williams and co. about privateering matters ; *sic transit gloria mundi.*

5. *Tuesday.* A cool morning. We dine with Mr.

and Mrs. Curwen at Mr. Goodale's, and W. Cabot there also ; we are highly entertained with Mr. Curwen's accounts, anecdotes, etc., from England.

6. *Wednesday.*   A cool day.   Mr. Curwen in a great rage ; says he is fit only for Bedlam.

7. *Thursday.*   Mr. Curwen goes in a pet to Boston ; says he can't pay 15/ in the pound.

8. *Friday.*   A fine, cool day.   Mr. Curwen returns in good spirits.

9. *Saturday.*   The town talk is of the Collector S. Webb's doings and rudeness in seizing the Widow Pickman's furniture for taxes ; every one sympathizes with her and her friends on account of the indignity.   W. Cabot calls to see us.   Mr. Noyes at tea ; Mr. Goodale, Wetmore, Mrs. Goodale, and Susan Higginson in the evening.

11. *Monday.*   Set out with Mr. Wetmore in his chaise for Newbury Court, and get there about 3 o'clock P. M. ; no Court.

12. *Tuesday.*   Mr. Oliver and Sally, with their two daughters, Mrs. Browne, and her daughter, and Mrs. Orne return from Providence.

13. *Wednesday.*   We get home from Ipswich to breakfast, and find Mrs. Browne, lady of Gov. Browne of Bermuda, with her daughter and servant, at our house ; her child ill — very ill ; Mrs. Orne also with them.

14. *Thursday.*   A letter from Mr. Deblois of Halifax. Mrs. Browne's daughter keeps chamber ; her servant is taken ill, and has a fire also in kitchen chamber, and keeps bed.

15. *Friday.*   Doct. Whitaker goes off, and his family are to go off at night ; people begin to sue for security, but find his doors shut.   A warm night this.

16. *Saturday.*   Cloudy morning, but warm day.   Mrs.

Browne's daughter and servant grow worse; at eve Mrs. Browne hath Mr. Fisher to pray with them, and is in very great distress. I move my books and papers this evening to Mrs. Chandler's room, next to Mr. Blyth's.

17. *Sunday.*   Cold, N. E. wind.   Mrs. Browne's daughter and servant grow worse; the servant's speech fails, and hiccough increases; a note at church and one at Mr. Barnard's meeting is put up for them; Mr. Blaney calls and tarries the forenoon with Mrs. Browne, dines with us, and tarries till night.   The [servant] grows better, and the daughter not worse; our hopes increase that she yet may revive.

18. *Monday.*   Morning at 4 o'clock Mrs. Pynchon was called up by Mrs. T. Lee, who watched with Miss Browne, and found the child fainting; the child revived again soon; Dr. H[olyoke] too was called up and came. The servant-girl grows better apace; this circumstance affords much consolation to Mrs. B.

19. *Tuesday.*   Cloudy and warm.   I purchase a cord of walnut wood and bark for my new office.   This morning Miss Browne is apparently relieved.

21. *Thursday.*   Cool.   Last night we were called up again, and the doctor called up to Miss Browne, who grew worse.

23. *Saturday.*   A fine, moderate day.   I set out for Woburn on Mr. Sparhawk's business, and lodge at Toy's.

24. *Sunday.*   Morning I go to Billerica and put up at Pollard's; tea at Mr. White's.

25. *Monday.*   Return to Woburn to inquire further of Mr. Wyeth as to Stoddard's and Sparhawk's affairs. At night I return home, and find Mrs. Browne's daughter and servant grown better.   Sarah Martin taken ill of a cold.

26. *Tuesday.* Clear and cold.   The sick mending gradually.   Mrs. H. Derby to see Mrs. Browne in the evening.   Mr. Blaney here, complaining that, notwithstanding his great attachment to the ladies, he could persuade none to marry him.   Miss Gerrish was asked if she could not recommend him to some [one] who would accept him; she answered that she could.   But will she go and live at Wenham?   She answered that the lady would.   He desired the favour of her name; she answered it was A. Gerrish; can you object?   Oh, no, Miss Gerrish, but does Miss G. know that there are bears at Wenham?   She answered in the affirmative, and silenced him.

27. *Wednesday.* The sick folk grow better.   News that M. De La Fayette is coming to Salem.

28. *Thursday.*   Mr. Wheeler at Mr. Fisher's.   Prim. Goodale hath his hands full; no rest by day or night; the Marquis is coming!

29. *Friday.*   Cloudy morning.   The Marquis La Fayette comes to town attended by . . . coaches [and] other carriages, [and] young gentlemen on horseback; they alight at Mr. Goodale's and take some refreshment, and chat awhile; then the company, clergymen, including the modest Dr. W., and merchants and mechanics, walk through the streets, the rabble giving them three cheers at each corner, the co[mpany] all having their hats on except the Marquis; the co[mpany] dine at the Assembly Room, [and] Judge John Pickering reads off a speech to the Marquis; he returns it *memoriter*; the musick was . . . . ; they drank tea at S. Page's, and had a ball at the A. Room [in the] evening.   Mr. and Mrs. Oliver return from the ball; the French Chevalier walks a minuet with Miss Williams; the Marquis hath a stiff knee and danceth none; the room was full of ladies and gentlemen; they break up at half past 12 o'clock.

30. *Saturday.*   Cloudy and some wet.   The Marquis and suit went out of town at 5 A. M., to dine at Portsmouth.   The employment of each circle, club, and tea-table in Salem is in finding and proving and disputing as to neglects and affronts respecting the entertainments and ball for the Marquis.

31. *Sunday.*   Mrs. Sargent and Patty Pynchon come after meeting to see Mrs. Browne; Mr. Blaney comes also [as] mediator, and all goes on smoothly and cleverly.

November 1. *Monday.*   Mrs. Anne Clark died.[1]

2. *Tuesday.*   Clear and fair.   Mr. and Mrs. Cur[wen] differ; they sign contract.[2]

3. *Wednesday.*   A fine morning.   Miss C. Browne grows better daily.   See in Hall's paper the malicious publication of the 2d instant.

4. *Thursday.*   A fine day.   In the frolic at Marblehead they all get groggy as soon as the Marquis left them, having broken his windows.

5. *Friday.*   Cool and fair.   Daland goes to Providence.   Dr. Paine and wife and child come from Halifax.

---

[1] Mrs. Clark was the relict of Captain John Clark.

[2] Although disturbed by the political troubles of the time, Mr. Curwen was much depressed and embittered by a domestic cloud that cast a shadow over the later years of his life.   The following extract from a letter from London, dated September 16, 1785, was addressed to a friend in Salem : —

" Should she [Mrs. Curwen] obstinately resolve to live and die in Salem, though that period, notwithstanding her hystericky habit, will be more distant than mine, whenever it may arrive, 't is my express and peremptory order, command, and injunction on my heirs that on no consideration her dead body be entombed with my late niece or any of my family, being unwilling that her dust should be mixed with that of a family to which she bore enmity; and I should not be a little deranged in the Resurrection morning to find Abigail Curwen starting up by my side ; for I am very sure, however I may forgive, I cannot wholly forget the wrong she has done me ; and to be put out of sorts at a season so solemn and important is too mortifying a thought to indulge."

7. *Sunday.* Cool and fair. Mr. Curwen and Mrs. Browne at church; he leaves the Communion, she partakes. I see Miss H. Lynde at tea, the only sight I have had of her for 25 years.

8. *Monday.* A very clear and fine morning. Miss Browne grows stronger daily, and Mrs. Browne's affairs as to Blyth, the church, and meeting matters are in a fair way.

9. *Tuesday.* The Sup[erior] Court meet.

13. *Saturday.* Cloudy and wet; at night it rains. The Court sit, and at night receive in [a] verdict of acquittal of Welcom on [an] indictment for assaulting Palfrey; the Court dines at Mr. Wetmore's.

14. *Sunday.* Cloudy and wet, after a short space of sunshine this morning. Judges Cushing and Sewall go to Mr. Barnard's meeting with Mr. Paine and Mr. Goodhue; P. M., J. Cushing goes to church, and he, with Sewall, Paine, Blaney, Mr. Noyes, etc., drink tea with me; Mrs. Browne comes down and is introduced.

15. *Monday.* A fine, fair day. Mrs. Browne and daughter go up to Mr. Orne's in Daland's carriage, dine there, and return at night. Miss B. is unwell and feverish at night, but on the whole rests pretty well.

16. *Tuesday.* A very clear and fine morning. At about 11 o'clock Mrs. Browne and family, with Mr. Blaney, set out in Daland's coach for Providence; at parting Mrs. Browne was much overcome, so that she could not take leave in form of her friends. Mr. Murray here.

18. *Thursday.* A fine day; a few clouds P. M.; at night some rain. The Sup[erior] Court is still sitting, and this day Mat. Fairfield is on tryal for uttering counterfeit State notes.

19. *Friday.* Rain. Fairfield is acquitted. Haraden's cause comes on at evening.

20. *Saturday.* A fine, fair day. The Judges agree to dine with me to-morrow, with Mr. Lowell.

21. *Sunday.* Rain in the morning, and the Judges can't come. J. Sewall sets out for York. At evening Mr. Parsons and Wetmore come at tea.

22. *Monday.* A fine day. The Court meets, and at noon adjourns to 2d Tuesday [in] June.

23. *Tuesday.* A very fine day. Stevens sick, and very few writs to be served.

24. *Wednesday.* Mr. and Mrs. and Miss Wetmore here in the evening, and Miss Gerrish.

25. *Thursday.* Thanksgiving. Mr. and Mrs. Goodale keep house. We dine at F. Cabot's. News of Morris being robbed of his plate, and Continental Treasury of . . . dollars.

26. *Friday.* Rain and cloudy; N. E. wind. Last night the tide rose to greater height than any remember. Bacon says it was navel high on the bridge by Mr. Ward's; if so, it must have come up to the top of Bacon's yard wall.

December 4. *Saturday.* Andrews, the Collector, absconds.

7. *Tuesday.* I deliver to Capt. Brookhouse Mr. Curwen's and my letters for Judge Sewall at Bristol, *via* Liverpool.

9. *Thursday.* Very cold. I write to Mr. Oliver, and inclose my letter to Gov. Browne's lady at Newport, inclosing copies of Mrs. Sargent's two deeds made to her son Dudley.

10. *Friday.* Account of the failure of Cruger and Company at Bristol.

11. *Saturday.* Morning, the Court adjourns without day. I spend the evening at Mr. Curwen's very agreeably; all in good humour.

12. *Sunday.*   Mas. Williams and his bride go to church, attended by his daughter, and all is harmony . hitherto ; but mark the end.

13. *Monday.*   Mr. Stiles's sermon at Club.   Tom. Needham, Jr., absconds and

14. *Tuesday.* Is seen at his chamber window. Widow Pickering's funeral ;[1] Deacon Bickford, Gray, D. King.

16. *Thursday.* A fine morning. L. Seaver solicits letters of license for his bro[ther], T. Needham, who says many gentlemen [are] shut up for less than he.

19. *Sunday.* Morning, very windy and a snow-squall ; it clears off about 10 o'clock ; the evening was clear after 9 ; I spent it at T. Lee's with Mrs. Anderson.

20. *Monday.* Cloudy and cold. Messrs. Pulling and Osgood go to Boston. I go with Stevens on John Hunt's business to Dr. A. Putnam's.

21. *Tuesday.* Moderate weather. H. Derby threatens to ruin Carpenter and Clarke, declaring them not to be worth a groat, and that he would strip their shop. Mrs. Goodhue and Susan, W. Cabot, Carpenter, A. Gerrish, and co.

22. *Wednesday.* Snow, rain, hail, *vicissim.* Carpenter and co. propose making over shop and goods to secure themselves and creditors, and to prevent Derby's designs to break them up. Pulling and Osgood at Boston ; a thin Assembly. John at Ipswich. H. Derby and Carpenter and Clarke kick up a dust.

23. *Thursday.* A very cold night was the last. E. H. Derby threatens to seize all the goods of Carpenter and Clarke.

24. *Friday.* Very cold. Poultry sells for 5*d.* and 6*d.*, mutton 4*d.*, beef 3½*d.*

25. *Saturday.* Cold Christmas. Mrs. P. ill, and I

---

[1] Mrs. Mary, relict of Deacon Timothy Pickering ; her age was 76.

confined by a cold, we dine by ourselves at a good, warm fire. Mr. and Mrs. Curwen spend the evening with us. At night N. Rogers and co. and J. Peirce attach Carpenter and Clarke's store and goods. Query the event, if not removed.

27. *Monday.* Carpenter makes proposals to Derby.

29. *Wednesday.* Some snow. Mr. Sears in town. Carpenter rejects Derby's proposals, and brings him to consent to his own ; his uncle C——t talks high, and will not be bound for any man ; Carpenter tells him he had no thought of asking him.

30. *Thursday.* Carpenter's friends do not wholly desert him, but agree this day to be sureties for him. Mr. Barrett here.

31. *Friday.* Cloudy and cold, snow air. John has under consideration Mr. Wetmore's proposal of his office. Mr. William Amory here from Newburyport, and John sets out with him in the storm, and to return Saturday morning. This day John went over to Mr. Wetmore's office.

1785. *January* 1. *Saturday.* Mr. and Mrs. Cabot consented to our using the eastern room for an office, we to keep the floor covered, and keeping and using the room carefully ; and P. M. we moved all from Chapman's house.

4. *Tuesday.* Mr. Wetmore goes to Boston. John continues at his office. Mr. Blaney, Mrs. Wetmore, and Mr. Phillips here in the evening.

5. *Wednesday.* Good sledding ; wood from 18/ to 21/.

6. *Thursday.* S. Page and Fogarty begin a lawsuit and quarrel.

7. *Friday.* A fine day. Vast quantities of wood.

8. *Saturday.* A great quantity of turkeys and poultry brought to market, 4*d.* to 5*d.*

9. *Sunday.*   A fine day. At church P. M.   Mrs. Pynchon ill, and keeps chamber.

10. *Monday.*   Snow and rain by turns. Wood in plenty ; mutton 3*d.*, poultry 4 1/2 and 5*d.* I find my lost book, Hist. of Charles 5th, at Mr. Curwen's. Fogarty put to bail by S. Page for £3000 ; goes to jail.

11. *Tuesday.*   Fine sledding. Fogarty comes out of jail.

12. *Wednesday.*   Some wet and snow. Mr. Goodale and lady, Mr. and Mrs. Wetmore, here at tea in Mrs. Pynchon's chamber. Colo. Gallison here about Lee's estate and the execution.

13. *Thursday.*   Very cold and blustering ; plenty of wood and provisions, it being excellent sledding.

14. *Friday.*   Fine sledding and cold yet. Mr. Wetmore's father comes to town.

15. *Saturday.*   Cloudy. Mr. Wetmore and his father [and] Mr. Noyes here at tea and in the evening. Dr. Holyoke's papers are lost.

16. *Sunday.*   Windy and snow, and very cold. Mr. Wetmore, the father, spends the evening here. I write to brother Pynchon at Guilford by Mr. Wetmore.

18. *Tuesday.*   Rains and thaws. I find Dr. Holyoke's lost paper, *et gaudia quanta fuere !* Mrs. Pynchon comes below to dine.

20. *Thursday.*   Clear and cool, and sledding revives. I write to J. Abbot as to Sparhawk, and to the latter as to Abbot and Mr. Phillips.

22. *Saturday.*   News of trouble at Mr. Gould's as to boarders ; poor Noyes !

24. *Monday.*   Church meeting for sale of pews. At Mr. Curwen's in the evening ; R. Ward there with the Clubb. Mrs. Nimmo taken ill with [a] fit of fever and ague at my house. She settles with some of the rioters ; others stand out and threaten her.

25. *Tuesday.* Mrs. Nimmo goes home P. M. and meets with more trouble.

26. *Wednesday.* Mrs. Nimmo is carried to Beverly on warrant for false news.

28. *Friday.* A fine morning, cool and clear. Mr. and Mrs. Wetmore here at evening.

29. *Saturday.* Snow. Capt. Baker calls me up as to Thomas Porter's affairs. John Felt of Danvers dies.

30. *Sunday.* Very cold. I go to church A. M., but P. M. am detained by Capt. Bartlett on business of necessity. In the evening Dr. Lloyd came to see Mr. Dowse, who survived only long enough to know, without ability to speak to the Dr. John spends the evening with [the] ladies at Mr. Wetmore's.

31. *Monday.* A very cold day, though clear ; fine sledding. Mr. Paine [and] Mr. and Mrs. Orne dine here. News of the day is that Gov'r Hancock hath proposed to the Court to resign the Government ; Mr. Dana is nominated for Puisne Judge of [the] Superior Court. President Willard greatly endangered by [a] mad horse in the ferry-boat, which struck him down by his forefoot. Mr. Dowse's funeral to be on Thursday next.

February 1. *Tuesday.* Very cold, and some snow this morning. Dr. Paine sets off for Boston and Worcester. Much snow falls this night. Mr. and Mrs. Orne lodge at Mrs. Pickman's, not being able to come out for the snow.

2. *Wednesday.* The snow is deep and drifted, and it continues snowing. John spends the evening at T. Williams's, and part of it at Mrs. Wetmore's with the ladies ; *mirum !*

3. *Thursday.* It snows still. The storm prevents the funeral ; it to be next Monday.

4. *Friday.*   No wood and little provisions, by reason of the depth of the snow and its being much drifted.

5. *Saturday.*   The bearers for the funeral : —

Mr. Williams,	J. Ropes,
Mr. Pynchon,	Mr. Mackey,
G. Dodge,	Mr. Wait.

6. *Sunday.*   Excessive cold this morning.   P. M., I go to church.   Mr. Curwen spends the evening with me.

7. *Monday.*   Clear and moderate.   Dowse's funeral : some of his brother's family come from Boston ; the corpse is carried into the church ; a number of singers from the other meetings, men and women, with a bass viol ; a good discourse on mortality.

8. *Tuesday.*   Morn clear and moderate.   I receive Gen'l Warren's letter.

9. *Wednesday.*   Brother Stephen here.   John goes to the Assembly.

11. *Friday.*   Clear and moderate.   John Williams is at Boston.   T. F. Oliver comes.

12. *Saturday.*   Wet ; at night it snows.   S. Orne grows worse.   Mr. Oliver and Lynde dine with me ; the mutton very excellent.   J. Grafton grows worse.   John Williams is to attempt taking his seat in the House.

13. *Sunday.*   Snows and blows.   S. Orne very low indeed.   Mr. Oliver here in the evening, and Mr. Goodale.

14. *Monday.*   Clear and cold ; the snow much drifted and very deep.   Club at Dr. Holyoke's in the evening.

16. *Wednesday.*   Moderate, some snow A. M.   Wrote to Mrs. R. Browne and to J. Williams by Mr. Oliver, who sets out in the stage.

19. *Saturday.*   A fine, cool morning, and plenty of wood comes in.   I send to Dr. Wingate Gen'l Warren's costs, £3.12.0, by Mr. Payson.   *Sic ista mat. dormit.*   At

evening John Williams comes to town from Boston, having taken his seat in the House of Repps.

20. *Sunday.* Clear and cool. J. Williams comes A. M. to see us ; dines at Mr. Orne's. Mr. Green, from Beverly, visits John.

21. *Monday.* Moderate and cloudy weather. I wait on the Assessors with a general account, and they ask for more particulars ; query the event.

22. *Tuesday.* Clear and moderate. Bro. Mitchell comes ; is deeply disordered.

24. *Thursday.* S. Orne is buried. Bearers : —

N. Ropes,   J. Gardner,

J. Pynchon,   Mr. Hodges,

J. Sanders.

26. *Saturday.* News that N. Tracey's estate at Cambridge and at Newburyport is attached. Welch at Boston fails.

27. *Sunday.* At church P. M. J. Grafton better. Mrs. Waldo and Mr. Wetmore go to Boston.

28. *Monday.* News of Mr. Tracey's whole estate attached in Essex and Middlesex. Mitchell goes to Marblehead with John. The affair of Boston bridge settled in General Court. Mr. Blaney returns.

March 2. *Wednesday.* I go with Dr. Holyoke to the Assembly, and spend a most sociable and agreeable evening.

4. *Friday.* Plenty of wood, though bad sledding. Evening at Mr. Wetmore's.

5. *Saturday.* Snows and thaws ; wood from 22/ to 24/ per cord. Mr. Curwen [in] the evening at my house.

7. *Monday.* Mr. and Mrs. Curwen and Miss Atkins, afternoon and evening.

8. *Tuesday.* Evening, Mrs. Holyoke and Peggy at tea ; at evening, Mr. Blaney, S. Sewall, Kimball, and

J. Sanders ; Ste. tarries here.   Mr. Wilds comes, having been ill.

9. *Wednesday*.   Hail and rain.   Bro. Stephen goes to Marblehead, John to Ipswich ; Kimball here.   Letters from Virginia.

10. *Thursday*.   A fine, clear morning ; good sledding. John proposes a voyage to Baltimore.

11. *Friday*.   Spend the afternoon at Mr. Cabot's, and [drink] tea ; evening at Mrs. Reb. Cabot's.[1]

12. *Saturday*.   A fine, clear morning.   At Mr. Dowse's apprizement A. M., with Mess. Derby and Goodhue.

15. *Tuesday*.   A clear morning.   At town meeting yesterday ; a large majority of votes at a full town meeting were for demolishing the old town house and brick school house, and for erecting a spacious town house by the Tabernacle, and dividing the school, placing one at each end of the town.   W. Amory comes P. M. and lodges with John.   Mrs. Orne at 9 in the evening goes with Dr. Paine, Mrs. Paine, and Mrs. Pickman to see her husband, and lodgeth there ; returns to us in the morning.

16. *Wednesday*.   Cloudy, snows and blows.   Mrs. Orne comes home ; at night sends word by Dr. Paine to Mrs. Cabot that when wanted she is ready to go tend Mr. Orne.

17. *Thursday*.   Exceeding cold.   Mr. Ward here from Lancaster.

18. *Friday*.   Eayres here.   Mrs. Orne is sent for by Mrs. Cabot ; goes and tarries ; her letter was delivered by Emanuel this morning.

---

[1] Rebecca Orne, who married Joseph Cabot, was born July 17, 1748, and died November 17, 1818.   Their son, Joseph, married Esther Orne Paine, who, after Mr. Cabot's death in November, 1799, married Ichabod Tucker. One of the grandchildren, Joseph Sebastian, married, first, Martha Stearns, and secondly, Susan Burley Howes, who now resides in Boston.

19. *Saturday*. Cloudy and cool. Dr. Paine and Mrs. Paine set off for Boston yesterday. Mr. and Mrs. Lowell in Salem.

20. *Sunday*. At home all day. Mr. Curwen in the evening.

21. *Monday*. Stephen and Mitchell here at [a] meeting of the Social Library. Mr. and Mrs. Lowell return to Boston.

22. *Tuesday*. Bro. Mitchell comes from Mr. Goodale's and lodgeth with us.

23. *Wednesday*. Mitchell sets out for Portsmouth without notice.

24. *Thursday*. A fine, clear morning ; very cool. About 10 o'clock Jack set out for Virginia, and goes on board Schooner . . . , Capt. Peirce ; his dog was grieved to the heart that he could not go with his master.

25. *Friday*. Cloudy ; wind N. W. ; raw, cold. Dr. Tupper here the night.

26. *Saturday*. Clear and cool ; wind N. W. At Mrs. Higginson's in the evening.

27. *Sunday*. Cloudy and cool ; wind N. E. A good wind for Jack and co. Mr. Goodale, Noyes, Mrs. Goodale, and Miss Higginson, and Mrs. Orne, here in the evening, all wishing Jack a safe arrival in Baltimore.

28. *Monday*. Cloudy, and wind at S. W. F. Grant absconds.

29. *Tuesday*. Cheever takes poor Sorrel and carries him off ; the kitchen is in mourning ; Ah ! Sorrel ! what will thy master Jack say ? Hast thou too left me ? Alas ! poor Sorrel !

April 1. *Friday*. Fair weather. At one o'clock came through the street 2 officers and J. T., Esqr., with a rabble round them ; they were carrying Mr. T. to jail upon execution for £225 ; he was in his slippers, wading through mud and wet ; they stopped at the tavern, and the people were enraged at the officer ; the gentlemen directly undertook to be answerable for Mr. T., to deliver the body or the money or sufficient security by Saturday night ; Mr. S., of Boston, son-in-law to Mr. T., was sent for by Mrs. Gardner.

2. *Saturday.*   At 12 o'clock Mr. S. comes, and P. M. gives his security with J. Norris for debt and costs, and Mr. T. is relieved.

4. *Monday.*   Snow and foul weather.   Extraordinary things done to-day are the agreement made with Jos. Flint, Jr., and with Jos. Endicot.

5. *Tuesday.*   Mr. Pulling and I set out with Ben. Daland for Ipswich Court ; in many places the snow was higher than the walls by the way, and in some places no sign of the wall appeared ; we went in Daland's slay, 2 horses, and in about 6 hours got within a mile of the town, and hearing of the adjournment of the Court, we returned, and arrived at Salem about 1/2 after 6 o'clock.

6. *Wednesday.*   Mr. Tudor here.   A fine, fair morning. Mr. Parsons, Pulling, etc. here, P. M., and in the evening.

8. *Friday.*   Cloudy, rain and snow.   At evening Mr. Wetmore, Mrs. Orne, Smith, and W. Cabot here at whist.   Rains in the evening.

10. *Sunday.*   Clear and moderate.   Sa. Clough dreamt that Jack comes home in the Astræa before the mast ; Sar. Martin says she shall dream about him soon, and then can tell for *sarting* whether there is a jot of truth in Sar. Clough's dream.

11. *Monday.*   A clear day.   The roads in Wenham and Ipswich impassable on horseback ; the riders dismount and walk by their horses.

12. *Tuesday.*   A clear, cool morning.   Bad news from

England relating to our trade and want of success in the Com[mercial] Treaty with Britain.

13. *Wednesday.* A fair and cool day. I have [a] letter from R. Lechmere, Taunton, England, and of W. Cabot [with] the balloon news from Blanchard and Jeffries' tour from Dover to Calais.

14. *Thursday.* A fine day. News from Britain; letters from Mr. Bartlett as to his troubles.

15. *Friday.* Troubles yet in Boston.

16. *Saturday.* A fine day, cool air; snow deep in the country yet. S. H. grows very unpopular; every proposal he makes is opposed by the populace, and they propose sending home the Salem wizard.

18. *Monday.* A fine day. Miss Wetmore taken ill, and 't is feared may have a settled fever.

19. *Tuesday.* A cool, cloudy morning; rained hard at night. At Mr. Carpenter's in the evening and Mr. Blaney's.

20. *Wednesday.* Cloudy. Letters from J. Sewall and Frye; Miss Wetmore grows worse.

24. *Sunday.* A fine day. At church both parts of the day, and all very good.

25. *Monday.* Manuel Aston went away to get him a trade, and to live with Symonds, the baker.

26. *Tuesday.* Adjournment of Common Pleas; Court meets.

27. *Wednesday.* Wrote to A. Peabody, Portsmouth, as to Sam. Sawyer's debt to me, to know if he has received payment or security.

28. *Thursday.* Common Pleas and Sessions Causes; higgledy-piggledy, ding-dong.

29. *Friday.* The C. Justice having determined on Tuesday, breaks up the Court at Friday noon; about 300 new entries; no jury trial.

30. *Saturday.* Mr. Orne sent down his chaise with his daughter Caty, with his desire that Mrs. Orne should return home in the chaise to-day or to-morrow, as she should incline. I returned from Ipswich Court at one.

May 4. *Wednesday.* Mr. Curwen and I walk out on the Plains at evening.

5. *Thursday.* A fine, clear, and moderate day. At Mr. Fisher's ; at Mrs. Dowse's with D. Smith.

6. *Friday.* A very fine, warm morning ; P. M., the wind out at east. Mess. Curwen and Pulling set out with me on a visit to Mr. Orne at Danvers at 1/2 past two ; we return at 8, having had a pleasant walk ; Mrs. Gray and Mrs. Barnard there at tea.

9. *Monday.* A fine day. Mr. Wetmore returns from Boston with Mr. Waldo. Mrs. Safford, sister of Mrs. Goodale, is buried to-day.

10. *Tuesday.* Mr. Wetmore sets out for Falmouth with Mr. Waldo ; query, the roads.

11. *Wednesday.* A fine, clear morning. A fine time for Ordination at Beverly. Mr. Curwen, yesterday from Boston, gives an account of high doings there in canvassing for election ; the wizard is to be put up.

12. *Thursday.* We hear from Beverly that large provisions were prepared, and very few partakers, the boats being kept as ordered on the east side of the ferry ; the latter is improbable. At Boston, parties run high yet. Mr. Curwen and Dr. Smith call to see me.

13. *Friday.* A fine morning. Mr. Sparhawk here. Mr. Smith sets out for Petersham.

14. *Saturday.* Rains [a] good part of the day, and plentifully at night. Capt. Peirce returned in safety with son John. Peter Oliver and co. from Baltimore. Stephen Higginson and wife from Boston, where they must have had a belly full of politicks.

15. *Sunday.*   A fine day.   John at church ; Mr. Lee of Cambridge [1] and lady.   Rain at night.

17. *Tuesday.*   A fine, clear morning ; P. M., at the Fort with Mess. Curwen and Cabot.

21. *Saturday.*   J. Russell visits Mr. Curwen.

22. *Sunday.*   Cloudy.   Spent afternoon and evening at Mr. Curwen's with him *et ux.*, in good spirits ; Mr. Curwen concludes on going to England in Calahan.

23. *Monday.*   Cloudy and rain all day.   N. Ropes and Mr. Hastings from Halifax call to see me at tea. Dr. Prince, lady, and son and daughter come in from Halifax.

24. *Tuesday.*   Cloudy.   We go to see Mrs. Prince at J. Derby's.

25. *Wednesday.*   Mr. Oliver comes in from Providence.

26. *Thursday.*   Mr. Selkrig here.   Dr. Paine and family come from Boston.

27. *Friday.*   Mr. Curwen and I walk over to Waters' at evening.

28. *Saturday.*   Mr. Orne here.   I go with Stevens and Turell to Moriarty's, Danvers, as to the executions. Mr. Prince returns from Maryland.   S. Phillips, President of the Senate.

29. *Sunday.*   A fine day.   The church well filled. Yesterday morning Mrs. Pynchon set out for Providence in Mr. Grafton's chaise.

30. *Monday.*   A fine day ; warm P. M.   Mr. Curwen preparing for [his] voyage to England.

31. *Tuesday.*   A clear, fine day.   In the afternoon at Turner's dancing school with a large company.

June 1.   *Wednesday.*   A very pleasant, clear day.   A

---

[1] Judge Joseph Lee, H. C. 1722, was a loyalist, but moderate in his opinions.   He was a brother of Thomas Lee.

large company ; Mrs. Prince and co. dine at Mr. Good-ale's, and continue till evening, and sup there. Dr. Paine *et ux.* and Mrs. Prince at evening. Mr. Grafton returns from Providence without Mrs. Pynchon.

2. *Thursday.* At Newburyport, Tileston shuts up.

3. *Friday.* A pleasant day. Landlord Goodhue absconds, and all his estate attached.

4. *Saturday.* A fine, warm day. Dan'l Cheever fails and is attached. Last evening Mr. Oliver returns from Portsmouth, and to-day sets out for Newburyport.

5. *Sunday.* At church in the afternoon with Mr. C.

6. *Monday.* [While] at tea Mrs. Cabot was taken speechless suddenly and put to bed.

8. *Wednesday.* I went in Burrell's stage to Boston with Mr. Oliver and Polly.

9. *Thursday.* Meet the referees at Mr. Tudor's office ; again P. M.

10. *Friday.* Again A. M. Mrs. Nutting died ; P. M. I return in Newhall's stage.

12. *Sunday.* A clear, fine day. At church in the afternoon ; spend the evening at Mr. Oliver's.

13. *Monday.* A clear, warm day ; wind at S. W. Mrs. Cabot continues senseless. Mrs. Barrett Cabot and Miss Bromfield both come. Mrs. Nutting's funeral ; a very long procession. Bearers : —

Dr. Putnam,	Pynchon,
Dr. Holyoke,	G. Dodge,
John Sanders,	S. Holman.

14. *Tuesday.* A fine, cool morning. The Sup. Court meets on adjournment from November term.

16. *Thursday.* Mr. Parsons, etc., pass through town from Philadelphia. At night Mr. and Mrs. Lowell came to town. Mr. Amory dines with us.

17. *Friday.* Very warm A. M., but afternoon cloudy ;

thunder and rain. Mrs. Cabot's[1] funeral P. M.   It rains and thunders at 3 o'clock.

18. *Saturday.*   A fine day.   Mrs. Pynchon and co. dine with Mrs. Orne at Danvers ; also John Smith and co.

19. *Sunday.*   A fine day.   Mrs. Pynchon at Mr. Barnard's meeting ; he preached a good sermon upon mortality ; Mrs. Nutting and Mrs. Cabot both dead.

20. *Monday.*   A very warm day.   Mr. Bromfield comes for his sister Betsy.

21. *Tuesday.*   I go with Mr. Wetmore in his carriage to Ipswich Court.

25. *Saturday.*   The Court ended.

27. *Monday.*   Williams and co. begin again upon Captain Haraden with actions.

28. *Tuesday.*   The last day of suing for July Court. B. Pickman, Jr., came to my office to study law at the usual terms for studying agreed on, being £100.00.

29. *Wednesday.*   Mr. and Mrs. Wetmore set out for Falmouth.

30. *Thursday.*   I receive a friendly letter from my townsman and old friend, Colo. Worthington, at Boston, who hath borne, and continues to bear, indignities and insolence from pretended patriots and hypocrites with the fortitude of a brave man, detesting and despising the duplicity and meanness of many who, by cringing and crawling, have wriggled themselves into office and power.   L. Deblois, Jr., of Halifax, son of Lewis De-blois, dined here, and upon (hearing) of the sufferings of Mrs. Grant and family most generously and genteelly slip't a Jac[obus] into Mrs. P.'s hand for Mrs. Grant.

July 2. *Saturday.*   Very warm and dry.   Mr. Lee continues very ill.

---

[1] Mrs. Elizabeth, wife of Francis Cabot ; she was 68 years of age.

3. *Sunday.* Cloudy; in the afternoon a fine, moderate rain. Early this morning Mrs. Orne and Anne Grafton come from the Farm, and spend the day and return at night. W. Amory comes from Newburyport and returns at night.

4. *Monday.* A fine, cool day. At Mr. Goodale's in the evening with Mr. Cutts, B. Pickman, etc. Mr. Dwight with Mr. Dane called on me early in the morning.

5. *Tuesday.* A very fine day. F. Clarke calls loudly again. It rains finely in the night.

9. *Saturday.* A large company go to Mr. Orne's, some on foot and others in carriages and on horses, and spend the afternoon.

10. *Sunday.* A very fine day. Letters from Mr. Oliver respecting his taking orders ; and certificates and recommendations from the clergy to Bishop Seabury for the purpose.

12. *Tuesday.* A pleasant, warm day. The Court come into town about 12, and meet in Mr. Barnard's meeting-house at one o'clock.

14. *Thursday.* Sessions day, and hot. The meeting-house thronged with publicans, sinners, innholders, retailers, and justices ; no room for lawyers.

15. *Friday.* Pell-mell, helter-skelter, some for Sessions business, others for Common Pleas; some for the Grand Jury, others for the petit Jury. In commanding silence the H. Sheriff overstrains, which brings all to a loud laugh, and so to good humour.

16. *Saturday.* A very fine day. Mr. Deblois sets out for Boston. The Court adjourns without day in tolerable humour by noon. Miss Atkins leaves us ; we part with her reluctantly.

18. *Monday.* A fine, clear day. Dr. Holyoke raiseth a new story to his house.

19. *Tuesday.* Fine weather. We hear of Walker; he is going apace to the dogs.

20. *Wednesday.* About 5 o'clock Mess. W. Pickman, Barnard, Davis, L. Oliver, and self set out in Burrell's coach for Commencement. Arrive there at 9. The performances at meeting so so ; an English oration by Ware[1] well composed, delivered with plainness. Gov. Bowdoin is courteous and growing very popular. We return to Salem about 10 at evening.

22. *Friday.* A warm day. Mr. Hitchcock and wife here from Providence.

23. *Saturday.* A warm day. Mr. Hitchcock makes us a visit, also T. Parsons ; he reads us Gov. Bowdoin's answer to the address ; it is long and learned. Yesterday, the town at a meeting, by a very full vote, concur with the Sessions as to building a court-house, and to pull down the brick school-house and the old town-house ; fears that the Courts may be removed to Ipswich effected what, it seems, nothing else could ; but to spoil all, they propose to sell the land where the old town-house stood. At night Mr. Parker,[2] a collegian, here.

24. *Sunday.* A fine, clear morning ; wind N. W. Mess. S. Higginson and Dickinson, agent of Lanes and Co., go to Beverly on affairs of accounts, and call here at Mr. Cabot's. S. Page died P. M., about 5 o'clock. Mr. Greenwood *et ux.* part ; she goes to Wenham.

25. *Monday.* A very fine day ; wind N. W. Brother Stephen Sewall *et ux.* and son call on us in the morning; he in ill health. The workmen are preparing to pull down the school-house and the old town-house ; the library is removed to Capt. J. Derby's house.

---

[1] Rev. Dr. Henry Ware, afterwards Hollis professor at Cambridge. He died in 1845.

[2] Isaac Parker, H. C. 1786, afterward Chief Justice of the Superior Court, and representative to Congress. He died in 1830.

27. *Wednesday*. Mrs. Curwen moves into Mrs. Hays', western end of Clark's house.

28. *Thursday*. Mess. Parker, Bass,[1] and Fisher call and drink punch with me. Plentiful rain in the night.

29. *Friday* Rain in the morning and parts of the day. Young Mr. Gannet calls here P. M.

30. *Saturday*. A fine, cool day. Debo. Cabot and Mrs. George Cabot here, and return at evening. Young Mr. Cabot is taken with a severe fit of nervous headache. This morning I send to Boston a letter for Mr. Curwen in London.

31. *Sunday*. Fair and cool in the morning. Mrs. Pynchon at home all day, but her *mari* at church all day ! ! !

August 1. *Monday*. A fine, warm, and clear day. Church meeting for sale of pews adjourned to the 15th day.

2. *Tuesday*. A fine, pleasant day, warm ; cloudy P. M. Mr. Barnard and I go to Woburn in his carriage on his business as to Execution *v.* Edwards, Tidd *et al.*, and get to Richardson's in the evening.

3. *Wednesday*. We return to Salem by 2. The weather warm.   Town-meeting P. M. ; vote to sell the land on which the old town-house stood ; 43 against 29. Mr. and Mrs. Lowell and 4 children at Mr. Cabot's. Mr. Reed, from Cambridge, with Mr. Noyes, here.

4. *Thursday*. Clear and very pleasant. Mess. Lowell and company set out for Portsmouth in the morning. Mr. Blaney here last evening. Mrs. Williams, wife of John Williams, died.

5. *Friday*. A pleasant day. Mr. Blaney here in the evening. Mrs. Pynchon at Mrs. Lynde's and Mrs. Holyoke's.

---

[1] Edward Bass was the first, and Samuel Parker the second, bishop of Massachusetts.

6. *Saturday.* A fine rain. I take tea first at Mr. Cabot's, then at Mrs. Pickman's with the girls, and brother Blaney not there !!! Clerk Osgood is very good in Dane and Blanchard. I write further to Mr. Robie, Mr. Walter, and Mr. Deblois, and Mrs. Pynchon to Mrs. Cotnam.

7. *Sunday.* A fine, cool day ; wind S. W. Wyatt ready to sail for Halifax with Mrs. Prince and family and Miss P. Walter. Mr. L. Oliver sets out for Boston this morning in his way to Providence, his brother being taken ill. W. Amory here and returns P. M. to Newbury.

8. *Monday.* A cool and clear day. Wyatt sails with Mr. Prince. Mr. Cabot burns his will with some appearance of malediction. Vans scrambles with Mr. Wetmore.

9. *Tuesday.* We have letter by Mr. and Mrs. Jenkins of Providence from daughter Sally. Vans scrambles and scolds at Wetmore.

10. *Wednesday.* A very fine morning. Mr. Jenkins sets out early for Newbury. A company go to Lynn ; Phillips to spend the day ; Smith, Pickman, and Jack to Burdock's.

11. *Thursday.* Convention of Church Clergy proposed, to promote uniformity of publick worship and make needful alterations in the Church Service, especially to shorten the morning service. Mr. Lowell and family.

12. *Friday.* Moderate and cool. Mr. Lowell and company go for Boston. P. M., cloudy and rain.

16. *Tuesday.* A fine, clear morning ; wind S. W. Mr. Waldo comes from Falmouth. Billy Wetmore goes to Ipswich school.

17. *Wednesday.* Smith, Pickman, Jack, and co. go for Flax Pond to spend the day ; Jack does right as to partner !!

18. *Thursday.*   D. Smith comes ; sells Mr. Dowse's house at auction.   Mr. Watson and co. here.

19. *Friday.*   Cloudy and wind N. W., and cool.   Jack went to Danvers on a fishing and fowling match on Wednesday evening, and is not yet returned.

20. *Saturday.*   A fine, pleasant day.   Mr. Cabot ill yet, is daily in pain ; his friends grow fearful of his disorder.   S. Higginson *et ux.* come to town.   L. Oliver returns from Providence with a letter from his brother. All there as well as usual.   He brings no news of J. Grafton and Patty ; they, to be sure, had some business in the other road to Newport.   Mr. and Mrs. Wetmore return from Mr. Cutler's ; leave little Billy very well and contented at school there.   .

21. *Sunday.*   A very clear and fine morning.   S. Higginson at Mr. Cabot's in the evening.

22. *Monday.*   A fine morning ; wind south.   Mr. and Mrs. Jenkins from Newbury call and lodge with us. The land on which the old town-house stood is sold.

23. *Tuesday.*   Our guests depart for Providence. A cloudy day, but the wished for rain cometh not. J. Grafton returns from sea, better.

24. *Wednesday.*   A fine, clear morning; all signs of rain fail.   The new town-house rises apace with the growling of the people about taxes.   Fogarty and Watkins keep close.

25. *Thursday.*   Cloudy P. M., and rain in the evening. A turtle frolick at Leach's.   Vans grows impudent and intolerable.

26. *Friday.*   Fine and cool morning.   Jos. Grafton and Patty Pynchon return from Providence.

27. *Saturday.*   A fine, clear, warm morning.   The streets full of provisions, but I have not a copper to lay out.   My neighbours in like circumstances and can't

lend me any.   Can there be a plainer case?   We must surely be content to go without any.   What a fine thing it is to have company in streights!   Whether it be so in times of wealth and plenty we know it.

28. *Sunday.*   A fine day.   Dr. Putnam at church A. M. P. Oliver P. M.   Some rain at night.   I find my cane at Southick's.

29. *Monday.*   Billy Wetmore went to Mr. Cutler's at Ipswich.   The Club at Colo. Pickman's in the evening.

30. *Tuesday.*   Cloudy and little rain ; in the evening a plentiful rain.   Mr. Cabot and Mrs. Pynchon ride out, also Mr. West and Sophia Cabot.

September 1.   *Thursday.*   Mr. and Mrs. Wetmore and the child set out for Boston.

2. *Friday.*   John goes to Mr. Orne's with F. Goodale in his father's carriage, in order for his tour with Mrs. Orne to Providence.   Some rain in the night.   Sophia Cabot leaves Salem.

3. *Saturday.*   Cloudy ; wind N. E., with some rain. As we hear nothing from Danvers we presume that John and Mrs. O. set out for Providence.   Gen'l Farley here about Estey's affair in the week past.   Watkins, Frost, Maj. Eppes, Ben. Eppes ; inhabitants of Marblehead in a rage at Mr. Robie's suit.

4. *Sunday.*   Cloudy ; wind N. E.   Mr. Fisher's child is this day christened by himself (Elizabeth).   Sponsors : Mr. Bowditch, Mrs. Ingersoll, Miss M. Hathorn.   His subject was the vanity of the world, showing that all was not vanity.   News of Dr. Orne from sea, and he is no better.   Alas, poor Orne!

5. *Monday.*   A fine day.   We hear that Mr. Wetmore has agreed for a house at Boston.   Mr. Blaney's misfortunes commence.   Club at my house.

8. *Thursday.*   Mr. Orne came ; dined here with Mrs. Mascarene and Mrs. Higginson.

9. *Friday.* A fine, clear, and moderate day. N. Sparhawk here. Early this morning Mr. Smith sets out for Windham, and Mr. Pickman for Oxford on Mr. Blancy's affairs.

12. *Monday.* The Club meets at Dr. Putnam's house in School Street for the first time.

15. *Thursday.* Mr. Winthrop, Misses Temple and Waldo come to town.

16. *Friday.* Miss Fiske [1] was buried with great pomp; a great concourse of respectable people.

17. *Saturday.* Cloudy and some rain. Mr. Winthrop and co. set off P. M. for Boston. Billy Wetmore comes from Mr. Cutler's on a visit. Last evening Mrs. Goodale began to raise blood; all are alarmed at it, she especially. John rides out to Danvers with Mr. Graäm; he returns and lodges with John.

18. *Sunday.* Rain and fogs and wet in plenty. Church full to-day; no meeting at Mr. Prince's house to-day. Mr. Graäm [and] Billy Wetmore visit us. Evening, John goes up to Mr. Orne's, sups at Mr. Graäm's. Primus brings down the horse and chaise for John's tour to Providence. He and Eb. Putnam are to set out to-morrow.

19. *Monday.* Nathan Browne's affair hurries him to extremes — to the law; I throw water to cool him.

20. *Tuesday.* Browne's heat increaseth; Lander's subsides.

21. *Wednesday.* Rain. Mrs. H. Lloyd at Mrs. Higginson's. By him I write to Dr. Lloyd.

22. *Thursday.* Marblehead town-meeting in an uproar as to S. S.

23. *Friday.* Eb. Putnam returns from Providence in

---

[1] Lydia, daughter of General John and Lydia (Phippen) Fiske. She was 17 years of age.

the evening.   Very cold.   This day Mr. Turner's furniture is sold at auction.

24. *Saturday.*   Cloudy.   At evening John and Mrs. Orne come in from Providence with a letter from Brother Pynchon and one from Mrs. Oliver.   Brother Pynchon sends a new account with the heirs.   Browne and Lander and Watson meet at my office.

25. *Sunday.*   Church and meetings begin 1/4 past ... A. M. and ... past 2 P. M.   Mr. Fisher, after church service, P. M., explains to us the doings of the church clergy at Boston Convention.

27. *Tuesday.*   Set out for Newbury Court with Mr. Wetmore in his carriage ; get there at two with a tired horse.   Mr. Hitchborn generously offers me his servant's horse, on which I finish my journey into Newburyport ; dine at Davenport's.

29. *Thursday.*   Dine at Parsons'.   News of Dr. Story's failing at Boston.

30. *Friday.*   Dine at Mr. Dalton's.

October 1.   *Saturday.*   Dine at brother Bradbury's. Set out after noon and reach Adams' at the Hamlet.

2. *Sunday.*   Reach Salem by 9 A. M.

3. *Monday.*   Cloudy and cold.   John to Reading ; Just. Browne's Court.

11. *Tuesday.*   I set out for Newbury with Mr. Wetmore in his chaise, Stevens' horse.

13. *Thursday.*   The Court at evening adjourns without day.

14. *Friday.*   Morn, I return from Newbury Court. Miss S. Lowell and Miss Atkins come.

15. *Saturday.*   News of J. Timmins' death from London.

16. *Sunday.*   All day at church.

17. *Monday.*   M. Sparhawk and son come here.

18. *Tuesday.* P. M., Mr. Sparhawk and son go to Boston.

19. *Wednesday.* The Assembly matters come on.

21. *Friday.* Mr. Abbot of Andover here to pay Mr. Sparhawk. Mr. Cabot agrees to go with me to Springfield, and to carry a servant ; he hath letters from Mr. Savage, London, and account that Mr. Curwen, failing of his pension, is expected to return hither this fall. The Pension List is said to decrease. Wind N. E., and cold, and rains all day.

24. *Monday.* Cloudy A. M. At 9 o'clock Mr. Cabot and I, with servant Joe, set out at Salem for Springfield ; dine at Watertown, lodge at Sudbury, at Butler's ; very poor lodgings.

25. *Tuesday.* We breakfast at How's, Marlboro, dine at Worcester ; I visit Mrs. Flagg ; we lodge at Leicester.

26. *Wednesday.* Breakfast at Brookfield. A very cold day. Dine at Graves' and lodge there, Palmer.

27. *Thursday.* Breakfast at Bliss's, Wilbraham ; dine at Parsons's, Springfield, and lodge there. Visit Mr. M. Bliss, Mrs. J. Dwight ; tea at G. Pynchon's, with Mrs. Platt's and Colo. Worthington's family.

28. *Friday.* Take Mr. Pynchon's horse and go over the river with Mr. Cabot and Bliss, and meet Ben. Ely at Stebbin's, where Mr. C. finds a young female attendant, and not engaged ; all dine at my expense ; return to east side of the river, lodge at Parsons's ; in the evening visit Mr. Hayward at J. Dwight's, and spend the remainder of the evening at Mr. Bliss's with his family and Colo. Worthington. A. M., in waiting for the boat, I call at Dr. Brewer's and make a visit there ; also call at widow Charles Pynchon's to see them, and at W. Pynchon's, the Registrar.[1]

---

[1] William Pynchon was the son of John, and a cousin of our author.

29. *Saturday.* We set out at 9 o'clock after breakfast, dine at Scott's, lodge at Brookfield, Lincoln's.

30. *Sunday.* Breakfast at Mason's, Spencer ; go to meeting, hear Mr. Pope, and set out at the meeting-house and dine at Leicester ; lodge at Patch's, Worcester.

31. *Monday.* Breakfast at Farrar's, Shrewsbury ; dine at Colo. How's, Marlboro — good roast beef, fine horse-radish, catchup, fine butter, apple pye, and cheese ; a pretty female attendant, her face muffled up for the ague ; Mr. C. prescribes flannel for it, I red baize, but we can't get off the muffler. Sup and lodge at Sudbury, at Barker's ; a fine female attendant without a muffler, and so young it is presumed by Mr. C. that she is not engaged, but he is to pop the question to her at night.

November 1. *Tuesday.* A fine morning. We break fast at Bradshaw's, Medford ; dine at Wait's, Malden ; drink coffee P. M. at Salem, and find all well. The Court meets and sits in Mr. Barnard's meeting-house.

2. *Wednesday.* Mr. Hopkins prays with the Court ; cause tried.

5. *Saturday.* Mr. Hues, Lincoln, Bradbury, dine here. At night, self *et ux.* wait on Mr. and Mrs. Sumner at their lodgings, at Goodhue's.

6. *Sunday.* Judges Cushing, Dana, and Sumner, with Mrs. Sumner, dine with us, Judge Sargeant and lady being out of town, and they go P. M. to Mr. Prince's meeting.

7, 8, 9, 10, 11. Trials.

12. *Saturday.* Mr. Bradbury, Parsons, and Mr. Watson eat fish with me ; Lincoln declined. Hibbett's case tried.

13. *Sunday.* Mr. and Mrs. Sumner, Paine, and Parsons at church P. M., and drink tea at Mr. Goodale's ; Mr. Wetmore goes home.

14. *Monday.*   A cold, clear day.   Mr. and Mrs. Sumner, Bradbury, and clerk Osgood at tea at my house.

15. *Tuesday.*   The Court breaks up P. M.

22. *Tuesday.*   Rain.   Mr. Orne and Mr. Selkrig come at evening ; the latter lodgeth here.

23. *Wednesday.*   Cloudy and windy.   Selkrig goes to Boston in the stage.   Letters come from Colo. Frye and Mr. Deblois of Halifax.

24. *Thursday.*   I went to Cambridge with Mr. Mascarene, and to Boston, and lodged at Mr. Wetmore's.

25. *Friday.*   I returned home — it rained ; I brought Billy Wetmore with me.

26. *Saturday.*   A fair day and cold.   Letters from Mr. Curwen and J. Sewall, by Calahan.

December 4.   *Sunday.*   Snow-storm.   Mr. Orne and Williams here in the evening.

5. *Monday.*   Clear and moderate.   Mr. Williams sets out for Deerfield with letter for Walker, writ, summons, and an order on Carpenter and Clarke.

6. *Tuesday.*   The Court meet at Robinson's.   At evening Mr. Wetmore comes in the stage and puts up with us.

9. *Friday.*   Very cold.   The Court still at Robinson's. At evening the Court adjourns without day in tolerable humour.

10. *Saturday.*   Wet and cloudy.   Mrs. Johnson, sister of Aq. Wilkins, here.   Confusions at Mr. Cabot's between him and son.

11. *Sunday.*   Cloudy and small rain.   Having a swelled face and bad cold, I tarry at home ; all ill of Sunday disorder — laziness.   At evening Mr. Watson of Providence, and Mr. Goodale here.

13. *Tuesday.*   Cloudy and wet.   Mr. Elkanah Watson breakfasts with me.   Mr. Graham, L. Oliver, Osgood, and B. P. at tea.   Mrs. Pynchon visits Mrs. H. Derby.

14. *Wednesday.* Clear and cold morning. O. Peabody called on me yesterday, and comes again on Mr. Cabot's and Mrs. Orne's affairs. Mrs. Orne, Peggy, and Caty come to Thanksgiving and lodge with us. John is ill of the asthma and pleurisy. Mr. Sparhawk here.

15. *Thursday.* Clear and cold. Mr. Orne comes, and his family, to dine at Mrs. Cabot's ; mine (except Jack, who is ill) to dine at F. Cabot's. John's pleurisy continues.

16. *Friday.* A fine day ; it rains in the evening ; a wonder ! F. Cabot, Esq., and son, and Mrs. Mascarene dine at Mr. Goodale's. Mr. Prescott [1] sits up with John.

18. *Sunday.* A fine, clear day, but John is confined in his chamber and I in the office all day.

20. *Tuesday.* Moriarty returns to Danvers. Mr. Graham dines with us in the office.

21. *Wednesday.* Cloudy morning. Brother Mitchell comes in the Portsmouth stage ; a dark cloud over his visage, his eyes wild ;[2] at evening he goes to Mr. Goodale's to lodge, John and I both being ill.

[1] Mr. Prescott was a classmate of John Pynchon.

[2] Mitchell Sewall, so often mentioned in this Diary, was a son of Mitchell Sewall. He was born in 1748, and was adopted by his uncle, Judge Stephen Sewall, and became a student of law. In 1774 he was made Register of Probate in Grafton County, New Hampshire. He afterward removed to Portsmouth, where he died in March, 1808, at the age of 59. He was a man of gloomy temperament, but of marked poetical ability, and a volume of his poems was published in 1801. His ode on war and Washington was quite celebrated, and was sung during the war. He was noted for his wit and social qualities. In his epilogue to the tragedy of Cato, written in 1778, occurs the well-known couplet : —

> " No pent-up Utica contracts our powers,
> But the whole boundless continent is ours."

In 1788 he delivered the Fourth of July oration in Portsmouth, which was published.

22. *Thursday.*   Cloudy.   Mrs. Vans here in the evening.

23. *Friday.*   A fine, clear morning.   N. Sparhawk, Esq., here on road to Portsmouth.   John Pynchon comes down.

24. *Saturday.*   It rains all day.   Flora Gilchrist here.

25. *Sunday*, and Christmas Day.   Fine, clear, and moderate.

27. *Tuesday.*   Rains, snows, and blows.   A number of unruly fishermen are put into jail for taxes, and they utterly refuse to pay them or to let them be paid.

31. *Saturday.*   I went out to Mr. Osgood's office and called in at Mr. Goodale's ; Mitchell was gone forth to musick.   I give to Daniel Oliver letters to be put into Lloyd's bag at Boston for London, to S. Curwen.

1786. *January* 1. *Sunday.*   Cold.   At evening I went to Mr. Oliver's and spent the evening.

2. *Monday.*   Snow-storm ; N. E. wind.   Club at my house.

3. *Tuesday.*   Mr. James Warren comes with letters from Mrs. Browne, of Virginia ; dines and sups with us ; Mr. Goodale [and] J. Grafton here with him at tea.

4. *Wednesday.*   A fine, clear day.   Mrs. Fisher in a fit falls into the fire.

5. *Thursday.*   Snow.   Mr. Warren goes to Marblehead in the snow-storm.

6. *Friday morning.*   Mr. Warren returns, dines, and spends the whole day ; in the evening goes for his horse, etc., for his journey.   I write again to Mr. Curwen.

9. *Monday.*   A fine, clear day.   Good sledding.   Oak wood at 15/ and 16/ a cord.   Club at Dr. Putnam's. P. M., John, B. Pickman, and co. go with the Misses to Mrs. Orne's.

12. *Thursday.*   I went to Boston with Mr. Warren in Burrell's stage ; very cold air.

13. *Friday.*   Mitchell Sewall set out with his servant for Portsmouth.

14. *Saturday.*   A fine, clear day.   I dine at Mr. Wetmore's, and at half after two o'clock P. M. set off for the ferry, and arrive at Salem in less than 4 hours.

18. *Wednesday.*   Letters by Mr. Ward from Mrs. Browne, Virginia.

19. *Thursday.*   The ferries at Charlestown and Chelsea frozen and impassable.

20. *Friday.*   Stage don't go ; the ferries impassable.

21. *Saturday.*   The stage goes.   The weather moderated ; fine rain.

23. *Monday.*   Thaws still ; in the afternoon the ice is all carried off from the ferry by the tide.   Portsmouth stage comes from Charlestown to-day by 2 o'clock, though the horses slump to the bottom of the snow.   ʼ

24. *Tuesday.*   Mr. Prescott, of Beverly, here, and lodges with John.   Andrew Cabot here about Knowlton.

26. *Thursday.*   A fine, clear, cool morning.   P. M., at Madam Lynde's lecture.   Mr. Osgood here at tea, and Mrs. Curwen and company.

27. *Friday.*   A fine, cool morning.   Mr. Townsend, of Newbury, comes at tea and lodgeth with John, and they, with Pickman, go over to Beverly to see Prescott, and tarry there on Saturday night.   Dr. Orne dies. We spend the evening at Dr. H[olyoke's] with Mrs. Mascarene.

28. *Saturday.*   A fine day.   The match goes on by fits and starts.   " Now I will marry, and then I will not, but will keep my estate for my children."   Mr. Townsend and John remain at Beverly.   Ab. Gerrish tells of suspicions as to Goodale's leaving the Sacrament on account of the tittle-tattle of the town as to feminine matters.

29. *Sunday.*   A very fine morning.   Mr. Fisher calls here.   At half after ten John returns from Beverly in great haste, and goes to church to play a voluntary. Mr. G. not at the Sacrament at meeting to-day.

30. *Monday.*   Rains and thaws ; S. W. wind.   Club at Mr. Pickman's.   Mr. Cabot in tears ; Mrs. M. Coy and matters go on heavily.

31. *Tuesday.*   Cloudy ; wind still at S. W.   The sledding very poor.   Dr. Jos. Orne[1] was buried P. M.   The bearers : —

    Dr. Osgood,   B. Goodhue,   J. Ashton.

February 1.   *Wednesday.*   A pleasant day.   Mrs. Pynchon goes out to Mrs. Goodale's, John to the Assembly.   Mrs. Henderson is abused by lads in the street.

2. *Thursday.*   Cloudy day.   Mr. Goodale and I accompany Mr. Cabot up to Morris's farm, which he liketh ; the tide catcheth us at the bridge and we sail over North River.

3. *Friday.*   Mr. Cabot proposeth that his son W., in order to get the farm a pennyworth, take the widow with it.

4. *Saturday.*   A very fine, clear morning ; a moderate S. W. wind.   Mr. Cabot walketh toward the house of the widow Good, the owner of the farm, and to offer to take both at a certain sum by the acre, as farmers purchase in the country all farms by the acre, allowing nothing for buildings and barn ; and in this case Mr. Cabot is to ask for the widow to be thrown into the bargain, as a barn would be.

5. *Sunday.*   Snow and N. E. wind.   All hands are

---

[1] Dr. Joseph Orne was a son of Jonathan Orne, whose first wife was Elizabeth Putnam.   He was born in 1749.   He married, first, Polly, daughter of Rev. Dudley Leavitt, and secondly, Teresa Emery, of Exeter, leaving issue.   He was a second cousin of Timothy Orne, who married Elizabeth Pynchon.

going to church to-day to hear John's voluntary on the
organ ; I go too late and hear nothing ; he refused to
play, as Young did not call him.

6. *Monday.* Clouds and some snow, and rain at times.
Billy Wetmore comes with Bob, in his way to Cutler's
school.   Club here.

7. *Tuesday.*   Cloudy.   Billy Wetmore and Bob set
out for Cutler's school.   I call on Stephens again for
his account (present, B. Pickman) ; he says I shall have
it.   John goes to Boston with Bob.

8. *Wednesday.*   A fine, clear, and pleasant day.   I
dine at Mr. Goodale's with Dr. Putnam, Holyoke, J.
Derby, B. and W. Pickman, J. Grafton, Mr. Noyes ; all
very cheerful.

9. *Thursday.*   A fine, moderate, clear day.   Justice
Holten, at the solicitation of B. Stevens, comes to J.
Pickering's with him to administer the oaths to me and
R. Manning as Justices.

10. *Friday.*   A fine, clear, and moderate day.   Great
struggle at G. Assembly for naval office, Marblehead ;
candidates, S. Sewall and Gerry.

11. *Saturday.*   A cold day, and very windy.   Mr.
Cabot and I go over to Northfield to Mr. Diman's high
land.   John returns by the stage in the evening with
Capt. Williams.

12. *Sunday.*   Clear and cold.   I go to church both
parts of the day.   P. M., I hear Jack play on the organ.
Through the scarcity of cash, scarce a dollar is collected
at Communion.   I spend the evening at Mr. Fisher's.

13. *Monday.*   A cool, clear day.   Spend the evening
with Dr. Eliot at Dr. Putnam's with the Club.   John
and co. begin their Club at my house this evening ; long
may their motives in forming it continue, and may the
advantages arising from it be as durable as I wish them ;

may every seed and every virtuous sprout or shoot in those youths meet with due encouragement and produce plentiful crops.

14. *Tuesday.*   Wind; a snow-storm this morning. Jeremy Nowland comes to visit his friends, and is a new man.

15. *Wednesday.*   A very fine, clear morning; west wind. Balsted, Gregory, and co., *et al.*, musicians, spend the morning with John, and with them Jeremy Nowland. James Hughes, Esq., in town.   In a letter from Mr. Wetmore we have notice of the choice of Stephen Sewall to the office Naval at Marblehead; the joyfullest news we have had, but less on account of the value of the office than of defeating the plot of Moloch.   Long life, health, and happiness to Mr. Gill, S. Higginson, Wetmore, and all the humane who exerted themselves on the occasion of Stephen's choice.

16. *Thursday.*   Cloudy morning, but moderate.   I write by D. Oliver to Mr. Tudor and to S. Gridley: to the former on Mr. Oliver's affairs, to the latter for the balance due to me on Moriarty's affair.

20. *Monday.*   Snow-storm continues.   A fire is seen at Marblehead, and the engine company, with great numbers of young men, set out on horseback and on foot for their assistance; but the sail loft is burnt down before they get over.   W. Cabot and I go almost half way; the snow very deep.

21. *Tuesday.*   A fine, clear day.   Mr. Smith[1] sets out

---

[1] The Mr. Smith here referred to was the Hon. Jeremiah Smith, afterwards so distinguished as a jurist in New Hampshire. He entered Harvard College in 1777, but enlisted in the army for a short time and fought at Bennington. He graduated at Queen's College, New Jersey. While reading law with Mr. Pynchon he taught a small school of young ladies, and he mentions this as "one of the happiest portions of his life." He afterwards reached the highest position on the New Hampshire bench, was for a year governor of that State, and represented her in Congress.

for Portsmouth. I give him a memorandum of his studying with me from May, 1784, and of his having been studying at Barnstable, so that in my opinion he is qualified for admittance to the office of an attorney.

22. *Wednesday.* Cloudy but moderate weather. John goes to work in the office, Pickman to diversion ! General Glover comes and complains of his loss by fire.

23. *Thursday.* Snow. J. Grafton, Patty, and co. go to Mr. Cutler's exhibition at Wenham.

24. *Friday.* More snow ; wind N. E. General Farley comes to town. Billy Wetmore comes home with Patty in the stage. I write to Mr. Wetmore as to the exhibition, and as to Billy coming hither from school, and as to Mr. Fitch's money, and acknowledgment as to brother Stephen. The subscription for Mitchell's poems goes on rapidly. Mr. Cabot grows worse.

25. *Saturday.* Clear and cold. Mr. Cabot grows worse, and is thought to be in danger. Mr. Graham and Mr. Pickman at tea here.

26. *Sunday.* Clear and chilly; S. W. wind. Mr. Cabot has no relief yet. Billy writes to Mr. Lowell of the dangerous state his father is in.

27. *Monday.* I write to Mr. Lowell. Mr. Cabot's pains still continue.

28. *Tuesday.* A fine day. Numbers of young people come from Boston and other towns to the Assembly, and at evening make a brilliant appearance. Mr. Cabot is greatly relieved.

March 1. *Wednesday.* Wrote to Mr. and Mrs. Oliver, and answered his letter in substance.

2. *Thursday.* Some snow and wet. Mr. S. Sparhawk here from Portsmouth.

3. *Friday.* Scarcity of cash is alarming, and the Court is about redeeming the State notes at 6/8 the pound.

4. *Saturday.* Rain and wet part of the day. S. Sparhawk returns to Portsmouth. His kinsman, N. Sparhawk, is bound for England, and offers his furniture to sale.

5. *Sunday.* High wind and rain all last night; some snow in the morning. Storms arise in the skies and political feuds at Court; commerce ruined, cash is fled; debts to France, Holland, and Spain must be paid.

6. *Monday.* I go to Marblehead with clerk Osgood. Tea at Mr. Sewall's.

7. *Tuesday.* S. Sparhawk here. Doane's famous cause heard at Boston.

8. *Wednesday.* A fine, clear, moderate day. S. Sparhawk takes tea with me. Mrs. P. at Mrs. Barton's.

9. *Thursday.* I write to N. Sparhawk, Esq., and to J. Peirce, Esq., by S. Sparhawk, as to Dodge's affair and as to Mr. Fisher's.

11. *Saturday.* A fine day. This day the first cause was tried before me as a Justice of Peace, Manning *v.* Page.

13. *Monday.* Pleasant weather. Mr. Cabot grows worse. Town-meeting.

14. *Tuesday.* A fine, fair day. I write to Mr. S. Bradstreet, Boston.

15. *Wednesday.* Cloudy morning. Sent by Charles Hall to Mr. Wetmore, Boston, Judge Greenleaf's certificate for my debt against Colo. Browne's estate for $£15.0.3\frac{3}{4}$.

16. *Thursday.* Cloudy and wet. The stage does not go to-day to Boston. Mitchell sets out for Portsmouth.

18. *Saturday.* A fine day. Mr. Lowell comes at night and lodgeth with us.

22. *Wednesday.* Bright northern light.

25. *Saturday.* A very fine, spring - like morning. Mr. Cabot grows worse.

27. *Monday.* A fine day. Write Mr. Robie and George Deblois of Halifax. Mr. Cabot sends for me.

28. *Tuesday.* A very fine day. Tea at Dr. Plummer's.

29. *Wednesday.* Cloudy. Mr. Lowell comes; Mr. Cabot declines.

30. *Thursday.* Mr. Cabot makes his will, [and] makes ample provision for Mrs. Mascarene during her widowhood.

31. *Friday.* Cloudy and rain. The old folk are invited by tickets to the Assembly. Mr. Lowell goes out of town. Mrs. Orne comes to the Assembly.

April 1. *Saturday.* Bright aurora in the evening. Messrs. Frenchman and Diman dined with us. A storm, and it blew all night very violently and snowed.

2. *Sunday.* Snows and blows still, so that people tarried at home from meeting and from church. Fr[enchman] and Diman at tea and supper.

3. *Monday.* Mr. Cabot grows weaker. Ab. Waters put into jail for taxes.

4. *Tuesday.* A fine day; the snow thaws. Mr. Cabot free from pain. Frenchman goes to Boston.

5. *Wednesday.* A fine, warm day; the snow goes off rapidly. Mr. Cabot's pains come on again; he grows weaker daily.

6. *Thursday.* Being Fast Day, we go to church at eleven. John plays a fine, grave piece on the organ; p. m., Mr. Fisher goes with me to hear Mr. Bentley, and we are much entertained. Mr. Barnard prays with Mr. Cabot, who grows weaker daily. Mr. Goodwin, of Cambridge, calls.

7. *Friday.* A fine morning, though cloudy and windy. I send by Burrell to Dr. Loring as to Dabney's debt; to J. Hunt as to Dr. Putnam's debt; I send to Mr. Wetmore N. Abbot's money per letter.

8. *Saturday.*   A fair, windy day.   Mr. Lowell comes in the afternoon.

16. *Sunday.*   Cloudy; wind S. W. and cool.   Fra. Cabot, Esq., is buried.   The bearers : —

Dr. Putnam,	J. Blaney,
Mas. Williams,	G. Dodge,
Jona. Gardner,	W. West.

Finding no partner among the relations, I walk with Joshua Ward, who is so obliging as to accompany me.

17. *Monday.*   Cloudy.   Mr. N. Sparhawk dines with me ; Mr. and Mrs. Higginson invited, but go to Beverly.

18. *Tuesday.*   N. E. wind.   Poor Still, 't is said, was starved to death in the ship Africa.

19. *Wednesday.*   Fine rain.   Mr. Higginson and Goodale dine with me ; Mrs. Higginson unwell, could not come.   Capt. Revell's character suffers on account of Still.

20. *Thursday.*   N. E. wind, cold, and rain.   President Willard and Professor Williams in town.

21. *Friday.*   Rain and N. E. wind all day.   Tea at Mrs. Gerrish's.   J. Grafton takes coffee at my office.   A fire in [the] E. Parish.

22. *Saturday.*   N. E. storm, rain, and cold.   Shocking account of the treatment of negroes on board the ship Africa.

23. *Sunday.*   Cloudy, and N. E. wind continues. The account [comes] of Capt. Revell's behaviour and great cruelty to his men, starving and beating Still to death.

24. *Monday.*   Rain all day ; wind at N. E.   I go with John to Just. Putnam's ; he gives me an account of Ab. Waters' B. sale.   Capt. Buffington gives an account of Walker's doings and plans.   Club is at Colo. Pickman's ; I am too busy to go.

25. *Tuesday*. Rain and cloudy. Mr. N. and Samuel Sparhawk and W. Cabot dine with us. S. Sewall and Hinckley spend the afternoon on a very agreeable errand, respecting Providence matters. I visit Ab. Waters, Danvers, and he gives me reason to hope for security for my due. Mr. N. Sparhawk mentions his reasons for going to Europe, and they are at least plausible.

26. *Wednesday*. At 9 o'clock the weather clears up, and the sun appears again, having disappeared for days past, except on Friday morning last, [when] it appeared for a few minutes only. Write to Mr. Oliver, Mr. Wetmore, and to Sam. Gridley, Esq., by B. Stevens.

27. *Thursday*. A fine, clear morning. B. Pickman and John walk to Marblehead, and dine there at S. Sewall's; at evening Mrs. P. at Mr. Goodale's. Mr. Pulling and I at J. Pickering's to swear him as County Register.

28. *Friday*. Mr. Kimball lodgeth here.

29. *Saturday*. Clear and cold. This day brother Stephen and son, W. Pynchon, called on us at breakfast, in their way to Manchester. Kimball is here all day fiddling and tooting with John. Mrs. Mascarene and servant leave W. Cabot's house; a cool parting this! Mr. Kimball lodges here.

30. *Sunday*. Cloudy and cool. Brother Stephen and son Stephen come over and, with W. Cabot, dine with us; tea at Mr. Goodale's; [they] go home in Mr. Goodale's chaise. Kimball returns and lodges with John.

May 1. *Monday*. Cloudy and some rain, and some sunshine. Mr. Fisher spends the evening with the Club at my house. Kimball here. I write again to Mr. O. and to Mr. Hughes by D. O.

2. *Tuesday*. Cloudy and cool. Bro. Stephen *et ux.* and little Mitchell and Billy at Mr. Goodale's at tea;

Kimball remains and raiseth a company of musicians in the evening.

5. *Friday.* Clear and cold. Mrs. Mascarene and Mrs. H. call on us. S. Barnard came to town from Deerfield.

6. *Saturday.* Cloudy and cold. Wrote to Stephen Higginson as to Smith's debt. S. Barnard calls to see me, and takes a letter to J. Williams respecting his concerns with executors of F. Cabot and the money sent by me to him.

7. *Sunday.* At church all day ; it rained, and Mr. F. preached in his surplice. At night Mrs. Pynchon tells me of Mr. Goodale's remarks ; *et tu, Brute !*

8. *Monday.* Cold and clear. I write to Samuel Sewall, Esq., by Wait.

9. *Tuesday.* Clear and pleasant. I call at Dr. Holyoke's, and see Mrs. Mascarene.

10. *Wednesday.* [In the] morning at Dr. Holyoke's again, and write to Dr. Kneeland and to Calef ; see Mrs. Mascarene and invite her to spend the day.

11. *Thursday.* Clear and cool. At [the] funeral of F. Cabot's child.

12. *Friday.* Cloudy. Yesterday W. Cabot desired me to inquire as to rent of the house.

13. *Saturday.* A fine, clear, and warm day. J. Jeffry and I walk to Mrs. Orne's farm, and find John and F. Goodale there at tea ; at evening we walk home. W. Cabot shows us his present from Capt. Carpenter of a cane and a pair of Persian slippers, wrought with gold on a scarlet cloth ; all rich and grand.

16. *Tuesday.* A cool, fine morning. Mr. Pick[man], Osgood, and I, at half past six, set out for Andover ; arrive at half past ten ; the reference between Wingate and Mulliken, Mr. Phillips, B. Bartlett, and myself, ref-

erees. The parties meet in the evening, and, we not concluding, adjourn to July Court, Salem.

19. *Friday.* Pleasant. Mr. Fisher hath letters from Mr. Wren, Portsmouth, whose letters are worth reading ; his example, goodness of disposition, his life and conduct, worth every one's attention and imitation.

20. *Saturday.* Cloudy and wet. I write to Ben. Eaton as to Mr. Cary's debts. Mr. Amory, Otis, John, and co. spend the evening with B. P. No news yet from Mr. O.

21. *Sunday.* Cloudy, but moderate, cool weather ; wind still N. E. We daily hear of great uneasiness and turbulence in country towns on account of taxes ; of declarations that they will not pay them.

22. *Monday.* Wrote to Sheriff Moulton, inclosing execution, Carpenter *v.* Cole, with orders to take effects sufficient, and in that case need not incommode or make further costs to Cole ; if half the cash can be had, and personal security for the rest, it may do ; sent by post.

24. *Wednesday.* Dr. Plummer's horse threw and hurt him.

25. *Thursday.* Coomes examined as to murder of his wife. Mr. Parker and Mr. Hughes come and lodge at my house. Mrs. Derby was buried. Bearers :—

Fiske,　　　　　　Cleveland,

W. Pickman,　　　　S. Blyth,

B. Goodhue.

27. *Saturday.* Cloudy and rain. Isaac Coomes, in jail for murder, confesseth the charge under his hand.

28. *Sunday.* A pleasant day. I go to church without cloak.

31. *Wednesday.* Election Day. I go with W. Cabot to see Mr. Orne ; drink tea there. Mr. Cabot takes cold and has a nervous headache in the evening. At

evening [John] has a company of singers, and they go about serenading. The lawyers are, most of them, turned or left out of the General Assembly, and are vilified in the public prints. We hear from Mr. Oliver that he can't come before the first week of June.

June 2. *Friday.* Capt. Moseley sails and leaves my books behind. Such is my luck in life! Behind! behind!

3. *Saturday.* A fine, clear morning. Wrote to D. Cheever, Esq., as to Putnam's debt. Very hot at noon, and cloudy P. M. J. Williams comes from Boston; J. Lee and *ux.* from Cambridge.

4. *Sunday.* A fine, pleasant, and clear morning. It being Whitsunday, John is to give us a voluntary. Very hot day. Tea at Mr. Grafton's.

5. *Monday.* A fine, clear morning; wind at N. E. and cold. Mr. Williams sets out in the stage for Boston, having seen Mr. Cabot, and is to write to brother Pynchon in order for adjustment of accounts of our estates.

8. *Thursday.* A very warm day. At evening Mr. Oliver, Sally, and Miss Chase come in the stage. Madam Pickman dies.[1]

10. *Saturday.* A fine, cool day. P. M., S. Sewall, Esq., calls to see Mr. Oliver and to ask him to preach at Marblehead to-morrow. I write to B. Bradish and to Eb. Tuck as to Mr. Deblois.

11. *Sunday.* Clear and cool. Mr. Oliver goes to Marblehead in Mr. Lee's chaise, which was sent for him.

12. *Monday.* A fine day, at times fair, at others cloudy. I go to Boston on Mr. Oliver's and my own business, with Daland's horse and carriage ; bring home the magazines from Mr. Russell's store, where Capt. Lyde left

---

[1] Mrs. Pickman was the wife of Colonel Benjamin Pickman ; her maiden name was Love Rawlins.

them. I lodge at Mr. Wetmore's, breakfast at Mr. Lowell's.

13. *Tuesday.* Mr. Oliver and Miss Chase go to Portsmouth. I bring home from Boston the magazines and the "Beauties of Shakespeare," etc. The weather is warm. Last evening Mrs. Pickman was buried.

14. *Wednesday.* The magazines are disposed of. The bearers to Madam Pickman, Mr. Turner and Dr. Putnam.

16. *Friday.* A fine day, but cloudy, and rain at night. Mr. Oliver and Miss Chase from Portsmouth.

17. *Saturday.* Cloudy and rain in the morning, but clears up, and carriages, horses, and chaises in plenty for Charlestown to meet the crowd, and to pass Charlestown bridge. General Farley, Estey, and Stephens meet at my office in order for a settlement of his execution for [the] June term. John and Ward set out at half past eleven for the bridge.

18. *Sunday.* Cloudy morning; some rain in the afternoon, but it clears up again. Mr. Fenno takes the S. W. corner pew at church. Mrs. Oliver and Miss Chase return from Marblehead at eve[ning]; Mr. O. remains there. John and Ward return early this morning.

20. *Tuesday.* Clear day. I meet with difficulty to get an horse for Ipswich Court; at length John and I set out with Cheever's horse and carriage.

21. *Wednesday.* Comes on the trial of Murray's cause, of Gloucester, with the parish officers, and I set out with Mr. Sewall's lady for Salem, and return to Ipswich that night.

22. *Thursday.* Isaac Coomes, the Indian, is arraigned for murder of his wife, and pleads not guilty, and trial to be to-morrow.

23. *Friday.*   Come on the capital trials of Coomes for murder, of . . . for burglary and theft, and of . . . for theft.

24. *Saturday.*   A fine day.   At 4 o'clock A. M. the Jury agree on a verdict of guilty as to Coomes, and, being tired and in want of air and rest, some of them walked out by the door to take the air, and went among people in other rooms in the tavern, and talked with some persons they had met about the power and duty of the Jury as to verdicts, of manslaughter, and of murder, and inquired people's opinions out of doors ; and this was objected to by Coomes's counsel before verdict, and, at the Court's instance, done in writing, signed by the counsel ; but the verdict was given in and affirmed ; and on considering that there were no books nor cases produced exactly similar to the present, the Court continued the Indictment to next term, notwithstanding the urgency of Attorney-General Paine for sentence.   Judge Sewall and lady set out from Salem and dine at Ipswich ; B. Pickman and Mrs. Pynchon with them.   Mr. Oliver goes to Boston and exchangeth with Mr. Parker ; he to Providence.   At evening Mrs. Pynchon returned home with me, Pickman and John in their chaise.

July 1.   *Saturday.*   A fine, pleasant day.   I dine at Mr. Goodale's with Mitchell Sewall and Dr. Holyoke. P. M., I go to the Fort and spend the afternoon with J. Grafton and others ; we walk down, all but Mitchell and J. Grafton ; the latter carrieth me back in his chaise.

2. *Sunday.*   A fine, clear, and cool morning.   Mr. Oliver and Fitch go to Marblehead in Mr. Stacey's chaise, and return at evening.   I go home with Mrs. Orne and lodge there, to walk home in the morning.

3. *Monday.*   A fine, pleasant day.   I get home from Danvers by half past six o'clock in the morning.

5. *Wednesday.*   A cool, clear day.   Mr. Oliver goes to Boston.   I go to widow A. Waters's with Mr. Noyes in the afternoon ; she concludes to administer on his estate.

6. *Thursday.*   A fine, cool morning; wind N. W. Last evening agreed with Burrell to pay him five dollars a year for carrying all letters and packets to and from Boston, including small bundles only.   [In the] morning fire is cried with great vehemence ; the eastern bell rings terribly, and sets the rest a-jingling ; the street is instantly filled ; all cry fire, save a drunken fellow and a fishmonger ; the one cries murder, the other, fresh fish fit for the pan ; the engines are dragged furiously along the street, but no fire is to be seen ; a quarrel ensues ; one party affirms there was no fire, one of the other side offered to swear that he smelt it.   So all return laughing [and] in good humour.

7. *Friday.*   A cool, pleasant day.   Mitchell Sewall returns from Boston with the bad news of brother Stephen's loss of the naval office at Marblehead.

8. *Saturday.*   Wind south ; in the afternoon a fine shower.   Brother Stephen came over by 6 o'clock this morning to see Mitchell, and tarryeth ; they dine at Mr. Goodale's.

9. *Sunday.*   A very fine day.   Mr. and Mrs. Oliver dine at Judge Oliver's, and go to church ; he preacheth all day ; Mitchell Sewall at church all day ; he and F. Goodale dine at W. Cabot's.   We hear [that] the General Assembly adjourns to next January, Stephens, the sheriff, having obtained an order for rehearing.

10. *Monday.*   A very fine morning.   Mitchell and Francis Goodale set off for Portsmouth.

11. *Tuesday.*   Common Pleas term begins.   A fine day, clear and pleasant.   I have a letter from P. Oliver, Esq., at Birmingham.

14. *Friday.*   The Court being pressed in business of the Sessions, the Common Pleas declare it to be time the Court adjourn without day.

15. *Saturday.*   Mr. and Mrs. Oliver return from Ipswich to breakfast, having been at the exhibition there. Mr. Oliver and his brother Lynde set out for Marblehead.

16. *Sunday.*   No church to-day, Mr. Fisher being ill. I spend the evening with Dr. Holyoke and S. Higginson at F. Cabot's.

18. *Tuesday.*   A fine rain; wind N. E. and cool.   All are preparing for Commencement.

19. *Wednesday.*   Cloudy morning and cool.   Mr. Goodale, F. Cabot, Davenport, and myself set out in Burrell's waggon at half past 5 o'clock for Cambridge ; we wear our cloaks and surtouts, and arrive at Cambridge at three quarters after 9 o'clock.   The sun breaks out, and the weather grew warm before noon.   The exercises, exhibitions, etc., continue till 3 o'clock ; the procession is preceded by musick, — 2 French horns, clarinets, etc., which go into the meeting-house and file off at the pulpit, go into the gallery, and there are joined by seven singers, and continue till the people are seated and the house filled.   At night Mr. Goodale, Winslow, and myself walk to Charlestown and lodge at Mr. Winslow's, and return to Salem the next evening in the waggon.

21. *Friday.*   Mr. and Mrs. Oliver set out in Burrell's stage for Boston, in order to go to Providence.

22. *Saturday.*   A warm day.   Mr. King, from Portsmouth, proposeth to come and settle in Salem.

24. *Monday.*   A clear, pleasant day.   N. Sparhawk and son here.   In the afternoon I go with T. Lee in his chaise to Cook's, Danvers, and stop at H. Derby's on our return at tea.

25. *Tuesday.*   Mr. Kimball dines with John, and lodgeth here.   R. Hooper's mortgage and bond to Bacon are missing.

26. *Wednesday.*   Mr. Cockle in town from Mt. Desert.   Mr. Reed from Cambridge.   Mr. Kimball lodges here.

27. *Thursday.*   A fine, moderate rain.   Mr. Pulling and I go to the prison house upon the affairs of Kimball and Poor.   Snow, from Springfield, calls on me ; by him I send letters to Boston.

28. *Friday.*   A fine, clear day.   J. Jackson calls.

29. *Saturday.*   A cold, fine morning.   Mr. Hooper's papers not found yet.   W. Cabot, Mrs. Pynchon, Miss Gerrish, and I go to Mr. Orne's, Danvers.   I have a letter from Mr. N. Sparhawk this day.

August 1.   *Tuesday.*   Mr. George Deblois comes in from Boston, where he arrived from Halifax, and set out for Newbury.

2. *Wednesday.*   Mr. Deblois returns from Newbury at night.

3. *Thursday.*   Mr. Deblois and I go to Mrs. Higginson's.

4. *Friday.*   Mr. Webster's lecture.   Mr. Deblois goes with me to the lecture, and about 26 were present and much entertained.   Mr. Amory lodgeth with John.

5. *Saturday.*   A very warm day.   I dine with Mr. Webster and others at F. Cabot's ; a genteel dinner and good company.   Mr. Deblois dines at Capt. Lee's ; John and Mr. Amory dine with B. Pickman.   Mr. Deblois goes to visit S. Williams' daughter Deblois.   Mr. Amory sets out for Newbury.

7. *Monday.*   A fine, warm day, as was yesterday also. Mr. Wetmore's lad came yesterday with a line acquainting us that Mrs. Wetmore had another daughter.

8. *Tuesday.* A fine, cool day. The Court of Sessions meet; Just. S. Choate presides; in the afternoon they adjourn without day. Mr. Deblois writes to Mr. Atherton; I to S. Phillips as to Wingate.

9. *Wednesday.* Cloudy; wind N. E. I write by Mr. Deblois to Mr. Oliver, Providence. Mr. Webster's lecture.

10. *Thursday.* A fine, clear day; cool air. Letters from Mr. Oliver; his to Stewart I send by Foster to Marblehead.

11. *Friday.* A clear morning. Mr. Webster's lecture this evening was entertaining and useful.

12. *Saturday.* A fine, cool day. Mr. Eliot comes to preach for Mr. Barnard. Mr. and Mrs. Lowell come with his daughter; she goes to Beverly, the parents to W. Cabot's. Daniel Oliver goes on board for Baltimore. Mr. Eliot spends the evening with us. John *et al.* go on board with D. Oliver at ten o'clock in the evening.

13. *Sunday.* I go to hear Mr. Eliot, and am much entertained.

14. *Monday.* A fine day. Mr. and Mrs. Lowell set out from Beverly for Portsmouth.

15. *Tuesday.* Mr. Webster lectured last evening at the school-house.

16.' *Wednesday.* Mr. Webster's lecture at evening, giving an account of his travels through the several Southern States and most of the Northern States of America; on Monday last his lecture was upon education of youths, male and female; he spends the evening at my house.

17. *Thursday.* A fine, moderate day. Agreed with Miss Ab. Gerrish for her house and appurtenances at £25 a year rent; and if her friends or neighbours say I ought to give more I am to give it, I to provide me a

chimney in the office at my own expense ; if our friends say that the rent is too high, it is to be reduced.   On yesterday morning John goes with Davenport to Beverly, thence to Gloucester, and returns this evening.

18. *Friday.* Cloudy morning.   I write to Mr. Wetmore as to Browne's executors.   R. Hooper, Esq., calls, and gives a dismal account of the credit of the neighbouring States ; all going together by the ears, poverty and distress are coming on, paper currency, party spirit, malice, mob's spite, and the Devil ; another revolution ; some adhere to France, some to Britain ; some curse the leaders, some the Whigs, others Tories.

19. *Saturday.* A fine, cool day. The mason, Graves's man goes to making mortar for the office chimney.

20. *Sunday.* A fine morning; wind south. At church all day ; *mirum !* Mr. Beal and lady at church.

21. *Monday.* Very warm. The masons, Stimson and Graves, begin on my office chimney.   Clerk Osgood moves his office to the Court House.

23. *Wednesday.*   We move from Mr. Cabot's to Mrs. Gerrish's house, and lodge there.

24. *Thursday.* Mr. Deblois and I set out for Amherst ; lodge at Merrimack.

25. *Friday.* We go into Amherst ; dine at Wilkins's ; I visit Mr. Dana, and Mr. D. and I ask Mr. Atherton to dine with us there ; he does so. We set out from Amherst, [and] lodge at Kendall's, Lichfield.

26. *Saturday.* We set out from Kendall's, lodge at Haverhill, Greenleaf's, [and] visit Judge Sargeant at evening.

27. *Sunday.* We set out for Topsfield, miss our way, and do not get there till eleven o'clock, too late for meeting ; dine at Baker's ; go to meeting, and after meeting set out for Salem.

29. *Tuesday.* Fair and warm. Wrote to Mr. Cary as to Eaton and Sheldon.

30. *Wednesday.* A very fine day. We make a fire in the new stove in my office. Sent to Chace, of Providence, the note he wrote for.

September 1. *Friday.* A fine, clear day. John returns home from his tour to Newbury, etc., with Davenport. News from North Hampton.

2. *Saturday.* Judge Sewall, of York, with Major Sewall, his brother, here with Mrs. Sewall; they go off for Boston.

3. *Sunday.* A fine day; a little sprinkling of rain. I go to church in the morning; at Judge Oliver's in the evening, and afterwards till eleven at Dr. Holyoke's.

4. *Monday.* Cloudy and warm. Mr. Willard, of Winchester, here.

5. *Tuesday.* The Court of Common Pleas is to meet at Amherst. Rumours prevail as to their being prevented by the populace, as well there as in other counties.

7. *Thursday.* J. C., of Beverly, owns S. C. for his natural son, and will support him according to his conduct.

8. *Friday.* Clear and cool. F. Cabot here, and W. Vans, Esq., on politicks.

9. *Saturday.* Fair, clear, and cool. A town meeting at Reading for tryal of the inclination of the people as to the militia going to protect [the] Concord Court. Mr. Oliver here at tea with Mrs. Oliver, Andrew, and Polly. We hear that Gov. Bowdoin is to march to Concord at the head of companies of artillery and militia from Suffolk and Middlesex. Query the tendency of cannons, arms, and apparatus of the kind, in the country and among people labouring under grievous taxes and bur-

dens? On Sunday the counter orders issue, and the militia not to muster.

10. *Sunday.* A very fine, clear, and warm day. Mr. Oliver read prayers at church.

11. *Monday.* Mr. Oliver goes over to Marblehead with Mr. Hinckley. It rained at evening.

12. *Tuesday.* The Court of Common Pleas stopped at Concord. Plentiful rain.

13. *Wednesday.* Mrs. Pynchon and Mrs. Vans go over to Marblehead. Rumour of wrangles with Parsons at Newburyport as to politics.

14. *Thursday.* Phealen goes to jail for house-break-ing. News from Newbury that the militia will support the Court.

15. *Friday.* Clear and cool. I go to Marblehead with W. Cabot, and breakfast with Mr. Oliver. Write to W. Wetmore, and send B. Bradish's debt to him by Burrell; also wrote to S. Chace, Esq., as to the note.

16. *Saturday.* A clear, fine day. Favourable news from Taunton; the Court sit and adjourn without doing business; the mob of 400 disperse, well pleased, as 't is said. In the afternoon news from G. Barrington that the mob have broken the gaols and let out the prisoners. Aq. Wilkins says we shall find no peace till justice be done to the soldiers who purchased our independence. Rumours of great uneasiness at Rowley as to the sitting of the Courts before redress of grievances.

17. *Sunday.* [In the] morning at church, Salem; afternoon at Marblehead. Mr. Fisher preached at Salem, Mr. Oliver at Marblehead; a full congregation.

18. *Monday.* A cloudy day. Mr. Jackson from Boston and Mr. Cary from Newbury. A countryman comes in with [a] new list of grievances. One was the cursed bank of money in Boston, where they let none of

it go into the country ; it ought to be divided, he said ; so offer was made him of a bank-note for his wood ; he would not take the cursed paper stuffe for his wood, not he ; they might give him the dollars, and keep the bills to themselves.   Another was the governor's salary, when he could find several [who] would serve as governor for half a crown a day.   Then the women of the governor's family lived without work, when they should go to work, as well as *his* wife and daughters.

19. *Tuesday*.   The Superior Court at Worcester sit, and the Grand Jury are charged to inquire as to the insurgents, and to prosecute them.

20. *Wednesday*.   Mr. Hooper and Mr. Bentley here at coffee.   Mr. Cabot brings news from Great Barrington of the extravagance of the rabble, abuses of the Court and lawyers, and preventing the sitting of the Court, and threats of the Superior Court.

21. *Thursday*.   A fine morning.   Judge Holten in town ; intends to be at Newbury Court.   I carry home to Marblehead Polly and Andrew Oliver, and bring back Mrs. Pynchon.   Write to Mr. Wetmore and Dr. Loring by Butler as to Dabney's debts, etc.

22. *Friday*.   A clear, cool morning.   Deacon Edmund Putnam is taken and committed on execution.

23. *Saturday*.   Cloudy and cool.   Deacon Edmund Putnam's son and another offered bonds for liberty of the yard, but are objected to by Stephens as insufficient. Rumours from New Hampshire that the insurgents against the Governor and against the General Assembly are dispersed by the militia, and 30 of them seized and thrown into prison.   Packet from New York comes as to bounds of Carolina and Georgia.

24. *Sunday*.   A fine, cool, and clear day.   At church in the afternoon.   Query the event of Stevens' suit

against Mr. Turner, on his promise to save Stevens harmless for not serving execution, etc., on his son in his lunacy.

25. *Monday.* A fine day. Mr. Wetmore comes, and I set out with him in his chaise for Newbury Court, and lodge at Adams's ; get breakfast at Homans', and get to Newbury before eleven, Tuesday.

26. *Tuesday.* [In the] morning before eleven we overtake Justice Phillips on the road to Court. At Newbury we find [an] artillery company mustered, [with] fifes and drums, and parading about the town to protect the Court in case of need, but all is quiet ; the Court opens and proceeds to business, but with many marks of timidity.

27. *Wednesday.* Fair weather. A continued action tried by the Jury, and some continued actions are defaulted, but not one new one, yet costs were given upon complaint of discontinuance. Query the reason, as it was in plaintiff's absence — timidity or selfishness? Mr. Phillips goes off to Boston, being President of the Senate.

28. *Thursday.* A fine, warm day. The Court go on with Sessions business, highways, licenses, etc. ; that done, [they] order all the new entries to stand continued to next term ; *quo jure? quâ ratione?* Why give judgment against plaintiff for costs on discontinuance, which for aught appears might have been owing to the present commotions, and not for him against his debtor, who declined payment for same reason ? Surely here are the signs of partiality, timidity, and disorder. At evening Mr. Wetmore and I set off from Newbury, and lodge at Ipswich, and next morning breakfast at Salem.

29. *Friday.* A clear, fine day. The clerk (Osgood) returns home, and says the Court of Pleas, etc., ad-

journed last evening without day.   Mrs. Orne goes over to see Mrs. Oliver at Marblehead with S. Sewall, Esq., in his carriage.

30. *Saturday.* A clear and very warm day.   Both creditors and debtors are dissatisfied at the Court's proceedings ; some have judgments, others not ; wretched timidity and partiality.

October 1. *Sunday.*   I go to church ; am introduced to the pew by John.   Brother Stephen has good news ; I write to President Phillips for his aid.

2. *Monday.*   A fine day.   Rumours of treason, riots, etc., etc.   Mrs. Orne returns hither from Marblehead.

3. *Tuesday.* Cloudy.   Superior Court, about returning from Springfield, durst not go to Great Barrington Court.   Rumours prevail to-day of great numbers in different parts of the State desiring to return to their old friends the Britons, and of a number of subscriptions handed about among the people for that end.

4. *Wednesday.*   We hear that the Superior Court arrived at Boston on Saturday last at evening, having adjourned on Thursday, and having done very little, if any, business ; no Grand Jury attended to do business.

5. *Thursday.* A fair day.   Mrs. Pynchon keeps chamber yet.

6. *Friday.*   Cloudy and rain most of the day.   We hear from Boston of the debates in General Court ; some for vigorous measures and for suspension of the *Habeas Corpus* Act ; others for a redress of grievances, and for all mild, soothing measures first.

7. *Saturday.*   Mr. Grafton brings a message from Boston from Barnard's ship.   Mr. Vans gives us good news from Boston as to brother Stephen's office, and news of confusions at Court and in the country, east to west.

8. *Sunday.*   A fine, clear day ; cool.   Mr. Fisher shews me the proceedings of the Bishops in England as to ordination of foreigners.

9. *Monday.* A very clear and fine day. Mr. Lane comes to town from Gloucester, where he landed.   He came in Capt. Barnard.   I write to Moses Hudson as to a mistake in [the] settlement of Mr. Cabot's and Gardner's suits, and to Theophilus Parsons as to Hawkes. Letters from R. Auchmuty and from S. Curwen, Esq., from London.   Mrs. Newhall, of Shelburn, and daughters here.

10. *Tuesday.* A fine day. Mr. Wetmore and Mrs. Pynchon set out in his chaise for Boston.

13. *Friday.*   Dr. Kneeland and lady come to town.

14. *Saturday.*   A fine morning.   Dr. Kneeland calls to see me.   W. Cabot and I, Mrs. G., and Ab. Gerrish go to Mr. Orne's farm.   Affairs of state go on heavily at General Court; they venture not to suspend the *Habeas Corpus* Act.

16. *Monday.*   A fine day. I set out in the stage with Colo. Pickman for Boston ; Mrs. Pynchon returns from thence in Mr. Orne's chaise by way of Charlestown.   I went over Winnisimet ferry and dined at Mr. Wetmore's, and received J. Oliver's letter.

17. *Tuesday.* Cloudy and rains. I set out in the rain for the ferry, and return to Salem at night.

20. *Friday.*   I write again to S. Curwen, Esq., as to Mr. Noyes's books and Dr. P.'s remittance.

23. *Monday.*   A fine, cool morning.   Mrs. Pynchon, in the afternoon, goes to Marblehead with Mr. Oliver in his chaise.

24. *Tuesday.* A clear, pleasant day. I write to Judge Oliver per ship Live Oak, [and] send it by Mr. Vans to Boston ; also write to Gen'l Farley by J. Hinckley as to Stevens's affair.

25. *Wednesday.* A fine morning ; moderate, but overcast. Wrote to Mr. Atherton and to Chase, for him and Darrah, as to their note. Mr. and Mrs. Orne dine with me ; we all sup at W. Cabot's.

27. *Friday.* Wait takes Boardman for Mrs. Cabot on Pickering's execution against him, returnable November, 1786.

28. *Saturday.* A very fine day. Eb. Hawkes dines with me. Mrs. Pynchon returns from Marblehead. Mr. Vans returns from Boston with news of the Riot Act and Tender Act and Lottery Act passed.

29. *Sunday.* Cool and windy. I go up to Mr. Orne's and lodge, acquainting him of the good news as to Boardman's debt.

30. *Monday.* Cloudy day. Mr. Orne comes to town, and lodges at Mrs. Pickman's.

31. *Tuesday.* A cool, clear day. Trial between Davenport and Graām before Justice Manning had this day. Graām is fined 5/ and pays costs, 16/. Davenport's letter, warrant, and horse hire cost him about 20/. News from the country that [there are] no insurgents nor opposition to the Court sitting at Cambridge ; and 't is said that 2000 militia, etc., are ready equipped there to support the Court.

November 1. *Wednesday.* A cool day. Mr. Orne returns home ; in his way goes to vendue of Felt's farm. No insurgents yet at Cambridge, and [the] Court proceeds to business.

2. *Thursday.* A cool day. I go to Beverly with S. Blyth ; tea at A. Cabot's ; visit Mrs. Higginson and her daughter Cabot at G. Cabot's ; speak with C. Wallis as to lad ; return in the evening by fine moonlight. Evening at Mr. Goodale's and part at Dr. Holyoke's.

4. *Saturday.* A fine, clear morning. John sets off in the stage for Boston on business of importance.

6. *Monday.*   Judge Cushing and J. Sewall come to town, also J. Dana, and have lodgings to seek.

7. *Tuesday.*   The Superior Court meet in the new Court House ; the Chief Justice mentions its elegance and convenience, and compliments the town and county upon it, accounting it the most elegant, etc., in the State ; he expatiates warmly against the conduct of the insurgents against the Judicial Courts, and proceeds and charges the Grand Jury to indict them for all opposition in Essex.   Parson Fisher reads prayers.

8. *Wednesday.*   Mitchell Sewall and John went from Marblehead for Boston.   Mr. Mansfield dines here.

9. *Thursday.*   At night a ball was made at Concert Hall for the Courts ; the Chief Justice danced 2 country dances ; Mrs. Orne was at the ball.   Mess. Hitchborn, Tudor, and Wetmore dine here, and S. Sewall.

10. *Friday.*   A fair day.   I am detained from Court by a cold caught last evening in going to the ball and returning in the rain.

11. *Saturday.*   A fine, clear day.   Brother Mitchell and John return from Boston, the latter in good spirits. At evening Judge Sewall, Mr. Goodale, and brother Mitchell spend the evening here ; Mitchell and Kimball lodge here.

12. *Sunday.*   A fine day.   At church I find Judges Cushing and Sumner ; they, J. Sewall, and Attorney-General Paine dine with me.   In the afternoon J. Sewall goes to church with me ; the others go to other meetings.   At evening all sup at Maj. Sprague's with Sunday night Club.   W. Pickering tells a foolish story of Ad. to G. Gage.   Brother S. and Mitchell lodge with us.

13. *Monday.*   A cool day.   Stephen and Mitchell go home ; Mr. Wetmore and son William to Boston.   P. M.,

I have a duplicate of a letter from Congress. J. Pynchon hath encouraging news from Boston as to military matters.

16. *Thursday.*   The Court adjourns without day.

17. *Friday.*   Clear and cold.   Judge Sargeant called to see me, and not being at home, he was to call to-morrow morning.

18. *Saturday.*   A clear and very cold, disagreeable air.   J. Sargeant does not call again.

19. *Sunday.*   A very cold day.   News that J. Williams succeeds in his plans for [the] bridge at Deerfield, and for regulations in Hampshire matters.

21. *Tuesday.*   Last of arresting for December Court, and I had but 2 writs to draw.

22. *Wednesday.*   Fresh news from Shays and the insurgents of a design against Cambridge Court.

23. *Thursday.*   Snow and cold.   Orders to Salem militia from [the] Governor to be ready in case [of need].

24. *Friday.*   Cloudy and cold A. M.   Warmer and clear P. M.   I go on Stevens's horse to Beverly, and see Edward Dodge as to execution *v.* Dale, and Mr. Dane as to tour to New York.   Stevens returns at evening from Boston.

25. *Saturday.*   Morning very cold.   News from Boston that Shays and co. are expected to be at Cambridge to stop the Court of Common Pleas.   Mrs. P. spends the evening at Vans' ; I go before 9, and am unluckily irritated at Vans' insolence and falsehood, and plainly tell him of it, and hurt the feelings of the company, and, since, my own feelings.

26. *Sunday.*   A fine, clear day, but cold.   I go with Mr. Fisher to see Capt. Britton ; very ill.

27. *Monday.*   South wind ; thaws, and wet walking.

News at night that 2 regiments of insurgents were on their march for Cambridge to stop the Court of Common Pleas, and [of] another body coming to support them. 'T is said Worcester Court of Common Pleas was stopped last week by insurgents.

28. *Tuesday.* Exceeding cold and windy. No news to-day of [the] insurgents. To-day Wait paid a part of Boardman's money to Mrs. Cabot.

29. *Wednesday.* P. M., I went to Beverly and visited A. Cabot, J. Cabot, G. Cabot, and Mrs. Higginson.

30. *Thursday.* A fine, moderate day. P. M. comes the news that the troop of about 80 horse, under Colo. Hitchborn, go from Boston to Middlesex and take Shattuck and . . . , and bring them, on charge of traitorous conduct, to prison to Boston ; this, 't is supposed, must soon bring our publick disturbances to a crisis. Capt. Britton still continues ill of dysentery.

December 1. *Friday.* A fine, moderate day. News of the taking Shattuck by the troop from Boston, etc., and of the triumphant return of the troop with the prisoners into Boston. Dr. Holyoke, lady, and daughter, Dr. Plummer and lady, *et al.*, and J. Grafton at tea here.

2. *Saturday.* A fine, cool morning, and clear. Mrs. Hinckley and Mrs. Oliver come from Marblehead and dine. At evening Mr. Bartlett comes to us at Mr. Goodale's, John being at Danvers at Mr. Orne's.

3. *Sunday.* A pleasant day. General Lincoln and other officers advise the Governor as to sending out the militia to protect the Justices at Worcester Court next Tuesday, but a majority of the Council is against it. J. Bartlett comes and dines here ; P. M., sets out for Mr. Orne's to see John, and thence goes to Boston.

4. *Monday.* Very cold. John sets out in the stage for Boston to wait on the Governor and Gen'l Jackson

17

for Ensign's Commission, and returns at evening with it, having seen Gen'l Jackson and Mr. Wetmore, and not the Governor. Brings news that the insurgents at Worcester County have shut up the Justices of the Common Pleas in their houses, to prevent the sitting of the Court, but McGill escaped, and got into Boston, this morning before sunrise; express is sent to General Lincoln at Hingham to go directly for Boston, and thence for Worcester. It snows and blows in the evening so that neither militia, nor Court, nor insurgents can well meet or proceed. Mrs. Pynchon, with Mr. Gerrish's horse and Mr. Cabot's chaise, goes with him up to Mr. Orne's, and she remains there. Dr. Plummer [1] joins the Monday Night Club, and spends the evening with them at my house. Shattuck and co. remain in good spirits at Boston jail. Mr. Wright moved into Dr. Putnam's house, next mine, a day or two ago.

5. *Tuesday.* Wind at E., and a most violent snow-storm, exceeding any remembered so early in the year; so deep and drifted is the snow that it is almost impracticable to ride in the roads. Judge Phillips calls in the afternoon, and, with J. Pickering, adjourns the Court by proclamation. Pickering is confined at his house, and J. Holten at his house, and both unable to attend Court.

6. *Wednesday.* The Justices Pickering and Phillips, having in vain waited for Just. Greenleaf's coming, meet P. M., and adjourn Common Pleas and Sessions to 3d Tuesday of January, 1787.

---

[1] Dr. Joshua Plummer was born in Gloucester, January 25, 1756, and was graduated at Harvard College in 1773. He was the son of Samuel and Elizabeth (Gee) Plummer, a daughter of Rev. Joshua Gee, of Boston. He removed to Salem in 1785, where he died in 1791. He was much esteemed by scholars and professional men, and had a high repute as a surgeon. His daughter, Caroline, was the founder of the Plummer Institute, established a professorship to Harvard College, and made many other generous gifts.

7. *Thursday.*   I walk down to Beverly ferry, and find the way blocked up by snow and impassable for horses.

8. *Friday.*   Cloudy, and south wind, and warm. Tarbell brings news from Mrs. Orne of her being very ill of slow fever, and calls on Dr. Holyoke, and he goes up and returns in the afternoon. The roads almost impassable without help from shovelling and the help of several sleds and 12 yoke of oxen. Mess. Otis and W. Amory spend the evening with John, Mr. Graham and B. Pickman also, and Graham lodges here. More news in the newspapers from Shays and co., insurgents, but their numbers rather decrease. However, Worcester Common Pleas and Sessions are put by again. A new snow-storm ariseth, wind N. E., and lasts all night.

9. *Saturday.*   Storm continues, and yet considerable provisions were brought to market. John enlisteth a soldier from Woburn, and, it being stormy, keeps him, and dieteth and lodgeth him.

10. *Sunday morn.*   The storm continues until 11 o'clock ; the sun breaks out, but the wind continueth ; the snow drifts in front of my house, and just admits of a view from my office window of Pike's garret window and of Hathorne's eastern garret window. No meeting to-day for public worship, the drifts of snow not admitting it.

11. *Monday.*   Clear, windy, and cold. The people go out on all sides of the town to clear the ways ; some sleighs pass, but with very great difficulty, through the streets ; none from the country ; it is said to be impassable for horses beyond the Bell tavern. The Club meet at Dr. Plummer's for the first time. John hath another soldier enlisted.

12. *Tuesday.*   Clear and extreme cold. The cold in the night was so great that few could sleep. In the

afternoon S. Gerrish and I go to Mr. Orne's farm, and find Mrs. O. better than she was; Mr. O. and Mrs. Pynchon well walled in with snow. I go on Daland's horse; we find the road very good from Salem to Procter's, very deep snow-banks from King's to Mr. O.'s.

13. *Wednesday.* Cloudy and more moderate air. John goes to Danvers for men, [and] tarries there the night. It rains.

15. *Friday.* Cloudy and clear by turns; the air rather warm and the travelling wet. John enlists H. Handly, and agrees with Scudder, a prisoner.

16. *Saturday.* Cloudy. Ensign Pynchon sets off on Stevens's horse for Boston with his 4 recruits — stout, brave soldiers! We hear from Mrs. Pynchon and Mrs. Orne and the family; all growing better; from Shays and co. that they are inclined to be penitent and sue for pardon on terms. The . . . here from Saturday, the 9th; the next from Monday, the 4th; the third from yesterday, the 15th; the fourth from this morning, the 16th. I sent the newspaper to Mr. Orne, and two volumes of the " Citizen of the World " to Mrs. Pynchon. The roads are to be cleared from Mr. O.'s to King's for carriages to-day.

17. *Sunday.* Cloudy and foggy; no wind. The snow goes off apace. P. M., I go to church, and find many more there than could be expected in so wet walking. Ensign Higginson in town on recruiting business. At tea Ensign Pynchon returns from Boston, having arrived there with his recruits last evening, being the first which had been returned from the country; all passed muster well.

18. *Monday.* Cloudy; toward evening cold. J. Higginson comes, and agrees to tarry recruiting at Salem and Beverly, instead of going on to Newbury, as was proposed.

19. *Tuesday.* Cold morning. John goes to Marblehead. Nat. Needham (*al.* Wilkes) leaves me to pay the money to F. Cabot, who advanced it for his family when in want of bread to eat ; no wonder Nat. should often be talking of the duties of religion and piety, of hearing heavenly prayers and sermons. John enlists another man, Hood.

20. *Wednesday.* A fine, clear day. John enlists another, Banks.

21. *Thursday.* A very clear, moderate, and fine morning. This day appointed for hanging Isaac Coombs for murder. Ensigns Pynchon and Higginson beat up for recruits in Salem. In the afternoon the artillery company, Tad. Buffinton the leader, escorted Isaac Coombs from the jail to the gallows, where he was hung in a bungling manner by Sheriff Farley in person. I hear from Mrs. Orne and Mrs. Pynchon that the former is growing better. The roads grow better by slow degrees.

22. *Friday.* It rains. Jackson, of Danvers, comes to enlist with John. Last evening, J. Turner, Esq.'s,[1] funeral. Bearers : —

G. Dodge,	Jona. Ropes,
Pynchon,	Jona. Gardner,
Dr. Holyoke,	W. Vans.

News from Mr. Orne's, Danvers, that Mrs. Pynchon is well and desirous of coming home. In the morning Ensign Pynchon sets off for Boston with 3 recruits, Hood, Banks, and . . . ; and Mr. Graäm sends Jackson for one more, with advice respecting another.

23. *Saturday.* Rain and snow. P. M., I set out for

---

[1] John Turner, who died on the 19th, was an eminent merchant of Salem. His daughter, Mary, married Daniel, the seventh son of Colonel Epes Sargent, and father of the late Lucius Manlius Sargent.

Danvers, and bring home Mrs. Pynchon. Higginson enlists more recruits. It begins to snow again in the evening. John returns from Boston.

25. *Monday.* Very cold. Church not full ; the musick by Young on the organ and the singing good. P. M., Mr. Britton's funeral ; he was carried into church, and a sermon on mortality ; no character attempted. Mrs. Pynchon, John, and I dine at W. Cabot's, and had a most excellent and tasty dinner done by Miss Gerrish.

26. *Tuesday.* A fine morning, clear and moderate. The sledding grows better hourly. Much poultry brought into market, and goes at $3\frac{1}{2}$/ and under per pound.

27. *Wednesday.* A very fine, clear morning, air moderate ; plenty of marketing, and sledding good in Salem. John has encouraging accounts from Boston *via* Bartlett.

28. *Thursday.* A fine day, good sledding, clear air. Young Mr. Gill here. Mr. Oliver comes here in the evening.

29. *Friday.* A cold, clear morning. John and his 3 recruits set out for Boston in good season, as did John Higginson. Mr. Lane with me in the evening, also Mr. F. and L. Oliver ; they say that Fenno brings accounts from Boston this evening that Gen'l Lincoln is collecting men, militia, etc., to accompany him to Worcester for protecting the Court to sit there, and to disperse the insurgents next week.

30. *Saturday.* Cloudy. The sledding continues very good ; rain expected soon to spoil it. John Pynchon and J. Higginson return from Boston ; each mortified at having one recruit of each rejected. News that Shays and insurgents continue in motion ; that they prevented Springfield Courts proceeding in November, and intend

to do the like at Worcester next week; Gen'l Lincoln, 't is said, is to go thither with the militia. John is lame by a fall at Boston.

1787. *January* 1. *Monday.* Letters from Mr. Curwen. Club at Colo. Pickman's in the evening with J. Lane. Warm, and thaw continues.

2. *Tuesday.* Plentiful markets. General Shays enlisting men in Connecticut.

3. *Wednesday.* Wet and bad travelling. From Hampshire, etc., they apply for aid from Government.

6. *Saturday.* Books are brought from Boston, Guthrie and Memoirs.

7. *Sunday.* Subscription is sent to town to raise money for paying militia.

8. *Monday.* Fine weather and good sledding. [The] militia to be raised is for supporting Courts of Justice.

9. *Tuesday.* Another snow-storm begins this morning, being Tuesday. The subscription, it is said, goes on; H. D. £100, J. A., W. G., B. P., £30 each. A snow-storm seems to be coming on, and keeps up the price of wood at 14/ and 15/.

10. *Wednesday.* Wind N. E., and snow. The stage goes to Boston and returns this day.

11. *Thursday.* Snow-storm continues. General . . . comes to town about raising men to march under Gen'l Lincoln to Worcester. Wrote to Mr. Wetmore as to Browne's affair; to S. Gridley as to my account; to C. Cushing for executions.

12. *Friday.* Mr. Eb'r Putnam, son of Judge Putnam, comes on Gov. Browne's business. John goes to Boston in the stage on recruiting business. A clear, cold day; the sledding grows good again.

13. *Saturday.* Clear and cold. Great number of loads of wood come to market to-day; oak at 14/ to 16/,

some at 12/. John returns from Boston with news that Shays, with great number of men, is to appear at Worcester to prevent the sitting of the Court of Common Pleas, and that he, John, hath encouragement to go with the militia ; he hears of his recruit, Clark, the deserter, who enlisted again at Boston, and left the officer there also, so that John is to be allowed his enlisting money.

16. *Tuesday.* Ipswich Court, which was adjourned to this day, is, by order of the General Court, adjourned to April 1.

17. *Wednesday.* John receives a line from Capt. Ramsdell.

18. *Thursday.* A fine, fair day, and appointed for the march of Capt. Ramsdell's company to Woburn, to be led by Ensign Pynchon. News comes that General Shays and company are gone off to Vermont, and in the afternoon Ensign Pynchon and Moses and co. march at half after one o'clock toward Reading ; dine at the sign of the Bell in Danvers, and after dinner a large company of gentlemen and others from Salem and Danvers give the company three cheers, and off they set in high spirits. Mess. Goodale, S. Gerrish, and myself take tea at Mr. Holt's, and return in a sudden squall of snow which overtook us. The night is excessive cold.

19. *Friday.* Clear and exceeding cold still. We hear that Ramsdell's company was met by [a] Lynnfield man upon a trot towards Reading ; saw Lieut. Moses and company at Woburn before night, appearing well and in good order.

20. *Saturday.* The air grows moderate, and snowstorm comes on. We hear again of Ramsdell's company, that he could not raise the Lynn company, and that Capt. Breed, a continental officer, was appointed captain

in Ramsdell's stead. In the afternoon a company from Gloucester passed through the town with fife and drum. Mr. Goodale and I dine at W. Cabot's upon an invitation to the family of each.

21. *Sunday.* Snows, and then fine rain ; wind N. E., and then it turns to snow again. Mrs. P. dines and spends the day at W. Cabot's. Small flights of snow and fine rain all day and in the evening.

23. *Tuesday.* Cloudy and cold. We hear from Woburn that John and co. got to Colo. Baldwin's by [the] middle of the afternoon, and lodged there.

25. *Thursday.* A very fine, clear morning. Mr. Vans brings news that the troops are at Worcester, and no appearance of an insurgent ; and the Court goes on as usual. One innholder is taken up and sent to jail for discouraging the militia from enlisting to support the Courts and Commonwealth. Dr. Waldo, from Worcester, called to see us, and mentioned his having yesterday seen F. Cabot, John Pynchon, and others from Salem, and that the army of 2000 and upwards were in high spirits ; that Shays and the insurgents were in 3 divisions ; a corps of 800 under Day, at Palmer Bridge, to cut off the communication between Shepard and Lincoln. A draft of 500 are ordered from Lincoln's troops to the relief of Shepard, who was stationed at Springfield with 800. Colo. Drury was taken and carried from Worcester to Boston jail.

26. *Friday.* Cloudy, and thaws. News comes that Shays is on his march for Springfield to attack Gen'l Shepard, having superior numbers to Shepard.

27. *Saturday.* A fine day. By the Centinel we have accounts of the number and situation of Lincoln's army at Brookfield, and of Shays's army at Springfield, and of Gen'l Shepard's firing on Shays's men and killing three men and wounding one badly.

28. *Sunday.* A fine, cold day, and clear. Brother Stephen came in the afternoon. Mrs. Goodale came and dined with us, and tarried the afternoon and evening. No express from Gen'l Lincoln's army ; all suppose it must have been intercepted by Shays's party ; no news from the army is now deemed a good event, as it must have reached Boston, had there been a battle, or had there been any very bad news ; Shepard's cannon and Lincoln's must have been heard at Brookfield or Worcester, and none were heard after his firing the first. J. Bartlett and co. are allowed to march from Boston to join Gen'l Lincoln.

29. *Monday.* A fine, clear, and cool morning. No further news ; no expresses till Jona. Jackson's arrival at Boston, P. M., this day ; his account is that Shays and co. were dispersed and gone over Chicopee River, 500 only keeping company with Shays ; that Gen'l Lincoln and Shepard were pursuing them ; that Shepard had dispersed Day's party of 3 or 400, and had taken about 40 prisoners ; that Shays had shot and killed his adjutant-general and 2 others.

30. *Tuesday.* B. Daland returned from Springfield with a letter from John.

31. *Wednesday.* Fine weather, some snow, good sledding. Many rumours as to Shays's and Lincoln's armies.

February 1. *Thursday.* Some snow and cold air. Beverly Commissary came home, as it is said.

2. *Friday.* A fine day. Mr. Pool brings a letter from John, dated the 28th, and a little after that by Daland, but mentioning the pursuit after Day and insurgents. By the papers we find terms offered by Gen'l Lincoln to Capt. Shays, and Shays answers them.

3. *Saturday.* Cloudy and cold. Vast quantities of

wood are brought in from the country. No account from the army, whether it is at Hadley or at Pelham, near Shays's and Wheeler. Gen'l Lincoln's proposals were answered well by Shays on the 30 January from Pelham.

4. *Sunday.*   Clear, and excessive cold ; wind N. W., and very high. Yesterday, Mr. Orne, Mrs. Pynchon, and I dine at W. Cabot's on venison.

5. *Monday.*   Exceeding cold, and some clouds. By Mr. Wright, from Boston, at one o'clock, we hear the vote of Legislative Assembly is that there is a rebellion in the western counties in the State, and that pardon be offered to the privates and non-commissioned officers under Shays and co. on terms of submission to Government and taking the oaths of [allegiance] ; we also hear that two more regiments are to march in aid of Gen'l Lincoln against the rebels at Pelham.   At evening Mr. Goodale shows me a letter from Fra. Cabot at Hadley, shewing the great danger of loss from an attack upon Shays, encamped with about 2000 men upon Pelham Hill.

6. *Tuesday.*   Clear, cold day. Major F. Cabot returns from Gen'l Lincoln's army with an account of Shays's army being dispersed, and retiring to Petersham from Pelham on last Friday evening, and of Gen'l Lincoln's following him in a severe snow-storm, in which his army marched 30 miles between 8 o'clock on Friday evening and 9 on Sunday morning without any refreshment, the severity of the storm not admitting of their stopping ; there were taken 150 prisoners.

7. *Wednesday.*   Clear, fine day. News of Shays and co. being reduced to 100 men, and of their wandering toward New Hampshire, where it is supposed some, if not all, of them will be arrested.

8. *Thursday.* Cloudy ; snow in [the] afternoon and all the evening. W. Cabot here [in] the evening. B. Daland set out A. M. for camp.

9. *Friday.* Fine, clear morning, and a moderate air. By a line from Mr. Vans, at Boston, we find he saw Major Harkin there, and that he left John Pynchon well at camp 2 days after Major Cabot's departure from thence, viz., on the 5th instant. Mr. Smith here A. M. and in the evening, and several of the soldiers' wives, to inquire the news.

10. *Saturday.* A fine, cool, and clear morning. Some of the Salem militia return and tell that Ensign Pynchon is lame with the last severe march, and set off on Wednesday last from Petersham for Hadley in a sleigh ; that others are dismissed for want of shoes, etc. ; that the allowance was so scanty they were forced to beg, and some pilfer, on the road ; that the whole company will return next week ; that the Ensign treated the company with grog, for their assistance in taking the company of insurgents prisoners, and for their spirited conduct toward the insurgents, who charged them with pilfering at Concord, by which treatment the Ensign became considerably popular among them ; that there had been a good understanding among the officers, and between them and their company, during the tour.

11. *Sunday.* Cloudy and severe cold. Bott married to Miss Hawthorn this morning at church. Mr. Templeman gives [an] account of Dr. Chauncy's death.

12. *Monday.* Clear and moderate. G. Cabot here, having spoken with Major Haskell at Boston, [and] gives account of [the] Salem company and of the 12 who took a captain and company of 40 men prisoners.

13. *Tuesday.* Clear and moderate weather. Townsend and Sibley, two of Ramsdell's company, call to ac-

quaint us of their leaving camp last Wednesday at Petersham ; that Ensign Pynchon was lame, and went in the waggon to Hadley, in the rout to Berkshire, to support Gen'l Patterson. Mr. J. Smith here at breakfast. B. Pickman, from Boston, says that the rumour at Boston is that Gen'l Patterson had made . . . composition with Wiley and the insurgents at Berkshire, each army to disperse, and Patterson to endeavour to obtain a pardon for Wiley and co. ; that Ensign Pynchon was not frozen in the feet, as had been reported, but was well at Petersham last Tuesday, save only a swelling in his ankles ; that the General Court were unanimous in their proceedings against the insurgents.

14. *Wednesday.* A fine, cool, and clear morning. Great quantities of wood in the market. P. M., snow, then rain, and in the evening it rains very hard. A letter from Ensign Pynchon of the 9th instant, giving account of Gen'l Patterson's composition with the insurgents at Lenox, and that Gen'l Lincoln was in full march from North Hampton for Lenox.

15. *Thursday.* Clear and warm. The snow decreaseth apace. Capt. Peabody here ; he went as a soldier from Middleton to West Springfield against Shays and Day.

16. *Friday.* Clear and cold. At evening I receive a letter from John Pynchon at Pittsfield, who is in high health and in good spirits, but wholly uncertain when the army may return, they being now busy in taking up insurgents and in dispersing their companies and corps which are found wandering about.

17. *Saturday.* Cloudy morning. No news of B. Daland, save rumours that he is taken by the insurgents ; no mention of him in John Pynchon's letter of the 12th (Monday) ; at 10 o'clock this evening we hear that he is in Boston, on his return homeward. I go to Boston, and

return at evening.   Dine at Mr. Wetmore's with Major
Ervins, Mrs. Weld's son Samuel, and young Mr. Ervins,
J. Williams, and Elbridge Gerry, Esqr.   Gen'l Patterson's character is cleared in the Centinel from the lies
raised and propagated against him.   I spoke with W.
Deblois as to his letter, and he agrees to wait for my
convenience.

18. *Sunday.*   Clear and moderate.   At noon B. Daland returns from the army with a letter from John
Pynchon, and account of his being well, etc.

19. *Monday.*   Clear, moderate weather; the snow goes
off apace.   Mr. Goodale and I dine at W. Cabot's on
venison.   Mr. Lowell came in at half past two, and set
out for Boston with his daughter.   Neighbour V. is
ready to give up his confidence in the public measures ;
thinks that Congress can hardly be held together, and
that our public affairs will be desperate unless the Continental Convention enlargeth the powers of Congress,
[and] amend the Confederation System, etc., etc., which
are hardly to be expected.   Dr. H. at Club gives his
political sentiments more fully than ever before.

20. *Tuesday.*   Cloudy and rain, which carries off the
snow rapidly.   Mr. Oliver, of Marblehead, took 43 of
Mr. McGilchrist's old sermons to read, and to return
them.

21. *Wednesday.*   Clear and cold.   News that an insurgent at the westward shot a light horseman, but was
taken with his party by the rest.   See the Nourse's
paper.

22. *Thursday.*   Clear and very cold.   I forward letters
to John Pynchon to care of Mr. Bartlett, Boston, by
Burrell.

23. *Friday.*   Clear and cold.   My letters to John
Pynchon went from Boston this morning by an express.

24. *Saturday*. Clear and moderate. Nat. Holt comes, having enlisted with John Pynchon for the Continental army. The snow goes off rapidly. More news from the army !

25. *Sunday*. Clear and moderate ; the snow goes off fast. By Mr. Higginson, from Boston, we hear that John Pynchon had been taken prisoner by the insurgents in New York State, but soon was dismissed on shewing that he was a Continental officer ; Wheeler, being taken in that State by R. Tyler and co., was rescued.

26. *Monday*. A fine, clear day. Mr. Oliver comes with Mr. Clarke, a young divine, and lodgeth with us ; spends the evening here with Mr. O. and Mr. Fisher.

27. *Tuesday*. Snow-storm ; wind N. E. Mr. Clarke sets out in stage for Boston. Mr. O. continues in town, and dines with us.

March 1. *Thursday*. A fine, warm day. Primus sets out with F. Goodale in R. Daland's carriage sleigh, with 2 horses, to bring home Moses and the Lieut. John Pynchon ; he meets them at Newhall's, and brings them home A. M. ; Mr. Goodale *et al.* with me.

3. *Saturday*. Another N. E. storm and snow. No man living among us remembers so many and so severe snow-storms in any year as in this.

5. *Monday*. Snow continues by turns ; the weather moderate ; at evening the wind comes in. News that a skirmish happened between Gen'l Lincoln's scouting party and a party of insurgents, in which the leader of the latter (supposed Maj. Downing) was killed, and several of Lincoln's [men] killed and wounded. Ensign Pynchon treats his men, who behaved well in the tour westward.

6. *Tuesday*. A fine, clear morning. News from the westward of several skirmishes between the inhabitants

and the insurgents ; of . . . killed on the part of the inhabitants and 62 prisoners ; . . . killed on the part of the insurgents and 62 taken prisoners ; but that the inhabitants were aided by some of Gen'l Patterson's troops ; that Shays and co. were arrived at . . . and much discountenanced by the Canadians.   Some snow to-day.

7. *Wednesday.*   A fine, clear, cool morning.   Never forget F. Cabot's humanity and kindness on a certain occasion, nor Maj. Sprague.

9. *Friday.*   A fine, clear morning, but some rain and snow in the afternoon and evening.   No strangers at the ball ; twice the number of ladies to the gentlemen.

10. *Saturday.*   A clear, fine morning ; the snow goes off apace.   Political squibs, serpents, and crackers in the papers announce the approach of electioneering business.

11. *Sunday.*   A clear and fine day ; the thaw carries off the snow apace.   News from Gen'l Shepard, at Springfield, that Capt. Shays is taken in Canada by order of Government there.   I receive a comfortable letter from Coz. J. Williams respecting family concerns.

12. *Monday.*   A fine, clear day.   John goes to Boston with his men, Carrel and co., for Continental army ; he gets there by 12, they about 2 o'clock.

13. *Tuesday.*   Cloudy and rain ; the snow goes off apace.   John returns at evening with Newhall ; the riding excessive bad.   Judge Dana taken with a paralytic disorder, and dangerously ill.

16. *Friday.*   Mr. Graham dines here.   Mr. Bartlett comes and takes lodgings with John.   A fine day.

17. *Saturday.*   John and J. Higginson go and spend the day at Mr. Orne's.   Tea at Mr. Cabot's.   Mr. Bartlett dines with us.   A fine, clear day.   The night-watch ceaseth ; thieving and house-breaking commenceth.

18. *Sunday.* Cloudy. Mr. Bartlett sets out for Boston A. M.   I at church P. M.

19. *Monday.* A fine, warm day. Political confusions prevail more and more, by accounts in the papers.

20. *Tuesday.* A fine, pleasant morning. Mrs. P. and I [spend] the evening at Dr. Holyoke's.

21. *Wednesday.* Clear and cool. Convention men and friends of the insurgents are using all their arts and endeavours to turn out of administration the present rulers. N. Holt comes.

22. *Thursday.* Cloudy. Jack and co. set out for Boston, being Fast Day. Mr. Osgood and I go to Mr. Orne's ; the going very good ; the snow almost gone.

23. *Friday.* Rain and clouds ; the snow is now all gone. News from Boston that Rhode Island State, by vote of their Lower House, had offered protection to the insurgents.

24. *Saturday.* Clear and cold. Mrs. Waters comes to my office to-day to scold about the suits against her, but makes default at Justice Pulling's. I go to settle with A. Cabot at Beverly.

25. *Sunday.* Clear and cold. John and B. Pickman set out for Beverly on a visit to Prescott. The Centinel and Friday papers are full of wrangling and reflecting pieces as to election of Governor, Senate, etc., etc. Bad news from Rhode Island as to Congress and as to insurgents ; that Government inclines to encourage the latter, and get rid of the former. At evening at Mr. Goodale's and at Mr. Cabot's.

27. *Tuesday.* A clear and cool day. John goes with Capt. Porter for Boston.

28. *Wednesday.* A fine, clear, and cool morning. Capt. Buffinton exercises his company at Pierce's house.

29. *Thursday.* Cloudy ; N. E. wind and cold. I set

out for Newbury on the reference between Wingate and Mulliken, on a dispute about an apprentice. Wingate's statement of his case, with explanations, notes, and observations, takes up 116 pages, folio, foolscap paper, closely written, which he insists upon reading and remarking on as he reads ; all interruptions or objections were in vain, so we let him go on, the referees taking liberty to sleep as they had occasion.

31. *Saturday.* At half past one Wingate ended, declaring he had a great deal to say, but, for want of time and through impatience of the gentlemen, he should then say no more. At half past seven in the evening I arrived at Salem, to hear political preachments and to read electioneering sermons in the newspapers. This day I have letters from Mrs. Browne, of Virginia, and from Mr. Curwen, in London. I return by the way of the ferry, because of the very deep snow-drifts ; on the road around in Beverly and in Danvers it is difficult to pass with carriages ; the ruts are so very deep that a person scarce can keep in the carriage in passing through the snow-banks.

April 1. *Sunday.* A fine, clear, and cool morning. The first day of a week *full, very full,* of importance.

3. *Tuesday.* The Court meet at Ipswich. The Bar meet at Perkins's, and agree on the admission of Mess. Andrews, Prescott, and Pynchon to the bar, and [that they] be recommended to the Court. I go in Stevens's chaise with him.

4. *Wednesday.* Very warm day. Andrews and Prescott admitted, but not sworn.

5. *Thursday.* Clear and pleasant. Mr. Greenleaf ill, and orders, with the consent of the Court, that the jury be dismissed, and no trials ; Andrews, Prescott, and Pynchon all sworn.

6. *Friday.* Clear and cool. J. Greenleaf and others go off for Newbury. p. m., the Court breaks up.

7. *Saturday.* A very fine day, clear and moderate. Salem and Marblehead parties set out from Ipswich ; the clerk with Mr. Stevens, and I with Mr. Mansfield. I find Mr. Lowell at Salem, and dine at Mr. Cabot's with him and Mr. Goodale. Mrs. Pynchon spends the day at Marblehead. See election witticisms in the Centinel.

8. *Sunday.* A fine, clear morning ; a plentiful rain in the night, with thunder. Mr. Spalding leaped out at chamber window in his sleep, dreaming, as it was said, that, being an angel of light, he could fly ; but he fell down by a stone wall, like a fallen angel, and was wet to his skin.

9. *Monday.* Cloudy and blowing weather ; some gusts of rain and hail, the latter so large as to break many glass windows, mine among others ; S. Gerrish had 6 squares broken.

14. *Saturday.* Miss Wetmore and Waldo come and dine with us. I go with W. Cabot to Mr. Orne's farm.

15. *Sunday.* A fine day. Mr. Oliver at church here.

17. *Tuesday.* A fine, clear, and moderate morning. News of the insurgents collecting in Berkshire to the number of 300, and, it is supposed, for rescuing the convicts in prison for treason, etc. ; query the event of present measures. See the papers respecting Rhode Island confusions and those at South Carolina.

18. *Wednesday.* Clear, cool day. John with Miss Waldo, and B. Pickman with Miss Wetmore, go to Danvers to tea at Mrs. Orne's. I have letters from Judge Oliver, S. Curwen, Esq., [and] N. Sparhawk, Esq., London.

19. *Thursday.* News that the Federal troops are dis-

charged ; that this is one of the last struggles of Congress.   All grow uneasy, disaffected.

20. *Friday.*   Lieut. Porter here ; he and John set out for Boston at 3.   Boston appears to be on fire in the evening.

21. *Saturday.*   Morning, fair winds and clear.   News from Boston that 60 houses were burnt last evening. Mr. Lovejoy here.   John Pynchon returns with news of the fire at Boston ; 60 dwelling-houses and stores, shops, etc., and Byles's meeting-house.   Mr. Amory comes at tea.

22. *Sunday.*   Snow in the morning.   At church all day.   John unwell.   Carrell comes from the Castle with letters for John.

23. *Monday.*   Cloudy.   John Pynchon goes to Boston about business of recruits, etc.

24. *Tuesday.*   A fine, clear, moderate day.   John returns from Boston ; brings no good news.

27. *Friday.*   A fine, clear day.   Judge and Mrs. Greenleaf go out of town.   Mr. Wingate here, and goes home.   Misses Waldo and Wetmore go from Salem for Boston.

28. *Saturday.*   Clear and cool.   Harvey[1] sat this week on the gallows, and was expelled the House of Representatives.

29. *Sunday.*   Cloudy and some rain.   John proposes to open an office in Salem.

May 1. *Tuesday.*   Cloudy ; thunder and rain.   By help of the storm and S. G.'s oratory, I buy good pig pork at 3*d.*

2. *Wednesday.*   Cloudy morning ; cool day.   Jack

---

[1] Moses Harvey was punished for exciting and stirring up sedition and insurrection in the Commonwealth, in connection with the rebellion under Shays.   See *Hampshire Gazette*, April 25, 1787.

lays the turf in the back yard. Mrs. P. and I at W. Cabot's at tea.

3. *Thursday.* A fine, fair morning. John goes to Boston with R. Derby. Mr. Lane here. Mr. L. goes to Portsmouth.

4. *Friday.* Clear, fine day. I go to Marblehead with J. Grafton in his chaise, and return at noon ; visit there at Justice Mansfield's.

5. *Saturday.* John Pynchon agrees for an office at Mr. Ropes'.

6. *Sunday.* At church all day with Mrs. Pynchon.

7. *Monday.* Vestry meeting ; vote a composition as to taxes of Britton's pew. I set out for Andover, and lodge there at Mr. Lovejoy's.

8. *Tuesday.* Mr. Lovejoy and I set out in his chaise for Haverhill, on reference between Wingate and Mulliken ; lodge and dine at B. Bartlett's ; go in the evening to visit Judge Sargeant.

9. *Wednesday.* Set out from Haverhill for Andover ; dine at Mr. Lovejoy's, and at 3 P. M. set out for Salem, and arrive at about 7 o'clock. In this journey I lost my bundle of linen out of my surtout.

10. *Thursday.* Town meeting for new representatives : R. Ward, R. Manning, Eb. Bickford, Ed. Pulling. It rains.

11. *Friday.* Rained last night and most of this day. W. Cabot and I go to visit John's office.

12. *Saturday.* Rain continues ; when over, Mr. Vans is expected from Boston ; what can reconcile him, since a lawyer is chosen representative and he left out, notwithstanding his exertions against the order, his declamatory speeches, etc. ?

13. *Sunday.* Rains, and all tarry at home A. M. save John. P. M., it rains, and I go to church.

14. *Monday.*   Cold, N. E. wind.   Mr. Pulling puts an odd query to me, with many half excuses respecting Pickman and his office.   Mr. Pearce calls me home from [the] Club.

15. *Tuesday.*   Some rain ; cold, N. E. wind.   Mr. Vans from Boston.   News that the insurgents intend to rescue the convicts westward.

17. *Thursday.*   Cold ; wind N. E.   Ascension Day. A sermon at Mr. O.'s church, Marblehead, and musick.

19. *Saturday.*   A fine, clear, and pleasant day.   Mr. Hooper here an hour, and almost suffocates me.

21. *Monday.*   A fine morning.   Colo. Pickman and lady go to Boston, and the Club here.   Mr. Jackson here in the evening.

22. *Tuesday.*   Some rain.   News of Shattuck's trial, and conviction of treason.

23. *Wednesday.*   A fine day.   Judge Sewall calls, and lodgeth with us.   Artillery company train, and make a fine show.

24. *Thursday.*   [In the] morning Judge Sewall sets out for Portsmouth and York.

26. *Saturday.*   A fine day.   Went in the afternoon to Mrs. Lynde's, who was gracious.   I take tea at Mr. Goodale's ; [he and she gone] with Miss Higginson.

28. *Monday.*   A fine day.   I adjusted account with clerk Osgood.   Young Mr. Lane calls on me with notice that his father will be here to-morrow.

29. *Tuesday.*   A clear, fine morning.   Mr. Lowell and Mr. Lane meet in Salem on affairs of Mr. Oliver.

30. *Wednesday.*   Election Day.   T. F. Oliver calls, and dines with us and his son.   Mr. Lowell dines at W. Cabot's.   It rains all day.

31. *Thursday.*   Cloudy ; it rained most of the last night ; wind S. E.   Mess. Lane and Lowell set out in the afternoon for Boston.   Mr. Oliver goes home.

June 1. *Friday.* Some rain and clouds, and in the afternoon sunshine. I go up to Dr. A. Putnam's about his deposition as to A. Waters. John Pynchon returns from Boston with R. Derby in Daland's carriage.

2. *Saturday.* John and Capt. Abbot go to Danvers and tarry all day, suppose at Capt. Porter's.

4. *Monday.* John goes to Middleton with Mr. Ropes. Dr. Boyce here, and takes a memorandum as to Ballard's fees on writ as to Mr. Turner's title to the 100-acre lot, and takes a note for him and his two sons to sign for Nichols, and Boyce's debt on note.

7. *Thursday.* Rain prevents training.

8. *Friday.* The Salem Cadets muster.

9. *Saturday.* I go to Topsfield with Daniel Esty.

10. *Sunday.* Mr. Fisher preacheth two excellent sermons.

11. *Monday.* Warm day. B. Pickman, Jr., goes for the eastward.

12. *Tuesday.* Cloudy ; wind S. E. I set out with J. Grafton for Boston ; dine with him at Mrs. Gray's ; lodge at Mr. Wetmore's ; go into the gallery to hear the debates of the House of Representatives. Mitchell Sewall comes. Putnam,[1] son of Gideon, proposeth to study law.

13. *Wednesday.* A warm day. I go into the lobby to hear the debates as to general pardon, and as to raising of troops ; return at evening [at] half past 9 o'clock.

14. *Thursday.* Very warm. Primus Lynde's funeral. Mrs. Goodale ill ; hath hysterical fits.

15. *Friday.* Warm. Dr. Masury a few days ago had a paralytic shock. A pardon to go with the troops to the westward.

16. *Saturday.* A fine, clear, cool morning. We hear

[1] Samuel Putnam, afterwards one of the Justices of the Supreme Court.

from Boston that 2 companies of artillery are to go forward to the western counties to support the Executive for the proposed execution of the traitors.

20. *Wednesday.* Morning, I set off for Danvers to attend Endicot's and Patch's reference at Leach's tavern, and attend till 5, and then set off with Stevens for Ipswich Court.

21. *Thursday.* Evening, the Chief Justice comes and meets us at Sheriff Farley's, and tells us of the escape of the criminals in Hampshire, etc.

22. *Friday.* The Court adjourns without day.

23. *Saturday.* A warm day. Mrs. Nimmo (*alias* Tate) goes off bag and baggage to Boston.

25. *Monday.* Cloudy and warm ; wind S. E., and some rain A. M. Town meeting for the bridge.

26. *Tuesday.* Clear and cool. Bridge ! bridge ! is all the conversation.

28. *Thursday.* Clear and cool. Turtle feast at Lynn Beach, [by] J. Gardner's invitation ; John and co. do not go.

29. *Friday.* Petitions go in for the bridge, the bridge !

30. *Saturday.* Mr. Turell and brother Stephen Sewall dine with me on fish. The ferry-way bridge scheme seems in best credit.

July 4. *Wednesday.* Grand exhibition at Boston on this day ; oration by Daws in Chapel, and Gen'l Brooks to the Cincinnati.

5. *Thursday.* Warm. Mr. Bourn and Mr. Oliver dine here, and Mrs. Oliver and son ; Mr. and Mrs. O. go to Danvers, and tarry at night.

6. *Friday.* Clear and warm. Mr. Bourn returns in the stage to Boston. Mr. and Mrs. O. return and take tea with us, and from hence go to Marblehead.

10. *Tuesday.* The Court.

11. *Wednesday.* Wait, D. Sheriff, being pressed with demands, agrees to serve no longer the Ju. Court. Mr. Wetmore and Billy come at evening.

12. *Thursday.* They dine with me, also Just. Lovejoy ; in the afternoon they return for Boston, and Maj. Erwin comes and takes tea with us.

13. *Friday.* The major goes to B. Island and takes possession on Mr. Turner's mortgage.

14. *Saturday.* The major goes to Boston in the stage.

15. *Sunday.* A fine day. No church. I go to hear Mr. Bentley at Mr. Prince's meeting.

17. *Tuesday.* J. Derby hath Dr. Putnam and the elderly people, gentlemen and ladies, at his house at the Neck, and [they] spend there the afternoon ; it was very cool, and the greater part of the company, gentlemen and ladies, walk back.

18. *Wednesday.* Commencement. The morning was so cold that many were discouraged from setting out for Cambridge ; at several places was considerable ice and frost. The guards at Cambridge were mounted all on white horses, and had handsome uniforms, scarlet and blue. The exhibitions of the candidates were said to be exceedingly good. The President's house broken [into] in the night, but the robbers were driven off.

19. *Thursday.* The watch patrol the streets, and several of other companies go into Lynn woods in quest of thieves and robbers, but find none. This a fine, clear, cool day. I have a letter from N. Sparhawk, Esq., and answer it, and write to Judge Oliver by Jenks ; also to S. Curwen, and send 42s. 8d. to him in a letter on account.

20. *Friday.* A fine, clear, cool morning. Mr. Fisher returns from Falmouth.

21. *Saturday.*   A fine, cool day.   Mrs. Pynchon goes with W. Cabot to Mr. Orne's, and returns at evening, and finds Mr. and Mrs. Wetmore and Billy here.

22. *Sunday.*   Cloudy and cool.   Mr. and Mrs. W. and Mrs. P. sup at Mr. Goodale's.

23. *Monday.*   Mr. and Mrs. Wetmore and our family dine at Mr. Goodale's.

24. *Tuesday.*   Mr. and Mrs. Wetmore and Mrs. Pynchon and Mrs. Goodale go to Marblehead.

27. *Friday.*   Cloudy.   Two straggling, suspicious persons are taken up by 2 negroes, and complained of for idleness and disturbing the peace.

28. *Saturday.*   Cloudy.   I dine at W. Cabot's.   See the hum in the papers as to American trade.   Mrs. Curwen returns in the new chariot.

29. *Sunday.*   Cool, but cloudy.   Mrs. Orne comes down and goes to church at Marblehead.

30. *Monday.*   Cloudy, and cooler than often in February ; at night people are uncomfortable abed without warming.   Ed. Putnam disappointed again as to swearing out of jail.

August 1. *Wednesday.*   Cadet company agree to exercise at 5 in the evening.   An attempt to rob at Lynn Plains.

2. *Thursday.*   Warmer and cloudy.   I write to Gen'l Glover, Rob. Foster, N. Silsbee, as to speedy settlement of account with N. Sparhawk, [and] Ezra Putnam for settlement with W. Wetmore immediately.   Bank-bills counterfeited, and passing at Boston ; a Nova Scotian suspected, and is followed eastward.

3. *Friday.*   Cold.   Secret correspondence of S. H. with G. Lincoln comes out.

4. *Saturday.*   I dine at W. Cabot's, and go with him to Mr. Orne's at tea.   H. Gardner returns from sea.

5. *Sunday.* Very warm and clear. I go to Marblehead ; dine at Mr. Oliver's. Most excellent singing at church in forenoon and afternoon.[1]

9. *Thursday.* Mr. and Mrs. Wright at tea with my family. Weather very hot.

10. *Friday.* Cloudy, and a fine rain A. M. Lecture at Spaulding's meeting-house.

12. *Sunday.* Warm. At church A. M. Mrs. Orne comes with Mrs. Pynchon, and the three girls return.

13. *Monday.* Rumours and surmises as to defaulters at Congress, Convention, etc. Brother Stephen comes and lodges with us.

14. *Tuesday.* A fine morning. The Court of Sessions adjourns.

17. *Friday.* Clear and warm. Last night neighbour Lang left open his shop window and doors, and this morning was missing his glass case, which some of the neighbouring wags took away, and were busy with Lang in searching for it, and advising to advertisements, search-warrants, etc., etc., till poor Lang was half crazy and bewildered ; his boy was shewing the neighbours and inquisitive folk the place where and how the thieves got in, which hook and bolt they drew and drove in again, till the spectators were ready to burst their sides.

18. *Saturday.* A fine, clear day. I drink tea at Mr. Fisher's. Hear by Mr. Vans of Dr. Holten's return from Congress, and of his want of confidence in the grand convention.

19. *Sunday.* A very fine, clear, and cool day. At church ; Mr. Fisher preacheth.

---

[1] The music at St. Michael's at this time was in advance of that in most churches. It was at this church that, four months later, on the eve of Christmas, the first chanting was heard in the American Church, and many persons often went from Salem to be present at the services.

20. *Monday.* Cool and cloudy ; rain at night. Mrs. Blyth dies P. M.

21. *Tuesday.* Rains hard in the morning. Wrote to T. Fuller for Mr. C., H. Gardner, M. Gardner, B. Felt, and D. Smith. French officers come to town from Boston.

22. *Wednesday.* Cloudy. Mrs. Blyth's funeral ; singers come from Marblehead ; J. P. plays a dirge.

24. *Friday.* A clear, warm day. Mr. Osgood and I go to wait on Dr. Holten, lately returned from Congress ; he had rode out, and we went to see Mr. Wadsworth's new house and meeting-house. At evening I take tea at Mr. Sanders's.

25. *Saturday.* A fine, warm morning. Several gentlemen from Nova Scotia come to town.

26. *Sunday.* A fine day. At church all day. P. M., Mr. Allen *et al.*, from Nova Scotia, at church ; their behaviour very decent and exemplary ; they go to Mr. Fisher's at tea.

27. *Monday.* Clear and cool. Letter from J. Sewall.

28. *Tuesday.* Mr. Osgood, of Haverhill, and his son here.

30. *Thursday.* Fair and cool. Dr. Walter and family come.

31. *Friday.* Clear and cool. I make a visit to Dr. Walter ; Mrs. W. is much fatigued with her passage and her journey from Boston to Salem, [and] keeps her room ; Mr. Grafton goes with me. Mrs. Pynchon goes to Marblehead with Mr. Oliver.

September 1. *Saturday.* A fine morning. I go with Mr. Fisher to see Dr. Walter and lady, and meet them both, and we are very cordially and respectfully received by them.

2. *Sunday.* Dr. Walter preacheth at Marblehead for

Mr. Oliver; his lady goes with him. Mrs. Orne also goes over, and spends the day most agreeably, as, on her return this evening, she tells us. Mr. Fisher gives us a most useful and entertaining sermon at church; his delivering it was excellent, distinct, etc.

3. *Monday.* A fine, moderate day. John goes to Topsfield and Reading on actions before Justice Cleaveland and Justice Browne, and succeeds to his wishes.

4. *Tuesday.* Fair, good weather. I incur the displeasure of masters and merchants by judgment in favour of a sailor. Mr. Oliver and brother here in the evening, and Dr. Holyoke on business.

5. *Wednesday.* Cloudy and rain; in the afternoon it clears off, and I go to Marblehead, and lodge at Mr. Oliver's; return, and write to Mr. Atherton, of Amherst, by Sheriff Stevens.

6. *Thursday.* Sup at Mr. Goodale's with Dr. Walter and lady and Jas. Jeffry.

9. *Sunday.* A very fine, clear morning. Dr. Walter preached in the morning and afternoon; Mr. Fisher read prayers; a very full church in afternoon; his address and delivery excellent in the pulpit, and his discourses and composition elegant.

10. *Monday.* Mr. Ogden, of Portsmouth, calls to see me. Mr. Osgood, of Haverhill, with the Club, is here in the evening.

11. *Tuesday.* A fine, cool day. Court of Sessions sit by adjournment; Justice Mansfield presides with dignity.

14. *Friday.* A general pardon of the convicts for treason, etc.

15. *Saturday.* A fine, cool day. I go with Mrs. Goodale to see Mrs. Orne and her daughter, Betsy; Dr. Holyoke and B. Pickman, Betsy Cabot and Miss Lander,

there at tea. See the Centinel and the satirical rap given by the reviewers to Doc. Adams's book on the American Constitution.[1] See the Governor satirized as to the pardons.

16. *Sunday.* Mr. and Mrs. Walter go to Marblehead. Mr. Ogden at church ; P. M., here. A fine, cool day. Joshua Grafton grows weaker and worse daily. Mess. Goodale and Grafton, Mr. Lynde Oliver, and I go over to the christening of Mr. Oliver's son, Daniel, and Mr. Goodale and co. kindly walk back for Mr. and Mrs. Walter and daughter to ride, Mr. Walter's horse having run off.

17. *Monday.* A clear, cool day. Spend a pleasant evening at Dr. Plummer's.

18. *Tuesday.* A cool, clear morning. Notice to-day from G. Williams of reference being Monday before Sept. Court, between Glover and Jewet. This day wrote again by post to Jewet as to reference. At adjournment of Court of Sessions this day I was called on to preside, being the only one of the quorum in town.

22. *Saturday.* Cloudy, and some rain and shine by intermission. Mrs. Pynchon goes with F. Goodale to Mr. Orne's, and returns at evening. Mrs. R. Cabot here.

23. *Sunday.* Fine weather. Mr. Fisher preacheth all day to crowded audiences ; Mr. Prince having a cold, his people go to church.

24. *Monday.* A fine day. At six o'clock clerk Osgood and I set out in S. Blyth's chaise for Newbury Court, and dine with the Court at Davis'.

25. *Tuesday.* Fine weather. I write to James, of Edgcomb, as to Glover's reference, by post.

---

[1] This paper was from the (London) *Critical Review* for April, 1787. See *Massachusetts Centinel* of September 22, 1787.

26. *Wednesday*. Good weather. Mr. Willis is not proposed for admission, the Bar not meeting.

27. *Thursday*. Fine weather. Mr. O. and I visit J. Greenleaf A. M., at 8 o'clock.

28. *Friday*. Murray, of Newburyport, recovers in case of taxation. A number of thieves confess and are sentenced. I visit Mr. Farnam, Mr. Cary, and Mr. Bass; dine at Mrs. Atkins's.

29. *Saturday*. Cloudy and rain. Mr. O. and I set out, and dine at Ipswich, overtaking Mr. Pulling.

30. *Sunday*. Fine weather. Mr. F. preacheth all day. Mr. Walter at Newburyport.

October 1. *Monday*. A fine day. At evening Club meet at Dr. H.'s, and Mr. Walter there.

2. *Tuesday*. A very fine day. I write by Mr. Walter to James Selkrig at Shelburne.

3. *Wednesday*. Clear and cool. I write to N. Sparhawk, Esq., S. Curwen, and Peter Frye by Folgier on Calahan, and to Mrs. Browne, of Virginia, by Dr. Oliver, who is to sail hence to-morrow.

4. *Thursday*. Cool and clear. Betsy Orne ill, and, we fear, upon the decline.

5. *Friday*. Mr. Grafton is said to be recovering from his illness.

6. *Saturday*. J. Grafton sent for his bearers, [and] ordered all matters as to his coffin, funeral, etc.; his aunts pronounced him delirious, his coz. Jos. to be sound and intelligent; an affray ensued, and he drove all out.

8. *Monday*. Delivered to coroner Cook, Salem, execution, Sar. Laurence *v*. Mich. Farley, dam. £35.5.4, costs £1.14.8, date 1 Oct. Dr. Paine[1] and family begin

---

[1] Dr. William Paine was the son of Timothy Paine. He was graduated at Harvard College in 1768, was proscribed in 1778, and became apothecary to the British forces in Rhode Island and New York. After the war he resided at St. John, but returned in 1787 to Salem. He went to Worcester to reside in 1793, and there died April 19, 1833.

housekeeping ; they came in last Friday. P. M., with Miss Prince, who brought letters from J. Sewall, who with his family has taken a house at St. John. Mr. Wetmore arrives from the eastward, and lodgeth with us.

9. *Tuesday.* I go to Jacob's, Danvers. Mr. Wetmore sets out in the stage for Boston. I go to see Dr. Paine, and spend the evening most agreeably in hearing accounts from New Brunswick. A. M., I went with Mr. Barnard to Mr. Diman's ; he confined by illness. Hans Newhall comes with many new and some of his old excuses ; W. Webb also comes ; and Israel Putnam comes about his father's enlargement.

10. *Wednesday.* Mr. Grafton continues better. Last evening I spend at Dr. Paine's, and am much entertained with accounts of friends at Nova Scotia. N. Sparhawk, Esq., and others arrive from England at Boston. John Derby brings home Mrs. Derby, and, with her, Miss Mayhew. Dr. Putnam goes out of jail.

11. *Thursday.* A very fine day. Mr. Diman disordered yet ; at times dividing his lands, at others solving paradoxes.

12. *Friday.* An exceeding fine morning. Mr. Diman finisheth his will and executeth it, and appears to be greatly relieved. Mr. Prince continueth ill.

13. *Saturday.* A fine, clear, cool day. Dine at W. Cabot's, and go with Mr. Goodale, Colo. Pickman, W. Cabot, and Mr. Noyes to the fort, and drink coffee.

15. *Monday.* A very fine, clear morning. A fine, cold collation at J. Derby's on the great occasion, young and old attending.

16. *Tuesday.* I write to R. Hooper, Esq., by Mr. Oliver as to settlement.

17. *Wednesday.* Windy and cool and clear. This being the day for training, the new militia company in

rifle uniforms turn out and make a very good appearance under Capt. Page, and they join in the exercises with the Cadets, and all are this day commanded by Capt. Abbot; the artillery company under Capt. Buffinton keep by themselves, insisting on firing their field pieces in School Street, whereby they broke Dr. Putnam's windows and greatly disturbed him, though ill. The wind blew all day, and raised the dust, so that it was difficult walking the street with eyes open.

18. *Thursday.* A fine, clear day; the wind continues. Professor Williams here yesterday with Mr. Barnard. Mr. Prince and Grafton continue ill yet, the latter far gone. Miss R. Pickman spends the afternoon and evening with Betsy Orne, and is very sociable.

19. *Friday.* A fine, clear morning. John and co. go to Reading, and are noticed by General Brooks, Hull, *et al.* I call at J. Grafton's; he died this evening.

20. *Saturday.* A fine day; cloudy at times. Mr. Oliver dines here. W. Pickman, John, and N. Ropes walk to Marblehead. Mrs. Pynchon visits at S. Grafton's.

22. *Monday.* A fine day. Mr. J. Grafton is buried, not carried into church. I. Osgood, from Haverhill, in town.

23. *Tuesday.* A fine day. Reference in Glover and Jewet's cause. Mr. Wetmore comes; the family on [a] visit at Mr. Paine's.

24. *Wednesday.* A very fine, warm day. Mr. Wetmore goes to Boston. N. Sparhawk, Esq., set out early this morning for Portsmouth; he came from Boston last evening and called to see me, and brought a letter and book from Judge Oliver.

25. *Thursday.* A fine, clear, warm day. Mrs. Pyn chon, Mrs. Orne, and Betsy spend the evening at Mrs. Anderson's; musick and dancing.

26. *Friday.* Fine, warm, clear morning; foggy P. M.

I go with neighbour Wright in his new chaise to Marblehead, and back at tea.   Mrs. Pynchon, Orne and co. spend the evening at Mrs. Pickman's; no dancing again.

27. *Saturday.*   A fine, clear, cool day.   We hear from Boston that a great majority of [the] General Court voted in favour of the new Constitution ; that the bridge over Beverly ferry is to be erected.

29. *Monday.*   A cool day.   Town meeting to obtain the mind of the inhabitants as to the bridge over Beverly ferry ; and the first motion made was to dismiss the meeting, in order to avoid the perpetuating of quarrels in the town ; and it passed in the affirmative by a majority of 15, the fullest meeting remembered in Salem.

31. *Wednesday.*   Cloudy and cool morning.   Sent by Dr. Paine Judge Oliver's present of a book to Colo. Worthington instead of S. Lyman, Esq., to whose care directed.   Mrs. Oliver came over on foot from Marblehead to see us ; dined and lodged with us.

November 1.   *Thursday.*   This day the dispute at General Court about the bridge came on warmly, and at evening (present 190 members) the vote was called and questioned, and on a division of the House . . . were for accepting the report of the Senate in favour of the bridge and . . . against it.

2. *Friday.*   Three swivels were fired in Northfield on account of the bridge news.

3. *Saturday.*   Fair, cool day.   Town-meeting is warned to be on Monday concerning the bridge ; the House of Representatives not concurring with the Senate, the matters rest before the Senate, and party spirit in Salem is at an high pitch ; S. Ward, the leader of up-in-town disputants, was by the Insurance Office voted out, and he tells them they will repent of their ill manners in doing it.

4. *Sunday.* A fine, clear morning, and cool, pleasant day. I walk to Marblehead in company with Mr. Turell ; go to church and hear their organ, lately repaired. Mrs. Ford is buried. At night I ride back with Mr. Oliver ; John walked with Mr. Turell.

5. *Monday.* A fine, moderate day. I go to Danvers before the Commission on Waters' estate, and put in my claim on judgment. The Superior Court meets here.

7. *Wednesday.* Mr. Symmes here.

8. *Thursday.* Mr. Wetmore comes with Billy.

9. *Friday.* A ball at Concert Hall ; the Judges Sargeant, Sumner, and Bradbury present, and a large company of ladies — about 55 ; Mr. Lane and son present also.

10. *Saturday.* P. M., the Superior Court adjourns without day. Judges Cushing and Sumner, with Mr. Sewall and the Sheriff, dine with us ; Mr. Lowell, Goodale, Prescott, and Mansfield disappoint us. S. Ward here at tea.

11. *Sunday.* Morning, Judges Cushing and Sumner go out of town early.

12. *Monday.* Dr. Paine is invited to be a member of the old Club, and spends the evening with them at Colo. Pickman's.

14. *Wednesday.* Cloudy and foggy. I spend the evening at Colo. Pickman's with Mr. Treadwell and W. Pickman ; our subject was the Connecticut Blue Laws ; [it is] said in the newspapers that they had the name given them from the blue cover they were stitched in. By the papers we find the Stadtholder, at the head of 15,000 Prussian troops, was reinstated.

15. *Thursday.* Warm and cloudy. Judge Mansfield and son here. W. Cabot and Ab. Gerrish dine here.

P. M., cloudy and rainy.   Mr. Goodale and I spend the evening at J. Grafton's.

16. *Friday.*   Rain, and dark weather.   Wrote to Jared Edgcomb as to Rep't Glover.

17. *Saturday.*   Clear and cool ; wind at N. W.   I go to Boston in Burrell's stage ; arrive at half after eleven ; dine at Mr. Wetmore's ; pass over Malden [bridge] for the first time ; I visit W. Deblois about the affairs of G. Deblois, of Halifax, and he appears to be well satisfied with my account of them, and is to write to him accordingly.   I return at evening by moonlight with G. Cabot, G. Williams, and Thorndike, and they entertain me with bridge news and General Court manœuvres.

18. *Sunday.*   A fine, clear morning.   W. Amory comes at evening and lodgeth with John Pynchon.

19. *Monday.*   Mr. Amory and co. dine with Master F. Goodale.

20. *Tuesday.*   They dine at Mr. Vans', [and] spend the evening at Mr. Pickman's.   Mr. and Mrs. Oliver with Miss Knight come to tea, having walked on foot from Marblehead.   Miss K. lodgeth at Mr. Wait's.   Mr. and Mrs. Oliver dine with us ; also Mr. Amory on Wednesday.

21. *Wednesday.*   P. M., it rains hard ; A. M., is cloudy. We go to Mr. Vans' for tea, and spend the evening, Mr. and Mrs. Oliver, Mr. Amory, Mrs. Pynchon, and I.

22. *Thursday.*   Cloudy and rain.   At evening I went to Insurance office, and was graciously received.

23. *Friday.*   Cloudy and rain.   I receive a letter from Colo. Pickman as to his son's discontinuing the study of law, etc., and answer it.

24. *Saturday.*   Cloudy and cool ; wind N. E. yet.   Mr. Pickman, Jr., calls to bid adieu to the office and to the study of the law, and takes away his desk, papers, etc.

27. *Tuesday.*   Cloudy.   Mr. and Mrs. Orne dine and lodge here; they, with Mr. and Mrs. Vans, spend the evening with us, and are very merry.

28. *Wednesday.*   Cloudy.   A full market for Thanksgiving ; poultry at 3*d.*

29. *Thursday.*   A fine, clear morning.   I write to Sheriff Wait by G. Peirce of Otisfield, for information as to W. Webb's security, payment of costs, etc., etc. The fiddler lodgeth and continues here, but sets out A. M. for Gloucester.   Mr. O. and Sally and two children dine at Madam Lynde's, but sup at Judge Oliver's.   Mrs. Gerrish is delivered in the night of twins.   We dine at W. Cabot's.   Wrote to Judge Oliver and Mr. Curwen.

December 1. *Saturday.*   Cloudy and cold ; the air seems full of snow, and doubtless will soon accommodate us with a part.

2. *Sunday.*   Clear and pleasant.   The fiddler dines here.

3. *Monday.*   Mr. F. Cabot, lady, and sister, afternoon and evening ; I at Mr. Goodale's ; Colo. Sargent there. Mr. Cutler here about Ohio.   Wrote to I. Osgood, Haverhill.

4. *Tuesday.*   Cloudy ; N. E. wind, and sky full of snow.   Write to Ezra Upton's widow, Danvers.   Wrote to brother Pynchon by Capt. White ; to John Williams to be at Springfield on 22d December, or early in the week after it, and to write me an answer of what time they can meet ; to Mr. Bliss, Esq., as to his account.

5. *Wednesday.*   A fine, clear day.   The fiddler comes in at one to dine.   Town-meeting for Convention men.

8. *Saturday.*   I go to Mr. A. Cabot's, Beverly ; spend part of the evening at George's.

14. *Friday.*   Clear and cool.   I write to Judge Oliver, Birmingham.

16. *Sunday.*   Clear and very cold.   Ink freezes on the stove in the office.   Mr. Fisher ill and does not preach.

17. *Monday.*   Clear and cold.   I have [a] letter from Mr. Walter, Shelburne.

18. *Tuesday.*   A clear, fine day ; cold.   I dine at Marblehead, [at] Sally's, and call on Mr. Hooper and on Mrs. Robie.

19. *Wednesday.*   Cool and cloudy.   Mrs. R. Cabot here in the evening on Mr. Osgood's affairs.

20. *Thursday.*   Cloudy, and snows.   Mr. Osgood, of Haverhill, calls again and again.

23. *Sunday.*   Cold.   John and I set out in Daland's carriage for Boston ; dine at Wait's ; tea at Wetmore's ; John returns ; I lodge at stage house.

24. *Monday.*   At half past five I set out in stage for Springfield ; breakfast at Willington's ; dine at Marlboro ; lodge at Worcester.

25. *Tuesday.*   Lodge at Scott's, Palmer.

26. *Wednesday.*   Meet John Williams at Parsons', and go with him to Ely's ; lodge at Mrs. Dwight's ; we cross the Connecticut River on the ice with sleigh and 2 horses.

27. *Thursday.*   Dine at Mrs. Dwight's ; lodge at G. Pynchon's ; (tea at Maj. Williams', who married Miss Pynchon, daughter of Doctor C. Pynchon).[1]

28. *Friday.*   Dine at Capt. Savage's ; spend the evening at Mr. Bliss's with Colo. Worthington.

29. *Saturday.*   Dine at G. Pynchon's ; lodge at Mrs. Dwight's ; tea at Maj. Williams'.

[1] Dr. Charles Pynchon was a son of the second John Pynchon, and a cousin of William Pynchon. He was a prominent physician of his day, and one of the founders of the Massachusetts Medical Society. He was at the capture of Louisburg, and at the battle near Lake George, when Colonel E. Williams was killed. Parkman mentions him in his *Montcalm and Wolfe.* He married Anna, a daughter of Henry Dwight, of Hatfield.

30. *Sunday.* Keep Sabbath, and sit with Mrs. Dwight's family.

31. *Monday.* I dine at Capt. Savage's with Lieut. Porter and the officers ; set out for Boston in New York stage. P. M., lodge at Scott's ; Gen'l R. Putnam there on his tour to the Ohio.

1788. *January* 1. *Tuesday.* Dine at Mason's, Spencer ; tea at Pearse's, Worcester, and lodge there.

2. *Wednesday.* Breakfast at Colo. How's ; dine at Flagg's, Weston ; bait at Willington's, Watertown ; lodge at Burrell's, Boston. N. B. Capt. Savage leaves us at Weston.

3. *Thursday.* Capt. Orne lends me his horse to ride on to Salem (the stage not going thither) ; I arrive and take tea at his house, and find my family well at home. Thus ends a pleasant tour to Springfield, unfortunate only in getting in no debts and not meeting brother Pynchon.

4. *Friday.* Very cold, and I see and feel signs of the rheumatism.

7. *Monday.* Cold and uncomfortable. J. Grafton with the Club at my house. Episcopal clergymen's protest against Freeman's ordination is found on [the] signpost.

8. *Tuesday.* The Convention meets at Boston.

10. *Thursday.* A severe, cold day. I set out in Burrell's stage for Boston with Mr. Bowles and another ; B. Pickman gets in at Newhall's and goes with us ; we are two and a half hours on the road from Salem to Boston. I dine at Mrs. Gray's ; lodge at Mr. Wetmore's.

11. *Friday.* Very cold. I dine at Mr. Wetmore's ; take tea at Dr. Loring's. We meet at Bunch of Grapes in the evening and begin the reference. I lodge at Mr. Wetmore's.

12. *Saturday.* Excessive cold. The referees meet at Mr. Wetmore's office and hear the parties. I dine at Loring's ; set out for Salem in Burrell's stage, and arrive at $\frac{1}{4}$ past six with Mr. Thorndike, Davis, and 2 others. Mr. Vans here. Cloudy, and cold E. wind.

13. *Sunday.* Very cold. I tarry at home. Mr. Gerrish's twin daughters die to-day, about six weeks old.

14. *Monday.* Cold continues. Mrs. R. Cabot tarries till my return from the Club, to consult as to Osgood and her affairs.

15. *Tuesday.* Cold still. Mr. Wooldridge brings Miss Robie to Mr. Goodale's.

16. *Wednesday.* It snows. Mr. Wooldridge sets out in the stage for Boston. In the afternoon it rains and blows. Mr. Gerrish's twins are this evening buried in one coffin and the same grave ; they were females, and their disorder a consumption. Wind changes to S. E., and grows warm.

17. *Thursday.* The snow disappears, and this looks like a spring day ; is warm and pleasant.

19. *Saturday.* Snow and rain P. M. Good news from the Convention ; a prospect that the Constitution may be accepted.

24. *Thursday.* A very fine, clear day ; cool. John goes to Boston. Hooper, of Newbury, goes to Boston.

25. *Friday.* Snows, blows, hails, and rains by turns. John returns, and goes to Marblehead to a ball.

26. *Saturday.* Clear and cold. Much wood brought, but at 14 shillings and upwards. At about 9 o'clock in the evening Peter Oliver and Hooper call for John, bound, as they say, to Marblehead. John asks II. to lodge with him in case he does not go to Marblehead ; but he goes to bed at Robinson's, and was found dead

in the morning, a broken pocket phyal by his bedside, and some laudanum at bottom.   Letter and books from S. Curwen.

27. *Sunday morning.*   Clear and cold.   News comes of B. Haw. Hooper's death ; the coroner's inquest find wilful self-murder ; the body was sent to Newbury to his friends there.   Who can withhold the compassionate tears from the disconsolate mother ?

28. *Monday.*   Fine, clear day.   Much wood is brought to market at 13/ and 14/ a cord.   John went to Boston in the stage, and returned at night.

30. *Wednesday.*   Mr. and Mrs. Oliver come and tarry. They dine at Mr. Vans' on Tuesday, and at Mr. Oliver's on Thursday.   Storm and snow to-day, and cold at night.

31. *Thursday.*   Fair, and good sledding.   News from Boston that the main question as to the Constitution is to come on in the Convention to-morrow, when Gov'r Hancock will be fully in favour of it.

February 1. *Friday.*   Cloudy, but good sledding.   Mr. and Mrs. Oliver go home in Mrs. Vans' sleigh.   Polly Bufton comes and spends the day.   Mrs. Goodale and Miss Su. Higginson spend the evening here with Mr. Orne.

2. *Saturday.*   Fine sledding.   Wood keeps at the price of 13 and 14/ for oak and 15/ and 16/ for walnut. Mr. O. dines with us, and goes home at night.   John Pynchon, Eb. Putnam, Reb. Cabot, and the Miss Pickmans at 12 set out for Danvers.   The Centinel of this day shews us a great probability of an acceptance of the Federal Constitution on Gov'r Hancock's proposals of amendment.   Andover calls a town-meeting, which refuses to instruct their representatives.

3. *Sunday.*   Warm and cloudy ; at night it rains ;

the snow is carried off, ice and mud only left. Mrs.
Ropes and daughter and Mr. Hodges spend the evening.

4. *Monday.* Cloudy and warm. The Club at Dr.
Paine's, who shows us the E. India pipe with a hose 8
or 10 feet long, through which the smoke is to be drawn.

5. *Tuesday.* The day appointed for finishing the debates of the Convention as to the new Constitution, but
nothing done, Boreas' blasts having equalled Gen'l
Thompson's.

6. *Wednesday.* Last night proved an exceeding cold
one ; this morning clear and cold, but the wind subsided
wholly this morning, and if the political blasts subside
also, we hope to have some good news from the Convention, Thompson's vehemence, 't is said, being somewhat abated. From Boston we hear, at 8 in the evening, that a vote passed in favour of the Constitution,
thus : —

$$
\left.
\begin{array}{ll}
\text{Voters in Convention,} & 355 \\
\text{For the Constitution,} & 187 \\
\text{Against it,} & 168
\end{array}
\right\} 355
$$

Majority of voters 19. All the bells in Boston rang on the
occasion.

7. *Thursday.* Cold. Great rejoicing at Boston ; a
grand and curious procession. See the papers and account of British flag !

8. *Friday.* The members of Convention return home.

9. *Saturday.* A fine day ; good sledding ; wood from
13 to 15 [shillings].

11. *Monday.* Very wet. Dr. Plummer takes the
Club.

12. *Tuesday.* I set out in [the] stage for Boston.

13. *Wednesday.* I go to see Mr. Lowell at Roxbury,
and Judge Sumner ; Mr. Russell and Mr. Lane, etc., at
Mr. Lowell's. I return to Boston at 9 o'clock to meet
Mr. Sparhawk ; he gone out.

14. *Thursday.* I set out in the stage from Burrell's, where I lodged, for Connecticut; lodge at Worcester; Major Haskell overtakes us.

15. *Friday.* Maj. Haskell and co. set out; dine at Colo. How's; lodge at Scott's, Palmer.

16. *Saturday.* Reach Springfield, [and] hear of John Williams being gone for Connecticut; we follow; dine at Hitchcock's, at Suffield, who recognizeth me with much heartiness and philanthropy; we lodge at Collier's, and go to hear Mr. Bōrdman on Sunday.

17. *Sunday.* At meeting A. M.; at home P. M. on politicks, with Mr. Dane and co.; spend the evening at Coz. Willys'[1] most cheerfully.

18. *Monday.* We proceed from Hartford in the sleigh through Weathersfield to Middletown; there see Gen'l Parsons, a very plain-dressed gentleman, and Mr. Wetmore's father, at the tavern; thence to Durham; at the tavern there meet Dr. Gutridge,[2] who married a Chauncy —my relation; he most kindly and urgently insisted on my calling to dine, on my return from Guilford. The stage sleigh left me there and proceeded to New Haven, and I set out in Mr. Morgan's sleigh for Guilford, but lodged at good Deacon . . . , 5 miles distant from it. The taverner and family are disobliging, and refuse me a horse for the 5 miles.

19. *Tuesday.* [In] morning early I set out with the good deacon's horse, and arrive at my brother's seat on

---

[1] Colonel Wyllys was the owner of the famous Charter Oak Place, and a cousin of William Pynchon, both being descended from Gov. George Wyllys.

[2] Dr. Gutridge was Dr. Goodrich, the minister of Durham, and a man of note among the Congregationalists. He married Catherine, daughter of Elihu Chauncy, of Durham, a third cousin of William Pynchon, both being great-grandchildren of Rev. Nathaniel Chauncy, of Hatfield. Dr. Goodrich was the ancestor of Professor Goodrich, of Yale College.

a beautiful hill; there find J. Williams in bed. We breakfast and spend the day most sociably together, not having met for 15 years before.

20. *Wednesday.*   We spend the day in chat — Dr. Pynchon [1] *et ux.*, and Mr. and Mrs. Rossiter and their children with us.

21. *Thursday.*   In afternoon all hands of us ride to town, and dine at Dr. Pynchon's; Dr. and Mrs. Ruggles spend the afternoon with us; at night we return to the farm. *Note:* Dr. Ruggles married [the] mother of Mr. Rossiter.

22. *Friday.*   We go, and are at Mr. Rossiter's, he being gone to New Haven Court; he returns at evening.

23. *Saturday.*   Dr. Pynchon and Mr. Rossiter take me in their sleigh and carry me to Durham; we all dine at Dr. Gutridge's, and visit old Mr. Chauncy's [2] and Capt. Chauncy's families; the former near 90 years old, and seeming like an old picture ready to leave the frame; thence we go to the stage house and bid adieu. I set out for Hartford, they for Guilford. At the stage house I meet Mr. Phillips, of Middletown, who married a Wetmore, and urged me to call on him at Middletown; in passing I called and saw Mrs. Phillips, who urged my

[1] Dr. Thomas Ruggles Pynchon, here mentioned, was the only son of Joseph Pynchon, and nephew of William Pynchon. He received his medical education in the hospitals of the British army in New York. He inherited by entail the property of his grandfather, Rev. Thomas Ruggles, of Guilford, and after peace was declared took possession of the property; his oldest sister, alluded to, married Mr. Rossiter. His son was Henry Ruggles Pynchon, whose son, Dr. Thomas Ruggles Pynchon, was the late president of Trinity College, Hartford, Connecticut.

[2] Elihu Chauncy, of Durham, the father of Mrs. Goodrich, and ancestor of the Philadelphia Chauncys, was a cousin of William Pynchon. Captain Chauncy was another member of the same family. Mr. Chauncy, of the Upper Houses, Middletown (now Cromwell), here mentioned, was a brother of Elihu Chauncy, of Durham, and the ancestor of the New York Chauncys, connected with the Alsops and Howlands.

tarrying ; I called on Mr. Chauncy at the Upper Houses, and he most cheerfully saluted me. At evening I arrived at Hartford and put up at Collier's ; meet Major Haskell.

24. *Sunday.* Go to meeting in the afternoon, and in the evening call again to see Secretary Willys and his son, who married the widow . . . , a daughter of Judge Dyar, and was acquainted with my daughter Oliver at Providence, where both had resided.

25. *Monday.* Major Webb, Mr. Pomeroy, grandson of Secretary Willys, and I set out for Springfield, where the stage leaves me and proceeds towards Boston ; I dine with them at Parsons's, but go and lodge at G. Pynchon's.

26. *Tuesday.* J. Williams comes to me at Springfield, and we go round to Dr. Brewer's, Dwight's, etc., to look over old accounts, but cannot settle, Dr. Brewer being absent at Brookfield ; we dine at Thomas Dwight's with a large company, Colo. Worthington's family, Judge Upham, and some ladies from Deerfield and Brookfield, in all 16 persons. They spend the day and evening there.

27. *Wednesday.* We dine again at Mrs. Dwight's, and I lodge at G. Pynchon's ; tea at W. Pynchon's.

28. *Thursday.* Williams leaves me. I call again on Thomas and Jonathan Dwight,[1] executor, who find bro. Pynchon's receipt to Colo. Dwight for the £30. At one Maj. Haskell, Mr. John Livingston, and Mr. Anderson, from New York, come in the stage from Hartford, and dine at Parsons's with Capt. Savage and Lieut. Porter,

---

[1] Thomas Dwight was the eldest son of Josiah Dwight, by his second wife (the first wife was Sarah, a sister of William Pynchon). He was a leading man, of influence and wealth. Jonathan Dwight was his first cousin, and the ancestor of Edmund Dwight, of Boston.

and [in the afternoon] we call and see the arms, stores, etc., at the Arsenal on the hill, and thence we proceed on our journey and lodge at Scott's.

29. *Friday.* We arrive at Worcester and lodge at Pease's tavern, where a company of young gentlemen and girls call with a fiddler, and dance ; Livingston and Anderson join the company and dance reels, etc., etc., till another company come and claim the fiddler and take him off. Anderson affects to cry, and the ladies pity him, not doubting his grief and tears to be sincere, and prevail on the fiddler to proceed for 2 dances more ; and upon their leaving him at last, he bawls out like a calf, at length recovering, falls a laughing and sneering at their simplicity — a true buffoon this !

March 1. *Saturday.* We quit Worcester, breakfast at Marlboro, dine at Weston, and go through Cambridge to Boston ; I lodge at Mr. Wetmore's, and deliver his father's letter.

2. *Sunday.* Very cold. I go to Charlestown, hire a carriage, etc., and reach Newhall's and dine there, and he in his carriage brings me to Salem. Thus ends the second unsuccessful tour to Springfield.

6. *Thursday.* Cold continued till this morning, and now the weather is pleasant and the sky clear. John goes to Marblehead Assembly.

7. *Friday.* Moderate, pleasant weather. House of Representatives uneasy at [the] Governor's message, as to [the] amendments of the Constitution. We spend the evening at Dr. Holyoke's.

8. *Saturday.* A fine, moderate day. Plenty of wood in the market at 13/, walnut 15/.

11. *Tuesday.* A fine day ; the snow goes off gradually. Mr. N. Sparhawk calls in the evening. Great lamentation at neighbour Wright's — his darling cock killed by a boy !

12. *Wednesday.*   Mr. N. Sparhawk dines with me and spends the day ; he calls at evening with his daughter Betsy.   John went early in the morning to Bradford. Cloudy.

13. *Thursday.*   A fine morning.   The Tender Act rejected at the Senate.

14. *Friday.*   Morn clear and pleasant.   John goes to Danvers, A. Putnam's Court ; does not return.   Mrs. Ropes here [in] the evening and sups.

15. *Saturday.*   A fine, clear, moderate morning, and pleasant day.   John returns in the evening at 9 o'clock from Marblehead, whither he went from Danvers.

17. *Monday.*   Clear and cool.   Jos. Flint's leg broken and his life in great danger.

18. *Tuesday.*   Cloudy A. M.   News of W. West's death, son of W. West.

20. *Thursday.*   A very fine day.   A. Oliver comes. Mrs. Pynchon goes to Marblehead.

21. *Friday.*   A fine, clear day, and cool.   The headache detains me from church.   Mr. Condy calls for John.

22. *Saturday.*   A fine, clear morning.   Mr. Condy calls again this morning, informing me of the army accounts.   Mr. Grafton and Patty Pynchon [1] married at church P. M.

23. *Sunday.*   A cloudy morning.   Mr. and Mrs. Graf-

---

[1] Martha Pynchon was married to William Pynchon, Jr., March 4, 1780. She was the daughter of Thomas Elkins and Elizabeth, daughter of John White, and after the death of her husband she married, on the date above given, Joseph Grafton ; and when again a widow, she became the wife of George Stewart Johonnot.   She died without issue on the 27th of May, 1840.   Her sister, Elizabeth, married Thomas Saunders, whose daughter, Elizabeth, married Hon. Leverett Saltonstall.   At the death of her third husband, Mrs. Johonnot was left with an ample fortune, which she bequeathed, as directed by his will, to the Insane Hospital at Worcester.

ton are out at church morning and afternoon. I dine at Mr. Vans'. Some rain P. M.

24. *Monday.* Mr. O. introduceth Bishop Seabury [1] and Mr. Moore, who, with Mr. Goodale, dine with us ; the Bishop calls upon Dr. Paine, but not upon Mr. Fisher !

27. *Thursday.* A clear and cold day. Mr. F. Cabot proposeth to solicit for sheriff's office in Essex ; Sheriff Farley says that he does not propose to resign it.

29. *Saturday.* I dine at Dr. Plummer's on salt fish, with Dr. Holyoke, Mr. Grafton, and co.

30. *Sunday.* Clear and cold. Mr. Ogden preacheth for Mr. Fisher.

April 1. *Tuesday.* John and I set out A. M. in Newhall's chaise for Ipswich Court ; arrive in season ; put up at Rogers's.

3. *Thursday.* Cool. Tea with Mr. Andrews at Perkins's. At night it rains.

4. *Friday.* Rains. John and I set out for Salem ; arrive at two and dine at home.

5. *Saturday.* Fine rain continues. Mr. Sargent and Dr. Plummer meet about their suit.

7. *Monday.* A fine, clear day, but the wind veers to the east, and very cold P. M. A full town-meeting to-day for choice of Governor, Lieut. Governor, and Senators, and a full meeting at N. Ropes', on account of J. Hodges' publishment. Mr. Nutting, about 95 years of age, comes in and sits down to bacon, beef, cheese, and olives.

8. *Tuesday.* Capt. Abbot and officers brought the window breakers before the justices at the Court House.

---

[1] It was on this visitation of Bishop Seabury to Massachusetts that he delivered the annual address before 'the Boston Episcopal Charitable Society at Trinity Church, Boston. At his first visitation, the preceding year, he confirmed 120 persons at St. Michael's, Marblehead.

9. *Wednesday.* Mrs. Pickman, Cabot, and Paine here.

10. *Thursday.* A fine morning. The window breakers recognized for July Court, begin to propose repairing the broken windows. Some rain P. M.

11. *Friday.* A fine, clear morning. Mr. and Mrs. Grafton with Mr. Goodale spend the evening here. Mrs. G. Cabot, of Beverly, is ill and declining.

13. *Sunday.* A fine, clear, warm morning. Mr. Turell and John set out in a chaise for Boston, to be left at Burrell's there for Webb. Mrs. Orne and the children dine at Dr. Paine's, and go home at evening.

14. *Monday.* A spring-like morning ; cloudy at noon. Club at Mr. G.'s. John and Mr. Turell return in the rain between 10 and 11 at night, wet to the skin, walking all the way.

17. *Thursday.* Fast Day ; fair and cool. At Mr. Fisher's church ; he preacheth in [the] forenoon only. Brother Stephen and son come, sup and lodge.

18. *Friday.* A fine rain. John goes over to Marblehead in a sulky and tarries at the dancing-school. Thunder and rain in the night.

20. *Sunday.* Cool day. At evening Williams comes and sups with John.

22. *Tuesday.* Cool. The farmers, though busy at the plough, yet send their wood to market at 11*s.* and 12*s.* a cord. News of war in Europe, [the] Emperor against the Turk.

23. *Wednesday.* By the papers, G. Lincoln is to be Lt. Governor ; Hancock, Governor.

24. *Thursday.* An affray between the Governor of New York and the people ; several killed on both sides.[1]

---

[1] This disturbance arose from an attack upon certain prominent physicians, who were unjustly suspected of unlawfully obtaining subjects for anatomical dissection. See Lamb's *History of New York*, pp. 306, 307. This riot was known as the " Doctors' mob."

25. *Friday.*   Rain, but warm.   Mr. Willes dines here. News from Marblehead that the dancers were not dispersed at sunrise this morning ; their carriages were sent home in the rain.   Dr. Holyoke calls in the evening ; informs [us] of Jay's being dangerously wounded in the skirmish at New York, and several other gentlemen hurt ; who would not prefer a democratick government to any other among virtuous subjects ?

26. *Saturday.*   Cloudy.   The dancing party have all returned from Marblehead.   Some rain toward evening.

27. *Sunday.*   Cloudy ; wind N. E., but not cold ; P. M., the wind is N. E.   Mrs. Gold is buried after meeting this evening.

29. *Tuesday.*   A fine, cool, clear day.   All is hurry and confusion, preparing for training to-morrow and for a ball at evening.

30. *Wednesday.*   A fine day.   The two companies of this town in uniform were reviewed, as per flattering accounts in the newspapers.

May 1. *Thursday.*   Mrs. Goodale and I, Mr. and Mrs. Grafton, go to Marblehead, and go to church, [it] being Ascension Day ; John goes on foot.   It rains in [the] evening.

2. *Friday.*   Cloudy ; P. M., it rains plentifully.   Mrs. Higginson, daughter, Miss Prince, and Miss Robie, and Miss Polly Goodale here at tea and in the evening.

5. *Monday.*   I go with Mrs. Vans in their chaise to Justice Putnam's, at Danvers ; on our return we find 6 representatives chosen for General Court : —

Manning,	Bickford,	F. Cabot,
Pulling,	Gray,	W. Pickman.

I find Mr. Condy with John Pynchon at the office upon a melancholy errand.   R. Ward much chagrined that he could not with his utmost efforts obtain a single vote for representative.

6. *Tuesday.* A fine, clear day ; P. M., the wind very high at N. W. Mrs. Orne is taken ill ; has the disorder of the phthisick to a higher degree than ever, but is greatly relieved by bleeding ; Dr. Paine goes up to tend her as physician.

7. *Wednesday.* Mrs. Orne grows better. Mrs. Oliver comes from Marblehead, and goes with Mrs. Pynchon, and they tarry with her.

12. *Monday.* Fair and fine day. Dr. Paine goes to Mr. Orne's and dines there. N. Sparhawk, Esq., from Portsmouth, calls on me, and takes Calef's note and account.

13. *Tuesday.* A fine morning. Good news of Maryland's accepting the Federal Constitution.

14. *Wednesday.* Fine day. Mr. Cabot and I set out P. M. for Chelmsford ; lodge at Billerica. Memo. sent to Dr. Kneeland Calef's note and account by Mr. Sparhawk last Monday.

15. *Thursday.* A most serene and fine morning. We go over to Chelmsford, and return to Billerica and dine at Pollard's ; set out after dinner, and arrive at Salem at evening.

17. *Saturday.* Cloudy, and warm ; wind at S. W. Primus brings willows for John.

19. *Monday.* Rain. Mr. Smith, of Cambridge, in town, and calls at my house, and spends the evening at Dr. Plummer's. John goes to Danvers on account of the riot, and his client is acquitted, at least is discharged by referees. News that Judge Wendell resigned the Probate Office, and Judge Sullivan [is] appointed in his stead.

20. *Tuesday.*   Cloudy and wet.   Rumours as to Prof. Willard's misconduct at Cambridge.

21. *Wednesday.*   A very fine, warm day.   All the town are employed about the bridges, and walking and riding out, some to Danvers bridge, others to Salem bridge : the former to be fit for use next week at election, the latter in September next.   Judge Sargeant in town.

23. *Friday.*   Rains all day.   The stage does not go to Boston to-day.

24. *Saturday.*   Some rain; cloudy.   I set out for Boston in the stage with two ladies from Gloucester ; meet G. Deblois at Boston ; dine at Mrs. Waldo's with Mrs. Wetmore and daughter.   Mrs. Higginson's life is despaired of.   All rejoice at the prospect of a good House of Representatives and a good Senate this election.

25. *Sunday.*   A very clear and fine morning.   Reb. Cabot calls in after meeting.

27. *Tuesday.*   I go to Marblehead with Mr. Stevens in his chaise and see Mr. Hooper there ; find Mr. Oliver at home and take tea there ; Miss Chace came with him from Providence.

28. *Wednesday.*   Cloudy ; wind S. W.   All hands merry and gay, running up and down [the] streets. Clerk Osgood, J. Grafton, and I walk to Danvers new bridge, and find the piers all put up, but no planks put down ; we return to election at Primus's flag, and take ale and pies, and see the dances.

29. *Thursday.*   A fine day.   I go with neighbours Pike and Gerrish to the vendue at Waters's.   Shillaber bids for the benefit of the creditors.

30. *Friday.*   The carousing, musick, etc., etc., go on with spirit in Northfield and in Southfield, at Danvers

and Marblehead.   Titus and Primus and attendants are getting money apace.

31. *Saturday.*   By the papers it appears that there is a better Senate, House, [and] Council, and better Governor than have been elected for years past ; a Court of Federalists.   At evening John Pynchon goes to Marblehead with Danish Captain.   Mr. Vans returns from Boston with very favourable news as to public matters.

June 1. *Sunday.*   Cloudy, cool, and windy.   Mr. Fisher preacheth all day.

2. *Monday.*   A fine day.   At evening Mr. Prince gives us an account of his tour to Springfield.   John and . . . set out for Probate Court at Ipswich A. M., and return with Graham and take tea.

4. *Wednesday.*   Mrs. Goodale and I go in her chaise up to Mr. Orne's, and return A. M.   Mr. Bartlett comes to town in the stage, and brings account of Fran. Goodale.

5. *Thursday.*   John takes possession of his new office with arms and ammunition.

6. *Friday.*   A very warm day.   I leave off my baize. Mr. Bartlett sets out for Boston with Burrell in the chaise.   Turner's dance is this night.   Fra. Goodale at Cambridge still.

7. *Saturday.*   A very clear, warm day.   Joyful news from New York that South Carolina hath accepted the Federal Constitution.

8. *Sunday.*   A fine day.   At church A. M.   I set out P. M. for Dr. Putnam to settle with Hill and Kettle, at Malden, and lodge at Mr. Hill's.

9. *Monday.*   At home all day.

10. *Tuesday.*   Kettle and Hill come from Malden to settle with me an account of Dr. Putnam.

11. *Wednesday.*   P. M., rains plentifully.   Mr. and

Mrs. Oliver, Miss Chace, and Billy came from Marble-head on a visit yesterday.

12. *Thursday.* Mrs. Oliver and Miss Chace dine here; Mr. Oliver dines with his parents. Mrs. Pynchon and Miss . . . spend the afternoon there, and I take tea with them.

14. *Saturday.* Mr. Motley here about G. Deblois's affair.

17. *Tuesday.* Morning, I set out with Stephen Cook in his chaise for Ipswich Court; they meet not till afternoon.

19. *Thursday.* S. Porter, Esq., passeth through Ipswich in the stage for Salem.

20. *Friday.* We hear of New Hampshire adopting the Federal Constitution.

21. *Saturday.* Comes on the trial of Peele and Farley, sheriffs, for misconduct as to execution of Haraden; Peele recovers interest and damages.

22. *Sunday.* A fine day. Mr. Porter goes to Mr. Barnard's meeting.

23. *Monday.* All hands prepare for rejoicing; in the midst I am called to Boston on G. Deblois's affairs; I go in the afternoon, and am wet to the skin by a plentiful rain; in the evening he calls at my lodgings.

24. *Tuesday.* A fine, clear morning. He sets sail in Capt. Davis. I return to Salem; call at Mr. Porter's lodgings, but do not meet him.

25. *Wednesday.* Rain and cold; N. E. wind. Mr. Nutting and daughter and Mrs. Vans at tea.

26. *Thursday.* A fine, cool morning. Mr. Porter calls on me. F. Cabot here. Miss Prince and brother are said to be bound to St. John.

27. *Friday.* Mr. Porter dines at my house. Mrs. Turner calls on us. Mr. Wetmore calls on his way to Falmouth.

28. *Saturday.* Cloudy and rain. Deacon Gatchell at the office. I dine at Esq. Vans' with S. Porter, Holyoke, and Goodale.

29. *Sunday.* Rains plentifully. Mr. Porter calls on me and goes to church with me.

30. *Monday.* Rain. The Club at Dr. Plummer's in the evening ; J. Jackson there. Things look gloomy at Virginia and New York as to [the] Federal Constitution.

July 2. *Wednesday.* Rain. Mr. Orne very ill. Mr. Hooper writes that he will soon send me some coppers ! When ?

3. *Thursday.* A very warm and fine day. Mr. Oliver and Miss Chace come. Politicians! politicians! scramble, turn, hoist, beg, pray, lie, twist, for offices.

4. *Friday.* Cloudy, and rain A. M. The Cadets and Artillery company turn out to-day, and are attended on the common by Colo. Fiske, Abbot, and Maj. Waldo, and go through their firing ; P. M., pass through paved street, firing [by] platoons ; street firing in the evening ; rockets were fired from houses in the common. Mr. Noyes and I go to Beverly bridge. News comes of Virginia's having accepted the Federal Constitution, which increaseth the general joy. Mr. Porter here.

5. *Saturday.* Cloudy and rain. J. Parker here, with news of Gen'l Browne.

6. *Sunday.* A pleasant day. Much talk of alterations of the Courts of Sessions and of Common Pleas ; scramble, ye politicians !

7. *Monday.* Fair and warm. Confusion in judicial matters as to filing causes sent up by Justices of the Peace to Court of Common Pleas.

8. *Tuesday.* Warm day. The Court of Common Pleas meet.

9. *Wednesday.* The Court goes on Jehu like.

10. *Thursday.* No licenses before noon.

12. *Saturday.* A fine day. I go to take tea at Mr. Vans'.

13. *Sunday.* A fine day. I go to church P. M., and to the bridge in the evening.

14. *Monday.* A most delightful morning induces eager desires, various plans, and schemes for Commencement. J. goes with Gerrish, Pike, and others a-gunning, and have both diversion and luck ; one gets a squunk, another gets a woodchuck, and by a majority vote it was determined to dress and eat the latter only. Mr. Wetmore comes from the eastward and dines with us.

15. *Tuesday.* Plentiful rain early this morning. Billy Wetmore comes in at breakfast ; [he] was caught in the shower in coming from Boston this morning. News from N. York that the Federal Constitution may not be accepted there.

16. *Wednesday.* Commencement at Cambridge ; I go in Newhall's hack with Maj. Haskell *et al.*, and return at half past eleven at night.

17. *Thursday.* A fine, cool day. I tarry all day at home.

19. *Saturday.* Mr. Appleton and family and Mrs. Ropes and family, Mr. Goodale, and others go to the Fort, with Mrs. Pynchon *et ipse.*

21. *Monday.* A fine day. High entertainment at Colo. Pickman's. With Mr. Porter in the evening.

22. *Tuesday.* Cloudy all day and some rain. Yesterday John distinguished himself in law distinctions at Mr. Osgood's, in construction of law of reference. Mrs. Curwen here.

23. *Wednesday.* Doct. Hitchcock calls to see me with Mr. Barnard.

24. *Thursday*. Cloudy. Mr. Vans, among other wise observations, this day, and for several days past, publisheth in a promiscuous company of G. B. and ladies [that] Parson Gilchrist, Jos. Blaney, and most other commonly called philosophers and men of learning are no better than so many fools; the first two he called idiots, and not one whit better as to living in the world.

25. *Friday*. I set out on Gerrish's mare, and her waywardness and wildness discourage me at North bridge, and I return her and take Daland's horse, and go to Ipswich on Dr. Rogers' request.

27. *Sunday*. Warm and cloudy. Mr. Amory, at breakfast with John, mentions his intention of residing at Salem in law business. Take tea at Mr. Goodale's, meet with S. Higginson, from Boston, and sup there.

28. *Monday*. Cloudy. I send Mr. Sparhawk's account unfinished, and give him the reason of it — my fatiguing journey to Ipswich.

29. *Tuesday*. Cool and cloudy. Mr. Amory calls and stays a part of the morning. Two turtles are dressed to-day, one at the Fort and one at Robinson's; John and Amory at the latter. John, in Symonds *v.* Foster, succeeds before Judges Batchelder and Osgood, and gains continuance to next Monday; S. Sewall for Foster.

31. *Thursday*. We hear that Symonds and Foster have compounded, the latter making confession of lies and abuses.

August 4. *Monday*. A cool morning; wind east. J. figures away before Just. O. in replevin; *ne quid nimis*.

10. *Sunday*. A cool and very fine day. Church-meeting in vain; no wardens chosen; the meeting adjourned. Dr. Paine *et ux.* and Mr. and Mrs. Grafton here in the evening.

12. *Tuesday*. Adjournment of the Court of Sessions.

Dr. Eben. Putnam died this day.[1] J. returns from Marblehead, having compounded with Capt. Madison and others concerned as to the libel for the sailor's wages. Jona. Mason calls, and repeats and renews his agreement as to a speedy adjournment of O.'s accounts. Mess. Jeffry, Pulling, and self dine with S. Porter, Esq. — a plentiful dinner.

13. *Wednesday.* A fine, cool day for the military muster of the militia and undisciplined soldiers ; on the common were 20 tents, with cake and other eatables, and drinks of all kinds ; there were 4 companies, Capt. Page's in a rifle dress uniform.

14. *Thursday.* A fine, pleasant day. Bro. Porter sets out for Ipswich with his baggage.

15. *Friday.* All hands go to the dance at the Assembly rooms.

16. *Saturday.* At 6 I set out for Boston on the reference, — Apthorp *v.* Bowdoin, — and find the dew was very great last evening ; people who set out at 4 were wet quite thro' all their clothes ; not finishing the business, I return at night by 1/2 past ten ; I refuse dining at Mrs. Waldo's for obvious reasons. It rains plentifully most of the night, and refresheth the surface and all upon the ground ; the produce, corn, etc., were nearly spoiled by the drought.

17. *Sunday.* No church to-day, Mr. Fisher being unwell. Dr. Putnam's pall-bearers [were] H. Derby, Ward, and Dr. Holyoke.

---

[1] Dr. Ebenezer Putnam was a prominent physician of Salem. He was graduated at Harvard College in 1739, and married, October 28, 1764, Margaret Scollay, who was born in Marblehead in 1724. He was a great-great-grandson of John Putnam, who died in 1662. His son, Ebenezer, was a merchant of Salem, and his grandson, Ebenezer, born September, 1797, was the postmaster in Salem. His great-grandson is Professor Fred Ward Putnam, of Harvard University.

18. *Monday.* A fine rain. Gov. Hancock is expected in Salem, but is stopped by the rain till 8 in the evening, and then comes in and puts up at Colo. Fiske's; some rode out to meet him, but were caught in the rain, and returned without his excellency.

19. *Tuesday.* Most of the gentlemen in the town wait on the Governor at Mr. Fiske's, and 13 carriages were driven out in the morning to attend him in his tour from Salem to Marblehead, and there were just 3 saddled horses with 13 riders on them.

20. *Wednesday.* Clear and warm; the earth with us wears a new and pleasing face; the gardens laugh, and the fields with the birds rejoice and sing together.

22. *Friday.* A clear, cool morning. I write to Mr. Whittredge of [my] intention to call on him to-morrow with Dr. Holyoke.

23. *Saturday.* A fine, warm day; at noon it rained plentifully. At 3 Dr. Holyoke and I set out for Danvers to see Mr. Whittredge; he was absent from home, and we returned. Mrs. P. goes to Vanburg with Mrs. Vans, and I take tea at Mr. Grafton's.

24. *Sunday.* A fine day. At church all day ; Mess. Turner, Osgood, and Cabot in my pew. In the evening the church proprietors meet at Mr. Blyth's respecting the affairs of the organ and Mr. Deblois' claim ; Mr. F. and Colo. A. conclude to go to Boston about it.

25. *Monday.* A good day. At Dr. Holyoke's in the evening, where Bro. Porter's letter to Salem Selectmen is read, and Sawyer's love-letter.

26. *Tuesday.* Shillaber and I go over to Waters' on business of the estate. Received a silly letter from R. Hooper, Esq.

30. *Saturday.* Overcast. Jno. and Amory, Osgood and co. go to Mr. Orne's in good spirits ; Amory dines with us.

31. *Sunday.* A fine day. At church P. M. ; the wardens, Colo. Abbot and Blyth, take the wardens' seats after much persuasion and many thanks of the proprietors. It rains at night.

September 2. Tuesday. Clear. I go over to Hutchinson and Page's about Waters' matter. Tea at Mr. Vans' ; she declining in health.

3. *Wednesday.* Clear and cool. Colo. Pickman and others at Mr. Treadwell's. Mr. Bradish, from Cambridge, and Mrs. Paine, from Worcester.

4. *Thursday.* A fine morning. At noon Mr. Pullen and I go to see the bridge and the placing a pier ; the regularity of the proceeding and quick despatch were highly pleasing. At evening Mrs. Paine and family go to dancing-school, and are much entertained there.

5. *Friday.* A fine, clear, warm day. I received Mr. Hooper's proposals at evening.

6. *Saturday.* Give notice to Mr. Hooper to attend Wednesday next.

7. *Sunday.* Turner, the dancing master, left the school and his scholars in tears last . . . Messrs. Goodale and comp. return from their visit to the French fleet. Seventeen colours at Beverly bridge, and crowds.

9. *Tuesday.* This day Mrs. Fr. Cabot died.[1]

10. *Wednesday.* A fine, fair day. I go to Marblehead to settle accounts with Mr. Hooper, Esq. I dine at Mr. Oliver's.

11. *Thursday.* A fine day. P. M., at Mrs. Lynde's and Mr. Oliver's. Mrs. Cabot is buried ; I could not attend the funeral.

12. *Friday.* Cloudy. I call to see Dr. Putnam's family, who are yet deeply impressed with grief at the

---

[1] Mrs. Cabot was Anna, daughter of John Clarke and Sarah Pickering, and sister of Rev. John Clarke, minister of First Church, Boston.

Dr.'s death. Billy Cabot and I ride up to Danvers bridge and back to Essex bridge, which we pass on foot, the planking and railing not yet being completed.

13. *Saturday.* A cloudy day. Mr. Vans takes W. Cabot and myself to his seat, Northfield, where we and some ladies spend the afternoon.

14. *Sunday.* A fine, cool, and clear day. At church all day. Mr. Porter dines with me.

17. *Wednesday.* A fine, cool day. The Cadet company are trained P. M. I go with Ja. Jeffry to Essex bridge and we pass it; the plank is laid nearly over the whole of the timber.

18. *Thursday.* Wm. Cabot is called on for fine for not training. Mr. Porter and Amory with me in the evening.

19. *Friday.* I spend the evening at Mr. Goodale's.

20. *Saturday.* A fine, clear day. At evening I walk to the bridge, and the planking was complete and the railing nearly so ; most of the posts for the lamps were put up. At half past eight in the evening I receive Mr. Oliver's invitation to spend the afternoon at the christening of his son to-morrow at Marblehead.

21. *Sunday.* A fine morning, tho' very cool. My cold caught at the Essex bridge last evening keeps me at home to-day.

24. *Wednesday.* A fine day. Essex bridge finished and prepared for passing and for payment of toll ; memo. what *each cattle is to pay ;* a great concourse resorted thither to pass, as it was to be free of toll this day ; the workmen had a procession from the bridge to Leach's, at Beverly, each with the tools of his trade.[1]

25. *Thursday.* At 6 A. M. Mr. Pullen and I set out for Ipswich, on affairs of Potter and Nelson, executors.

---

[1] This bridge, at the time of its erection, was regarded "as one of the modern wonders."

26. *Friday.* A fine day. We return and find the lamps lighted at Essex bridge.

28. *Sunday.* A fine, cool day. Mr. Porter and Goodale at church. At F. Cabot's to wait on Lt. Gov. Lincoln.

29. *Monday.* Colo. F. and John go to Boston for instructions as to rank, etc., on the day of review, and return at night, satisfied with Gov. H.'s politeness.

30. *Tuesday.* Rain. I set out with Stevens in his chaise for Newbury Ct. ; dine at Ipswich with Potter and co. ; arrive at Newbury P. M., and meet with the Court at the Court House in season.

October 1. *Wednesday.* A fine day. I dine at Mr. Parsons'.

3. *Friday.* I dine at Dr. Smith's ; all genteel and delicate, except the invitation.

4. *Saturday.* Small rain. At 12 Stephen and J. Sewall and Prescott set out from Court and dine at Ipswich ; reach Essex bridge at 6 and saw the lamps lighted.

6. *Monday.* A pleasant day, though cool. At Dr. Holyoke's in the evening ; how came J. G. there ? Will he be a member *nol. volentis ?*

8. *Wednesday.* Cloudy, and rain A. M. Rev. Mr. Diman [1] died this day.

9. *Thursday.* A very clear and fine morning. Capt. N. Ramsdell, of Lynn, calls to see us.

10. *Friday.* A very fine day. Mr. Grafton here.

11. *Saturday.* Rain [all day], and till night. Mr. Amory dines with us, takes tea, and sups with John. Mrs. P. and I spend the evening at Mr. Vans'. I call at Mr. Fisher's to see him and Bro. Porter.

12. *Sunday.* Clear and cool. Jack sets out early for Middleton.

---

[1] Rev. James Diman, H. C. 1730.

13. *Monday.*   A fine day.   Mr. J. Bartlett comes at tea and lodgeth with us ; Mr. Hooper cometh not.   Mr. Diman's funeral to-day ; he is carried to the meeting-house.

14. *Tuesday.*   A clear and cool day.   Mr. Bartlett, Jno., and Amory set out for Marblehead.   Mr. Sparhawk calls to see us.

15. *Wednesday.*   A clear, fine day.   Mrs. Pynchon and I go to Marblehead, and carry Wm. Oliver with us, and there meet Mr. Harris,[1] the schoolmaster, our kinsman.

16. *Thursday.*   A very clear and fine day.   Mr. Hooper spends the morning at Mr. Osgood's office upon entries, etc.

17. *Friday.*   A fine morning.   Jno. ill ; Dr. Griffin calls to see him ; Dr. Holyoke also calls in the evening.

18. *Saturday.*   Cloudy, but moderate.   Mrs. Pynchon with Mrs. Vans set out on their tour for Essex bridge ; it is proposed that they get out of the carriage and walk over it, as at some period of time it doubtless must fall to decay, and no mortal knows but that time may be whilst these two Amazons are walking over it.   *It is prudent always to be prudent ;* they quote Judge Lynde.

19. *Sunday.*   A fine, cool morning.   A letter from Judge Oliver.

20. *Monday.*   Cloudy morn.   Mr. Amory gives particulars of the publication as to Judge Greenleaf's cruelty. A plentiful rain this evening.

21. *Tuesday.*   Rain in the morning, and high winds.

---

[1] William Harris had been a student of medicine under Dr. Holyoke, but, becoming interested in the Church, had abandoned physic, and was now preparing for Holy Orders. He succeeded Mr. Oliver at St. Michael's, where he officiated for eleven years.   He afterwards became distinguished as President of Columbia College.

I spend the evening with J. Grafton at Clerk Osgood's ;
Dr. Plummer there also.

23. *Thursday.*   Mr. and Mrs. Gannett call to see us ;
they put up at Mrs. Derby's.

24. *Friday.*   Mrs. Gannett and Mrs. Derby call A. M.
and spend an hour.   Mr. Gannett and I go and spend
part of the evening at Mr. Fisher's, where we meet with
Bro. Porter ; those three classmates [1] were in high spirits
at the meeting.   The weather was fine to-day.

25. *Saturday.*   A summer-like day.   Mrs. Pynchon
and company, Miss Gerrish, Mr. Pickman, and Carpenter set out in Newhall's hack for Beverly, and to go over
Danvers new bridge ; W. Pickman and W. Cabot and
myself walk over, and take tea with them at Mrs. Higginson's, and all return over Essex bridge save Mrs.
Pynchon ; she tarries with her aunt and Mrs. Cabot.

26. *Sunday.*   Cloudy.   I am kept at home by a cold
caught in passing the bridge in the damp evening.   Jno.
came home from M. head, and set out in a carriage for
a review at Braintree.   G. Cabot politely invited me to
dine with him at Beverly, and sent his servant on purpose to ask me ; I could not go.

27. *Monday.*   A cloudy day.   The military companies
and great numbers went for Boston for the review at
Braintree.

28. *Tuesday.*   The militia return from Braintree to
Boston.   Mrs. P. returns from Beverly in Mr. Lee's carriage.

30. *Thursday.*   Excessively cold ; people's roots were
frozen in the garret.

31. *Friday.*   Somewhat more moderate ; a clear day.
Mr. and Mrs. Murray here to see us, and stayed most of
the forenoon.   Mr. Grafton here before noon and all the

------

[1] Of the class of 1763.

afternoon and evening ; Mr. Goodale and Amory also here.

November 1. *Saturday.* A cold morning, but clear. Stevens brings news of the adjournment of the Superior Court to December, the third Tuesday, to the joy of many.

2. *Sunday.* A fine, pleasant day. I go to church A. M. Mr. Grafton here after church upon his and bro. Wood's concerns.

4. *Tuesday.* Mr. Barnard and Mr. Haraden here about Mr. Diman's will. At 12 Mr. Oliver and I set out to visit Mr. Cutler, returned from Muskingum.

6. *Thursday.* Jas. Diman, witness of his father's will, examined.

7. *Friday.* The witnesses examined as to Mr. Diman's will. A fine day ; some clouds and wind ; rain at evening.

8. *Saturday.* Windy. Judge Greenleaf writes to Colo. Hutchison and Capt. Page respecting their commission on Waters' estate, and to make return, and that the Adm. ought to discount with Mr. Shillaber and me ; on seeing them, she and her son grew high and provoking ; Mr. Shillaber and I were there and at Mr. Waters' a considerable time.

10. *Monday.* Windy, cloudy, and cold. Mrs. Gibbs, Curwen, Mrs. Paine, and others spend the evening here, also Mr. Gibbs, at cards. At 9 I go to Mr. Goodale's ; at Club till past 10 ; much talk of Greenleaf's trial and of Federal Court.

11. *Tuesday.* Bro. Porter calls. It rains plentifully, and the wind very high at evening ; it drove in Mr. Vans' south chamber window quite across the chamber and through the panels of the door.

13. *Thursday.* Cool and clear. Mr. Hichborn and J. Allen and Mr. Rowe at Robinson's.

16. *Sunday.*   Mr. Paine, of Worcester, in town.   We spend the evening at Dr. Paine's.

18. *Tuesday.*   Cloudy and cool.   Mr. Sparhawk here, going to Boston and to sail for London in Scot the latter end of next week.   *Mihi gaudia quanta fuere!*   And I am to direct to the care of Isaac Winslow, merchant, Boston.

19. *Wednesday.*   Cloudy and cool.   T. Goodale takes me in his chaise to Marblehead, where I visit Mr. Hooper; call on Messrs. Mansfield and Sewall ; take tea at Mr. Oliver's ; he at Boston.

21. *Friday.*   Cloudy, and rain most of the day.   Sergt. Daniels gets into another scrape, and escapes from the officer and warrant.

23. *Sunday.*   Cloudy, and rain.   I tarry at home, ill of the rheumatism.   I send to Mr. Bowdoin, to desire a meeting of Wardens and Vestry after services as to Mr. Deblois' account of the organ.

24. *Monday.*   Rain and clouds.   Mess. Briant and Vaughn meet at my office at ten o'clock, the one from Boston, the other from Portland, upon a suit.   Mess. Cabot and Shillaber meet to settle.

26. *Wednesday.*   Clouds and rain.   Mess. Haraden and Amory call about Mr. Diman's will.

27. *Thursday.*   Rains plentifully this morning, as it did most of last night, and lo, the gloominess of this Thanksgiving day, the mists and clouds impending on all our publick manœuvres, measures, and concerns.   We dine to-day at Mr. Goodale's, and John goes too.   At present the town seems generally employed about Mr. Diman's will ; they condemn it as unequal, unfair, and deceitful in the testator, and in his family and legatees, in excluding his daughter Haraden, and would have it set aside as being made when he was under the legatee's

influence, advice, and direction ; . . . suppose it was prefaced with these influences, and that his devises were made upon his considering of these influences and advice, would it be worse, or more illegal ? Mrs. P. and I dine at Mr. Goodale's with W. Cabot and Ab. Gerrish.

28. *Friday.* Wet and cloudy. Mr. Osgood, Mrs. Dalton, G. Cabot, F. Cabot, also Mr. Amory, Mrs. Mellan.

29. *Saturday.* At eve. Mr. and Mrs. Vans and niece Langdon were here. Mr. Haraden, Amory, etc., at the examination of witnesses as to Mr. Diman's will.

30. *Sunday.* Cloudy. At church P. M. Lefavor and Bowdoin to meet at eve. upon Mr. Deblois' demand for the organ.

December 1. *Monday.* Rains all day. I go to Ipswich on affairs of Waters' estate for W. Shillaber and myself ; also on concerns of Jas. Diman as to proof of his father's will ; it was approved, and an approval claimed by Haraden ; we return at night.

2. *Tuesday.* Cold and very windy. I went to Mad. Lynde's and to Mr. Oliver's.

3. *Wednesday.* Very windy and cold all day. At eve. Mr. Fisher and some of the vestry call about Mr. Deblois' demand for the organ. Three sailors call for wills and powers, they being bound with Capt. Lambert to the Cape of Good Hope ; having paid me generously, as they supposed, they desired me, being an old gentleman, to pray for them.

4. *Thursday.* Windy and cold. I set out for Boston in S. Williams' chaise, and arrive before night ; lodge at Mrs. Wetmore's at the new house ; find them all well, dressing for the Assembly.

5. *Friday.* I go to the Governor's to see Mrs. Sewall from St. John ; I meet her and Mrs. Hancock together ;

the Governor ill of the gout in his chamber. Last evening I spend with Dr. Loring *et ux.*, and I return home at night in a snow-storm. It clears up by 8 o'clock.

6. *Saturday.* A fair day. We find J. G.'s disposition to knavery, and instead of leaving goods for our security, his views were to carry them off with him.

7. *Sunday.* Cloudy morning. Mr. Fisher advises to a private application to Mess. Fisher and L. Deblois in London respecting church debts, and respecting the organ.

8. *Monday.* Cloudy, and some rain. Divers messages pass between J. Grafton *et ipse* as to the goods which were attached. At length Mr. Sanders gave us his covenant to indemnify us to pay off the goods and exōn. on notice.

10. *Wednesday.* I set out in the stage with Burrell and five others ; arrived at Boston before two and dined at Mrs. Wetmore's ; met Mess. Gorham and Lowell at Mr. Wetmore's office in the evening, and agree on a report in Apthorp and Bowdoin's suit.

11. *Thursday.* I set out in the stage from Boston at 1/2 past one and arrived at Salem at 5. The Superior Court continues sitting at Boston, and slander and ribaldry go on briskly in the newspapers.

12. *Friday.* At home all day. Jno. goes to Beverly on Mrs. Cabot's business, and thence to Marblehead in the evening.

14. *Sunday.* A fair day. I at church P. M.

15. *Monday.* Judge Sewall at [the] Club at Dr. Plummer's, and we spend a pleasant evening. In the morning Jno. sets off for Lynnfield after Ste. Rolfe, and Justice Perkins' Court.

16. *Tuesday.* A very fine morning. The Superior Court meet to-day, but call no debtors before noon.

17. *Wednesday.* Snow, and is very windy and cold ; the ink freezeth in the office.

19. *Friday.* Clear and cold morning. A very numerous company at the ball ; the aged tarry till 12 or 1, the younger till 3 and 4 ; in the morning the Judges and 2 of their ladies there.

20. *Saturday.* Very cold. Mess. Lowell and Atkins dine with me on fish. The Court sit in the evening.

21. *Sunday.* All tarry at home ; I very ill. Mr. Lowell spends the day here. Judges Sargeant and Sumner and his lady dine at Mr. Goodale's.

22. *Monday.* The Court meet at eleven. Mr. Lowell spends the evening with the Club at Mr. Goodale's.

23. *Tuesday.* Wind So. and very chilly. The Court (3 only) sit in the evening.

24. *Wednesday.* Clear and cold. I spend the evening agreeably at Rea's, Mr. Sullivan's lodgings ; he invites me to go with him to see Mr. Adams at Braintree. This evening Ez. Putnam's cause with Middleton is tried, and goes in favor of Middleton.

25. *Thursday.* I go with T. Goodale in his chaise to Marblehead ; we and his father dine at Mr. Oliver's with Peggy Orne. The music at church is very fine.

26. *Friday.* Cloudy and cold. Court sit till 9 in the evening.

27. *Saturday.* Clear and cold. Court sit [till] six in the evening and adjourn without day ; more suits at this term (the clerk says) than ever before in Essex Sup. Court.

28. *Sunday.* Stormy, snow, and high E. wind. J. Sumner, Sargeant, and Lowell go out of town at 9 ; I have a bad headache and tarry at home.

31. *Wednesday.* Cloudy, wet, and unpleasant. Vans and co. set out for the General Court.

1789. *January* 1. *Thursday*. A very fine morning, clear and pleasant ; as Mr. G. says, 't is beautiful, beautiful. Justice Perkins in tribulation as to fines. I go to the scholars' exhibition, under Master Harris, and am highly entertained with parts of the " Haunted House," acted there. I send Sheldon's papers to Clerk Cushing, Boston.

2. *Friday*. A fine, clear day, but cool. Jno. Pynchon sets out from [his] sick room for Marblehead to defend the rioters in the Shimmington affair, and returns at evening at the exhibition by the rope dancer here.

3. *Saturday*. Cloudy, and snow. Jno. goes to Marblehead again for the rioters. Wood to-day at 15/ to 17/ per cord.

6. *Tuesday*. I set out for Wilmington for Foster *v.* Rolfe, a reference.

7. *Wednesday*. I lodged last eve. at Mr. Orne's, and get home this morning.

9. *Friday*. Cold. Provisions in plenty, and from N. Hampshire.

11. *Sunday*. A cold day. I go to church all day ; *mirum !* Says the parson, " I took you for Dr. Gould." Says bro. Porter, " You certainly have on the deacon's wig." Says my witty brother, " As the Dr. wears his hair he may well spare his wig." Says brother . . . , " How long has the Dr. wore his hair ? " " All his days," says brother . . . " How came he ever to think of getting a wig ? " " 'T is one he bought at vendue," says brother . . .

12. *Monday*. Norris' goods seized for false entry and for duties.

13. *Tuesday*. Jno. goes to Boston on F. Cabot's affair ; lodges at Mr. Lowell's.

16. *Friday*. A very clear, warm day. Wood 13/ to 15/. Mrs. Ropes spends the evening here.

18. *Sunday.*   A fine day.   I at church P. M.

19. *Monday.*   Cloudy and cool.   Plenty of wood, the price from 12/ to 14/, oak.

24. *Saturday.*   Jno. and I went to Mr. Orne's and took tea, and returned in the evening.

25. *Sunday.*   Snow, and N. E. wind.   I go to church ; Mr. Wm. Turner at church in my pew ; he took tea at my house.   I go to Mr. Fisher's in the evening, and meet there Capt. Ingersoll and Bro. Porter.   The Lt. Governor's salary of £160 pleaseth neither party.

27. *Tuesday.*   Some snow.   Wood at 11/ to 13/.

28. *Wednesday.*   Cloudy.   Mess. Oliver and Amory dine with John.   At evening Mrs. Higginson here, and gives orders as to W. West.

29. *Thursday.*   Rain.   Town-meeting for choice of Representatives ; there were 521 voters ; B. Goodhue, Esq., had a majority.   Neighbour Wright *et ux.,* Mrs. Vans, and her niece spend the evening here at cards ; bad walking, and Peter and David pushed them over the way in the sleigh.

31. *Saturday.*   Snow-storm, and N. E. wind.   Little doing at Gen'l Court.

February 1. *Sunday.*   Clear and cold ; the snow considerably drifted.   Mr. Goodale here in the evening. Jno. returns on foot from Marblehead ; the ways impassable with horses.

2. *Monday.*   Extreme cold the last night.   Write to Mr. Sparhawk, but through delay miss the stage, to my great disappointment ; beware of delays in future ; my losses by delays insupportable.

3. *Tuesday.*   Clear and cold.   Plenty of wood, 12/ for oak, 14/ for walnut.   Mr. Amory and Mr. Turner's son dine with John.

4. *Wednesday.*   Clear, cold morning, but cloudy at noon.   Mr. Ward, of Lancaster, here in the evening.

5. *Thursday.* Clear and cold. Mr. Orne comes early in the morning; sleeps here. Ball.

6. *Friday.* The company small at ball last evening. Mr. Apthorp there from Halifax; come to fight Moreton.

12. *Thursday.* Mr. Oliver comes and lodges at his father's. Mrs. Goodale spits up blood, and is much alarmed and weakened.

15. *Sunday.* Cold morning, but clear. At home all day. Mr. T. Cabot with us in the afternoon, with an account of his tour in the stage to and from N. York. Mr. Goodale here, and none else in the evening.

16. *Monday.* John Pynchon goes to Marblehead, and carries Garnet, the fiddler. I at Madam Lynde's part of the evening.

18. *Wednesday.* A cold day, and clear. I write again to Mr. Hooper for adjustment.

19. *Thursday.* Mr. Oliver returns from Boston, and with him a Mr. Jones; they take tea and go to Marblehead.

20. *Friday.* Snow-storm; N. E. wind; snow much drifted. Amory and Jno. set out for Gloucester.

21. *Saturday.* Clear and moderate. Mrs. Abbot's daughter, Priscilla, dies about 6 P. M., her only child; all her earthly hopes were concentrated in her, and fail at once, and she rendered inconsolable.

22. *Sunday.* Cloudy and warm; wet walking, and rain. I at home all day. In the evening John Pynchon returns wet and fatigued from Newbury.

27. *Friday.* Moderate and cloudy. Capt. Ramsdell dines here to-day.

28. *Saturday.* Moderate weather, and thaws, but the sledding good, and wood is brought in plenty; many loads remain in the street from A. M. to 2 and 3 o'clock.

Mr. Otis calls at the office for John, not yet returned ; Mr. and Mrs. Vans and Caty set out for Danvers in his sleigh.

March 2. *Monday.* A fine, moderate day. John goes to Marblehead on Otis' affair, and remains all night.

On the Saturday following the above Monday, my father was taken in the morning with a most violent fever, supposed to be rheumatic ; he continued ill until Saturday, the 14th ; he died on that day at 12 o'clock. He was, during his whole illness, attended by Drs. Paine and Holyoke, and was the greater part of the time delirious. His memory I shall not cease to cherish while my heart vibrates with a spark of life. His funeral was attended by a very numerous and most respectable train of mourners and friends.

J. P.

INDEX.